Keeping a Christmas Secret
Ducks Disappearing
I Can't Take You Anywhere
Sweet Strawberries
Please DO Feed the Bears

Books for Young Readers
Josie's Troubles
How Lazy Can You Get?
All Because I'm Older
Maudie in the Middle
One of the Third-Grade Thonkers
Roxie and the Hooligans

Books for Middle Readers
Walking Through the Dark
How I Came to Be a Writer
Eddie, Incorporated
The Solomon System
The Keeper
Beetles, Lightly Toasted
The Fear Place
Being Danny's Dog
Danny's Desert Rats
Walker's Crossing

Books for Older Readers
A String of Chances
Night Cry
The Dark of the Tunnel
The Year of the Gopher
Send No Blessings
Ice
Sang Spell
Jade Green
Blizzard's Wake
Cricket Man

I LIKE HIM, HE LIKES HER

BOOKS BY PHYLLIS REYNOLDS NAYLOR

Shiloh Books
Shiloh
Shiloh Season
Saving Shiloh

The Alice Books
Starting with Alice
Alice in Blunderland
Lovingly Alice
The Agony of Alice
Alice in Rapture, Sort of
Reluctantly Alice
All But Alice
Alice in April
Alice In-Between
Alice the Brave
Alice in Lace
Outrageously Alice
Achingly Alice
Alice on the Outside
The Grooming of Alice
Alice Alone
Simply Alice
Patiently Alice
Including Alice
Alice on Her Way
Alice in the Know
Dangerously Alice
Almost Alice
Intensely Alice
Alice in Charge

The Bernie Magruder Books
Bernie Magruder and the Case
   of the Big Stink
Bernie Magruder and the
   Disappearing Bodies

Bernie Magruder and the
   Haunted Hotel
Bernie Magruder and the
   Drive-thru Funeral Parlor
Bernie Magruder and the Bus
   Station Blowup
Bernie Magruder and the
   Pirate's Treasure
Bernie Magruder and the
   Parachute Peril
Bernie Magruder and the Bats
   in the Belfry

The Cat Pack Books
The Grand Escape
The Healing of Texas Jake
Carlotta's Kittens
Polo's Mother

The York Trilogy
Shadows on the Wall
Faces in the Water
Footprints at the Window

The Witch Books
Witch's Sister
Witch Water
The Witch Herself
The Witch's Eye
Witch Weed
The Witch Returns

Picture Books
King of the Playground
The Boy with the Helium Head
Old Sadie and the Christmas
   Bear

I LIKE HIM, HE LIKES HER

Alice Alone

Simply Alice

Patiently Alice

PHYLLIS REYNOLDS NAYLOR

Atheneum Books for Young Readers
New York • London • Toronto • Sydney

ATHENEUM BOOKS FOR YOUNG READERS
An imprint of Simon & Schuster Children's Publishing Division
1230 Avenue of the Americas, New York, New York 10020
Alice Alone copyright © 2001 by Phyllis Reynolds Naylor
Simply Alice copyright © 2002 by Phyllis Reynolds Naylor
Patiently Alice copyright © 2003 by Phyllis Reynolds Naylor
For information about special discounts for bulk purchases, please contact Simon & Schuster Special Sales at 1-866-506-1949 or business@simonandschuster.com.
The Simon & Schuster Speakers Bureau can bring authors to your live event.
For more information or to book an event, contact the Simon & Schuster Speakers Bureau at 1-866-248-3049 or visit our website at www.simonspeakers.com.
Book design by Mike Rosamilia
The text for this book is set in Berkeley Oldstyle Book.
Manufactured in the United States of America
This Atheneum Books for Young Readers paperback edition May 2010
8 10 9
The Library of Congress has cataloged the hardcover editions as follows:
Naylor, Phyllis Reynolds.
Alice alone / Phyllis Reynolds Naylor—1st ed.
p. cm.
Summary: Alice's first year in high school gets off to a difficult start when her boyfriend Patrick becomes interested in someone else, but with the help of her father, older brother, and best friends, she gains a better sense of her own self-worth.
ISBN 978-0-689-82634-4 (hc.)
[1. Interpersonal relations—Fiction. 2. Self-esteem—Fiction. 3. High schools—Fiction. 4. Schools—Fiction. 5. Single-parent families—Fiction. 6. Friendship—Fiction.] I. Title.
PZ7.N24 Ah 2001
[Fic]—dc21 00-040143

Naylor, Phyllis Reynolds.
Simply Alice / Phyllis Reynolds Naylor—1st ed.
p. cm.
Summary: In her freshman year, fourteen-year-old Alice experiences changes and challenges with her friends, family, and school activities, which leave her feeling better about herself than ever before.
ISBN 978-0-689-82635-1 (hc.)
[1. Interpersonal relations—Fiction. 2. Brothers and sisters—Fiction. 3. High schools—Fiction. 4. Schools—Fiction. 5. Theater—Fiction.]. I. Title
PZ7.N24 Si 2002
[Fic]—dc21 2001035539

Naylor, Phyllis Reynolds.
Patiently Alice / Phyllis Reynolds Naylor—1st ed.
p. cm.
Summary: The summer after ninth grade, Alice and her friends spend three weeks working as assistant counselors at a camp for disadvantaged children and cope with all kinds of changes.
ISBN 978-0-689-82636-8 (hc.)
[1. Camps—Fiction. 2. Poverty—Fiction. 3. Friendship—Fiction. 4. Remarriage—Fiction. 5. Family life—Fiction. 6. Single parent families—Fiction.] I. Title.
PZ7.N24 Pat 2003
[Fic]—dc21 2002012887

ISBN 978-1-4424-0978-1 (bind-up pbk)
These titles were previously published individually.

Alice Alone

To the memory of my former editor, Jean Karl,

who helped me raise Alice,

and who taught me as much about life

as she taught about writing.

Contents

1

HOMECOMING

September has always felt more like New Year's to me than January first. It's such a brand-new start—new classes, new friends, new teachers, new clothes. . . . This September I was entering a school almost twice the size of our old one, and it was scary to think about being one of the youngest kids again instead of a seasoned eighth grader. I hated the thought that I wouldn't be considered sophisticated anymore, and I'd probably feel as awkward as I used to.

"Hey, no sweat!" Lester, my soon-to-be-twenty-two-year-old brother said. "You'll get used to it in no time—the leftover infirmary food, the—"

"What?" I said. We were sitting out on the front steps sharing a bag of microwave popcorn on the very last day of August. In fact, we'd just made a lunch of hot dogs and popcorn.

"Didn't you know?" he said. "The food in the high school cafeteria is leftover stuff from the prison infirmary. But it won't kill you. Of course, there isn't any hot water in the showers, and—"

"What?" I bleated again.

"And the showers, you know, are coed."

"Lester!" I scolded. If anything would drive my friend Elizabeth to an all-girls' school, it was rumors like that.

"Hey, look around you," Lester said, taking another handful of popcorn and spilling some on the steps. "Do you realize that practically every person you meet over the age of eighteen went to high school and lived to tell about it?"

"I know I'll survive, Les, but when I think of all the embarrassing things I'll probably do, all the humiliating stuff just waiting to happen . . ."

"But what about all the good stuff? The *great* stuff? What's the next good thing on the agenda, for example?"

"Dad coming home this afternoon."

"See? What else?"

"Patrick gets back on Saturday."

"There you are," Lester said.

He was being pretty nice to me, I decided, considering that he'd just broken up with his latest girlfriend, Eva, for which I was secretly glad, because I don't think she was his type. She certainly wasn't mine. She had starved herself skinny and was always finding fault with Lester. If they ever married, I figured it would be only a matter of time before she started criticizing me.

"Are you picking Dad up?" I asked. Lester's working on a master's degree in philosophy at the University of Maryland. His summer school courses were finished, but he works part time.

"Yeah. I got the afternoon off from the shoe store. I figured Dad deserves a welcoming committee. Want to come?"

"Yes. But first I want to bake him something," I said.

I'd already bought the ingredients because I'd planned this cake in advance. I once found a note on a recipe card of Mom's for pineapple upside-down cake, saying it was Dad's favorite, so I decided to make that.

Mom died of leukemia when I was in kindergarten, so it's just been Dad and Lester and me ever since. Except that Dad's going to marry my former English teacher, Sylvia Summers, who's in England for a year on an exchange program, and Dad was just coming back from a two-week trip to see her. *One* of the reasons Miss Summers went to England was to give her time to decide between Dad and Jim Sorringer, the assistant principal back in my junior high school. She and Jim dated for a long time—until she met Dad. But I guess she decided she didn't need a year to think it over after all, because when Dad went to visit her, they became engaged.

Pineapple upside-down cake is really easy, especially if you use a cake mix. All you do is melt a stick of butter in a large baking pan, stir in a cup of brown sugar, add canned pineapple slices, and then the cake batter. I had the phone tucked under my ear and was explaining all this to Pamela, my other "best" friend, while I worked.

". . . and when you take it out of the oven, you turn the pan upside down on a big platter." And then I added, "Why don't you make one for *your* dad? Surprise him." If ever a girl and her dad needed to learn to get along, it was Pamela and Mr. Jones. Ever since Pamela's mom ran off with her NordicTrack instructor, Pamela's been angry with both her parents, but she and her dad are trying hard to make it work.

"Maybe I will," said Pamela. "You have any pineapple I could borrow?"

"I think so," I said.

"We may not have enough butter."

"You could borrow that, too."

"Brown sugar?"

"Well . . . maybe."

"Would you happen to have a cake mix?"

"Pamela!" I said.

"Never mind. I'll go to the store," she told me.

While the cake was baking, I did a quick cleanup of the house. I dusted the tops of all the furniture, ran an electric broom over the rug, made the beds, and wiped out the sinks— sort of like counting to one hundred by fives, skipping all the numbers in between.

Lester did the laundry and the dishes, just so the place wouldn't smell like sour milk and dirty socks when Dad walked in. Miss Summers always has the most wonderful scent, and I could guarantee that her flat in England didn't stink.

Of course, what I wanted most to know was where Dad had been sleeping while he was there, but I'm old enough now that I don't just pop those questions at him. I'll admit I've imagined the two of them having sex, though. If I ever get *near* the topic, he says, "Al!" My full name is Alice Kathleen McKinley, but Dad and Lester call me Al.

We had things pretty much in order by 3:45—the cake cooling on the counter, the laundry folded and put away. I decided to put on something a little more feminine than my old cutoffs, so I dressed in a purple tank top and a sheer cotton broomstick skirt. It was lavender with little purple and yellow flowers all over it, yards and yards of gauzy material that swished and swirled about my legs when I walked. I stood in front of the mirror, whirling around, and the skirt billowed out in a huge circle. Even Lester was impressed when he saw me.

"Madame?" he said, holding out his arm, and we descended grandly down the front steps.

Dad's plane was landing at Dulles International, so we had to drive way over into Virginia to pick him up. I sat beside Lester, my legs crossed, feeling very alluring and grown-up. I was wearing string sandals, and my toenails were painted dusky rose.

"It's going to be awkward, isn't it, after Miss Summers moves in," I said as Lester expertly navigated the beltway.

"I can't eat breakfast in my boxers anymore, I'll tell you that," he said.

"I guess she won't exactly be eating breakfast in *her* under-wear, either," I said. "Gosh, Lester, I hardly even remember Mom. I don't know what it's like to have a woman around. I'm so used to being the only female in the house."

"Don't feel sorry for you, feel sorry for *me*," said Lester. "Imagine having *two* females here, taking over!"

The plane was going to be fifty minutes late, we discovered when we got to the airport, so Lester bought us two giant-size lemonades. We sat on a high stool in a little bar while we drank them, my feet crossed at the ankles, and my four-tiered skirt cascading all the way down to the floor.

Then we ambled around, looking in shops, until I realized that the lemonade was going right through me.

Lester waited outside the restroom, and when I came out again, I told him I wanted to check out a little gift shop I'd seen earlier. I was already thinking of what to buy Miss Summers for Christmas, and hurried on ahead so I could look around before Dad's plane came in. Two guys, maybe a year older than me, came up behind me and, as they passed, one of them said, "Cute butterflies."

What? I thought.

An older man passed on the other side of me and smiled.

Then, "Al," came Lester's voice. "Wait."

I glanced around and saw Lester walking rapidly up behind me.

"Stop!" he whispered urgently, taking hold of my arm, and

I felt the fingers of his other hand fumbling with the waistband of my underwear.

"Lester!" I said, jerking away from him, but he gave a final tug, and suddenly I realized I had walked out of the restroom with the hem of my skirt caught in the waistband of my yellow butterfly bikini.

"Oh, my gosh!" I cried, covering my face with both hands as several more people walked by us smiling.

"Just pretend it happens every day," Lester commanded, urging me forward again.

"Everyone *saw*!" I croaked, feeling the heat of my face against my palms.

"Al," he said, "people are far more interested in catching a plane than they are in your underpants. The world does *not* revolve around you. Keep walking."

I uncovered my eyes. "Is this what it's going to be like living with a philosopher?"

He shrugged. "Would you rather go the rest of your life with your hands over your face?"

I took a deep breath, and we made our way to the gate.

We had to wait till Dad went through customs, of course, and then he would take a shuttle to the main terminal. But at last the passengers were coming up the ramp and through the exit, and there he was in his rumpled shirt, a wrinkled jacket thrown over his arm, a trace of beard on his face, a man without sleep. But I don't think I'd ever seen him look so happy.

I threw my arms around him as Les reached out for his carry-on bag.

"Oh, Dad!" I said.

"Home!" he sighed in my ear. "And what a welcome! Good of you to meet me, Les!" Then he and Lester hugged.

"Bet you're ready for some sleep," Les said, grinning.

"The bed will feel pretty good, all right," said Dad. "How *are* you guys, anyway?"

We chattered all the way down the escalator to the baggage claim area, and Dad and I watched for his nylon bag to come around the conveyor belt while Les went to get the car.

"So what do you think, Al?" Dad asked, grinning at me as we retrieved his bag, then leaned against the wall by an exit, waiting for Lester. "Think you'll get along with your new mom?"

"Oh, Dad, it's the most wonderful news in the world," I said. "You don't know how long I've wanted you and Miss Summers to get engaged. I can't wait!"

"Neither can we. This separation's going to be hard, but we'll manage," he said.

"Will you be getting married next June?"

"July, maybe. We haven't worked out all the details yet." He gave my shoulder a squeeze. "So how did you and Lester get along without me?"

"Okay. He broke up with Eva, you know. And Marilyn's back in the picture. Sort of. They're just friends, Lester says."

"Well, that's good. I've always liked Marilyn. Is Patrick back yet?"

"Saturday," I told him.

I asked him about Miss Summer's flat in England, and he described the rooms, and what the town of Chester looked like, and then we saw Lester's car pull up outside.

I crawled in back and let Dad have the passenger seat. But there was so much to tell. As Lester drove, I rattled on about how Aunt Sally had flown over from Chicago to make sure Lester and I were okay, and how we got her to leave again, and how Pamela had gone to Colorado to live with her mother, then came back again to be with her dad, and how I got my string sandals at a half-price sale, and. . . .

"Al," said Les.

I stopped. "What?" Was I acting like the world revolved around me again?

He nodded toward Dad. Dad's head was leaning against the window, and he was sound asleep. Smiling, still.

Elizabeth and Pamela and I sat on my couch Saturday afternoon, our bare feet propped on the coffee table, gluing little decals to our toenails. Elizabeth was putting roses on hers, I was gluing stars, and Pamela was gluing on signs of the zodiac.

"I don't know," I said. "We may just look freakish. Maybe they don't wear toenail decorations in high school."

"Are you kidding?" said Pamela. "They do anything they want in high school. You see all kinds of stuff. You can be as old-fashioned or individual as you like."

"I thought we *were* individual," I said. Pamela now had a

blue streak right down the middle of her short blond hair. It made her head look sort of like a horse's mane. Elizabeth would probably have to be tortured before she would do anything to her long dark hair.

"So if we're individuals, why are the three of us sitting here all gluing decals on our toenails?" Elizabeth asked.

"Good question," I said.

She leaned back and stared at her feet. "I'm scared," she told us. "I'm afraid I'll get lost in high school and be late to class or I'll wander into some part of the school reserved for seniors or I'll start my period and the restroom will be out of Kotex, or—"

"Elizabeth, shut up," said Pamela. "If you're going to begin high school no different than you were when you started junior high, then what's the point?"

I gave Pamela a look, because Elizabeth went through a sort of anorexic period over the summer, and we think she's beginning to pull out of it, but we're not sure. I didn't want Pamela to say anything that would set her off again.

"What she means is you've got too many big things going for you to worry about all the small stuff," I told Elizabeth. "Lester says if you just look around, you'll realize that almost everybody over the age of eighteen . . ." I stopped right then, because my eye caught something moving outside the window, and when I looked out, I saw Patrick riding up on the lawn on his bike.

"It's Patrick!" I cried, thinking he wasn't due back till evening. I grabbed my can of Sprite and sloshed some around in my mouth before I got up and went out on the porch to meet him.

He looked as though he'd grown another inch—taller, somehow, in his white Polo shirt and khaki shorts. Patrick has red hair, so he doesn't really tan, but his skin looked a deeper red. "Hi," he said, smiling at me.

"Hi," I said, feeling shy all of a sudden.

"You wanted me to bring you the perfect shell," he said, handing me a little box.

"Is it? Really?" I lifted the lid.

It was a beautiful shell, curved at one end, a beige color with little white spots all over it, and ivory on the inside.

"It's not perfect," he said, pointing out a small chip on the edge, "but it was the best I could find." Then he pulled me toward him. "How about the perfect kiss?"

I loved the feel of his arms around me. It was broad daylight there on the porch, but I didn't care. I put my arms around his neck and turned my face up to his. He pressed his lips against mine—softly at first, then hard and firm, and his fingers spread out across my back. It was a long, slow, beautiful kiss.

He let me go long enough to breathe, and asked, "Well, how was it?"

"It'll do," I said, and we kissed again.

"Ahhhhhhhhh!" came a long, loud sigh from the window. We jerked around in time to see two heads disappearing, one brunette, one blond, followed by the rapid thud of footsteps going upstairs.

2
GETTING STARTED

For my first day of ninth grade, I wore a necklace that Dad and Miss Summers had picked out together. It was a black velvet ribbon that hooked in back, worn snugly around the neck, covered with antique lace and tiny dewdrop pearls sewn here and there. It was just right to go with the scoop-neck black jersey top I'd chosen to wear my first day with a great pair of jeans. I thought I looked stunning.

"Don't I look ravishing, Lester?" I asked, standing in his doorway.

Lester lifted one eyebrow as he sorted through his shirts. "How come the top half of you looks like it's going to a party and the bottom half looks like you're going fishing?" he asked.

"It's the style, Lester!" I said. "I'd look like a geek if everything matched."

"Is that why one ear's lower than the other?" he said.

"What?" I asked, walking over to his mirror.

"And one eye's crooked?"

"*Lester!*"

"Hey, relax. It's only high school, not boot camp. Dad never told you he got you on sale, huh? Fifty percent off."

I gave him a look and went down to breakfast. Dad was eating a bowl of Wheat Chex.

"You look great, Al," he told me. "Black's a good color on you. Sylvia said it would be."

"Were you and Sylvia shopping together?" I asked. "For a ring, perhaps?"

"As a matter of fact, we were," he said, and smiled over his toast.

"Describe it," I said eagerly.

"Well, it's round, of course."

"The *diamond*," I said. "Is it one large stone, or . . . ?"

"It isn't a diamond at all, Al. We chose matching gold bands, sort of a woven look."

I stopped chewing. "You didn't buy Sylvia a diamond?"

"No. She said she didn't want to feel responsible for it. She said she'd be continually checking to see if it was still there, and it would catch on things—"

"But . . . but diamonds are forever!" I squeaked. "Enduring love!"

"What's this, a singing commercial?" Lester asked, coming into the kitchen.

"She's upset because I didn't buy Sylvia a diamond," Dad told him. "When *you* get married, Al, you can have diamonds on your toes, for all I care. You can even have a diamond in your navel. But Sylvia and I wanted matching gold bands."

"So she doesn't have any kind of an engagement ring?" I asked.

"No. Just a wedding band, after we're married."

I took another bite of cereal and thought it over. "Well, at least you'll *both* be wearing them. I'm suspicious of any man who wants his wife to wear a ring but won't wear one himself. Now maybe Janice Sherman will understand that you are really, truly taken." Janice Sherman is assistant manager at the Melody Inn, where Dad's manager, and she's had a crush on him ever since we moved to Silver Spring.

Dad merely grunted, and turned to the editorial page. "Watch the clock, Al," he said. "You have to catch the bus ten minutes earlier, remember."

I'd already been through orientation at high school. All the new ninth graders had gone to school for a half day to find our classrooms and try our lockers and get a floor plan of the whole building. But we weren't nervous about locks and floor plans; we were nervous about the sophomores, juniors, and seniors, and today they'd be out in force.

Elizabeth was already waiting when I got outside. The new bus stop was three blocks away, so we'd be walking together. She was wearing her long dark hair pulled back away from her face, with a few curls hanging down at the temples, and the rest scooped up with a scrunchie in back. Elizabeth's got the most gorgeous skin and eyelashes and, except for shoulders and knees that still look too bony, she's beautiful, only she'd never believe it.

"You look great," I told her, eyeing her royal blue shirt and off-white jeans.

But she was looking at my collar necklace. "Where'd you get it?"

"Dad and Sylvia gave it to me. She chose it, I'll bet. They were shopping for wedding bands."

"Then it's official," Elizabeth said. "Gosh, Alice, aren't you excited?"

"It's still a long way off," I told her. "Right now I'm excited about ninth grade!"

"Well, I'm nervous!" Elizabeth said.

Except for algebra and possibly Spanish, I didn't think there would be any subject I couldn't handle this year, but Elizabeth is pretty wired about grades. She's always made good ones, of course—better than either Pamela's or mine. But from ninth grade on, we'd heard, your grades appear on your transcript when you apply to college, and Elizabeth kept saying she had "too much on her plate," which was an interesting way of putting it.

"I've made up my mind," she said as we crossed the first street. "I'm giving up ballet and taking modern dance instead. It's much less rigid, and it will be enough to keep me exercising without having to audition for *The Nutcracker* every year." She'd already given up gymnastics last spring, and tap the year before.

"If it's what you really want to do," I told her.

"But I also want to drop piano, and that upsets my folks. I just don't like that practice hanging over me every day. Mom wants me to start with a new teacher. She says I've outgrown Mrs. Ralston, and I'm probably just bored, so she's signed me up with Mr. Hedges, who's supposed to be the best in Silver Spring."

"Well it's up to you," I said again.

"I told Mom I'd take a couple of lessons just to see, but I already know how I feel about it. They just act so . . . so *disappointed* in me . . ."

It's not easy being Elizabeth, I know. She'd been an only child for thirteen years of her life—until Nathan Paul was born last year—so she'd had her parents' whole attention—adoration, really—all to herself. At the same time, they expect a lot of her, or maybe she just demands a lot of herself in order to please them—but she's had about every kind of lesson there is and wants to be good at everything. And perhaps she's just beginning to realize how impossible that is.

At the bus stop there were some older kids we didn't know, but when the bus came, a lot of our crowd was already on, and they were laughing.

"There's Alice," I heard someone say. I wondered what the

big deal was and looked around for Patrick, and then I saw him in the third row, with a short, curly-haired girl sitting in his lap. Patrick was laughing, too, and his face was red.

I stared. It was Penny, the new girl who had worked at Baskin-Robbins over the summer, the place we went for ice cream, the dimpled girl the guys liked to tease.

"Oh, Patrick, you're in for it now!" Brian hollered.

Penny looked around, then bounced off Patrick's lap, her eyes dancing. "Oops!" she said apologetically to me. "Sorry, but I was pushed."

"Mark pushed her," called out Jill.

I didn't know what to say, so I just laughed, too, and sat down beside Patrick.

"She sort of fell on me," he explained.

The tenth, eleventh, and twelfth graders were watching us with bored amusement, like we were a playpen full of toddlers. I gave Patrick a quick kiss. "Were you able to change your lunch to fourth period?" I asked.

"No. I couldn't swing it."

"Oh, Patrick! We won't be eating together!" I said.

"I know, but with the accelerated program, I'll have to grab a sandwich when I can." Patrick had mentioned the possibility of an accelerated program before, but in such an offhand way, it hadn't really sunk in.

"You're actually going to do it? Four years of high school in three?"

"If I can hack it."

"Why?"

"So I can get a jump on things. Go to college one year earlier, get out one year earlier, get a job, make a start—"

"What's the hurry?" I asked.

"Life," said Patrick.

"But *this* is life, too! What about all the fun stuff in high school? What about the senior prom? You won't even be here!" What I was really asking was, *What about me?*

"So I'll come back for the prom," Patrick said, smiling. "Wherever I am, I'll come back and take you to the prom. Okay?"

That was a commitment if ever I heard one. I slipped my fingers through his, and he caressed my thumb the way I like, and I was very happy to see that Penny noticed and looked the other way.

I'm not very good at math and science. Dad's not either, actually. Lester's probably better at both than we are, but one of the reasons I'd been dreading high school was algebra. I'd put off taking it as long as I could, but anyone expecting to go to college had to pass it: algebra, geometry, physics. I got stomachaches just thinking about it. Patrick said he'd help, though. Patrick, the whiz-at-everything guy.

Biology I could handle, though. It made pictures in my mind that algebra didn't. U.S. history I could handle. English. Even Spanish, I discovered. Then there was P.E. and health, and, for my extracurricular stuff, I signed up to be one of the freshmen roving reporters for the school newspaper, *The Edge.*

I'd even be able to take photos sometimes. Pamela signed up for the drama club, and so did I. Except she wanted a leading role, and I wanted to be part of the stage crew.

I sailed through most of the day, all right. The only class I had with Pamela was history, and the only ones I had with Elizabeth were health and P.E. None with Patrick. It was the lunch hour that I missed him most, though. A lot of our old gang was there, so we grabbed a table for ourselves, but I felt odd man out without Patrick.

"Hey, listen!" Karen called from her end of the table. "How about a coed sleepover, my place, Saturday night."

"Coed?" I asked.

"Yes. *Every*body! Bring a sleeping bag and we'll take over the living room."

"Cool!" said Brian. "Your mom going to be there?"

"Of course!"

"Darn!" said Brian, and we laughed.

"She won't mind," said Karen. Her folks are divorced, and she spends every other weekend at her father's. I figured her mom was just trying to make the weekends Karen spent with her extra special.

But Elizabeth was still staring at Karen. "Everyone on the floor together?" she asked.

"Well, I suppose the girls could lie on top of the guys, if you'd prefer," Pamela joked. Everybody laughed. Sometimes I wish Pamela wouldn't do that—embarrass Elizabeth in front of everyone.

"We had a coed sleepover at our church once," Karen explained. "Our youth group had this project—we were going to scrub down all the pews in the sanctuary and repolish them—so we had an overnight first, and then the minister and his wife made breakfast for us the next morning and we cleaned the pews."

"Hey, the library had a sleepover when I was in sixth grade," Brian told us. "They called it a Read-all-Night-athon, and about fifty kids showed up. There were sleeping bags over the whole floor. They turned out the lights at one in the morning, though."

I liked the idea of sleeping on the floor next to Patrick. Sleeping *anywhere* next to Patrick, actually. I told him about it after school.

"Ummm," he said, putting his arm around me and kissing my hair.

Everyone seemed to be in a good mood at dinner that evening. Dad had been on cloud nine since he got back from England, and Lester came home from the university to say that he got a real "babe" for a professor in his Schopenhauer course. *I* was in a good mood because Dad had bought Chinese takeout for dinner, and the whole kitchen smelled of shrimp in garlic sauce.

"Have you told Janice Sherman about your engagement yet?" I asked Dad.

He chewed thoughtfully for a moment. "Guess I haven't. I did mention it to Marilyn because she more or less asked. What she asked was if Sylvia and I were still an 'item,' which is a strange way of putting it, I think, so naturally I told her we were engaged."

I studied my father. There are times he seems to be living on a different planet entirely. "Dad, Janice Sherman has been your assistant manager for . . . what? Seven years? Marilyn has been a part-time employee for maybe one, and you told Marilyn before you told Janice. *Why?*"

"Self-preservation," Lester murmured, looking amused.

Dad seemed perplexed. "Because Janice didn't *ask*," he said. "She asked what it was like in Chester, so I described the countryside. I thought that's what she wanted to know."

I flung back my head and screeched at the ceiling. "Dad, you are so *dense*! Janice Sherman doesn't care about Chester, she cares about you! She doesn't want to know what you and Sylvia did in the countryside, she really wants to know what you did under the covers."

"Al!" Dad said. "Now that's just—!"

"It's true! She only asked about the countryside because she thought maybe she could learn how serious the relationship is."

"Well, now, how am I supposed to know *that*?" Dad shot back. "If a woman asks me if there are as many sheep in England as the postcards make them out to be, how am I supposed to know she's really asking about Sylvia?"

Lester laughed. "Because the woman's had a major crush on you since day one," he said.

"Major, *major*!" I added. "Dad, if you ever asked Janice Sherman to marry you, she'd be in a bridal gown by six that evening."

"You two are exaggerating," Dad said. "Janice may have had a mild interest in me at one time, but she's dated a number of men over the years."

"Mostly music instructors there at the Melody Inn just to make you jealous," I told him.

"Nonsense," said Dad. "Anyway, *Marilyn* seemed quite happy about it." He smiled. "What she *said* was, 'It'll be nice to have someone sharing your pillow again, Mr. M., won't it?' Now in my day I wouldn't have dared say something like that to my boss."

"That's Marilyn!" said Lester, and all three of us laughed.

And then I did the stupidest thing. With all this talk of sharing pillows, I brought up the coed sleepover. "Well, guess what I'm going to do on Saturday? I'm going to a coed sleepover," I said, my brain on vacation.

And without missing a beat, Dad said, "Over my dead body."

"Everyone's going to be there—the whole gang."

"Everyone but you. I don't care if the Pope and all his cardinals will be there. You are not going to a coed sleepover. I never heard of such of dumb idea," Dad said.

"Al, *I* never went to a coed sleepover," Lester said, siding with Dad.

I couldn't believe that things could go downhill so fast. One minute we'd all been eating fried rice and talking about Dad's engagement, and the next minute the bottom had dropped out of my world.

I had promised myself that when I started high school I was going to act more mature. When Dad and I disagreed about something, I was going to discuss it with him calmly. No more breaking into tears and running upstairs to slam my door. So what did I do? Break into tears. All I could think of was that everyone would be there—Patrick would be there, probably—and I wouldn't.

"I can't believe you!" I sobbed. "Y-you don't know anything about it, *either* of you. You just have these knee-jerk reactions, and think that just because a bunch of kids are in sleeping bags, something's going to happen."

My outburst took us all by surprise, I guess. We'd all been feeling mellow, and now this. But if *I* wasn't sleeping on the floor next to Patrick, who would be?

"Al," Dad said, trying to sound reasonable. "What adults in their right minds would allow a bunch of fourteen-year-old boys and girls to spend the night together? *Think!*"

"Churches do it! Libraries do it! It's no big deal," I told him, wiping my eyes and trying to sound more grown up. "All you can think about is sex! Everyone simply brings a sleeping bag and we watch TV and eat popcorn and talk and play cards, and then everyone goes to sleep in his own sleeping bag. Do you actually think some guy is going to crawl into a girl's bag with a dozen other kids lying only two feet away?"

"At two o'clock in the morning in a dark room? Yep!" put in Lester.

I turned on him then. "Karen said her church group had one and they all got up the next morning and scrubbed down the pews."

"What'd they do the night before? Have a food fight?" Lester asked.

"No! It was a work project, but they started with a sleepover. Mark said the public library had one when he was in sixth grade, and the librarians slept right there with the kids."

Dad sighed. "So what adult is going to sleep on the floor with *you*?"

"Karen's mom, I suppose."

"Where's her father?"

"They're divorced."

"Al, if you are going to be sleeping on the floor with a bunch of guys around, it's going to be under *our* roof, not off in some divorced mother's apartment where things could get beyond her control."

I hardly even stopped for breath. "Then can we have the party here?"

Dad blinked.

"We've got more room than Karen, we wouldn't be sleeping so close together, and if you want you can sit on the couch all night with a broom and poke anyone who gets out of line," I said, knowing full well that Dad can't stay awake very long.

Lester looked at Dad. "She's gotcha there, Pop."

Dad looked as though he'd just been hit with a brick. "Al, I am going to count the days until you leave for college," he said, half under his breath.

"How do you know I won't live at home and go to the University of Maryland like Lester?" I chirped.

He turned helplessly to Lester.

Les shrugged. "I don't know. If churches and libraries do it . . ."

"Even *Elizabeth* can do it!" I said, not at all sure.

At that precise moment, like a message from God, the phone rang, and when I picked it up in the hall, Karen said, "Alice, Mom won't let me have the party. I can't believe this! I was sure she'd say yes."

"I'll call you back," I said quickly, and hung up.

"Okay, Lester, you've got to help me out here," Dad was saying. "Al can have the party, and I'll make the popcorn and order the pizza, but after I go to bed, you're in charge."

"What?" yelled Lester.

"You know I can't stay awake past eleven. It's a Saturday night, your classes have only begun at the U, so you can't have too much to do yet. I need you. Once Sylvia and I get married, we'll handle things like this."

Lester gave a howl of pain.

"Thanks, Dad," I said.

I went upstairs and phoned Karen. "The party's still on. Dad says we can have the sleepover here."

"Really?" she cried. "Oh, Alice, your dad is so cool!"

3
A SUDDEN ANNOUNCEMENT

Once the word got out that Lester was in charge, everyone, it seemed, was coming. Even Elizabeth. We got a lot of calls, though—parents wanting to talk to Dad to make sure he was going to be here. This only made Dad more nervous, and Lester berserk.

"I really appreciate this, Les," I said. "Maybe I can make it up to you somehow."

"You can hire ten vestal virgins to massage my feet and feed me grapes, but you'll still owe me," he growled.

As Elizabeth and I walked to the bus stop the next morning, she said, "Mom said I could come if I put my sleeping bag next to Lester and not off in some dark corner with one of the guys."

"Poor Les," I said. "And to think his birthday's on Sunday."

Elizabeth stopped walking. "His birthday's Sunday?"

"So?" I said.

"Alice, we've got to get him a cake! He's giving up one whole night of his life just for us."

Every day is sacred to Elizabeth Price. She knows exactly what she plans to do every hour of the day, and how much she expects to accomplish by the time she goes to bed. Maybe I'm envious of her, because too often I just let things happen to me. I react to whatever comes along instead of *making* things happen. She used to think she was going to join a convent, but lately she's been talking about marriage and motherhood and even a career. By thirty, she says, she wants to be "settled in." Career or marriage or both, she wants to be settled.

No matter how much she tells you, though, you always get the feeling that she's holding back. That you never quite know the real Elizabeth. Maybe everyone's like that to a certain degree. Maybe we never tell our friends *every*thing there is to know about us.

There was no stopping her where Lester was concerned, however. As soon as we got on the bus, Elizabeth told Pamela and Pamela told Brian, and soon everyone knew that we were planning a surprise party for Lester on Saturday.

I didn't get involved. If they wanted to give Lester a cake, it was okay by me. I'd have my hands full just making sure the bathroom was clean and the house straightened up, and helping Dad with the food. That, and algebra.

I was really having trouble with that subject. I worried so much about not understanding it when the teacher wrote things on the board that I concentrated more on the worrying than the problem. But every time I walked in the classroom, my stomach churned. Whenever I had to put a problem on the board, I could feel perspiration trickling down my sides.

In junior high, I would have leaned my head on Patrick's shoulder going home and told him how scared I was, and he would have put his arm around me and volunteered to come over and help me with my homework. But now, if Patrick wasn't staying after school for band practice or something, he was doing extra work in the library for his accelerated program. I missed him.

"I might as well not even have a boyfriend," I complained to Gwen, the friend who'd helped me with general math back in eighth grade. She had a boyfriend too, and his nickname was Legs. He goes out for track every spring with Patrick.

"Yeah? Tell me about it," she joked.

"I never see him! He's always got fifty other things to do!"

"He calls, doesn't he?"

"It's not the same as talking to him in person."

"Well, you can't carry a guy around in your pocket," Gwen said.

"What's that supposed to mean?"

"You've each got to have your own space."

"It's like we've each got a ball field of space around us now! What more does he need?" I asked.

She laughed. "A whole city block. Some boys need a whole block just to themselves."

I didn't think that applied to Patrick. He'd never said anything about needing more space. He was simply too busy with all he had going on in his life. I should be proud of him, I told myself—somebody as smart and motivated as he was. Most of the time I'd let him decide where we should go and what we should do. He always had the best ideas.

When Gwen and I walked down the hall together, we had the habit of leaning toward each other, our arms touching. I walk that way with Pamela, too, but Elizabeth doesn't like people leaning on her. Gwen's chocolate-colored skin against my pinkish-cream made Legs think of candy, he said—the kind his grandma kept in her candy dish.

"If you need help with algebra, I could come over sometime," Gwen offered when we reached the stairwell.

"I don't just need it sometimes, I need it all the time. Every day," I told her. "I don't think I'm going to pass this course."

"You said the same thing about general math. Don't play dumb on me," Gwen said.

The fact was, I wasn't playing. If a textbook says, *The widest part of North America is from Labrador to British Columbia*, I can see a picture of it in my head. If I read that *The clam has gills that hang into the mantle cavity on each side of the foot*, I know exactly what the book is telling me. I see pictures in my mind. But if

I read that *The coefficient is the multiplier of a variable or number, usually written next to the variable*, or [5a+6a={5a-a+7a}-a], I might as well be looking at pigeon tracks in the snow. I can almost feel my eyes roll back and my brain go on hold.

"That's life, Al. L-I-F-E. Some things are harder than others," Lester said that evening as we made taco salad for dinner. The Melody Inn stays open late on Thursday nights, but it was Janice Sherman's turn to stay at the store, and we wanted to have dinner ready for Dad when he got home.

"Well, life stinks," I said. "I don't want to go through four years of high school scared to death I'm going to flunk."

"What's the worst that can happen if you do?"

"I'd have to take algebra I again next semester, which means I'd have to go to summer school for algebra II."

"And . . . ?"

"And there are other ways I want to spend my summer!"

"If that's the worst thing that can ever happen to you, be grateful," said my brother, the philosopher, as he sprinkled cheese over the ground beef.

"But after algebra, there's geometry, and after geometry, physics!" I cried. "Tell me one single way algebra can help me if I decide to become a psychologist." I had already narrowed my career options to a counselor or a psychologist rather than psychiatrist, because if I went into psychiatry, I'd have to go to medical school, and if I went to medical school, I'd have to take chemistry and who knows what else.

"Because somewhere along the way, you'll have to take a course in statistics, and you can't enroll in that if you can't pass algebra and geometry, that's why," Lester said.

"Why would I have to take *statistics*?" I bellowed.

Lester handed me the shredder and the lettuce. "Let's say you read a study that says most men who commit suicide have sisters. Statistics can help you figure out if the results could have occurred by chance, whether sisters are the actual cause of their brothers' demise, or . . ."

I didn't get to hear the rest, because the phone rang just then and I answered in the hall. It was Aunt Sally in Chicago. She took care of us for a while after Mom died, and I keep mixing up early memories of Mom with her. This sort of freaks Dad out. Aunt Sally calls every so often because she feels responsible for us, I guess. She even flew out for a few days to see how we were doing when Dad was in England.

"So what's new?" asked Aunt Sally.

She used to say, "Alice, how *are* you?" implying that she suspected the worst. But because I often clammed up when she asked that, she's learned to say, "What's new?"

"Well, Dad's on cloud nine," I told her. "I don't know when he and Sylvia are getting married—next July, maybe—but he's really happy these days, and busy as usual at the store. Lester's back at the U, and I started high school this week."

"Sounds as though you've all got your work cut out for you," said Aunt Sally. "So what are you doing for fun?"

No matter how she tries to disguise it, whenever Aunt Sally

opens her mouth, you know exactly what's eating her. She's not concerned about our work and our studies; she's concerned about what Lester and I are doing for fun, because fun and trouble are never that far apart in Aunt Sally's mind. It's hard to believe that Carol is her daughter, because there's no resemblance between Aunt Sally and my grown cousin.

"Well, Les isn't going with anyone at present. We're celebrating his birthday this Sunday."

"Yes, I've sent him a card. Twenty-two! Can you believe it, Alice? Lester? Twenty-two years old?"

"Yep, I believe it. In fact, he's going to chaperone the coed sleepover I'm having here Saturday night," I said.

I don't know why I do that. There's something about me that loves to torture Aunt Sally.

"Alice, ex-*cuse* me, but I though you said a *coed* sleepover!" she gasped.

"That's right. There will be about a dozen of us, if everyone shows."

There was a long pause. Then: "Is your father absolutely, positively out of his mind? Lester, the ultimate playboy, is going to chaperone a dozen hormone-crazed kids on a . . ." She paused again long enough to breathe. "Where are you all going to sleep?"

"On the floor. In sleeping bags. *Individual* sleeping bags," I said, laughing.

"Well, all I can say is that things have certainly changed since I was a girl," Aunt Sally said. "Marie and I couldn't even spend the night with a girlfriend unless Mother knew exactly who would be there. And I would never have considered letting Carol go to a coed sleepover. Ever!"

"So she eloped with a sailor," I said, and knew immediately I'd been unfair.

But Aunt Sally just sighed. "Yes, eloped, and divorced two years later." Another pause. "I suppose Patrick will be at this sleepover?"

"Of course."

"Alice, let me give you one little piece of advice: Familiarity breeds contempt."

"Huh?"

"It's true. The more familiar you let a boy get with you, the more favors you give him, the less respect he will have for you."

Familiar? Favors?

"Then I guess after people marry they absolutely hate each other," I reasoned.

"Oh, I didn't mean that! I just mean there's a lot of truth in the saying that if a girl lets a boy go all the way, he won't respect her in the morning."

"How about halfway?" I teased. I couldn't help myself.

"Now, Alice . . ."

"A third of the way? Three-eighths?"

"Alice . . ."

"Aunt Sally," I said, "picture this: Twelve guys and girls, each in his or her own sleeping bag, sprawled out on the rug in our living room, with Lester right smack in the middle of us, listening for every sound, watching for any move . . ."

"What *I* see is Lester snoring away, surrounded by a dozen fourteen-year-olds, who . . . well, I've said all I'm going to say on the subject, Alice. But have fun!"

Have *fun*? I knew at least one person I could count on to stay awake Saturday night: Aunt Sally. I always tell Dad he doesn't have to lose any sleep over Lester and me. Aunt Sally will do it for him. I went back out in the kitchen.

"What did Sal have to say?" asked Lester.

"Familiarity breeds contempt," I said.

Lester grinned. "She's got that right," he said. "Every time you wash your undies and drape them over my towel in the bathroom, kiddo, I want to toss you out the window along with them."

We had dinner ready when Dad got home around six thirty, and I spent the rest of the evening at the dining room table doing my homework. Lester did the dishes, then went up to his room to read, and Dad sat on the couch, his feet on the coffee table, a clipboard on his lap, writing to Sylvia Summers.

About nine thirty, I'd just gone out in the kitchen to get some chocolate grahams when the doorbell rang, and a few moments later I heard Dad's voice in the hallway. "Janice!"

Janice's voice: "I know it's late, Ben, but could I come in for a few minutes?"

"Of course! Something happen at the store this evening?"

I heard the door close and their feet crossing the hallway into the living room.

"That for me?" Lester yelled from upstairs.

"No, Les. Janice just dropped by," said Dad.

I didn't know what to do. I couldn't very well take my graham crackers back into the dining room and sit there chewing while they talked. But if I stayed in the kitchen I'd be eavesdropping. What I should have done was go upstairs, but I didn't.

Dad: "You look upset."

Janice: "I *am* upset. I didn't want to bring this up at the store, Ben, so I decided to come by and tell you in person. I'll be leaving the Melody Inn at the end of September."

"Janice! Why on earth?"

"I've asked the main office for a transfer, and they'll let me know. I can't go on working for a man I don't trust."

"What? Janice, sit down. Please!"

More footsteps, then a pause. Then the squeak of the couch springs.

"I've worked for you for six years, Ben. Longer than any of your other employees, and the store has had its ups and downs. But I thought we made a good team."

"We did, Janice! We do! What do you mean, you don't trust me?"

"I don't expect you to tell me everything that goes on in your life," Janice said, and now her voice was trembling. "But when it's a subject as intimate as marriage, and I have to hear about it from a part-time employee . . ."

"Ah." It was a cross between a sigh and an exclamation, and

Dad paused. "Marilyn told you that Sylvia and I are engaged. Right?"

"Can you understand how that made me feel, Ben? Hearing it from her? She gets the news and I don't?"

"Janice, I swear. I know I'm a fool when it comes to social relations sometimes, but it was only because she came right out and asked. I mean, these young women, they just ask these things, so I told her. I didn't think . . . I honestly didn't think you'd be that interested."

Out in the kitchen I clutched my head and closed my eyes. Even I didn't think my dad would say something quite so stupid.

"Y-you didn't think I'd be *interested*? I'm speechless," said Janice.

Dad didn't answer.

"All these years of loving you . . . ," she said quietly.

"Janice!"

"And I knew it wasn't reciprocated. I can't blame you for that."

"Janice, I've always been fond of you. You know that."

"'Fond' won't do it, Ben. But I did think you'd have the courtesy—the decency—to let me know first if you became engaged to another woman."

"I was thoughtless and stupid not to tell you first, and I apologize. But is this reason enough for you to leave? Move somewhere else?"

"I think so. I may even make manager at another store, who knows?"

"Well, if that happens, it will be my great loss and another's gain, Janice. I can only wish you the best of luck, and I mean that sincerely. You'll do a great job wherever you are. I'm just sorry you feel this way."

"So am I, Ben."

I moved my head an inch at a time until I could just see around the doorway into the living room. Janice was getting up from the couch, her purse tucked under her arm like a rifle. She walked stiffly across the room toward the front door. I edged back again until I heard my father's footsteps, too, in the hall. Then I peeked again.

"Can I count on you until the end of the month?" he asked.

"Yes. You can count on that," Janice said. "Good-bye, Ben." Suddenly she threw her arms around Dad's neck, her purse dropping to the floor, and pressed her mouth against his. Dad stood as stiff as a broom handle, his palms resting lightly against her waist, but his fingers bent back away from her, afraid, it seemed, to touch her any more than necessary.

Before he could say a word, she turned again, swooped down to pick up her purse, then went out the front door, closing it behind her.

Dad didn't move.

Les was coming downstairs in his stocking feet. I emerged from the kitchen, and we joined Dad there in the hallway. I didn't know what to say, so I let Les do the talking. He grinned a little ruefully at Dad and said, "Well, Pops, you win some, you lose some."

Dad shook his head. "Can you imagine? And all because Marilyn found out before she did."

But Lester said, "I think it was the only excuse she could come up with. It was only a matter of time before she left. It would have been unbearable for her, once you were married, to have to listen to *Sylvia and I did this*, and *Sylvia and I did that.*"

"You're probably right, but I'd no idea she was this unhappy. What am I going to do? Who will I find to replace her? Janice knows the store almost better than I do. She's a terrific asset!"

"Won't the corporation send someone else?"

"They always give us a chance to find someone local first."

"Well, the advice you'd give me is to sleep on it, so why don't you?" Lester said.

"I guess I will." But Dad still didn't move; he just stood in the hallway with a dazed look on his face. "Will somebody please explain why the major problems in this household concern romance?" he asked plaintively.

"'Cause love makes the world go around, Dad," I told him.

"And it makes me dizzy," Dad said.

4
THE BIG NIGHT

There were even more people on Saturday than I'd expected. Kids invited other kids, I guess. The usual crowd was there, the ones who hang out at Mark Stedmeister's pool in the summer: Patrick, Elizabeth and Pamela, Brian and Mark, Karen and Jill and, lately, Gwen and her boyfriend, Legs. I'd invited two friends from school, Lori Haynes and her friend Leslie, mostly because some of the girls had been so awful to them back in eighth grade, but I wanted to know Lori better.

Justin Collier came, of course—the guy who likes Elizabeth—but I was surprised when Sam Mayer showed up with his girlfriend, Jennifer. Sam had asked me to the eighth-grade semiformal last spring, not realizing, I guess, that Patrick and I were a couple. That made fifteen people, and Mark had invited Penny, so that was sixteen. Penny's dad actually came to the door to make sure an adult was present. But the biggest surprise of all was that an hour after everyone else had got there, Donald Sheavers rang the doorbell.

Pamela was peering out the window. "It's him!" I heard her squeal, and Elizabeth started laughing.

I looked out. "Who invited *Donald*?" I asked. *"Pamela!"*

"He's cute!" she said.

Donald Sheavers used to be my boyfriend back in fourth and fifth grades when we were renting a house in Takoma Park. He doesn't even go to our school, and I'd never thought he had much between the ears because he always did whatever I told him. If I'd said, *Donald, jump out the window*, he probably would have jumped. But Pamela met him when we bumped into him at the mall, and then she invited him to the eighth grade semiformal, and he'd seemed a lot smarter then.

I wasn't exactly wild to have him at the sleepover, though, since he didn't know most of the other kids. Or maybe I remembered the way he always gave a Tarzan yell when he saw me, just because we used to play Tarzan together. Really dumb. It didn't matter where we were—at school, the mall, the playground—whenever Donald saw me, he'd beat his chest and give a Tarzan yell, and it embarrassed me to death.

I opened the door. Donald started beating his chest and opened his mouth, and just as suddenly he closed it again and grinned. "Just kidding," he said.

I laughed and held the door open for him. He had a sleeping bag under one arm. "So where's the party? We all going to sleep in the same bed or what?"

"Shhhh," I said. "Dad's freaking out as it is."

"Don-ald!" Pamela cried dramatically, throwing her arms around his neck, and introducing him to the other kids.

There were already three different card games in progress, but the TV was going, too, and there was the smell of popcorn coming from the kitchen. A car with a Domino's sign on top stopped out front, and a man came to the door carrying five large pizzas.

I guess I'd never seen so many people in our house at one time. Wall-to-wall people. Somebody had a boom box playing softly in one corner, competing with the TV, Karen was snapping Polaroid pictures of everybody, Jill was dancing with Justin Collier and Mark, both at the same time, Penny was strutting around in red flannel pj's with a drop seat, making us all laugh, and Patrick was imitating David Letterman. It was simply loud and fun and busy, just the way a party should be. Donald seemed to fit right in.

Dad wasn't used to cooking for more than four or five people at a time. If we had one other person at the table besides our family, we figured we had a full house. Now Dad couldn't even carry a pizza into the room without stepping over or around bodies—on the floor, in chairs, under chairs, leaning over the back of the sofa.

I guess it was the first time I could remember that I'd had a real party. I mean, more than a few friends in for birthday cake. The first time I'd had music and TV and guys and girls all at the same time. Most definitely the first time I'd ever spent the whole night with guys in the room.

The thing about having a party at your place, though, you feel like you have to be responsible for everybody. You have to keep checking to make sure everyone's having a good time. I was mostly concerned about Lori and Leslie, because I wasn't sure how the other kids felt about them. I noticed that while they stuck pretty close to each other, they didn't hold hands with everyone watching, and certainly didn't kiss. That's the one thing I felt sad about, that Lori and Leslie didn't feel they could be themselves in my home.

The other person I was watching was Elizabeth, mainly to see if she was eating anything. She was doing okay, I guess. I still saw her pause before every bite, as though debating whether she could afford to let herself eat it. But she ate most of a slice of pizza and some grapes and a couple of chips, which was a lot more than she had allowed herself last summer.

"Penny's wild," Pamela said to me as we passed on the stairs. With only one bathroom, and gallons of Coke and Sprite, people were going up and down all evening.

"What do you mean?"

"Just fun and crazy. Mark's going ape over her."

"Do you care?" I asked, because Pamela used to go with Mark when she wasn't going with Brian.

"No way. I'm keeping my options open," Pamela said.

I went back down to the living room. Penny was sort of crazy in a fun way. Still wearing those red flannel pj's, she was teaching Donald Sheavers a new dance, and Brian kept trying to get in the act and mess it up. Patrick was sitting on the couch doing one of his magic tricks for Lori, using Legs as his assistant, while Sam and Jennifer watched TV—Jennifer on his lap.

I slipped out to the kitchen to see if Dad needed any help. He had the harried look of the Old Woman Who Lived in the Shoe, like seventeen homeless kids had just shown up on his doorstep.

"Need anything, Dad?" I asked.

"About three more hands," he said. "I made a big pot of chicken gumbo in case people are still hungry after the pizza, but I thought we had more crackers, and—"

"Oh, Dad, you're wonderful!" I said, and gave him a hug. His eyes lit up like a flashlight. Every so often it hits me that grown-ups—parents, anyway—need to be told they're doing okay, that they're loved and appreciated. You'd think they wouldn't need that anymore once they're grown, but they do.

Mark had brought a video of one of those old horror movies, *Invasion of the Body Snatchers*, so about ten thirty we decided to put that on and we all settled down to watch, heads leaning on shoulders, legs over legs, pillows everywhere, till everyone was comfortable. It would have been terrifying if I was watching alone, but Mark and Justin kept making crazy remarks, so we laughed all the while it was on.

At some point I realized the light had gone off in the kitchen and Dad wasn't around anymore. Then I noticed Lester sitting at the back of the room, eating a bowl of gumbo and watching the movie with us.

We clapped and brayed and whistled when the movie was over, and then the girls discovered that Lester was there and started cozying up to him. It's really amazing to watch. Girls' voices change when they talk to Lester. Their smiles are different. They laugh differently. I caught Lester's eye and made a gagging gesture, and he grinned.

"Hey! Anybody want an egg cream, made by the World's Best Egg Creamer?" Lester said, as much to get Jill and Pamela off the back of his chair as to have something to do, I think.

"What's an egg cream?" asked Brian.

"Ha! Come out to the kitchen and watch a genius at work," Lester said, so everyone traipsed out to the kitchen. He dramatically rolled up his sleeves. "Anybody here who doesn't want one?"

"So what is it?" Pamela asked.

"A drink," said Les.

The guys looked surprised.

"Count me in," said Brian, and everyone wanted to try one, eighteen in all, counting Les.

Lester got out our tall iced-tea glasses, then the water glasses, then a couple beer steins, and finally a mason jar. He went over to Dad's cupboard and took out the chrome seltzer dispenser, then a box of cream chargers. He slipped one of the chargers, which looked like a miniature propane tank, into the top of the dispenser, then filled the bottom with seltzer water. All the guys were fascinated.

After that he took a jar of U-Bet chocolate-flavored syrup from the cupboard and a half gallon of milk from the fridge.

"That's it?" asked Karen.

"Oh, and a spoon. Very important, the spoon!" Lester said, and took one from the drawer. Then, with a flourish, he said, "Observe!"

He carefully spooned an inch of chocolate syrup into the bottom of each glass. When they were all filled, the beer steins and the mason jar, too, he added an inch of whole milk on top of the syrup, going from one glass to the next. Then he took the first glass, tilted it, inserted the spoon and, with his other hand, sprayed the seltzer from the pressurized dispenser directly onto the spoon so that he got a big chocolatey head. He stirred and handed the first glass to Elizabeth.

"Enjoy!" he said.

I don't know what fascinated me most—the way Elizabeth's cheeks turned pink as she took the glass from his hands, or the way the other kids were watching. This was not a treat Elizabeth would ordinarily have allowed herself, certainly not last summer, but Lester had chosen her—*her*—to get the first glass. So she lifted it to her lips and drank.

"It's *wonderful*!" she said. And then, as though counting calories, "It's only milk and syrup and seltzer?"

"You got it!"

"Where does the egg come in?" asked Penny.

"Search me," said Lester. "It's an old New York drink. Some say it comes from Russia. But is that good or is that good?" He handed the second glass to Penny.

"Ummmm! It's good," she said. And offered Patrick a sip until he got his. I was glad Les served Patrick next.

We migrated back into the living room and sat around savoring the egg creams. There are times I absolutely love my brother. He was the hit of the evening. It was going on one o'clock, and when Les came in with his own egg cream in the mason jar, he said, "Ah, yes! An excellent bedtime drink," hoping we'd take the hint.

"In your dreams," said Pamela

"We're good for another three hours!" said Justin.

"Besides . . . ," Elizabeth added, and looked at Karen and Jill. Suddenly looks traveled all around the room, and Elizabeth and Karen went upstairs to my bedroom and came back down carrying a cake with lighted candles. They'd ordered it from the Giant, and on the frosting, in blue letters, it said, TO OUR NO. 1 STUD. The girls started singing "Happy Birthday" and everyone joined in, even the ones who didn't know what it was all about. "Happy birthday to you, happy birthday . . ."

I was sitting on Patrick's lap on the couch, and we started singing too. Patrick did, anyway. I never sing "Happy Birthday" because I can't carry a tune.

"Happy birthday, dear Studly . . . ," sang Pamela.

As soon as the cake was in Lester's hands, Karen took a picture.

Lester looked a little embarrassed. "Stud?" he said, looking around. "Somebody here named Stud?" Then he laughed.

"Make a wish!" Penny instructed. "Make a wish with all us gorgeous girls around you, and maybe it will come true."

"You mean I can wish this party was over, and you'll all go home?" Lester teased.

"Better than that. Maybe one of us could be your teddy bear for the night," said Pamela.

"Pamela!" Elizabeth scolded. We all laughed again.

"I don't know about that. My old teddy bear had one ear chewed off and an eye missing," Lester said.

"Blow, Lester! The wax is dripping," Gwen told him.

Lester blew out all twenty-two candles, everyone clapped, and then Jill got a knife and cut the cake into twenty pieces. We all dug in.

"Presents! Presents!" cried Pamela. I looked around in surprise. I'd expected the cake, but no one had said anything about presents. I stared as the girls—all except Leslie and Lori, who hadn't know about it, either—retrieved little packages from their sleeping bags, some flat, some in tiny balls, some in small boxes, and gave them to Lester.

"What's this? What's this?" he asked.

"Open them!" said Elizabeth. "You have to open them in front of everyone."

"Uh-oh," said Lester. "I don't like the sound of that." But he did, and we shrieked as he unwrapped or unrolled, untied or unwound, pair after pair of boxer shorts, each one wilder than the one before. Boxers that looked like newsprint; boxers with ants painted all over them; boxers in a leopard print, boxers with lipstick marks . . .

Les looked around at the girls. "Somebody trying to tell me to change my underwear more often?" he joked.

"No, we want you to model them!" Pamela said, and all the girls laughed.

"Hey, we came empty-handed!" Patrick said. "No one told us about presents, Les, but I'll give you the shorts off my bottom if you like."

"No. Thanks, anyway," said Lester.

"How about mine?" said Brian. He stood up and lowered his jeans just enough to show us three inches of bright purple boxer shorts with yellow zigzag lines on them.

"I can top those," said Donald Sheavers, showing off his racing car boxers, and suddenly all the guys were lowering their jeans and all the girls were screeching, and Lester looked relieved when I slipped another movie in the VCR and eventually everyone turned around to watch.

We weren't ready for sleep, though. Lester went upstairs to put in a half hour of study while we goofed off. Elizabeth and I were gathering up glasses and washing silverware—stepping over bodies and carrying stuff to the kitchen—when we heard a lot of muffled laughter coming from the next room and I wondered what I was missing. But after all the work Dad had put into the food for the party, I didn't want him to come down the next morning to a sink full of dirty dishes. I went back to the living room for a final check and heard Jill whisper, "There's Alice!" and instantly all heads in the living room jerked toward me with grins on their faces.

"Yeah? What?" I said, laughing.

"Nothing! Nothing!" Brian said.

"Just a little innovative photography," Justin added.

Actually, some of the kids had already staked out spots for their sleeping bags—under the dining room table, beside the couch, behind my beanbag chair, *on* my beanbag chair. I put in still another video while the girls trooped upstairs in twos and threes to change in my room and brush their teeth. Most of us just took off our jeans and pulled on shorts or sweatpants, but it felt so daring, somehow, to come downstairs with our sleeping bags and put them down next to the boys' on the rug.

There was always a short line outside the bathroom, and the boys were joking about going out in the yard to pee. By the time Lester came back downstairs, almost everyone had found a spot to roll out his sleeping bag, and he went around turning off lamps while the movies on the VCR played on, the volume low.

Patrick had saved a spot for me under the grand piano next to him, so I crawled in my sleeping bag, and he rolled over and kissed me on the mouth.

"Hey! Hey! None of that!" Mark called. "Hey, Les! Over here, man! Sex alert! Sex alert!"

Lester, on the couch, sleepily raised one eyebrow, gave me a look, and rolled over on his side.

We were all pretty tired. It was almost three o'clock, and

I knew that Dad probably hadn't had much sleep yet and was hoping we'd all quiet down. The music, the movie, the food, the warmth of the sleeping bag . . . Patrick and I kissed a while longer, and I was thinking how it would feel if Les wasn't here and we really did both crawl in the same bag. But he fell asleep even before I did, and for most of the night, I slept. So did everyone else, though I woke up briefly around four and was aware that Lester had turned on a table lamp and left it on. I guess he figured that the next best thing to his staying awake all night was the light from a lamp.

I woke again about eight to whispers and giggles, and lifted my head to look around. Lester was sound asleep on the couch, his mouth agape, snoring peacefully, but Pamela and Jill were slowly, delicately propping Q-tips at odd angles in his thick brown hair.

Other kids began to stir and when they saw what Jill and Pamela were up to, they began to giggle. Jennifer took some dental floss out of her overnight bag, and Jill unwound it and wrapped it around the Q-tips, draping it from stick to stick, turning her head away so she wouldn't breathe or giggle in Lester's face. It looked sort of like a crown. Pamela went out to the kitchen and returned with a sheet of foil. She tore off little pieces and carefully squeezed them over the ends of each Q-tip so that they looked like silver. Both Patrick and I were each sitting up on one elbow now, laughing silently. Karen took a Polaroid picture.

Les gave a sigh and opened his mouth even wider. Penny

got in the act and stuck one finger in his mouth. Then she turned to the other kids, most of whom were awake now, all but Donald Sheavers, and mimed that she was going to stick two fingers in without touching the sides of Lester's mouth. Lester snored on. Penny's dimples grew even deeper as she indicated three fingers and gently guided them in without waking Lester. Somebody clapped. This time Penny held up four fingers, but at that moment Lester's mouth snapped shut, and then his eyes opened. He gave a snort, and Penny sat back on her heels.

"Wha'sup?" Lester said groggily. He saw Pamela and Jill and Jennifer all looking at him and laughing. Les swung his legs off the couch and looked around. As he did so, one of the Q-tips slipped and dangled over his eyes. "What the . . . ?" Lester cried, running his hand over his hair. Then he leaped up. "Oh, for crying out loud," he said as the crown fell off, and everyone laughed.

Dad stepped in from the kitchen. "Anybody for waffles and sausage?" he said.

"They're all yours, Dad. I'm outta here," Les said, bolting up the stairs with his blanket and pillow.

Some of the girls went upstairs to shower, two and three crowding into the bathtub at once to save time, a couple of guys went back to sleep, but by ten, half of us had eaten Dad's waffles and the other half were getting dressed. A few kids, Patrick included, had already gone home, and the rest drifted away, one by one, most of them telling me that they'd had a really great time, and I knew they meant it. You can just tell.

When the last person had gone, I went out in the kitchen to help with the dishes. Dad looked at me. I looked at him.

"Whew!" he said, and we both laughed.

"Thanks, Dad," I told him. "Everyone had a really great time. And there wasn't any sex going on, if that's what you're going to ask me next."

"I wasn't, but I'm glad to hear it," he said.

I spent the next hour putting the house back in shape, running the vacuum over the rug and the dining room, cleaning the popcorn off the sofa and chairs, rearranging the furniture, carrying more glasses to the kitchen. There were Polaroid pictures all over the top of the piano, and I got myself a glass of orange juice and sat down on the sofa to enjoy them.

There was a photo of Brian eating a piece of pizza; Elizabeth carrying the birthday cake; Lori and Mark and Jill and Justin playing cards; Gwen and Legs watching the movie; me with my mouth open, eating popcorn; Lester holding up a pair of boxer shorts; Lester on the couch with Q-tips in his hair, and then . . . I suddenly felt like a block of ice without any heartbeat at all. Because there in my hand was a picture of Patrick and Penny with their arms around each other, kissing.

5

THAT SINKING FEELING

I couldn't breathe for a moment, and then I sank down on the couch, not taking my eyes from the picture.

On this couch, this very couch where I was sitting, Penny and Patrick were turned toward each other in the photo. She had one hand on his shoulder, he had a hand on her waist, and their faces were turned at an angle so you could see most of the back of Patrick's head and one side of Penny's face.

How *could* they? How could *he*?

My eyes were brimming over, and tears spilled down my cheeks. I felt humiliated, angry, and lost. How could they do this in my very own house? Here at my *party*? Why had Karen taken their picture? And then I remembered when I'd walked in the living room once and heard someone whisper, "There's Alice," as though a secret was traveling around the place. Everyone was in on it but me.

I leaned back against the sofa cushions, covered my face with my hands, and sobbed. Maybe Karen had left it behind just so I'd find out. Maybe Patrick had been seeing Penny for weeks and no one had the nerve to tell me.

The phone rang, but I didn't want to answer. Lester was still sleeping, though, and Dad was outside raking leaves. So I got up, swallowed, and walked to the phone in the hall.

"Hello?" I said, but it didn't sound like me.

There was a pause.

"Al?" Pamela's starting to mimic Lester now, calling me "Al."

"Yeah? What do you want?" I said hoarsely.

"My gosh, it doesn't sound like you at all. I think I left my sweater at your place. I'm on my way over to pick it up, okay?"

"All right."

Another pause. "You sound like you've been crying."

I swallowed again.

"Alice, have you been crying?" she asked.

"Pamela!" I bawled. I couldn't hold back any longer.

"What's the matter? What's *happened*?" And then, before I could say anything, she said, "You saw the picture, I'll bet."

Everybody knew, then! Everyone was waiting. All the kids knew that Patrick was falling for Penny, and no one knew how to tell me, least of all Patrick.

"I'll be right over," Pamela said, and hung up.

I sat down on the stairs, too weak to do anything else. Yesterday had been so wonderful. I'd felt attractive and popular and clever and fun. Now I felt like old news, yesterday's leftovers. I felt tricked and pitied.

I knew I should go wash my face before Pamela got here, but I couldn't even make myself do that. Now that she said she was coming, I wanted her to hurry and get here. I wanted to know how long she'd known Patrick was cheating on me and how many of the other kids knew.

When her footsteps sounded on the porch, I heard voices and realized that Elizabeth was with her. They'd come together to let me know that Patrick was breaking up with me, to be with me in my time of need. I didn't *want* to be pitied. I didn't *want* to be sad. Yet here I was, and the minute I opened the door, I started crying again.

Instantly Elizabeth put her arms around me, but Pamela was saying, "Al, it was a joke! That's all it was, just a joke."

"Well, if th-that was a joke, I don't get it," I sobbed. "How long have you known something was going on?"

"I didn't know anything until Pamela came over and got me and said you were upset about a picture," said Elizabeth. "*What* picture?"

We were an odd-looking lot. Elizabeth had obviously just gotten home from Mass, because she was wearing a dark green dress. Pamela had changed to shorts, even though it was only sixty degrees out, and I was still dressed in the clothes I'd worn yesterday. Wordlessly I led them into the living room and handed Elizabeth the photo.

She stared at it, then at Pamela. "Where was *I* when they took this picture?" she asked.

"I don't know. You and Alice were off in the kitchen somewhere, and Karen was just being . . . well, Karen. She was telling us how you could make pictures lie so it looked like something was happening that wasn't and she'd seen someone take a picture at a party where it looked like a couple was kissing when they weren't, and Penny said, 'Let's try it!' and chose Patrick. It was supposed to be a *joke*, Alice!"

Pamela was calling me Alice again, so I knew she was serious. But the words "chose Patrick" rang in my ears. Why not Mark or Brian or Donald or Justin? Why did she choose a guy who was actually going with someone? And then, the question that hurt even more, why had Patrick agreed to do it?

"Look!" Pamela explained. "They weren't even touching. I helped arrange them."

"*You?*" I cried.

Pamela looked chagrined. "Well, if they're going to do it, wouldn't you rather have one of your friends calling the shots to be sure it's legit? We had them arranged so that their lips were two inches apart, their hands weren't touching each other, but from across the room, in the camera, it looked like a real kiss."

"That's a scream," I wept. "I never saw anything so funny in my life."

"Forgive and forget," Elizabeth said quickly, trying to be helpful.

When Pamela went upstairs to get her sweater, Elizabeth said, "Patrick probably couldn't help himself. All the guys are nuts about Penny. It's just hormones, that's all it is."

That was supposed to make me feel better?

When Pamela came back down, we went out to sit in the sunshine on the front steps. We could hear the quiet *scrape, scrape* of Dad's rake at the side of the house.

"This was supposed to be a beautiful September," I said ruefully. "I wanted it to be an autumn I'd always remember—my first year of high school. I'll remember it, all right."

"Seventy times seven," said Elizabeth.

"What? What are we doing now, the multiplication tables?"

"That's how many times you're supposed to forgive someone."

"Great!" I said. "Patrick gets to kiss her four hundred and ninety times more." I guess I'm pretty good at arithmetic when it's important.

"He didn't *kiss* her!" Pamela insisted.

No, he hadn't kissed her, but he'd been two inches away from her lips, I thought. He had smelled the scent of her hair, looked into her eyes. If he hadn't kissed her, I'll bet he'd wanted to.

I leaned back on my elbows. "She's like a magnet," I said. "What is it about small, petite girls, anyway? The boys go crazy over them, and it makes the rest of us feel like elephants."

"I don't feel like an elephant. You're exaggerating," said Pamela. "And you have to admit she's a lot of fun. You'd better take it as a joke, Al, because everyone else is."

"I know. I'm making a mountain out of a molehill. I guess I just wanted it to be the perfect party, and this was the part that wasn't so perfect," I said.

"I've got to go have lunch," said Elizabeth. "I'll see you later, guys."

We watched her cross the street.

"I have to go, too," said Pamela. "Dad's taking me to an Orioles game."

I glanced over at her. "Sounds like you're getting along better!"

"We're making 'a conscious effort,' as Dad puts it. Anyway, it'll get me out of the house when Mom calls. She always calls on Sunday afternoons, and I don't much feel like talking to her. Then I've got a ton of homework to do."

"Me too," I told her. I'd thought the homework in junior high was awful, but it was nothing like what they give you in high school.

I sat on the porch a while longer and let the sun warm my legs as Pamela went back down the block. Finally I heard Lester in the kitchen, making something gross in the blender, so I went back inside. He was pouring some kind of skim milk/banana/oatmeal mixture into a glass, and he seemed only half awake.

"Shut up," he said, before I even opened my mouth.

"Happy birthday, dear Les-ter . . . ," I warbled off-key.

"Oh, geez, don't ruin it," he said.

"I just wanted you to know that Dad and I are taking you out to dinner tonight, and as my present to you, I'm doing all the dishes this week, even though you're on kitchen duty."

That perked him up a little. "My laundry, too?"

"Don't push it," I said. I watched him glug down the concoction, then stick an English muffin in the toaster. He was wearing an old pair of boxer shorts with lemons on them, and a ripped T-shirt.

I felt like crying again, but I didn't. "Lester," I said. "If there was this girl you had really, really liked for a long time—"

"Don't start," he said.

"No, I need to know. And let's say there was this party and all your friends were there, and it was going on all night, everybody having a good time . . ."

Lester reached into the fridge and took out the butter carton.

". . . and the next morning you found a Polaroid picture somebody had taken of"—I didn't want to say "kissing" because Lester probably wouldn't be bothered by a kiss—"of this girl lying naked on the couch with a naked guy on top of her, and—"

"What?" Lester yelled, dropping the butter.

". . . and you found out it was all trick photography to make them *look* like they were having sex, but they weren't, would . . . ?"

Lester grabbed me by one arm. "Who was it? Pamela? Jill?"

I shook my head. "Nobody."

"Al, did anyone get naked last night while I was sleeping?"

"No."

"Did anyone have sex with their clothes *on*?"

"No."

"Then will you please get out of my face and let me enjoy my breakfast in peace?"

"Lester, really! I need your advice!" I said, sitting down across from him, and told him about the photo of Patrick and Penny.

"So if it's all a joke, what's the big deal?" he asked.

"It *hurts*, Lester!"

"Maybe so, but the best thing you can do is laugh and forget it."

"I can't."

"Okay, then. Get on the bus tomorrow and go claw Patrick's eyes out. That'll really endear you to him. C'mon, Al. Snap out of it."

"I guess you're right," I said, and went upstairs.

For a while I managed to put the picture out of my mind, and worked on a paper for history. I went back down around two and ate part of a sandwich Dad had left and some pretzels, but when I started to go up again and saw the sofa where Patrick had been sitting with Penny, where everyone had been whispering, it started the feelings all over again.

I lay for a long time on my bed staring up at the ceiling, at the cobweb that was strung between my light fixture and the wall. It was beginning to collect dust, and looked like a cable on the Brooklyn Bridge. Was Karen trying to start a fight between Patrick and me? I wondered. Was Penny trying to come between us?

I heard the doorbell ring. Lester's footsteps in the down-stairs hall.

"Hey, Al! It's Patrick," he called.

Patrick! For a moment I didn't move. I wouldn't go down, I *couldn't*! Then I realized how weird it would seem if I didn't. I leaped up and yelled, "Be down in a sec." I brushed my teeth and put on a little eye makeup so my eyes wouldn't look puffy, then went downstairs. My smile felt about as false as Jill's eye-lashes or Karen's fingernails.

"Hi," I said. Even my voice sounded fake. It sounded as though it came from the tiny chest of a Barbie doll.

"Hi," said Patrick. "Want to walk over to the school or some-thing? Get some ice cream?"

The school is the elementary school nearby, where our gang still gathers sometimes. We sit on the rubber swings, talking to each other, whirling the swings around, scaring all the little kids away.

"Well, I'm not sure," I said. "I'm sort of busy. We're taking Lester out to dinner tonight, and I've got all this homework."

"So have I, but I've been at it all morning. Need a break," he said. A lock of red hair hung down over the left side of Patrick's forehead, and he seemed to have grown another two inches since the day before. He playfully jiggled my arm. "C'mon. It'll do you good."

"Okay," I said.

We went outside. Dad was still at it, transplanting azalea

bushes. He always seemed to be tinkering with the yard or the house since he came back from England, getting things ready for Miss Summers, of course.

"Going for a walk, Dad," I called.

He waved and bent over the azaleas again. Patrick and I started our typical slow walk down the sidewalk, his arm around my waist, but it didn't seem like old times anymore. Usually I lean against him in an easy, comfortable manner, but this time my body resisted, and I discovered I was walking with my arms folded in front of my chest, as though I were cold.

Patrick looked down at me. "My, aren't *we* friendly!" he said.

I managed a smile. "Sorry. Got homework on my mind," I lied.

"Algebra?"

"That's later. I haven't even started it yet."

"Want me to stick around and help?"

"No, I'll manage. Lester's here if I've got any questions."

We walked a little farther. "Great party last night," Patrick said. "Everyone had a good time."

"Evidently." Why is it that even when you *know* what not to say, you end up saying it?

Patrick gave my waist a little tug. "What's the matter with you, anyway?"

There was no use in pretending. "I found a photo of you and Penny, Patrick. That's what's the matter."

"Didn't anyone explain about that picture?" he asked, with not a trace of guilt.

"Well, you certainly didn't."

"It was all a pose, Alice! We weren't even touching! We were just horsing around for laughs."

"Ho-ho-ho."

"Karen was going to show it to you, and then you put in another video and I guess we just forgot."

"And it didn't occur to you to tell me about it?"

"I *forgot* about it! Why are you getting so upset?"

I felt stupid and silly, yet still betrayed. "I don't know. How would you feel if after a party at your place, you found a picture of me kissing Justin or Donald Sheavers?"

"We weren't kissing!"

"I know it, but—"

"If I found a picture like that, I'd probably pick up the phone and ask you about it."

"So I'm asking. How come Penny picked you?"

"I don't know. I just went along for the ride."

Patrick let his arm drop, and a space developed between us there on the sidewalk. "What is this? The third degree? We were just having fun. Isn't that allowed?"

I felt awful then. Deserted. "Of course, Patrick! It's just that everyone seems so secretive about it, as though there's something between you and Penny I'm not supposed to know."

"There's nothing secret. She's just fun, that's all." And when I didn't answer, he said, "Hey! She's not you, Alice."

"I wonder why that doesn't help." I knew I shouldn't have said that.

Patrick thrust his hands in his pockets, and we walked a few minutes in silence. The *thrub* of my heart seemed to echo in my ears.

"We're not married, you know," Patrick said finally, without smiling. "I think I'm still allowed to have friends."

"Of course you are," I said, beginning to regret the whole conversation. "I guess I'm acting dumb about it."

I thought he'd put his arm around me then, glad to be forgiven, but he didn't.

"I . . . I don't want you to think you have to have my permission every time you want to talk to another girl," I added.

He didn't answer for a while. We just walked on slowly, a foot apart, but finally he moved closer and then he put one arm around my shoulder. "I'm going to be graduating a year before you do," he said. "I'll be away at college. I'll meet new people, and so will you. We've both got to be free to make friends, Alice."

I could feel tears gathering behind my eyelids, but I managed to hold them back. "I know," I said. And then, trying to be funny, I added, "but remember our date for New Year's Eve when we're both twenty-one. You'll call me, you said."

He just laughed. "I'll put it on the calendar," he promised.

6

MOVING ON

When I got on the bus the next morning, Patrick was sitting with guys in the last row, and Penny was up on her knees, leaning over the back of the seat, talking to Jill and Karen.

"Hi, everybody!" I said, my smile molded onto my face as though set in concrete.

"Hey, Al! Great party!" Mark called.

Some of the girls turned then, Penny included.

"Yeah, we had a great time!" said Jill.

"Lester's so *funny*!" said Penny.

"Was he wearing any of the shorts we gave him?" Karen asked.

I managed a laugh. "I don't keep track of his underwear," I said.

The sophomores, juniors, and seniors cast us curious glances, and Elizabeth giggled. Penny and Jill and Karen laughed, too. Then it was like we were all friends again, and Penny pulled me down on the seat next to her to see the little rosebud tattoo she got on her wrist, nonpermanent, of course, and Elizabeth squeezed in beside us.

"I've got this friend who has a tattoo on her butt," said Karen. "Permanent! She'll never get it off!"

"What kind is it?" Elizabeth wanted to know.

"Popeye! Can you imagine?"

"Can you imagine lying naked while a man tattoos you?" asked Elizabeth.

"Hey, that would be the best part!" said Penny, and we laughed some more. A senior in front of us glanced around with a bemused expression, and that set us off again.

"Hey, Alice, did you find the picture Karen took?" asked Jill.

I didn't miss a beat. "Yeah, Patrick told me about it. The artificial kiss," I said, and couldn't believe how natural I sounded. How comfortable and confident and easy.

"We were just acting up," Penny said. "I always get nutty around friends."

How did I know I wouldn't like this girl? I thought. How did I know she might not become one of my best friends? I felt one hundred percent better by the time we got to school. Two hundred percent better when Patrick came up behind me as we were getting off and slipped his hands around my waist, kissing me on the side of my neck. I nuzzled him in return. Everything was back to normal. I felt loved and secure.

The drama club met for the first time after school. Mostly we just sat around talking, the drama coach, Mr. Ellis, outlining his plans for the spring production, telling us some of the plays he was considering, as though we had a vote in the matter.

Pamela was the only person there I knew. She fit right in with that blue streak in her hair, because a lot of the kids wore black, with black makeup and purple lips and hair. But when one of the purple-lipped girls asked a question, she sounded intelligent. Even nice. Maybe my world was broadening, I thought. Maybe I could learn to get along with girls I was jealous of, and people who looked and dressed like they lived on another planet.

"Just so I can get some idea of what we have here to work with, how many of you are interested in acting, and how many are here for stage crew?" Mr. Ellis asked. "Let's see a show of hands for actors."

Most of the kids, Pamela included, wanted to act.

"When it's time to do casting, we have to open it to the whole school, of course, so there are no guarantees," Mr. Ellis said, "but I've found that the bulk of the major roles each year go to members of the drama club. Now, how about stage crew—set design, costumes, props, lighting—that kind of thing. Everyone else here for that?"

The rest of us raised our hands. There was only one other girl besides myself, I discovered, who wanted to be part of the crew. She was short and squat, dressed in overalls. Her hair was light brown—modified punk—and she had huge blue eyes. We gave each other sympathetic smiles when we realized all the rest of the crew were guys.

"Anyone here for something *other* than acting or stage crew?" Mr. Ellis asked, smiling. "Simple curiosity, maybe?"

A guy sitting to one side, dressed completely in black and purple, raised his hand. "Director," he joked, and we all laughed.

"Looks like we'll be seeing a lot of each other," the blue-eyed girl said when the session was over. "I'm Molly."

"I'm Alice," I said.

It felt good to be branching out—to feel myself *stretch*. Patrick wasn't the only one who had extra things to do and places to go after school.

At home, we could hardly keep up with Dad. All week long he had been relandscaping the whole yard, front and back, putting a dogwood tree in one place, a red maple in another, azaleas on both sides of the front steps, rhododendron, tiger lilies, ivy, a magnolia . . .

"How do you know Sylvia will like all this stuff?" I asked him as he came in with muddy work gloves to get a drink of water.

"Because I've chosen all her favorite plants and trees," he said.

"Are we going to keep living here, then, after you're married?"

"We've talked about it," Dad said. "She loves her own little place, but it's just too small for the four of us, so it makes sense that she move here." Dad smiled at the thought of it. "She'll certainly make the house a home, with all her little touches."

"It's already a home," I said, somewhat resentfully.

Dad looked over at me from the sink. "Of course it is, honey. But won't it be nice to have a mom around?"

"You know how much I've wanted this, Dad, but she's really not my mother. I don't think I can ever call her that."

"You don't have to. 'Sylvia' will do."

I continued nibbling a carrot. "Are you going to visit her again before she comes back in June?" I asked.

"I'd like to. We'll have to see."

"Christmas?"

"Not Christmas. That's our busiest time at the store, and I won't have Janice this year, remember. Besides, Sylvia plans to do a little traveling over the holidays, see a bit more of the country before her year is up."

How could two people in love stay away from each other that long? I wondered. A lot could happen in eight months.

It was my turn to make dinner, and I was having hamburgers, oven-made french fries, and a salad. As I scrubbed the potatoes and cut them in long strips, I tried to imagine another person living in our house. Dad's bedroom is the largest. He has two huge closets on either side of a bay window. There are clothes poles in only one of them, though. The other has built-in drawers at the back for blankets and stuff, and shelves along the sides, so I don't know where Sylvia's clothes would go. And we only have one bathroom. That could be a problem. It's *already* a problem!

I sprinkled the potato slices with olive oil and salt and stuck them in the oven while I looked around the kitchen, trying to see it through Sylvia's eyes.

It's a big, old-fashioned kitchen with lots of cupboards, but little counter space. We have a large dining room, a large living room, and a full basement. Dad uses a corner of our dining room for his office, but all that will change when he marries Sylvia, he says, because she'll need an office, too.

"I'm thinking of finishing the basement," Dad said at dinner. "Insulation, paneling, wall-to-wall carpet. . . . I want Sylvia to have plenty of room for her school things, and I could use a real honest-to-goodness desk. If I turned half of the basement into office space, would that be okay with you two?"

I dipped one of my french fries into a pool of catsup and thought about Miss Summers's house, the few times I'd been in it. I know how she liked having her desk by the back window overlooking the yard and bird feeder.

"How do you know she'll like working in a basement?" I asked.

"It's all we've got," Dad said simply. "But she can hang plants all over the place if she likes. Decorate the house any way she wants."

"Not my room!" I said. "I want my room exactly the way it is now." I guess you could call it jungle decor—the bedspread, the chair, the large rubber plant in one corner . . .

"I'm sure Sylvia isn't going to touch your room, Al. Or yours, either, Les. You can keep your rooms the way you want them."

"Seems to me the solution would be for me to get an apartment somewhere and let you and Sylvia use my room as an office," he said. "I've sponged off you long enough, Dad."

"For one thing, Sylvia wouldn't hear of it," Dad told him. "And for another, it saves us a lot of money, your living at home. Until you're out of school, Les, money's going to be tight, and we enjoy having you around."

"For what? The court jester?" Lester said. "If I could share an apartment with a bunch of guys, it might not be so expensive."

"Les, you are free to do whatever you want. But I think Sylvia would be very distressed if you moved out on her account. Why don't you live at home for at least another year while we all get acclimated to one another, become a family, and later, if you want to live somewhere else, you can make the decision then."

Somehow I'd never thought of Lester leaving home. Oh, if he married, of course. But living single somewhere else? Away from Dad and me? I wanted change, and I didn't. Looked forward to it and dreaded it both at the same time.

I was over at Elizabeth's when she and her mom had this argument. I've almost never heard of Liz and her mom arguing at all, and especially not in front of other people. She and I were sitting on the couch looking through a magazine and her mother had just put Nathan down for his nap.

Mrs. Price stopped in the doorway of the living room and said, "Did you get my note about your piano lesson? You said you couldn't make it Friday, so he's going to squeeze you in Saturday at one forty-five."

"I already called him and canceled," Elizabeth said, turning the page again to an article titled, "Does He Want You for Your Mind or Your Body?"

Mrs. Price was carrying an armload of Nathan's clothes to the basement, and she leaned against the door frame. *"What?"*

"I canceled. I've got a big paper to write this weekend."

"Elizabeth Ann, all you said was that you couldn't do it Friday, and Mr. Hedges has gone out of his way to move appointments around so he could take you."

"Well, he'll just have to move them back again. You never told me you were making it Saturday," said Elizabeth.

I pretended to be engrossed in men who want you for your mind, but I was right in the line of fire between Elizabeth and her mom.

"Why didn't you *say* you didn't want a lesson at all this weekend?" Mrs. Price asked in exasperation. "We are so lucky that Mr. Hedges accepted you at all, and now, after he's taken an interest in your playing, this seems so ungrateful."

"Well, I'm not having a lesson this weekend, Mother, and I've taken care of it," Elizabeth said, and I noticed her voice was shaking.

"I just wish you'd told me earlier," her mother snapped, and went on down to the basement.

Elizabeth didn't say any more, but I could see she was upset, and I went home shortly after that.

When I went to the Melody Inn the following Saturday to put in my three hours of work, I discovered that Janice Sherman was leaving sooner than she had expected. She had an offer to manage a Melody Inn in Toledo, Ohio, and wanted to go early to find a place to live. Dad said she could, that we'd make do somehow till he got a replacement. Everybody was being ultrapolite and friendly to her, and she was being her usual methodical self, putting Post-it notes on every shelf in her office, on every box and drawer, saying exactly where everything was so we wouldn't go bananas after she left.

"When did all this happen?" Marilyn whispered to me when I dusted the shelves in the Gift Shoppe, the little boutique under the stairs leading to the practice cubicles above. "Did she and your dad have a fight or something?"

I didn't want to say more than I should, so I just told her, "No, I think Janice figures it's time she moved on."

But Marilyn didn't buy it. "Move out, is more like it. Your dad comes back from England with the news that he and Sylvia Summers are engaged, and suddenly Janice Sherman is looking for a new place to work. We all know she's nuts about him." When I didn't answer, she asked, "Who's he going to get to replace her?"

"I don't know," I answered. "I suppose he'll advertise. Or maybe headquarters will send a replacement."

All day long the instructors stopped by Janice's office and stood in her doorway with their cups of coffee, making small talk, saying how they'd miss her, asking about the store in Toledo.

"I think living in Ohio will be a nice change of pace," she'd say.

I guess almost any place can be nice, but I don't think I would give up a job near Washington, D.C., for Toledo. Still, she seemed genuinely pleased that the instructors thought enough of her to ask, and Dad took her out to lunch.

When they got back, Marilyn and I had decorated Janice's office with good-bye balloons. We'd all chipped in to buy her a jacket from the shop next door, a red jacket that she'd mentioned to Marilyn she liked. I'd gone across the street for brownies and grapes, and Janice was delighted by the fuss we were making over her. I had to admire her for looking so cheerful when I knew she was leaving because it was hopeless to stick around a man who was in love with another woman.

Would I keep hanging around a guy who was in love with someone else? I wondered. Why did life have to be so complicated? Dad was in love with Miss Summers, but for a while she'd been in love with Jim Sorringer. Janice Sherman was in love with Dad, who didn't love her back. Marilyn was still in love with Lester, who wasn't in love with anyone at the moment. Wouldn't it be simpler if we were just assigned somebody when we reached the age of twenty-five? Maybe there was something to the custom of arranged marriages after all.

Marilyn and Dad took turns darting in and out of Janice's office to wait on customers, then they'd come back, and we all watched while Janice tried on the red jacket. The instructors stopped in between students for a cup of coffee and a brownie, but by two o'clock, it was past time for me to go.

"Good-bye, Janice," I said. "I hope you'll be really, really happy in Toledo." If only I'd stopped there. Why didn't I just say, "We'll probably hear that the Toledo store is leading all the others in sales, once you take over," or something. Instead, I said, "Next thing you know, we'll probably hear that you're married."

There was a three-second silence, but it seemed like three minutes to me. Everyone stared at me, then they all started talking at once, cleaning up cups, taking another grape, and Janice said, "I'm not going to Ohio to look for a husband, Alice; I'm going for the job."

I blushed and tried to avoid Dad's withering stare. "Of course! I just mean, that'll probably happen, too! I mean . . ." I tried to laugh it off. "You in that red jacket, well . . . Wow!"

"She does look great in it," one of the instructors said.

But Dad said, "If you hurry, Al, you can still make the two-twenty bus."

I gave Janice a quick hug and left the store, my cheeks burning. Why don't I think before I open my mouth? And yet, was it really so terrible?

* * *

Lester got home before Dad. He clerks at a men's shoe store on weekends—an upscale store, he says, where all the customers wear navy-blue dress socks up to their knees, and have tassels on their Italian-made loafers.

"We had a going-away party for Janice at the store today and I blew it," I told him.

Lester took off his jacket and dropped it on a chair. "What'd you do? Sneeze in the punch?"

I told him what I'd said about her marrying. "Why couldn't she take it as a compliment?" I asked, following him out to the refrigerator, where he stood taking things out one at a time, sniffing them, then setting them on the table. "We'd just given her a red jacket that made her look young and pretty, and everyone knows she's been disappointed in love, and—"

"That's exactly why you don't say something like that. Besides, aren't you doing a little stereotyping here? Janice can only be happy if she gets a man? You don't have to be part of a couple to be happy, you know."

"But look how happy Dad's been since he met Miss Summers!"

"He was missing Mom, of course. But you can be part of a couple and still be miserable. Or be single and happy. I'm not part of a couple at the moment, and I'm a heck of a lot happier than I was dating Eva Mecuri."

I thought of Lester's last girlfriend, and had to agree on that.

Six o'clock came, and Dad wasn't home, then six thirty. Lester and I made cheese omelettes for ourselves and left the egg and cheese and chive mixture in the refrigerator for Dad.

"Maybe he took Janice out to dinner, too," I said. "Maybe she became hysterical at the thought of never seeing him again, and—"

"Don't!" Lester said, and turned on the TV.

Six thirty became seven . . . then seven fifteen . . . seven thirty. I began to get worried. I called the Melody Inn, but no one answered.

At a quarter of eight, Dad pulled in the drive, and when he came in he apologized. "I should have called," he said. "Sorry. Hope you two weren't worried."

Lester turned off the TV. "We only called all the hospitals, the state police, and the National Guard," he told him.

"Did Janice Sherman change her mind about leaving?" I asked.

"No. I thought she was rather pleased with all the attention. *Loved* the red jacket. I think things are rather good between us, actually. No hard feelings."

"Then where . . . ?" I asked, and waited.

"A surprising new development," Dad said. "Actually, I took Marilyn Rawley to dinner."

One of Lester's feet slid off the coffee table, and he stared at Dad. Marilyn Rawley was an old girlfriend of Lester's—the first *serious* girlfriend, in fact, who had ever come to our house. She was "country" through and through—a sort of '60s flower child, with long straight brown hair. She was small and thin—the kind you could see walking barefoot through a meadow in a see-through cotton dress and no bra. A lot different from Crystal, with her short red hair and big breasts and her classical taste in music. But I'd liked Crystal, too!

"Yeah?" was all Lester said, but his eyes were fixed on Dad.

"As soon as Janice had left the store and Marilyn and I were cleaning up, Marilyn said to me point-blank, 'Mr. McKinley, I'd like to be considered for Janice's position.' Just like that."

"Really?" I cried.

"She's in *school*!" said Lester. "She's working on her degree."

"I know," said Dad. "I told her I needed someone full time to be assistant manager, and she said she was willing to drop her courses in order to get the job. I said I didn't think that was a good idea, but she told me she was on the verge of dropping out anyway, that college wasn't where she wanted to be."

"You're not going to let her, are you?" asked Les.

"I wasn't, but it turns out she had already talked to her adviser about leaving school. She said she was dropping out whether she got the position or not. So I suggested we talk about it more over dinner, and we went to that little Chinese place just off Georgia Avenue, and . . . to make a long story short . . . over beef and green peppers . . . I hired her."

Lester frowned, but I was delighted. "Great!" I said. I could see us now—one big, happy family: Dad and Sylvia, Lester and Marilyn, me and . . .

"She's good with customers, Les, and she does know music— classical as well as folk and rock. I suggested a three-month trial period—see how she likes the business end of it, shuffling papers. . . . If it doesn't work out, she can clerk full time and I'll hire someone else for assistant manager. What do you think?"

"*I* think it's a great idea!" I said.

"Maybe so," said Lester. "She's been less than motivated about getting a degree."

"Soooo," Dad said, relief in his voice. "Nice to have *that* settled. I guess today was a day of moving onward for Janice and upward for Marilyn."

I watched him hang his suit coat in the closet. "How was the final good-bye with Janice Sherman?" I asked.

"Cordial," said Dad.

"Cordial?" I teased. "Was there a kiss in that cordial?"

"Actually, yes. And a hug as well."

"On the lips or on the cheek?" I quizzed.

Dad laughed. "On the ear, as I remember. The kind that shows you're not too serious. But Janice did a lot for the Melody Inn, Al. Don't knock it."

"I won't, but Marilyn will do so much more!" I said.

"We'll see," said Dad.

I was glad he didn't yell at me for what I'd said to Janice about getting married. But I wondered if having Marilyn at the store full time would bring her and Lester together again.

It would be the best of all possible worlds for me, I thought. Elegant Sylvia Summers in her beautiful, soft clothes and wonderful perfumes, and Marilyn Rawley in her cotton dresses and bare feet. What one couldn't teach me about life, the other could. If Lester would only fall in love with Marilyn again, and marry her, Marilyn and I would be sisters-in-law, and she and Lester could have four children, all playing barefoot in the grass and wearing flowers in their hair and playing guitars and singing folk songs, and . . .

The phone rang, and I picked it up in the hall.

"Alice!" came Pamela's voice. "Are you going?"

"Going where?"

"Penny's Halloween party. Didn't she call you?"

There was that cold, sliding-down feeling again. "No . . ."

"Well, she will, I'm sure. At her house on Halloween. Costumes and everything. Elizabeth and I are going. All the guys have been invited, Brian told me."

My lips seemed to stick together. "Did you get . . . invitations in the mail, or what?"

"No. She called. Oh, you're invited, I know."

We talked for a few minutes, and then I made an excuse to go. I didn't want to tie up the phone.

But eight became nine, nine fifteen, nine thirty . . . I checked a few times to make sure no one was using the phone. It sat silently in the hallway, its buttons like little square eyes, mocking me. Twice I checked my e-mail. No message from Penny there, either.

And then, about a quarter of ten, Penny called.

"Hi, Alice. I wanted to be sure you knew about my party," she said, and told me the date and the time.

"Sure," I said. "Sounds great." But I couldn't help feeling she'd saved me till last, that I was at the very bottom of her list.

7

PANIC

Things were going to be all right. Penny was just what everyone said she was—cute as a penny, funny, friendly, and open, and it was okay that all the boys, Patrick included, liked her. How could they not? Just because Patrick liked her didn't mean he liked me less, or that I wasn't special to him.

I didn't want an ugly costume, though. Penny was also pretty and petite, and I wasn't about to go as a clown or something, with a big nose. I decided to go as a flapper, one of those 1920s girls in the short fringed skirt and headband. I told Pamela and Elizabeth, and we all decided to be flappers together. Mrs. Price said she'd help with the costumes, and we had a lot of fun getting the stuff together and trying it on.

"We've got to have plumes in our headbands!" Pamela said one afternoon, lifting some stuff out of a shopping bag. "I stopped at the fabric store and found the wildest stuff!"

I squealed as she handed me a green feather plume to stick in the sequined headband I'd be wearing, which matched the short, swishy dress Mrs. Price had made for me. It was tank-style, all one piece, no waist, with a fringe of the same color around the hem.

"And a garter!" Elizabeth said. "We've each got to have a garter. Pastel panty hose and a garter."

Mrs. Price had as much fun as any of us. We had to take turns watching Elizabeth's baby brother while her mom sewed the dresses on her machine. We tickled Nathan with our plumes while he crawled around the floor, trying to get away from us and giggling.

My dress was pale green, Elizabeth's was red, and Pamela's was purple, which made the blue streak in her hair stand out all the more. I bought the matching panty hose for all of us, and an hour before the party Saturday night, Pamela and Elizabeth came over to show our costumes to Dad and Lester.

Lester was getting ready to go down to Georgetown with some friends, where all the college kids gather on Halloween. At the moment, though, he was sitting on the couch reading *Newsweek* and eating an apple. Pamela had brought over a CD of the Charleston, and I put it on my portable player and set it out in the hall. As soon as the music began, tin-sounding and honky, we danced into the living room, our arms around one another's shoulders, kicking our legs out like the Rockettes, and then we each cut loose and did our own version of the Charleston.

Lester lowered his apple and grinned. "You girls dancing or swimming?" he asked, but he not only laughed, he clapped.

Dad got up from the dining room table, where he was going over mail orders from the Melody Inn, and stood in the doorway smiling at us. "Your mother certainly would have enjoyed this, Al," he said wistfully. "Let me get my camera."

I was delighted that we were making a hit with Dad and Lester. If they liked us, the guys at the party surely would.

Dad drove us over to Penny's. Her house was about the same as ours—old and big, with lots of trees around it.

Both her parents were on hand to meet us at the door, and Penny herself was dressed as a pirate—short black shorts, a red shirt and black sash, gold earrings, a red bandanna, and a patch over one eye. Adorable, was the only way to describe her, but then I felt adorable, too, so it didn't bother me as much as it might have.

Not everyone was there, but most of our crowd was. She hadn't invited Lori and Leslie, I noticed, or Sam and Jennifer, and she didn't even know Donald Sheavers, but Gwen and Legs had come, and the usual gang that hangs around Mark Stedmeister's pool in the summers. I guessed Penny would be a part of it now.

The guys all came as gangsters, every one of them. Well, all but Legs. He and Gwen came as Twinkies. Karen was a bag of potato chips and Jill was a French maid. We made quite a picture.

In fact, flashbulbs kept going off all evening, and Penny's folks took a number of group pictures.

Of course, everyone made us put on the Charleston CD and dance, and soon the whole gang was hoofing it up. The gangsters and the flappers together looked great, and I was having more fun than I'd had at my own party.

Patrick swung me around, tipped me back, and kissed me in front of everyone; it was just a glorious Halloween. Penny's dad drove some of the kids home afterward, Pamela's dad drove a bunch, too, and Lester came to pick up Elizabeth, Patrick, and me. Patrick kissed me again before he got out of the car.

"All that worry for nothing," Elizabeth said to me after Patrick got out. "He's still crazy for you, Alice."

"I guess so," I said. "How about you and Justin?"

"Oh, he likes all the girls," she said.

I couldn't help but wonder about Elizabeth as I dressed for bed. Justin is one of the best-looking guys in ninth grade. Nice, too, and nuts—or *was* nuts—about Elizabeth. But just because he made a remark last summer—a joking remark—about her getting chubby, she's been giving him the cold shoulder. It's almost as though she *looks* for reasons not to get too close to a boy. And she sure isn't chubby now. There are times I feel there will always be a part of Elizabeth I'll never know. I wonder if anyone feels that way about me.

I slept late the next morning and had a ton of homework, so I didn't go running. Pamela, Elizabeth, and I had started running every morning during the summer to tone up before we started high school, and I'd vowed to keep it up after school began. I enjoyed running even when Pamela and Elizabeth weren't with me. Sort of my own special time to think things over and plan my day.

But now I realized I'd let too much slip by while I was getting ready for Halloween, and began to panic that even if I stayed up all night I wouldn't be able to do it all. When I looked at the course outline for English, I discovered that a huge paper I had thought was due November 10 was due November 3, a week sooner.

"Don't anyone talk to me!" I bellowed, pushing Dad's stuff to one side of the dining room table and taking over the rest of the space for myself.

"A pleasure," said Lester. "Who rattled *your* cage?"

"High school is too much work!" I cried in despair. "Every teacher thinks his is the only subject there is—that you've got all the time in the world just to work on his assignments. Never mind what anyone else gives you."

"And you haven't even started college, much less grad school," said Lester, which didn't make me feel any better.

I had only done two problems in algebra when the phone rang.

"Al, it's Patrick," Dad called. "Should I say you'll call him back?"

"No, I'll take it," I mumbled. As I walked to the phone in the hall I wondered if I should ask him to come over and help me with the algebra, but I couldn't very well let him help and then tell him to go home. If he came, he'd want to stay awhile, and I'd lose an hour or two I just couldn't afford. "Hi," I said.

"Hi. How are the legs this morning?"

"Wobbly." I laughed. "It was a fun party, though."

"Sure was," he said. "Hey, today's the last day for that sci-fi movie at the Cinema. Want to go?"

Patrick is so smart, he can do his homework in half the time, even with his accelerated program. It's maddening. "Oh, Patrick, I can't!" I wailed. "I'm too far behind. Heart attack city! Can't we rent the video after it comes out?"

"I want to see it on the big screen, Dolby sound and everything," he said. "It's supposed to be really good. Karen and Brian and Penny and a bunch of us are going."

I was silent.

"Alice?" he said.

Maybe I should just go, I thought. Maybe I should forget the homework for once and go, be spontaneous, but I knew I couldn't. I should have planned better. I should have checked my assignment due dates. "I can't," I said flatly. "Have a good time."

"Sure?" he said.

"I'm positive. I've got a billion assignments, Patrick. I'd like to, but I can't."

"Okay," he said. "Talk to you later." And I heard him hang up.

I tried not to think about Patrick at the movies with Penny. There would always be a Penny. No matter what happened in life, there would always be a girl or a woman who was pretty and fun and popular and clever, and I had to get used to it. Patrick and I were an "item," so why did I worry about it so much?

I was relieved that I actually got through the first section of the algebra assignment by myself. The remaining problems were so hard and my patience so thin that I put them off until later to ask Lester. Then I read a chapter in history and started the essay questions at the end.

Elizabeth called to see if I had gone to the movies with Patrick. She'd stayed home to do her English assignment, too. I told her that I was uneasy about Penny being there with Patrick.

"It's broad daylight!" she said. "You never have to worry about a guy and a girl going anywhere in the afternoon, even the movies. That's so uncool, it doesn't even count."

I felt better, and made myself a peanut butter sandwich with bacon bits. After I was finished with history, around five o'clock, I ate an apple and painted my nails, and then I started the paper for English. I figured Patrick would call later and tell me about the movie, what I'd missed and what everybody did after. But the phone didn't ring. Just before I went to bed I checked my e-mail. No messages at all.

Patrick wasn't on the bus the next morning. Sometimes he has band practice before school, and his dad drives him over. Penny was there, though, talking about the movie and how scary it was.

Brian guffawed loudly and interrupted. "There was this part where the woman's in the cave, afraid to come out because the creature with all the tentacles is around somewhere, but she doesn't know it's been cloned, and there's another one back in the cave, and you see this tentacle sort of oozing, sliding across the rocks behind her . . ."

"And then Patrick puts his hands around Penny's neck!" laughed Mark.

"You should have heard her scream!" Brian said.

"Everyone in the theater turned and stared at me!" Penny went on, laughing at herself. "He was horrible!"

"A hundred-decibel scream," said Justin.

"Well, he *scared* me!" Penny said, laughing some more.

I slid onto the seat beside Pamela.

"I think you should have come," she whispered tentatively.

"*You* went?"

"Sure. I thought everyone was coming."

"I had tons and tons of work to do."

She just shrugged. "When the cat's away, the mice will play," she said.

"What's *that* supposed to mean?"

"Just that Patrick was fooling around. He was sitting right beside Penny."

"Well, he had to sit somewhere."

"I know. I'm just telling you."

I felt I was swimming against the tide. I felt as though a big steamroller was coming at me, or an avalanche or something.

"So . . . what else happened?" I asked.

"Nothing. That I know of."

"Meaning . . . ?"

"I don't *know*, Alice. I can't watch them every minute."

"Well, I can't either," I said. "And what's more, I shouldn't have to."

"Right," said Pamela.

I felt flat all day. Irritated. Anxious. But I made up my mind that I wasn't going to ask Patrick about it. I wasn't going to nag and question and put him through the third degree. If you had to do all that to keep a guy, what good was it?

He called that evening. He told me all about the movie, but he didn't mention Penny. Didn't say how he'd slipped his hands around her neck at the critical moment, made her scream. How he happened to be sitting right beside her.

I was proud of myself that I didn't ask. "I'm sorry I missed it," I said.

"Yeah, it was great," he said. "You want to stop by the band room after school tomorrow? Levinson's going to decide between me and another guy as to who gets to do the drum solo at the winter concert. We both have to audition, and I figure it wouldn't hurt to have my friends there."

"What time?"

"Three."

"Oh, Patrick! I've got an editorial meeting for the school newspaper! We get our assignments for the next month. Damn!"

"You can't skip?"

"If I do, I'll get stuck with the assignment nobody else wants. I've heard it's really, really important to be at the first meeting of every month."

"Well, that's the way the ball bounces," Patrick said.

"Look. I'll see if I can't get my assignment first and come right down to the band room," I told him.

"Okay. See you," he said.

I loved being one of the two freshmen roving reporters, and looked forward to the weekly meetings. Sam Mayer was only a freshman, too, but he'd moved right up to photographer. He was so good that he was sent to cover the first football game. The roving reporters got the fluff assignments, we call them, the kind you could either put in or leave out and it wouldn't make much difference. But some assignments were better than others, and they were fun.

Nick O'Connell, a senior, was editor in chief, and when I got to the meeting, there was a big argument in progress. Sara, the features editor, was complaining that none of her ideas were taken seriously, and that it was obvious to her that guys ran the newspaper, and girls didn't get much say about the way it was done. In spite of myself, I was about five minutes late coming in, and wasn't sure what the issue was. But Sara was so upset that her chin quivered, and I knew it sure wasn't the time to ask if I could choose my assignment and leave.

Some of the kids were taking Nick's side and some were taking Sara's, and then somebody brought up an issue that seemed totally unrelated to the problem, and everyone went off on that. By the time Nick got to the assignments, he started with the seniors instead of the freshmen, and finally—the very last—I got mine: I didn't even get a choice. Something about the "mystery meat" served in the school cafeteria.

Nick said it was okay for me to go then, so I grabbed my coat and book bag and ran down two flights of stairs, then the long corridor to the band room. But everyone had gone. The janitor was sweeping up. I took a city bus home and tried calling Patrick, but no one answered. When I called again around ten, his mom said he'd gone to bed.

Lester had to drive me to school early the next morning because I'd forgotten to pick up the new layout instructions for the school paper. At noon, they served the mystery meat again, and luckily I had my camera ready. There it was, the gray-looking patty swimming in a pool of greasy-looking gravy. I was careful not to take pictures of my friends—the newspaper frowns on cliques taking over the paper, the same kids getting their pictures in again and again. So I spent my lunch period walking around the cafeteria, going up to kids I didn't know and asking them what they thought they were eating, then photographed them taking a bite.

"Soy delight," said one girl.

"Squid," said another.

"Roadkill," said a guy.

"Skunk au jus."

"I don't want to think about it," said the last girl, and I hoped I got the face she made when she took a bite.

I stopped at a one-hour photo shop on my way home that afternoon, and at least four of the five pictures turned out well.

The fifth was a little fuzzy—I think she moved—but I wrote her up anyway, and did a layout for the paper. It was a lot of fun writing the piece, actually. I started off quoting Lester: "There's a rumor that the food in the cafeteria is leftover from the prison infirmary. . . ."

Later, I was just getting ready to take a bath when Jill called.

"What'cha doing?" she asked.

"Something really exciting: getting ready for a bath. Maybe even a pedicure. What are you doing?" I asked her.

"Just resting up. Finished a paper for social studies. . . . We missed you at lunch."

"Yeah. I was doing an assignment for *The Edge*," I told her.

There was a pause. "You should have been in the band room yesterday," she said.

"Yeah? How did Patrick do? I haven't seen him all day."

"Great. He got the solo. We were cheering like mad."

"I wish I'd been there! I had a newspaper meeting. Who all came?"

"Penny."

A panic spread through me, sharper than anything I'd felt so far. "Only you and Penny?" I asked.

"Well, there were a few of us, Alice, but, like I said, you should have been there."

"What are you saying?"

"Penny went up and hugged him after Levinson said he got the solo."

"She did?"

"I mean, you could have just called it a friendly hug, but . . . well, he didn't push her away, that's for sure."

"Well, of course not. Patrick's not rude," I told her.

"But she was *there* for him, Alice! That's what I'm saying. She was there at the movie the other day, too, and you weren't."

"Well, that's just great! I happened to have a ton of homework then, and it was important I be at that meeting today. There have been plenty of times I've wanted to do things with Patrick and *he's* been busy. That's life. We just have to make time for each other when we can."

"I understand! I understand! I'm just telling you as a friend, that's all. But things do happen, and I didn't want you to be the last to know."

"Well, thanks, but it's just something Patrick and I have to work out ourselves," I said.

"I guess I shouldn't have bothered," Jill said, and hung up.

Oh, boy. I slid down the wall and sat hugging my knees. I imagined Patrick auditioning for the solo, looking around to see which of his friends had shown up. I imagined Penny hugging him afterward. Patrick not pushing her away. Patrick hugging back. Patrick looking down at her and smiling.

And I wondered if, in the long run, it would have made any difference if I'd been there or not. If I'd been at the movie and the audition both. And for the first time, I sensed Patrick slipping away from me, and felt sick.

8
HEART-TO-HEART

I probably sat on the floor without moving for twenty minutes, and then I picked up the phone and called Patrick.

"Oh, hi, Alice," Mrs. Long said. "Just a minute. He's practicing."

I could hear Patrick's drums going in the background, booming up from the basement. I remembered with a pang the drum lesson he'd given me down there once, the way he'd touched me, the tingle I'd felt, the way I'd wanted him to touch me again. I swallowed.

The drumming stopped. I heard Patrick's footsteps on the stairs, the fumble of the phone in his hands. "Hello?"

"Hi, Patrick. I've been hearing good things about you," I said.

"Yeah, I got the solo part. I get about four minutes to improvise."

"That's wonderful! I really wanted to be there, but there was some big crisis at the meeting and I was the last one to get my assignment. I ran all the way down to the band room afterward, but everyone was gone. Why didn't you call me?"

"Well, I've been really busy."

I swallowed. "Yeah. Me too. I wondered if you wanted to come over some night. Just hang out."

"Tomorrow, maybe. We leave for a band competition Friday afternoon."

"I know. Tomorrow's fine."

We talked about this and that for another twenty minutes. Neither of us mentioned Penny. Maybe when you like a really popular guy you have to get used to groupies—to other girls liking him, too. Maybe it goes with the territory.

Patrick was on the bus the next morning, joking around with the guys in back like always, and Penny and Jill were sitting together when Elizabeth and I got on. Jill looked the other way when I said, "Hi." Penny said, "Hi," and went on talking to Karen, who was hanging over the back of the seat. Pamela and Brian and Mark were all squeezed together in one of the seats. She kept trying to wedge in between them, but they made her sit on their laps.

Elizabeth and I slid in a seat together behind some seniors who were arguing about a movie review.

"What's with you and Jill?" Elizabeth whispered.

"You noticed."

"Yes. She was, like, ignoring you."

"I don't know. I guess you'd have to ask her," I said.

I was miserable all day, and somehow the thought of seeing Patrick that night didn't help. I didn't feel as though he was mine anymore, and even though I knew he didn't *belong* to me—he wasn't a possession—I just didn't feel special any longer. The Snow Ball—the first formal dance of the year—was coming up in the middle of December, and I wanted to feel that we were that same special couple we used to be, comfortable in knowing we'd be going to it together.

I put on my best jeans and a rust-colored sweater that night, the gold locket that used to belong to my mom, with a little lock of her hair in it, and tiny gold earrings.

"Hello," Patrick said at the door, and smiled down at me.

I reached up and kissed him lightly on the lips. "Want to come in?"

"The leaves are blowing around like mad, and it's actually warm out. Let's walk," he said. "Have a leaf fight or something. Go get some ice cream."

I laughed and stepped out on the porch to check the temperature. It was warm for November. I put on my white windbreaker, and we went down the steps.

"Didn't you ever do that when you were little? Have a leaf fight?" he asked.

"I think I just jumped around in them. No natural aggression," I said.

"We used to try to stuff them down girls' necks."

"Typical," I said. "Always trying to get in a girl's shirt."

He laughed.

We walked out in the street in the gutter where the leaves had piled up, enjoying the crunching sound underfoot. I let him do the talking—the assignment he had to do for physics, his mom's birthday, the car his dad was going to buy, the sci-fi movie I'd missed, what a blast it had been. . . . He still, though, didn't mention Penny, and it began to annoy me that he wouldn't talk about her, almost as though he had something to hide.

"I hear you had quite a cheering section at your audition," I said finally, as lightly and casually as I could muster.

He didn't say anything for a moment. Then, "Yeah, some of the kids showed. I usually block everyone out when I'm playing, though."

"And afterward?"

"What?"

"Well, I heard you got quite a hug."

He smiled faintly. "Penny's real affectionate," he said. "It's just the way she is."

"I guess so," I said, hating the flat sound my voice took on. "You must have enjoyed it, though."

"Why not? I did what any normal guy would do—hugged her back. Something wrong with that?" Now *his* voice had an edge to it. I didn't trust myself to respond, and then he added, sort of jokingly, "She *likes* me! What can I do?"

"What else?" I said.

Patrick wasn't smiling anymore. "Is this what tonight's about? You wanted to lecture me about Penny?"

"What I really wanted was just an evening together—we haven't seen much of each other since school started. But if there's something I should know . . ."

"Why do I get the feeling that every time I'm within six feet of Penny I have to report back to you?" Patrick said.

"I don't know. Conscience, maybe?"

"What's that supposed to mean?"

I noticed that instead of taking the usual route to the grade school where we often sat on the swings and hand-walked the horizontal bars, we had turned at the next corner as though we were circling the block. As though my feet refused to go in a straight line that would, if we had passed the school and gone three blocks farther, have taken us to the ice-cream parlor where Penny may or may not have been working that night. I even wondered if that's why Patrick had mentioned getting ice cream, just so he could see her.

"I mean that I keep hearing things from other people about you and Penny, but I never hear about them from you. And if she's just a casual friend, why wouldn't you mention her along with everyone else? What's so secret if she's just another face in the crowd?"

Patrick looked straight ahead. "She's not just another 'face.' She's a good friend. She's fun to be with. I expect to have a lot of good friends, male and female, through high school and college, and you should too. The more the better."

We walked awhile without speaking. The truth of what he

said only cut a little deeper. So did the fact that we seemed to be heading right back to my house, because we turned again at the *next* corner. As though the relationship, as well as our feet, wasn't going anywhere.

"So why did I have to find out about that false 'kiss' between you and Penny from a photo on our piano? Why did I have to hear from someone else about you sitting beside her at the movie and making her scream? Why did Jill tell me about the way Penny went up and hugged you after your audition, but I didn't hear it from you?"

"Because Jill's a gossip, that's why."

"But you wouldn't have told me yourself? Once again, Alice is the last to know."

"What's to tell? She likes me, I like her. She's not you, she's just different."

Somehow, the way he said it, cut deepest of all. The last time Patrick had said, *She's not you, Alice*, it had made me feel special, as though Penny could never hold the place in his heart that was reserved for me. But now I heard something else: that Penny was different, and he liked that difference. That there were qualities he found in Penny that he didn't find in me. And while that was only natural and made common sense, it hurt like anything. What it meant to me was that Patrick found Penny fun and cute and full of life, and it made me feel large and unattractive and dull in comparison.

"What I'm hearing, Patrick, is that Penny's pretty special to you," I said, but my words came out all breathy.

He glanced over to see, I suppose, if I was going to cry. "But you are too," he said in answer.

I imagined Patrick kissing Penny the way he had kissed me; touching her the way he had touched me. "How can we *both* be special?" I asked angrily.

He shrugged. "You just are. You and I have been going out for two years."

"Just tell me this: Are we still a couple or not?" I asked, refusing to look at him, my feet plodding on ahead.

Patrick didn't answer for a moment. Then, "If you mean will we still go out, sure. If you mean I can't go out with Penny sometimes, then . . . ." He didn't finish.

My whole body felt like feet. I could feel each one hitting the sidewalk. The more I imagined Patrick and Penny together— petite Penny—the bigger my feet seemed to be. My legs, my hands, my head felt huge, and the more unattractive I felt, the angrier I got. I didn't want to be walking along beside this red-haired guy who didn't want me anymore. Not the way he used to.

When we turned again onto my street, I could see our porch six doors down. I didn't even want to walk past those six houses to get there. I wished I was there already, safe inside.

"Well, maybe if Penny's so special to you, you should just become a couple," I snapped.

Patrick stopped walking and stood absolutely still on the sidewalk, his hands in the pockets of his jacket. I'd never seen his face like it looked then. Reserved. Distant. "Are you asking me to choose?" he said.

"Yes," I told him. "Maybe you should just take her to the Snow Ball."

"Then, maybe I will," he said. And he turned and walked slowly off in the other direction.

I caught my breath, wanting to call after him, but I didn't. I could feel my heart racing, my tongue dry, the blood throbbing in my temples. I turned and walked as fast as I could back home, my eyes starting to close against the tears, my chin wobbling, and then I was running up the steps, crossing the porch, streaking up the stairs to my room, and collapsing on the rug beside my bed.

I don't know how long I cried. My room was full of Patrick—pictures and postcards and mementos of all the things we'd done. Pamela had even returned the Milky Way wrapper from the first candy bar Patrick ever gave me; I'd given it to her as my prized possession when we thought she was moving to Colorado. Most of my bulletin board was devoted to Patrick.

My memories were Patrick. My kisses were Patrick's. All my plans for weekends and summers had been built around him, and now there didn't seem to be anything left—any structure to pin things on. I'd had a boyfriend for so long that I didn't know what to do without one. How would I act, going everywhere by myself? Being a single in our gang? How did other girls manage this?

There was a light tap on the door. "Al?" said Dad.

I couldn't answer.

"Al?" he said again, louder. "May I come in?"

"Yes." Even my voice sounded small.

The door opened, and he stood there in his Dockers and flannel shirt, looking down at me. "What happened, honey?" he said, and came over to sit on the edge of my bed. I turned around and grabbed hold of one of his legs, burying my face in his pant leg, and cried some more.

"Something happen between you and Patrick?"

"I think w-we b-broke up," I sobbed. "Oh, Dad!"

I felt his hand on my forehead, his fingers brushing back the wet hair that clung to my temples. "Want to tell me about it?" he asked softly.

"It's . . . just . . . there's this girl, Penny, and she's been chasing him, and . . ." I couldn't go on. I was putting it all on Penny, I knew. I still couldn't face the fact that the feeling between her and Patrick was mutual.

Dad did it for me. "And he let himself be caught?"

I nodded vigorously and went on crying, curling up against his leg as though it were a pillow.

"Love is really hard sometimes," he said. And I was glad he said "love." I was glad he acknowledged that I loved Patrick, and didn't modify it with "puppy love" or "high school infatuation" or something.

"It's worse than being sick, worse than throwing up," I told him, my nose clogged.

"I know," said Dad.

"I feel like there's nothing left. That Patrick's gone and taken a part of me with him."

"In a way, I suppose he has," said Dad.

I was doubly grateful that he didn't immediately start talking me out of my crying jag, that he accepted how I felt.

"I feel alone and ugly and scared, like I don't know what to do next. Like . . . like I don't even know how to *act* without a boyfriend. It's all so stupid, and yet . . . oh, Dad, it hurts! It really hurts."

"I know, I know," he said.

Deep inside, however, I felt maybe it wasn't over. That Patrick would go home and feel as bad about this as I did. That he'd e-mail me, maybe, or the phone would ring about ten o'clock and his voice would be soft and gentle the way it often was after we'd argued. I could even imagine him saying, "Alice McKinley, may I have the honor of escorting you to the Snow Ball?" and I'd sort of giggle and maybe cry, and we'd both say how dumb the argument had been. He'd tell me how he couldn't bear to lose me, and I'd say I'd been insanely jealous, and everything would be okay again.

Except that the phone didn't ring and Patrick didn't e-mail. I had a horrible night. I looked incredibly awful the next morning— my eyes were all puffy. I wanted to stay home. I wanted Dad to write an excuse, say I needed sleep, but he wouldn't.

"Al, do you really want everybody to notice that you aren't on the bus? Do you want the news of your breakup to travel around, and everyone know that you're taking it hard?"

That, I realized, would be even worse than letting them see my puffy eyes. I wrapped some ice cubes in a dish towel and sat at the kitchen table, holding the ice to my eyes, taking deep breaths to quiet my nerves.

Lester came clattering down the stairs for breakfast. I saw him pause in the doorway, staring at me, and then, out of the corner of my swollen eyes, I saw Dad shake his head at him sternly. Les came on in the kitchen without a word to me, mumbling something about how his car needed gas and he'd just drink a little coffee and get a muffin on campus. Then he was gone.

When my face began to feel numb, I dumped the ice in the sink and went upstairs to shower. I knew I couldn't keep anything down if I tried to eat, so I skipped breakfast and concentrated on my face. I carefully put on foundation and blush and powder, dropped Murine in my eyes, blow-dried my hair, and dressed in a beige top and khakis. Walking beside Elizabeth to the bus stop, I kept my face turned away from her a little, and she didn't seem to notice my eyes.

She was talking about an English assignment and how she'd almost forgotten to wash her gym clothes the night before, how her shorts were still damp, and when the bus came, we got on and sat together across from Pamela. I could sense Patrick's presence at the back of the bus, but I didn't hear his voice and dared not look in his direction.

Pamela and Karen were sitting together comparing nail decals. This time the older kids on the bus were so loud that anything we said was drowned out. They were making up a new cheer for basketball games, with a lot of bawdy words in it, and of course all the ninth graders were drinking it in.

Elizabeth in her usual way was trying to carry on a conversation with me as though she weren't subjecting her ears to their banter. "I forgot to take them out of the dryer and they'll be a wrinkled mess," she was saying. She stopped and studied me for a moment, then leaned forward and looked directly into my face. "My gosh!" she said.

I could feel tears welling up again. "It's that bad, huh?"

"What's *happened*?" she asked softly.

I didn't answer, and she looked quickly around to see if anyone else was listening. "You and Patrick?" she asked again.

I nodded.

"You and *Patrick*?" she repeated, unbelieving. And when I didn't answer, she said, "You broke *up*?"

I leaned my head on her shoulder, swallowing and swallowing, till I'd managed to control my tears. She put one hand on mine and squeezed it, and I was never so glad for a friend.

9

PAIN

I didn't want anyone to pity me, though. I didn't want to feel like "poor, rejected Alice." I was pretty sure Elizabeth wouldn't tell anyone until I said she could, but it turned out that Jill asked Patrick if he was taking me to the Snow Ball, and he said, "Probably not."

That's when Jill told Karen and Karen told Pamela and Pamela cornered me outside the cafeteria and said, "Alice, what happened?"

"It was by mutual consent," I said.

"Was it Penny?" she asked.

"It was everything," I said, starting to move away before the bell. Before I started crying.

"I'll be over after school," Pamela called after me, and disappeared down the corridor.

How do you look cheerful when you're crying inside? How do you act interested in friends' conversations when all you can think about is what you said to Patrick and Patrick said to you and how he looked when he said it? How do you keep your mind on the blackboard and tomorrow's assignment when tomorrow seems about as bleak and colorless as a tomorrow ever seemed?

It's weird, but I was almost more depressed about breaking up with Patrick than I remember being over my mom dying, I think, because I was too young to understand what dying meant. That it was final. Forever. I remember everyone else crying at the funeral, but I kept thinking, "But when she's better, she'll come back!" The breakup with Patrick seemed pretty final to me because—even if we got back together sometime, how could it ever be the same? How could I ever feel that Patrick liked—loved—me best of all?

"Alice? Up here, please," my history teacher said, tapping the pointer against a wall map. "You can't see China out the window."

At lunchtime, I noticed Penny studying me warily from the end of the long table where we ate, but I avoided looking at her. I found myself laughing a little too readily at Mark's jokes, being flirtatious and silly with Brian, teasing Justin Collier. It was sickening. Exhausting. Pretending can wear you out, and so, about halfway through, I just stopped talking and concentrated on my chicken salad sandwich.

Patrick wasn't on the bus going home. The band had left for a state competition that afternoon, and I was glad of that. Pamela got off at the stop with Elizabeth and me, and we walked the block and a half to my house. I held up pretty well until we got up in my room, and then I lay down on my bed and started crying.

Pamela sat on one side of me, Elizabeth on the other. Pamela was stroking my hair, Elizabeth rubbing my back.

"Alice, it wasn't about 'everything,'" Pamela said. "Nothing is about 'everything.' It had to be more specific than that."

"We just . . . we had a big fight," I said. "He came over last night, and we argued and . . . and he left. I said some things . . . he said some things . . . and . . . it's over. We just . . . just grew apart, I guess."

Pamela fell back on the bed and stared up at the ceiling. "I *hate* those words! I hate 'we just grew apart.' People say that to explain things, and it doesn't explain anything at all. Mom said it when she decided to leave Dad for her NordicTrack instructor. I didn't like it, but it wasn't exactly a huge surprise because there always seemed to be a lot of friction going on between Mom and Dad. They were always fighting about something. But *you*! Alice, you and Patrick have been going together for so long, I almost began to believe in true love."

"We're only fourteen," Elizabeth reminded her. "How can we know what true love is when most of us have never been in love at all?"

I was sobbing again. "I *did* love Patrick," I said. "I don't know if it was real love or true love, but I really cared about him. And I thought he c-cared for me. And now he's going to ask Penny to the Snow Ball."

"He's *what*?" Pamela choked, sitting up again. "Just like that? Is that how he broke it to you? Just, 'I'm taking Penny to the Snow Ball'?"

"No. I . . . I told him to."

"You what?" cried Elizabeth.

I had to go over everything Patrick and I had said to each other. Every step we took. How we started out kicking leaves in the street and walked around our whole block, and by the time we were six houses from home, we'd broken up.

"Well, here we are," Elizabeth said at last, propping one of my pillows against the headboard and leaning back. "Just two months into high school, and all three of us are without boyfriends."

"It doesn't bother me," said Pamela. "I like playing the field. It just bothers me about Alice and Patrick, that's all. What about you and Justin?"

"I don't think I want a full-time boyfriend. That's just not in the picture right now," Elizabeth said.

Why couldn't I feel like they did—content to be unattached? Why did I feel so incomplete without Patrick liking me, calling me, kissing me, touching me, without being his special girl?

"What you have to do, Alice, is let the guys know you're available," said Pamela.

"What am I? A hooker?" I asked, blowing my nose.

"You know what I mean. Pretend you like things this way. Flirt with all of them. Act relieved it's over."

I shook my head. "Acting's no good, Pamela. I've got to be me."

"So what are you going to do? Cry in the cafeteria?"

"No, but I'm not going to try to get a boyfriend on the rebound."

"Good for you, Alice. That's the worst thing you could do," said Elizabeth encouragingly. "Just be yourself."

"My ugly, clumsy, overgrown self," I said.

"That's not true, and you know it," Elizabeth said, and I thought how recently, when she wasn't eating, we were saying the same thing to her.

"If people start talking about Patrick taking Penny to the Snow Ball, I'll tell them it was your idea," said Pamela.

"No, don't say anything. Don't go around making excuses for me, please," I said. "Just let it be. Let Patrick do the explaining."

I was almost glad my friends had come over, because the more they talked about Patrick and me, the more sick of it all I became.

I felt somewhat better after they went home, and even went down to the kitchen and made a Jell-O salad with fruit cocktail for dinner.

But by the time Lester got home from the university, I was near tears again. The house seemed so quiet. *Too* quiet, because one thing I knew: Patrick wouldn't call. He was at the state competition, of course, but even if he wasn't, he probably wouldn't have called. Perhaps not ever. I struggled not to cry through dinner. Dad was working at the Melody Inn till nine o'clock every night that week, going over work that Janice had left behind, so Lester and I were eating alone, and my eyes looked like two pink pillows. Every so often a tear slid down my cheek and chin, landing on my lasagna. I could see Les looking at me sideways.

"Is it . . . uh . . . too indelicate to ask what's wrong?" he said finally, almost gently.

I swallowed. "Patrick and I broke up last night."

"Ouch!" said Lester. "I'm really sorry, Al. Anything in particular, or was it just time?"

"You mean that a relationship just runs its course, and when it's time—when it runs out of steam—it's over?" I asked incredulously, my lips quivering.

"No, I just meant that in ninth grade, with four years of high school ahead of you and another four, at least, of college, you need to run through a number of relationships, and the longer you stick with one guy right now, the more you're going to have to hustle to work the others in later."

My face began to scrunch up again, and my voice became mouselike. "I don't *want* any other guys, Lester. I want P-Patrick! I never liked anyone as much as him."

"It's hard, kiddo. No doubt about it."

"He likes another girl. Penny. She's cute and fun and petite, and I feel like a horse around her. I can't stand that he likes her so much."

"He told you he does? That he likes her more than you?"

"No, but he likes her. He says he likes us both, that he and I should both have a lot of friends."

"Chalk one up for Patrick."

"We argued, and I told him if he liked Penny so much, maybe he should just take her to the Snow Ball instead of me, and he said maybe he would." I started crying again. "Half the time I want to run over to his house when he gets home and bang on the door, begging him to take me back, and the rest of the time I want to bang him on the head and ask how dare he do this to me."

"That's exactly why they should lock up girls around the age of fourteen and not let them out till they're twenty-one," said Lester.

We did the dishes together, putting some food away for Dad in case he hadn't taken time to eat, and Lester said that the pain of a breakup doesn't go away all at once, but it does go away in time.

After the kitchen was clean, he went up to his room to study and I went to mine. But I couldn't concentrate. I lay on my back, staring wide-eyed at the ceiling, and every so often a tear would trickle down and land in my ear. From Lester's room I heard a song on his radio that Patrick's combo played once at one of our junior high dances. I just didn't feel I could stand it. It used to be Dad who was the sad one in our family, with both Lester and me getting along in our love lives, and now it was Dad who was having all the luck, and Lester and me who were out in the cold.

Lester and me and Mr. Sorringer, the assistant principal, who was in love with Miss Summers and isn't over her yet.

And suddenly it seemed as though everybody in the world except Dad was grieving for someone, and that Lester and I might be loveless the rest of our lives. Weeping pitifully, I got up in my stocking feet and padded down the hall to Lester's room. He was propped up on his bed with text books scattered all around him.

"L-Lester," I wailed from the doorway.

He looked up, then reached over and turned the volume down on his radio. "Yeah?" he said.

"D-do you think we could be h-happy if you and I just grew old together?" I wept.

"*What?*" Lester said and turned the radio down even more.

"If we don't ever m-marry, Lester, we could always get a house together somewhere. I'd do all the cooking and you could take care of the yard and the p-plumbing, and at least we could look after each other in our old age," I sobbed.

Lester opened his mouth, then closed it again, and finally he said, "Correction: They should lock up girls when they're fourteen and not let them out till they're thirty. Whatever gave you a cockeyed idea like that?"

"I don't want to go the rest of my life alone!" I wailed.

"So get a roommate! Get a dog! Join the Peace Corps! Adopt some orphans! Al, there are as many ways to enjoy your life as there are people. Just because you're alone today doesn't mean you'll be alone tomorrow."

"But I want Patrick!" I cried. "If *he* doesn't want me anymore, how could anyone else?"

Lester pushed his books aside and motioned for me to come over and sit beside him. I was only too glad. I crawled up on the bed, leaning back against the pillows by the headboard, and snuggled up against him. He even put one arm around me.

"You're talking a little nutty, Al, you know? Aren't you the same person you were a couple weeks ago?" He lifted my face with his other hand as though looking me over. "I don't see any facial hair; don't see any fangs."

I just sniffled.

"Fourteen years ago," Les went on, "Patrick Long was just a squalling little blob of protoplasm in messy diapers who grew up to play the drums. He's just one of the three billion males on this planet, and—even assuming that he hates you, which I doubt—are you going to let that one sack of skin and blood and bones named Patrick make the decision about whether you are likable or not? Attractive or not? Are you going to let that one squalling blob of protoplasm just fourteen years out of diapers determine your self-esteem?"

I sniffled again. "I thought you l-liked Patrick."

"I do! But when did you let him have all this power over you? If *he* likes you, you're witty and beautiful; if he doesn't, you're dog doo. Am I right here?"

I just leaned against Lester and didn't answer, loving the closeness. He smelled of taco chips and beer. He handed me a Kleenex, and I blew my nose.

"The one thing about life, Al, is it's always changing. Bad things don't last forever. It's okay—it's normal—to feel depressed over this, but it won't last. Trust me."

"But if bad things don't last forever, if everything changes, that means good things don't last, either," I countered.

"True. People do die, after all. But most of us find some level at which we can be, if not deliriously happy most of the time— and nobody is—we can be reasonably content, with healthy spurts of excitement and joy. If you care about yourself, then the things that happen outside yourself, things you can't control, can hurt, but they can't destroy you. Philosophy 101."

I could tell from the way Lester shifted his body slightly that his arm was getting numb, but I went right on leaning against him. It was too comforting to give up. "Do you ever miss your old girlfriends?" I asked.

"Some of them."

"Crystal?"

"I think about her once in a while, and hope she's happy with Peter. I don't think it would have worked out if I'd married her."

"Eva?"

"I'm glad that's over."

"The dingbat?"

"Who?"

"Joy what's-her-name. Do you ever think about her?"

"Never. I've forgotten all about her."

"Marilyn?"

Lester withdrew his arm and rubbed his shoulder. "Yes, I think about her. But right now it's best if I stick to the books and forget the ladies for the time being. It's a difficult semester."

I blew my nose again. I was beginning to feel more like myself. "Now that you're twenty-two, Les, do you think you're any smarter? I mean, can a person *feel* himself getting wiser?"

"Definitely. All I wanted at eighteen was my own car, a pretty girl to ride around in it with me, a six-pack, and a good guitar. And right now, none of the above is my first priority."

I started to grin. "Are you, by chance, wearing any of the birthday shorts we gave you? Some of the girls have been asking."

Lester contemplated that for a moment, then pulled out the waistband of his jeans and peered down inside. "Yep," he said.

"Which ones? The boxers with newsprint on them? Ants in the pants? What does the well-dressed philosopher of twenty-two wear under his jeans?"

Lester grinned. "Daffy Duck," he said, and waved me out of his room.

10
ALONE

The phone rang about five minutes later, and I dragged it into my room and sat down on the bed. It was Jill.

"Alice, are you okay?" she asked. I guess this meant we were friends again.

"I suppose everyone's heard by now," I said in answer.

"Patrick's a jerk," she told me. "It's one thing to flirt with Penny, but another to break up with you."

I could feel tears welling up in my eyes again. "He's just . . . just being honest."

"How can you defend him like that?"

"Well, he can't help liking somebody."

"Of course, Penny's mostly to blame," said Jill.

I didn't want to get into this, because I knew she was goading me into saying something against Penny, and everything I said would get right back to her. "Maybe nobody's to blame," I said, my voice flat. "That's just the way it is. She likes him, he likes her."

"Oh, stop being so noble," Jill said. "She's been making a play for Patrick for months, and everyone knows it. Of course, Patrick could have ignored her, but—"

"Listen, Jill. I've got to go. I've got homework and stuff."

"But are you sure you're all right?"

"No, but I'll live," I said.

I hung up and sat with the phone in my lap, staring at myself in the mirror on the opposite wall. I looked a mess. My eyes were puffy, my cheeks streaked with tears. I wear hardly any mascara, but the eyeliner on my lower lids was smeared.

The phone rang again and I leaped, almost knocking it to the floor. I waited till the third ring, just in case it was Patrick. It was Gwen.

"How you doin', girl?" she said, in that wonderful, thick, comforting voice.

I started crying again. I couldn't *believe* it.

"Not so good, huh?" said Gwen.

"I'm pretty sad," I mewed, my chin wobbly. "I'm just . . . *really*, *really* sad."

"I know. I guess you and Patrick have been going together for so long, we sort of looked at you as Siamese twins. Insepa-rable," she said.

"That's the way I felt, too," I told her. "But we're not. And now I just feel strange and lost."

"Listen, if you ever need to talk, will you call me? Doesn't matter what time, day or night, you call."

"Thanks, Gwen. But I've got Dad and Lester. I wouldn't have to call you in the middle of the night. I'll be okay."

"Sure now?"

"No, but don't worry."

I put the phone on the floor and decided to take a bath. To soak awhile with a cold washcloth over my eyes, and try to let my mind go blank. But as soon as I settled down in the water, the washcloth slid down below one eye and I found myself staring at my knees sticking up out of the water.

They suddenly looked fat to me. Fat knees. How could I expect Patrick to like a girl with fat knees? I sucked in my breath and spread my fingers out over each kneecap. My fingers looked short and stubby, and my nails were uneven. How could Patrick like a girl with stubby fingers? It was just as Lester had said—now that Patrick didn't love me anymore, I must be unlovable. I was appealing and attractive up until I had said, "Maybe you should take Penny to the Snow Ball," and by the time he had said, "Maybe I will," I had metamorphosed into this ugly creature with swollen eyes and stubby fingers and fat knees.

The phone rang, and I heard Lester's footsteps out in the hall, then a tap on the bathroom door. "Hey, Al. It's Karen. You want to take it?"

"Yes, but don't look, Lester!" I yelped, spreading the washcloth over my breasts and doubling my legs up.

"Blindman's bluff!" he called as he slowly opened the door and emerged with his eyes closed, feeling his way with one hand, holding the cordless phone in the other.

I reached for the phone and grabbed it just as Lester's foot hit the side of the tub and he lost his balance, lurching forward. Both arms landed in the water up to his elbows. Water splashed all over the place.

"Lester!" I shrieked.

"What's happening?" came Karen's voice.

"Am I supposed to swim my way out, or what?" Lester asked, opening his eyes anyway.

"Don't look!" I yelped as he tried to wipe the water out of his eyes.

"Oh, my stars, she's *ne-kid*!" Lester cried, imitating Aunt Sally.

"Alice, what's going on?" came Karen's voice over the phone.

I was swinging the washcloth at Lester to get him out, and he was trying to get to his feet to find a towel. When the door finally closed behind him, I said, "Hello?"

"What in the world is happening?" asked Karen.

"Lester just fell in the tub," I said. "He tripped. I'm alone now."

"Well, I just called to see if you needed to talk," she said.

"I'm about talked out, Karen. Word sure travels fast. Everyone seems to know."

"I just wanted to make absolutely sure you're all right."

"I'm okay."

"But are you sure?"

"I'm not sure about anything! I thought I was sure about Patrick, and look what happened!" My face scrunched up. "I thought we were a *couple*, Karen! A real couple. That nothing could ever h-happen to us."

"But . . . surely you've had *some* interest in other guys, Alice! I'll bet you've flirted a little with other people once in a while, haven't you? That guy from Camera Club last year who used to like you. Sam Mayer?"

"But I never gave up Patrick for him."

"Well, maybe Patrick hasn't given you up for Penny. Maybe he wants to go on liking you both."

"I couldn't stand that!" I told her. "Not after being special to him all this time. To have to share him?"

"I don't know." Karen sighed. "I just don't know. But I want to be sure you're okay."

"I'll be all right," I said, impressed that so many people cared about me. Patrick wasn't my only true friend in the world, it seemed.

By the time I got my pajamas on and was back in my bedroom, the phone rang again. Pamela.

"All these phone calls!" I said, trying to button my pajamas with one hand and hold the phone with the other.

"Well, Elizabeth organized a suicide watch," Pamela told me.

"*What?*"

"She's divided the evening up into fifteen minute segments and one of us has to call you every fifteen minutes. I've got the nine-fifteen detail."

"*What?*" I cried again. "Pamela, I'm okay. Really! I'm sad and disillusioned and angry and confused and jealous, but I'm not going to kill myself. Penny, maybe, or Patrick, but not myself. Joke, joke! Please don't call 911."

I put the phone back in the hallway and climbed into bed. Lester came to the door and tapped.

"Can I open my eyes now?" he quipped.

"Very funny," I said.

"What's with all the phone calls?"

"Elizabeth's organized a suicide watch," I told him.

"Come again?"

"Somebody has to call me every fifteen minutes to be sure I'm still breathing."

The phone rang again. Lester reached around behind him in the hall and grabbed it. I could hear Elizabeth's voice asking about me. "Do you think I should come over and spend the night with her?" she asked.

"Lester to Elizabeth! Lester to Elizabeth!" Les said into the phone. "There is no cause for alarm. I repeat: No cause for alarm! Temperature's normal, pulse is normal, her pupils aren't dilated or anything, and I ask you, *beg* you, to call off the suicide watch. Okay? She needs some sleep tonight. We *all* need sleep."

"If you're sure, Lester," I heard her say. "You can never tell what a depressed person might do."

"I can tell you what *I* might do if this bloody phone doesn't stop ringing . . . ," said Lester.

"I'm sorry!" Elizabeth said. "We just wanted Alice to know we care."

"She knows! She knows! Good night!" Lester told her, and hung up. He turned around again. "So *are* you okay, Al?"

"Yes. Listen, Lester, how much did you see in the bathroom?"

"See of you, you mean? I saw two knobby knees, if you want the truth."

Knobby knees? I had *knobby* knees? Skinny, bony, knobby knees? If I thought they were fat and Lester thought they were knobby, they must be somewhere in between, which meant they were about right.

"Thank you, Lester," I said. "That was exactly what I needed to hear."

I didn't go to sleep right away, though. Dad came in late from the Melody Inn, and stopped by my room to say good night. "In bed already?" he asked. "You aren't sick, are you?"

"Sick with a broken heart," I said.

He sat down on the edge of the bed. "It's official, then?"

"I guess so."

"Want to talk about it?"

"Not really," I told him. "I'm about talked out. Penny made a play for Patrick, and he fell for it. Simple as that. I don't understand how a girl could flirt with a guy when she knows he's somebody's boyfriend."

"You've heard the saying, all's fair in love and war," Dad said.

"But *you* never . . ." I stopped, because I realized too late what the answer was, and didn't know how to retract the question.

"As a matter of fact, I did. Twice, it seems."

"But you didn't know that Miss Summers had been going with Jim Sorringer until after we'd taken her to the Messiah Sing-Along, right?"

"That's right. I didn't even know her until you invited her to go with us. She seemed to enjoy our company, because when I called and invited her out a second time, she said yes. It wasn't until the third date that she explained she'd been having a serious relationship with Jim Sorringer but was having second thoughts about it. And when a man is attracted to a woman who is having second thoughts about the guy she's been dating, well . . . it means you have a chance, and there's nothing immoral about giving her a choice."

"But you said you'd done this twice. Flirted with a woman who belonged to another man."

"Well, I don't think you could say that Sylvia 'belonged' to Jim Sorringer, any more than you could say he belonged to her. They weren't officially engaged yet. As for your mother and Charlie Snow . . ."

Charlie Snow. It was a name I had heard before, and knew only what Aunt Sally had told me. That she used to think she could never forgive Dad for taking Mom away from wealthy

Charlie Snow, and all because Dad wrote Mom such beautiful love letters.

"So tell me," I said.

"The truth is, your mother actually *was* engaged to Charlie when I met her. It was some kind of fraternity party at Charlie's college, and a bunch of us guys from Northwestern were invited. Marie was there, as Charlie's fiancée, and she danced with me just to be friendly; and we talked . . . danced and talked. . . . There was something about her eyes. Like we were talking more with our eyes than we were with our lips, but we caught ourselves looking at each other the rest of the evening, and finally it was as though our eyes were doing *all* the talking."

"Sounds more like infatuation to me than love," I put in, thinking of Patrick and Penny and wondering if they'd been talking to each other with their eyes.

"I had the same thought, believe it or not," Dad went on. "And I imagine it occurred to Marie as well. You can't go hopping from one man to another, one woman to another, just because you make good eye contact."

Dad sat staring at the wall as though his thoughts were a million miles away. "I couldn't get her out of my mind, though. I saw her again at a neighborhood theater with some girlfriends, and we couldn't stop staring at each other. So I wrote her a funny letter, and she replied, and I wrote another, more serious, saying that I knew she was spoken for, but if she wasn't entirely sure . . . and it turned out she wasn't entirely sure about Charlie. And so she gave his ring back."

I didn't know if I wanted to hear all this or not. "If she could ditch him for you, though, she could have ditched you for someone else," I said. "It doesn't show much loyalty."

"Very true. And don't think it didn't occur to me. But she never did ditch me. Never, to my knowledge, was unfaithful. I don't know if it was because we genuinely loved each other, which we did, or whether we were just lucky, or both. You never know about love."

"How did Charlie Snow take it?"

"He was furious, of course. I would be, too. But he was also a gentleman. He and I met and had a talk. We didn't do anything stupid like fight. He suggested that we go three months without either of us seeing Marie, and let her make up her mind, but a week later there was a knock on my door, and there stood Marie. She said, 'Ben McKinley, if you don't love me, I want to know now.' I took her in my arms and never had a single regret."

It was such a beautiful love story, I felt like crying all over again. I wanted to be loved like that. I wanted Patrick's arms around me. I wanted his light kisses on my lips, and the way he'd rub my shoulders sometimes when I was upset. Everything about him I loved. And now, Penny would have all the things that had been meant for me.

Dad reached over and pulled me to him. I cuddled against him like I used to do when I was five.

"I miss him a lot, Dad," I said.

"I know," he told me, and kissed the top of my head.

"Do you suppose I'll ever have a love story like that?"

"You may have one even better," he said. "Life is full of surprises, sweetheart."

I pulled away finally and blew my nose. "What am I going to say when I see Patrick and Penny together at school?"

"You're going to say 'Hi.'"

We both smiled a little.

"It's going to be hard, Al, but you can do this! It's a ritual we all have to experience before we're grown—the admission price to being an adult."

"But *you* always won out! You were never the loser."

"Oh, but I was. A couple of times. There was this brunette with gray eyes, for instance, and . . . well, the spark just wasn't there for her, and she was honest enough to tell me so."

"And you lived."

"Yes. And met someone even more wonderful: your mom."

I let out my breath and looked at my father. "Okay," I said. "I *can* do this! I can get on that bus Monday and not make a fool of myself."

"That a girl! Of course you can, honey."

"But I *still* wish I could just jump from here to being married, like you and Mom, and skip all the stuff in between."

"It doesn't work that way, Al." Dad smiled. "And you'd miss out on half the fun."

11

THE HARDEST PART

At least I had the weekend to recover, and the only place I had to go was the Melody Inn to put in my three hours Saturday morning. It wasn't until I saw Marilyn in a new dress and haircut that I realized she was now assistant manager. Instead of straight brown hair that hung halfway down her back, it was shoulder length and curled gently under at the ends. Instead of a peasant dress or jeans and a wool sweater, she was wearing a teal-colored jersey dress with Native American jewelry. She looked great.

"Gosh, Marilyn, you're gorgeous!" I said.

"Hope I don't look as nervous as I feel," she said. "There

is *so* much to learn. But your dad seems to think I can do it."

"Of course you can."

"What would really help, Alice, is if you could run the Gift Shoppe on Saturday mornings by yourself. In fact, if you're willing, I'm going to ask if we can't hire you for all day on Saturdays. It would sure make things easier for me."

I stared. "Of course! I'd *love* to! Except I don't know how to work the cash register and add tax and stuff."

"*That* I can teach you. C'mon," she said, and I had my first business lesson.

I got along fine, actually. I guess I'd watched Marilyn so much when she was working the Shoppe that I'd soaked up a lot by osmosis. Around eleven o'clock Dad came out of his office and said, "Marilyn told me she'd like to hire you full time on Saturdays, Al. What do you think?"

"*Please*, Dad! I need something to take my mind off things right now."

"All right. If you think you can spare the time."

I hesitated. "If something really big comes up once in a while, could I still get the day off?" I asked.

"We could probably arrange it," he said.

So I was hired from ten to six on Saturdays at minimum wage. I truly didn't think about Patrick again until I went back to the stockroom to eat a sandwich with Marilyn. I'd just been too busy. But we were sitting next to a brand-new five-piece Ludwig drum set that Dad hadn't put out on the floor yet, and it reminded me of Patrick. My eyes welled up, just like that.

"Alice?" Marilyn questioned. "Good grief, what's the matter?"

I pressed my fingers over my eyelids, determined I wouldn't cry, and kept swallowing until I had things under control.

"Alice?" she said again.

"Patrick and I broke up," I said finally.

"Oh, no." Marilyn sat back and looked at me, one hand dropping loosely into her lap. Then she gave me a little smile. "We're two sad sisters, aren't we?"

I dabbed at my eyes. "Do you still miss Lester?"

"All the time," she said.

"I cried so much yesterday that one of my friends posted a suicide watch," I told her.

"All needless, I hope. Alice, don't ever jump in the river over *any*body. It's an insult to the sisterhood, as though he's worth everything and your life isn't worth squat. At least I'm not as sad as I used to be. I *am* getting over him. Getting Janice's old job helped. Anything that builds your self-esteem helps."

She was right about that. I worked hard all afternoon and once I'd mastered the cash register and Maryland tax and counting change, I began to think of the Gift Shoppe as my own little place. I even put a pair of men's briefs on display, with *Beethoven* on the seat, and sold three pairs by five o'clock.

As good as I felt at the store, however, I felt awful after I got home. Saturday night, and I wasn't going out with Patrick. Of course, I wouldn't have been going out with him anyway, because he was in a band competition at Frostburg, but at least I could have fantasized that he was thinking about me.

Both Elizabeth and Pamela called and asked if I wanted to go to a movie or something, but I knew we'd just sit around afterward talking about Patrick and Penny, so I said that Dad and Les and I had plans. I put on all my favorite CDs and cleaned out my dresser drawers. Then I sorted through all the clothes in my closet and filled a couple of bags for Goodwill.

On Sunday I studied. I even read ahead in history, had a chance to go over my algebra homework twice, memorized the new vocabulary for Spanish, and did my nails. And all the while I had a pot roast on the stove, simmering with carrots and celery and onions. The house smelled wonderful. I'll admit I checked my e-mail about six times to see if Patrick was back; if he had, perhaps, sent a message.

And around nine o'clock, I found one:

> I really didn't want things to work out like this.
> I'd like to keep seeing you, but I need other
> people, too.

I e-mailed back:

> We all need other people, Patrick. That's not
> the point. I thought we were pretty special to
> each other, but Penny is obviously special, too.
> You can't be "special" to us both.

He called. I pulled the phone into my bedroom and sat on the floor, my back stiffly against the edge of my bed; I wasn't comfortably curled up on my rug with my pillow as I usually was when Patrick called.

"You want to talk?" he asked cautiously.

"About what?" I said, which was stupid, but I couldn't think of what else to say.

"About whether you're going to get over this or not."

"Why is it *my* problem, Patrick? You can do whatever you want, and I simply have to get *over* it?"

"All I'm trying to say is that I still like you a lot, but I also like Penny. I don't know where it will lead—maybe nowhere— but I still want to go out with you."

How can a guy as smart as Patrick be so *dense*? I wondered. "In other words, you want me to be here for you so that if things fall through with Penny, I'll welcome you back with open arms."

"That's not what I said."

Now I was really steamed. "Patrick, what can you be thinking? How are either Penny or I supposed to be happy with *this* arrangement?"

"Look. None of us is tied to anyone else. You and Penny can go out with anyone you want. In fact, maybe we should just all consider ourselves friends and forget this 'special' stuff."

"Is that what you want?" I asked, my chest already cold with the sound of it.

"I don't *know* what I want right now. I still want us to go out, but I don't want to be told who I can see and who I can't. It's that simple."

"Then the answer is simple, too, Patrick. We can't be like we were if you're going out with Penny, too. How could you even *expect* us to be?"

There was a long silence. It sounded as though Patrick was toying with the telephone cord. Then his voice sounded flat and distant. "Well, I guess we'll see each other around."

"I guess so," I said. And then we hung up, and I felt like an old milk carton, sour and empty on the inside.

I woke up Monday feeling bluer than blue. I knew that both Patrick and Penny would be on the bus, and that by now absolutely everyone would know that Patrick and I broke up. That now it was official. Patrick and Penny were free to be a couple, and even their names sounded right together: *Patrick and Penny; Penny and Patrick.* Just thinking about this hurt more than a smack across the face.

"Al," Dad called from my doorway. "You getting up? You're ten minutes late already. Better get a move on."

I forced myself out of bed and went into the bathroom to shower. What would I wear? Something Patrick loved, to make him regret we'd broken up? Something he hated, to show I didn't care? Something sexy, so other guys would pay attention to me in front of Patrick? Something drab and mousy, so nobody would look at me and I could blend into the background?

How about something *I* liked? I told myself finally, and put on a pair of black leggings, black mules, and a huge purplish sweater with a mock turtleneck collar. Also tiny purple earrings set in sterling.

"You look great, Al," Dad said at the table. I doubted he really liked what I was wearing, but I thanked him for the vote of confidence.

"Sort of like a huge grape," said Lester. If you want the truth, ask my brother.

Elizabeth was waiting for me when I went outside. She didn't want me to have to climb on the bus alone. There was a slight hush when I boarded—only the upperclassmen were talking—but among our friends—Karen and Jill and Mark and Brian—all eyes were on me. Patrick, to his credit, sat at the back of the bus with the guys again, not with Penny, but she was on her knees looking over the back of her seat, carrying on a conversation with him.

I gave a general "Hi" and a smile to everyone at once and sat down by Pamela, who had saved a seat for me. Elizabeth squeezed in beside us so that I was sandwiched between my two closest friends.

"Just ignore Patrick," Jill whispered over the back of the seat. "Don't even give him the time of day."

"Why?" I said. "We're not enemies."

"Well, I wouldn't call *Penny* your friend exactly," said Karen, which was ridiculous, because it was Karen who had engineered that photo of Penny and Patrick and the nonkiss. Why is it so difficult to tell who your friends are and who aren't? Is this just a problem among girls? Do guys act like this? I happened to know that Penny and Karen went shopping a lot together. Whose side was she on, anyway, or did she just enjoy starting a fight?

I changed the subject and, when the bus reached the school, was one of the first to get off. I wanted in the worst way to see whether Patrick and Penny were walking together, but I went on inside and straight down the hall to my locker.

One thing I noticed was that Mark and Brian and Justin and some of the other guys didn't know what to say to me all day. As though guys had to stick with guys and girls with girls. But I tried to stay as cheerful as I could. I said hello to the boys when I passed them in the hall, and even got through the bus ride home again, though this time I noticed that Penny had gone to the back to sit beside Patrick.

It was the next day that it hit. I had just come out of the library and Patrick and Penny were walking about fifteen feet ahead of me, holding hands. Penny seemed to be doing all the talking, and every so often, Patrick turned and looked down at her with the same smile I remembered, the affectionate smile he used to give me, the funny little smile that wrinkled the bridge of his nose. I whirled around and went in the opposite direction, a pain in my chest and throat as through I'd swallowed a tennis ball and it was stuck.

I began to feel that every corridor at school was a minefield. I didn't want to see Patrick at all, and I especially didn't want to see him with Penny. If either of them were coming and they hadn't seen me, I'd duck in a classroom or lean over a drinking fountain—do anything possible to make myself invisible. Twice I started up a flight of stairs to hear them coming down the flight above me, and I'd turn and go the other way.

This is ridiculous! I told myself. Wasn't it enough that Patrick liked someone else? Did I have to be a prisoner in my own school, too? I knew I couldn't go on hiding like this all year, but I just didn't feel strong enough, or wise enough, to face Patrick and not see his eyes light up anymore. To say hello to him in the hall and not hear any warmth in his voice. I just didn't think I could bear it.

But after I'd seen them together, it helped to simply expect it: Patrick standing by Penny's locker, his hands on her waist, her hands on his shoulders; Patrick at a table in the library, Penny next to him, his arm around her, and the worst—Patrick and Penny standing out on the steps, kissing lightly on the lips, the way *we* used to do.

It still hurt, but at least it didn't surprise me anymore. If they did this in public, though, what did they do in private? I wondered. How far did she let him go? How far did he want to? Was it possible they went all the way? If *I* had . . . ? I didn't finish the thought.

At home after school, all I wanted to do was curl up on my bed and listen to CDs. Sleep. I slept a lot. I also got my period, so I just dragged around the house and for the most part, Dad and Lester left me alone—didn't yell at me if I forgot it was my night to do the dishes, or if I left my shoes where someone could trip over them, or forgot to take the clothes out of the dryer.

I was glad I didn't have any classes with Patrick this semester. I'd been so disappointed in September when I'd found out I didn't, but now I was relieved. On Thursday, though, third period, I went in the library to check out a book, and Patrick was there at the desk, waiting, too. We were both embarrassed.

"Hi," he said. He was wearing a white sweatshirt, and a lock of his flaming orange-red hair hung carelessly down over one eye.

"Hi," I answered.

We both glanced in opposite directions. There wasn't any clerk at the desk.

"Nobody here?" I said finally.

"She's looking for a book I had on reserve. Said she'd be right back," Patrick told me.

"Oh," I said.

More silence. The librarian appeared, stared for a moment at the book in her hand, then must have realized it wasn't the right one and went back in her office. Patrick shifted his weight to the other foot.

I felt I would rather have a tooth filled than stand here like this beside Patrick. Have a tooth filled without Novocain, in fact. About the only thing worse would be if Penny came in, too, and they stood beside me, kissing. I wondered idly how Patrick would react if I reached out and touched him. Moved over and kissed him lightly on the cheek? *That cheek belongs to me!* I found myself thinking. After being my boyfriend for two years, would he push me away? Was there any of the old feeling left for me at all?

Finally I said, "How was the band competition last weekend?"

Patrick looked surprised. Startled, even. "Okay, I guess. We came in second in overall performance. We could have played better, though."

"Second sounds pretty good to me," I said.

The librarian returned with Patrick's book, stamped it, and he was done.

"See you," he said.

"Bye," I said.

I knew I'd done well. I knew things would be a little easier now that I had proved I wouldn't hold a grudge—that we could speak civilly to each other. But no one could possibly know how much it had hurt to stand there talking like strangers when once we would have leaned against each other, Patrick caressing my arms as we waited. When we used to French-kiss, he would run his hands up and down my sides, and my breasts tingled. Where did those feelings go when you had once been so special to each other? How could they just evaporate as though you'd never had them at all? They didn't. They stayed, and stayed, and stayed.

"Al, phone!" Dad called that evening.

"Hello," I said, thinking that *maybe* it was Patrick. Maybe my speaking to him had broken the ice, and he'd changed his mind about Penny. But it wasn't. It was Mrs. Price.

"Alice, I hope I'm not interrupting your studying or anything," she said, "but could we talk for a minute? Elizabeth's gone over to the library, so this is a good time for me."

I hate it when someone's parent does that—talks to me behind her back and tries to make me the go-between.

"It's okay," I said. What else could I do?

"I just don't know what's going on with her lately. With *us*, I should say, because she's irritable with her father, too. It's as though she's *looking* for ways to disagree with us. All we have to do is suggest something and she's against it. I didn't care so much when she gave up gymnastics and ballet, because they put too much emphasis on staying slim, and we all know the kind of trouble Elizabeth has had with that. But *piano*? Has she . . . well . . . said anything to you about that, Alice? I mean, anything that might help me understand?"

"Not really," I said. "What's happened?"

"She dropped piano. After all the work I went through to get Charles Hedges to take her on, and all the interest he's shown in her—he insists she's talented—she quit. She didn't even tell me." Mrs. Price's voice trembled. "He called and said it was a shame she didn't stay with it, because she'd make a really good pianist."

"Elizabeth could be good at almost anything," I said.

Mrs. Price sounded on the verge of tears. "I know. I just thought . . . if you could ask her about it. I mean, if I just *knew* why she's so uncooperative lately . . ."

"I sort of hate to go behind her back," I said.

"And I hate to ask it, but I'm . . . I'm just so *puzzled*!" she said, and sniffled. "It's as though she has a grudge against us or something."

"If I find out anything, I'll let you know," I said, but I didn't promise to pry.

"I appreciate it, Alice. You're the only one of her friends I felt I could ask. All I want is for things to be like they used to be between Elizabeth and me—between her and her dad, too. And I think she's making a horrible mistake giving up piano."

After I hung up, I knew I didn't want to get involved in this. When a parent says she wants things to be the way they used to be, what she is saying is that she doesn't want you to grow up, because that's what it's all about. Change. Elizabeth's been the perfect daughter for so long, she can't stand it, but her mom just doesn't see that.

There must have been a blowup over at Elizabeth's shortly after her mom talked to me, because Elizabeth was steamed all the way to the bus stop the next morning.

"I just get so tired of parents thinking they know what's best for you when they don't know what's best at all!" she raged. "All I hear is 'Mr. Hedges this' and 'Mr. Hedges that' . . . like he's some sort of god, and we're supposed to worship him just because he says I have talent."

"Maybe you really do," I said.

"That's not the *point*! I don't want to be a professional pianist. I can play well enough to suit me, and I don't care whether I ever get better than this or not. High school's a lot harder than junior high, and I've loads more work to do."

"Did you explain that to your folks?"

"They don't *care* how I feel. All they care about is how Mr. Hedges feels. 'He'll be so disappointed. He took such an inter-est in you. He'll think we're so ungrateful.' Who *cares* what he thinks? I'm their daughter!"

"I think you all need to improve your communication skills," I said, trying to make a joke of it.

"Mom puts on that hurt look, like I've let her down. And Dad just buries himself in the computer. 'If she wants to throw her talent away, let her,' he says. 'We gave her the best lessons money could buy, and if she doesn't care, it's her loss—all those years of practice.'"

"Maybe you could take a year's leave from piano," I sug-gested. "Then see how you feel—if you really miss it or not."

"They'll never give up," Elizabeth said, and I was astonished to see there were tears in her eyes. "They've got me on this guilt trip, and they have no idea what it's doing to me."

I guess they didn't. All I could figure was that this argument was about a whole lot more than piano lessons, but I didn't know what it was.

Everything seemed to depress me lately. Elizabeth and her folks, algebra, breaking up with Patrick. . . . At home that evening, Dad asked if he'd gotten any mail and I knew immediately he meant *any letters from Sylvia*, but there weren't any. Lester had put in a couple of hours at the shoe store after his classes at the U, and he was tired. Now that he'd broken up with Eva, he didn't seem to be having as much fun as he used to. He spent most of his time studying.

And suddenly I said to myself, *Alice, you're not the only one who's hurting here. You aren't the only one with problems. Concentrate on someone else for a change.*

It's what they say to do when you're depressed, you know. Walk in someone else's shoes for a while, and your own won't feel so tight. I wasn't too worried about Dad, because I knew his mood would improve the minute he heard from Sylvia. And he could always pick up the phone and call her in England if he wanted. But I wished I could do something for Lester. The holidays were coming up and he wasn't really dating anymore.

Of course, with Thanksgiving only a week off, what I *should* be doing, I thought, was concentrating on someone *really* needy— maybe by inviting a poor family to have Thanksgiving dinner with us, but I didn't know any poor families personally. I'd thought of inviting Pamela and her dad; they weren't poor, but they were sad, with Mrs. Jones having deserted the family. But Pamela had told me that her uncle and aunt would be in town, and they were all going out for Thanksgiving dinner at Normandy Farm.

So on Friday after school, I looked up the number for the Salvation Army and called. I said that I wanted to invite some people who might otherwise be alone on Thanksgiving. And then, thinking of Lester, I said maybe the Salvation Army knew of some young women who were working as maids or something, or were far away from their families this Thanksgiving, and might like to share our dinner with us.

How many people could we serve? they asked. I mentally counted the number of chairs. Six in the dining room, four in the kitchen. Then I realized I would be doing the cooking, and I'd never cooked for ten people in my life.

"Uh . . . three, I guess," I told them. That would be double the size of our family.

The Salvation Army said that mostly they had whole families of eight or nine needing a place to go on Thanksgiving, but if I got in touch with an organization called CCFO, perhaps they would know of some young women who would be glad for a refuge on Thanksgiving Day.

I liked that—a refuge. I liked thinking of our house that way. So I called the number he gave me, and was startled when a voice said, "Community Connections for Female Offenders, may I help you?"

I blinked, then swallowed and told them how the Salvation Army had given me their number, and that we had room at our table for three young women on Thanksgiving, and did they know of any ladies who didn't have anywhere to go?

The man on the phone asked if I knew anything about their organization, and I said no. He said that their purpose was to help women offenders, now out of prison, readjust to the community. To help them find places to live and jobs so they wouldn't return to a life of crime.

I gulped.

Then he assured me that he would not send us anyone who had been accused of a violent crime, and they would all have places to live, but that CCFO, for their part, needed assurances that we were what I claimed we were, simply a family who wanted to share our holiday, because they don't just send three young women out to anyone who asks. After they had checked on us, he would like to call my father at his place of employment, so I gave him Dad's number at the Melody Inn.

"Very good," he said. "We appreciate your call, and we'll be in touch."

At least it gave me something to take my mind off Patrick.

A letter from Sylvia had come that day, and Dad was in a good mood all evening. He always read her letters three or four times before he folded them up and put them away, and she must have said all the right things because he was still smiling when he tucked it back in the envelope.

"Dad," I said from across the room where I was slouched down in my favorite beanbag chair that he's been trying to get rid of. "I thought it would be nice if we invited some poor people to our house for Thanksgiving this year. I mean, people who ordinarily wouldn't have anyone to spend the holiday with."

Dad looked at me over the rims of his glasses. "That's a noble thought, Al. I think it's a fine idea. Do you know of a family?"

"Well, no, but I called the Salvation Army—just to see how we might go about it—and they referred me to another organization that knows of"—I remembered what the man at the Salvation Army had said about people needing a refuge—"refugees who would appreciate Thanksgiving in someone's home, and so I called and this man is going to phone you at work. He said

they always check people out first. They don't send . . . um . . .
refugees out to just anyone who asks."

"Of course not. Honey, I'm real proud of you. How many
did you say we would take?"

"Just three," I said quickly. "I wasn't sure how many I could
cook for." The fact was, I'd never roasted a turkey in my life.

"That's great. Les and I will help, of course. It's a fine idea."

I called Elizabeth and told her what I'd done and she said
it was a fine idea, too. Elizabeth goes for noble things. She said
they were having her grandparents for Thanksgiving, but she
could come over that day and help me out for a couple of hours,
that she wanted to do her part for the refugees, too.

"They speak English, don't they?" she asked.

"I'm sure of it," I said, and began to wish I hadn't said anything at all about refugees.

The next day at the Melody Inn, both Dad and Marilyn were
with customers and I was answering the phone when a call came
from CCFO.

"Dad," I said, going over to the center of the store where he
was showing a cello to a couple. "You have a phone call."

"I'm with a customer, Al. Can't you take it?"

"They have to speak to you," I said.

"Excuse me," Dad said to the couple, and went back to
the counter. "Hello?" I waited, holding my breath. "Yes, that's
correct. I'm her father, and she told me we'd be having guests.
We're delighted to have them. . . . Yes, that will be fine. . . .
Yes. . . . I wonder if I could put my daughter back on the line.

I'm with customers at the moment. . . ." He handed the phone back to me.

The man from CCFO wanted directions to our house and asked what time the women should be there. I hadn't even thought about it. I figured it would take most of the morning to cook, though, so I said maybe two o'clock.

"Well, we do appreciate your thoughtfulness," the man said. "It means a lot to former prisoners to experience Thanksgiving in a friendly home. One of the women will be driving the other two, and their names are Shirley, Charmaine, and Ginger."

12
EXPANDING MY HORIZONS

There are two ways that putting your mind on other people makes you feel better. First, it simply gives you something to do, and second, you don't feel so alone, as though fate singled you out to be more sad than anyone else you know.

As soon as I got home from the Melody Inn on Saturday—Dad always works an hour or two after closing on Saturdays—I called Aunt Sally in Chicago and asked her how to roast a turkey. I didn't want to get into who exactly we were having for dinner, so I told her we were having some refugees.

"My goodness, Alice, you are so grown up!" she said. "Your dad must be very proud of you."

"How big a turkey should we get?" I asked.

"It depends how long you want to eat leftovers."

We like leftovers at our house because, if the food was good to start with, it means nobody has to cook for as long as it lasts. I imagined us eating turkey sandwiches for a week after Thanksgiving, and I liked the idea a lot. "A long time," I said.

"Well, then, you certainly couldn't go wrong with a twelve-pound turkey. That's two pounds per person, but if you're serving refugees, no telling *how* much they'll eat. And it would be a really nice gesture to send each one of them home with a little package of turkey. Why, I'll bet even a sixteen-pound turkey wouldn't go to waste."

"Okay, but how do I roast it?" I asked.

"The important thing to remember is to remove the neck and gizzard."

"What? I have to *kill* it?" I cried.

"No, no, but it will come packaged with the dismembered neck stuffed in the neck cavity, and the heart and kidneys and gizzard stuffed in the cavity below," she said. If ever I had thought about being a vegetarian, I should have made a commitment right there. But Aunt Sally continued: "All you really have to do is follow the instructions on the wrapping and you shouldn't have any trouble. Rinse it well, and don't stuff it until you are just ready to pop it in the oven. You can find a recipe for stuffing on any package of croutons. You need to figure on a roasting time of about twenty minutes per pound of turkey. I'll be here all Thanksgiving Day if you need me."

"Thanks," I told her. And then, "Oh, one little piece of news: Patrick and I broke up."

There was silence at the other end. Then Aunt Sally said softly, "It was the sleepover, wasn't it?"

I thought back to the sleepover. In a way she was right. That was the night Karen took a picture of the fake kiss between Penny and Patrick, which led to the definitely unfake kisses ever since.

"Sort of," I told her.

"Oh, sweetheart, how I wish you'd listened to me. All those bodies together there on the floor . . . !"

"It wasn't that, Aunt Sally. Somebody was taking pictures," I said.

"Alice, do you mean to tell me that boys and girls were all over each other and someone was taking *pictures*? Where was your *father*? Where was Lester?"

"It's not what you think," I said. "It was Patrick and the new girl, and Karen arranged it so it only *looked* like they were doing it, but actually . . . ."

"*What?*" cried Aunt Sally.

I decided to quit before things got any worse. "Thanks for your help," I told her. "I really have to go. I'll let you know how the turkey comes out."

Another thing that helped was my job as one of the roving reporters for the school newspaper. My piece about the mystery meat in the school cafeteria turned out well. Everyone was laughing about it, and the result was that the cafeteria stopped serving it. They substituted turkey franks, which tasted a lot better, and I realized I had not only entertained, I had made a difference.

"Good job, Al!" Nick O'Connell said to me at our next meeting. He wasn't so pleased with the photos I'd taken, though, so on my next assignment, he sent Sam with me. We were to ask six different students what they would give our school as a Christmas present if they could give anything they wanted.

I liked being paired with Sam Mayer. He and Jennifer Sadler were going together, so it wasn't as though we were a couple or anything, but Sam had liked me in junior high school and we were still good friends.

"You always want to catch a person alone," Nick had told us. "If you ask somebody in front of his friends, he's more likely to give you a flip answer. Get him alone and he's more thoughtful. Makes better copy."

Sam and I decided to meet before school on Friday and just roam the halls, catching kids at their lockers, or at the juice and bagel bar in the cafeteria. I had to ask Lester to drive me there early, and he was grumpy.

"Lester," I said, balancing my book bag on my knees, "if you were in a position to give the university a Christmas present— anything you wanted—what would it be?"

"Al, it's seven forty-five, and I haven't had breakfast," he grumbled.

"Really, though," I said.

Lester slowed to a stop at the light. When it turned green he said, "A bike path to the university from every neighborhood in the metropolitan area, and a babe on every bike."

"What you need is female companionship," I told him.

"I don't even have time to clip my nails, and you want me to have a girlfriend," Les said.

I was on the verge of telling him about Shirley, Charmaine, and Ginger, but decided I'd better hold off. "I know you're taking extra courses this semester and don't have time for a serious relationship, but that doesn't mean you can't at least have some casual women friends," I said.

"Yeah, sure. So round me up some casual women friends," he muttered.

I just smiled and went on swinging my foot.

Sam and I met outside the cafeteria and found our first student sitting at a table, eating a bagel with cream cheese. We didn't want to embarrass him while his mouth was full, so while Sam adjusted his camera, I filled the guy in on what kind of a story we were doing for the paper and asked if he had any ideas of what would make a good present for our school.

"A swimming pool," he said. Then, after he swallowed, he added, "for skinny-dipping only."

I smiled and wrote it down while Sam took his picture, and we set out to find someone else.

"I heard about you and Patrick," Sam said.

"Yeah. About everyone in the whole school knows, I think."

"Patrick must have rocks in his head to let you go," said Sam.

"Well, it was more or less mutual," I told him, which wasn't entirely true. But it *was* partly because of something I had said, so I figured it was true enough. And then I added, "How are things with you and Jennifer?"

"Great!" he said, and I was glad that we saw a girl on ahead, standing at her locker, and zeroed in on her next, because I really didn't want to get in a discussion of Sam and Jennifer versus Patrick and me.

We had our six student comments done by the first bell, and all I had to do was condense or expand their replies to fill up half a page, with head shots. We got some interesting answers, though. The news editor had told us that two years ago they had asked the same question and got answers like, "Put belly dancers in the cafeteria," or, "Reduce the drinking age to fifteen." This time the kids said things like, "Repair the school restrooms and make sure there are doors on all the stalls," and, "Build a student lounge so the kids would have some place to gather in bad weather before and after school."

"I had an interesting assignment for the school newspaper," I told Dad and Lester at dinner, glad that I could talk about something pleasant for a change instead of moping around over Patrick. And I told them what Sam and I had done.

"Sounds as though you're enjoying ninth grade, Al," Dad said.

"*I* got an interesting assignment today, too," Lester said sardonically. "I have to compare the moral systems grounded in Kant's Categorical Imperative, Benthamite utilitarianism, and Aristotle's *Nicomachean Ethics* in terms of whether they commit the naturalistic fallacy."

"I'm never going to college," I said.

Dad raised an eyebrow.

"Well, I'm never majoring in philosophy," I told him.

Elizabeth's family was going to eat Thanksgiving dinner in the evening, so she promised to come over that morning and stay long enough to help me cook our meal. I hadn't told her that our guests had been in prison, only that I'd called the Salvation Army for suggestions. Besides, I thought, everyone deserves a break—we all make mistakes. If nobody knew they were ex-cons but me, maybe they'd be treated more like ordinary people and could put their past behind them.

Lester and I went out to buy a turkey the Monday before Thanksgiving, and I remembered what Aunt Sally had said about sending some home with each of the refugees when they left. Why stop at sixteen pounds? I thought. Why not get a twenty-pound turkey, and maybe Dad and Lester and I wouldn't have to cook for a month!

"Okay by me," said Lester. "You're the chef, babe."

I couldn't explain it, exactly, but there was something about doing a good job on that newspaper write-up, and now, learning to roast a turkey—to make a whole Thanksgiving dinner, in fact—that made me feel less lonely. Or maybe just not so dependent on Patrick to make me feel like a lovable, worthwhile person. Maybe this was a good time to try my own wings, to concentrate on learning new things. An Alice Time—all for myself.

Dad and Lester said they'd clean the house, since I was doing most of the cooking. Elizabeth arrived about seven Thanksgiving morning. At twenty minutes per pound for a twenty-pound turkey, we figured it would take six hours and forty minutes to roast. If I wanted to serve it at two thirty, it had to be in the oven by seven thirty.

We went down to the basement to get the turkey out of the freezer. It was so cold, I could hardly carry it, and it sounded like a rock when I dropped it on the table.

Elizabeth looked worried. "You know, Alice, I think you were supposed to defrost it first," she said.

I looked at the microwave. "So?" I said, pointing to the button that said *defrost*.

"I don't know . . . ," said Elizabeth.

I turned the turkey around and looked at the print on the wrapper. *Defrost in refrigerator 2 to 3 days prior to cooking*, it read, and I went weak in the knees.

"Oh, Alice!" said Elizabeth.

We took the shelf out of the microwave and tried to cram the turkey in, but it wouldn't fit. We were trying to turn it upside down when Lester came downstairs. "What the heck are you doing?" he asked, and that's when I lost it.

"Lester, it's supposed to defrost for two to three days, and the people are coming at two o'clock!" I wailed.

"Al, you blockhead!" Lester said, and that brought Dad to the kitchen.

Lester explained the problem. "What do you think?" he asked. "Chain saw or dynamite?"

The upshot was that they took the turkey outside, cut it in half lengthwise with Dad's power saw, and then we defrosted a half at a time in the microwave until it was merely icy. I didn't have to stick my hand into the neck or abdominal cavity to remove the innards because Dad had already sawed them in half.

Lester said he couldn't watch, but after we'd rinsed out the turkey, Dad stuck both halves together with duct tape so we could stuff it, and told me to remove the tape before we put it in the oven. Then he went upstairs to scrub the bathroom.

Elizabeth had been chopping the mushrooms and celery for the dressing, and I melted the butter and added the bread cubes. We looked at the turkey, its legs spread, and then at each other.

"It's positively obscene to have to stick your hand in there," Elizabeth said. "I am never going to have a baby."

"Relax," I told her. "When you have children, they won't cut your head off first." We took turns spooning the dressing into the turkey's cavity. Then, while I held the two parts together, Elizabeth removed the duct tape, and we used wooden skewers to sew the bird up. At a quarter of nine, we brushed it with melted butter, covered it with foil, and put it in the roasting pan.

It took both of us to get it in the oven, and I turned the heat up fifty degrees higher than it had said to allow for the fact that it was half frozen.

We did the pies next. Mrs. Price had sent over some ready-made piecrusts, so Elizabeth and I made the three easiest pies in the world: pumpkin, pecan, and mince. Even a six-year-old could make them. After that we tackled the sweet potatoes and mashed them with melted butter, cream, and orange rind.

Lester poked his head in the kitchen around eleven thirty. "What time will the turkey be done, Al?"

"Three thirty, if we're lucky," I told him.

"Three thirty? What time are the people coming?"

"Two," I said.

"What am I supposed to do with them until then?"

"*Talk* to them, Lester! Be sociable! I'm cooking the dinner. Do I have to tell you how to entertain, too?"

"Do you know what country they're from?"

"From here."

"Refugees from *here*? From *what*?"

"I don't know, Lester! I don't know where they were born. I'm doing the best I can, and if you—"

"Okay, okay," Les said. "Pipe down."

When he left the kitchen, Elizabeth said, "Don't you know anything at all about these women, Alice?"

My heart began to thump. She was looking at me suspiciously. "Liz," I said. We'd started calling each other nicknames since we began high school. "They're not . . . not exactly refugees in the ordinary sense. They're sort of . . . more like . . . well, troubled women looking for refuge in an uncertain world."

"What?" said Elizabeth.

"The Salvation Army referred me to an organization called CCFO, which turned out to be Community Connections for Female Offenders, and after I found that out I couldn't very well hang up, could I? They've all been in prison."

Elizabeth let her spoon fall into the sweet potatoes. "What?"

"Shhhh. It's okay. They haven't done anything violent."

"Alice, are you out of your mind?" she gasped.

"Probably," I told her.

13
REFUGEES

We had this plan: As soon as the turkey was out of the oven, I'd put the pies in to bake while we were eating the rest of the meal. I'd heat the peas and carrots on the stove, the sweet potatoes in the microwave, stick the rolls in the oven for a couple of minutes, open a can of cranberry sauce, and *voilà!* Dinner.

Elizabeth and I found my mom's best tablecloth in a drawer in one of Dad's closets. There were marks all along the creases, and the matching napkins had yellowed, but it looked better than a bare table. We also found a box of sterling silver candlesticks and ten little individual salt and pepper shakers to match the candle holders. Dad said they had been a wedding gift from

Aunt Sally and Uncle Milt. While I checked on spoons and serving dishes, Elizabeth polished the silver, and I'd never seen our dining room look so elegant.

Elizabeth said she'd stay till the women arrived, and followed me upstairs so I could comb my hair and change my shirt. I chose a long, moss-green shirt to wear with black leggings, and had just put some mauve blush on both cheeks and was fastening tiny gold hoop earrings when I heard Elizabeth say, "Oh . . . my . . . gosh!"

"What?" I turned around.

She was standing at the window, her hands on the sill, looking down at the street. I picked up the other earring and walked over in time to see the last of the three women coming up onto our porch. This one was dressed in a fake zebra-skin coat, five-inch heels, and was wearing enough jewelry to open a store.

"Wait till Lester gets a load of this!" Elizabeth said wide-eyed. Then she turned to me. "Alice, do you think they were *prostitutes*?"

I didn't know what their convictions were for. All I knew was that Dad was probably expecting Albanian refugees with kerchiefs on their heads, but at that moment the doorbell rang.

"Al?" Dad called from the kitchen. "You going to get that?"

"I've got it!" came Lester's voice. I could hear him walking across the living room toward the front door. The sound of the door opening.

There was a three-second silence so profound, it was as though Lester had lost the power of speech. And then the miracle happened. I heard my brother say, in his most gentlemanly voice, "Welcome to our home. I'm Lester. Please come in."

Elizabeth and I went downstairs together. The three women—two white, one African-American—were taking off their coats. They were probably in their late twenties or early thirties, and each smiled as she handed her wrap to Lester.

Elizabeth stuck around just long enough to hear the African-American say, "I'm Charmaine," the one in the leather jacket say, "I'm Shirley," and the one taking off her zebra-skin coat say, "I'm Ginger."

"And I'm Alice," I said. "This is my friend Elizabeth, who helped me make dinner. Only she's leaving now."

"Well, isn't that nice she could help you!" said Charmaine.

"Good-bye! Have a nice dinner!" Elizabeth said, slipping noiselessly past me, and whispered, "Good luck!" as she closed the door behind her.

Dad came out of the kitchen, and Lester introduced the women to him.

"You were so kind to invite us to dinner," Shirley said, pushing up the cuffs of her satin blouse, which she wore with designer jeans, and followed the others into the living room. "The CCFO has been wonderful to us."

"Excuse me?" said Dad.

But I chimed in with, "We're always glad to have company for dinner. Won't you sit down? Lester will see to the appetizers while I check the turkey." Then I made a beeline for the kitchen and opened the oven door. The thermometer still had a way to go before it reached the poultry mark, and I stared at it, trying to will the mercury to move. I grabbed a dish of black olives and a plate of cheese and crackers to take to the living room when Lester came around the corner.

"You're dead," he told me. "Al, who *are* those women?"

"Charmaine, Shirley, and Ginger." I gulped.

"I know that! Where did you find them?"

"I told you. I called the Salvation Army, and—"

"These are no Salvation Army bluebonnets, I'll tell you that."

". . . and they referred me to the CCFO," I added as Dad entered the kitchen.

"What is the CCFO?" Dad asked me.

"Community Connections for Female Offenders," I bleated.

"Holy Mother . . . !" Lester said prayerfully, and we're not even Catholic.

"Al," breathed Dad, "get out there and be friendly. Les, put the wine back and serve those women ginger ale if you have to drive ten miles to find some."

I took the cheese and olives to the living room and sat down across from Charmaine in her blue jersey dress. She seemed the most motherly of the lot. If you had met either Charmaine or Shirley on a bus, they wouldn't look different from anyone else, but Ginger . . . I figured if anyone had been a prostitute, it was she.

"So who all is in this family, Alice?" Shirley asked. "Just you and your dad and Lester?"

"Yes. Mom's dead," I told her, and instantly all three women stopped smiling and looked at me pityingly. "So we just wanted to . . . to have a feminine presence at the table this Thanksgiving, we miss her so," I fumbled, not knowing how to stop.

"Bless your little heart," Charmaine cooed.

Dad came back in the room then, and Ginger said they were sorry to hear about his wife. Dad looked quizzically at me, then at Ginger, and said simply, "Thank you."

Lester found some ginger ale and brought it in with a bucket of ice.

"All three of us are looking for jobs right now," said Charmaine. "The CCFO got us work in a warehouse, but we'd like something better, if we can get it."

"What kind of work are you looking for?" Dad inquired.

"Something that'll pay the rent. Something in sales, maybe. You put yourself out of circulation awhile, you're amazed at how much the rents have gone up," said Ginger.

"Shoot. Just blink your eyes and it's another thirty dollars a month," said Charmaine.

"Sales have their ups and downs," Lester told her. "I take some classes at the U and work part time selling shoes."

"*Do* you, now?" said Charmaine.

"A college boy!" said Ginger.

I went out in the kitchen again and turned the oven to 450 degrees. I decided I would get that turkey done if I had to blast it out of the oven. I fussed around, making sure everything else was ready to go, sat out in the living room for another fifteen minutes making small talk, and when I checked again, the needle had almost reached the poultry mark. I turned the oven down a little for the pies, and tried to figure out how to lift a twenty-pound turkey out of a roasting pan so I could set it on the carving board.

I thought of calling to Dad or Les for help, but Dad had just made a joke and the women were all laughing, and then Lester said something funny and they laughed some more. I figured I needed Dad and Lester to keep the conversation going more than I needed them in the kitchen.

I slid out the oven rack as far as I dared. Then I picked up two heavy meat forks, jabbed one in each side of the turkey like handles, and tried to lift it straight up out of the roasting pan. The skin was stuck to the pan, however, so I tried jerking upward to free it.

The skin gave, the turkey jerked free, and then, before I knew what happened, one fork slipped out of the side, and half the huge turkey fell to the floor with a greasy *whump* and *splat*, followed a second later by the other.

I don't know which was louder—the clatter of the pan as it clanked back on the rack or my scream.

Lester was the first one to reach me, Dad at his heels, and a moment later Ginger, Shirley, and Charmaine were all peering over Dad's shoulder at the spectacle there on the floor.

The turkey looked as though it had been cut in half with a power saw because it had, its legs and skewers akimbo, dressing strewn about the floor in clumps, the puddle of grease, like an oil slick, spreading slowly out beneath it.

I was on the verge of tears when Charmaine started to giggle.

I saw Shirley elbow her, and suddenly she gave a snort disguised as a sneeze, and then Ginger burst out in a fit of laughter. A moment later Dad joined in, then Lester, and suddenly we were all standing there in the kitchen, howling like hyenas.

Charmaine leaned against the door frame, clutching her ribs as though she, too, might split in half.

"Well," said Dad at last. "The only sides we can't eat are the sides that're on the floor. Ladies, would you care to take a seat at the table while we tend to things here?"

"Not until we help clean up," said Charmaine. "Just hand me a dishrag, Ben."

The next thing I knew, Dad had speared one half of the turkey, Les had speared the other, and they were lifting the twin carcasses onto the carving board. The three women, with towels and rags, were mopping up the floor, stopping every so often to laugh some more.

We were in fine spirits when we finally got the meal on the table. There was enough stuffing left in the turkey to salvage for dinner, and the sweet potatoes turned out well. So did the rolls and the peas and carrots, and I remembered to stick the three pies in the oven. Already we could detect the scent of mince-meat.

"Alice, you can cook me a turkey any day," said Shirley. When she smiled, she arched her eyebrows, which had been plucked into two thin half circles. "This sure beats jail food."

"Indeed it sure beats that," said Charmaine.

And then they began to talk. It was almost as though, once

I had made such a horrible mess of the turkey, it was easier for them to talk about their own mistakes. And since the women knew how we'd got their names, there was no need to hold back.

As it turned out, it wasn't Ginger in the dozen or so gold bangles who had been a prostitute, it was Shirley, but she'd been in prison on a drug charge. Both Ginger and Charmaine had done shoplifting big time.

Once, when Shirley referred to her former profession, she glanced at me and hesitated, but Dad said, "You can say anything you want around here, because that's the way we learn in this house."

"It's the way we *all* ought to have learned!" said Charmaine, wiping her fingers with the rose-colored nail polish on her napkin. "My mother didn't tell me *nothing*! Not a single thing I needed to know about myself. Everything I learned I learned from the neighbor boys in all the wrong ways. I ever ask my mother a question about sex, why, she'd crack me across the mouth, like how I shouldn't even be *thinking* about things like that."

Ginger nodded. "I'd ask my mother questions about sex, she'd just laugh. Big joke. *You'll find out soon enough*, my aunt would say, and she and mom would laugh some more."

Shirley, though, was more quiet than the rest. Then she said, "My mother told me everything I wanted to know about sex and more besides. Said she expected twenty dollars a week from me—a boarding fee—for our two-bedroom apartment. Now how in the world is a high-school girl supposed to get twenty dollars a week to pay for her own room? So I was taking boys up to my bedroom after school, making a whole lot more than twenty dollars, and that's when my mother said I didn't need to finish high school to make that, and didn't care if I never went back, so I didn't."

This was news to Charmaine and Ginger.

"Your very own mama?" Charmaine gasped.

"If you can call her that," Shirley continued. "She used the money for her drug habit. Then I got into drugs as a way of getting through the afternoons with the boys. Nobody is ever again going to mess with my body and my mind if I can help it."

"Good for you," said Dad.

All the women were looking at me now.

"You got a good home here, mother or no mother," said Charmaine.

"The kind of mothers *we* had, you can do without," said Shirley.

But Ginger disagreed. "Every girl needs a mother," she said.

Dad smiled around the group. "Well, Alice is about to get one, because I'm engaged to be married next summer."

All the women began to exclaim at once, and I had to tell them the story of how I'd invited Miss Summers to the Messiah Sing-Along and Dad didn't know about it, and Dad told about his trip to England, while Lester poured more ginger ale.

When I went out in the kitchen to rescue the pies, the edges were browning nicely. We sat around talking while the pies cooled, and then I set them out with a can of Reddi-wip and some plates and forks, and we all helped ourselves.

Dad said he'd do the dishes. The women wanted to help, but he said absolutely not, so the rest of us moved into the living room and sat around our big coffee table, playing crazy eights and poker, and some other kind of card game we'd never heard of that the women had learned in prison.

"That's one thing they give you plenty of in prison: time," said Shirley.

"Isn't *that* the truth?" said Charmaine. "You ever think the months are flying by too fast, you just spend a year in jail and you'll swear that clock don't move at all."

Ginger, who was closest to Lester's age, kept directing coy little remarks to him, I noticed, and fluttering impossibly thick black eyelashes, but he didn't fall for it. He was gallant and funny and helpful and attentive, and I could tell that none of the women wanted to leave as afternoon turned to evening, but they realized they should go.

Dad and Lester helped them on with their coats, and I remembered what Aunt Sally had suggested, and wrapped up a packet of turkey and some rolls for each of them.

"Thank you so much," Shirley said, shaking hands all around. "It was a wonderful afternoon."

Ginger lingered over Lester's handshake. "Don't you study too hard now, College Boy," she said. "You've got to have a little fun."

"I'll remember that," said Lester.

But it was Charmaine who hugged me as she went out the door. "Little girl," she said, "you don't know how lucky you are to have a home and a family like this."

I hugged her back. "Maybe I do," I said.

We watched them go down the sidewalk, Ginger in her five-inch heels that, according to Lester, would be considered instruments of torture back in the Dark Ages. And then, with a little toot of the horn, the old Buick turned around and headed back down the street.

I wondered if Dad and Lester were going to jump all over me once the women were gone, but Lester simply hit me on the head with the newspaper he was rolling up to restart the fire.

"Knucklehead," he told me, trying not to smile. "Salvation Army, Community Connections for Female Offenders. Who are you inviting next year, Al? The Mafia Wives Club?"

"Why didn't you *tell* us about those women, Al?" asked Dad.

"I thought maybe if you didn't know they were ex-cons, it would be easier to treat them like ordinary people," I said.

"Well, fortunately, they seemed to feel comfortable enough here to talk about their past, and let's hope it really is past," said Dad. "Actually, I think you did a fine thing, Al. Your mother used to do things like that—invite a neighbor in who had lost her husband. Take dinner to a friend going through chemotherapy— that sort of thing. I just wish you'd let me in on these schemes *before* they happen."

"You guys were really wonderful," I said. "You made them feel right at home. You were great."

"Yeah, well don't go pressing your luck," Lester growled.

I went back to the dining room to help put things away. The women had been careful not to spill anything on Mom's linen tablecloth, but I decided to wash it anyway, to see if I could get rid of the yellow lines. I carefully picked up the candlesticks that Elizabeth and I had polished, and then the little sets of silver salt and pepper shakers. And suddenly I froze and stared at the table. Five sets of shakers. One was missing.

I stood there, my throat too tight even to swallow, blood rushing to my head. I tried to picture where each woman had been sitting, and realized that the set of shakers by Charmaine's place were gone.

How *could* she? How could she accept our invitation to eat at our table and share our hospitality and then walk off with one of the few things I had left that had belonged to my mother? How could she hug me there at the door with those shakers stuffed in a pocket?

My eyes filled with tears. Angry tears. How could people come into our house and just *take* things? First my boyfriend. Now my mother's shakers. I didn't want to admit to Dad that I never should have invited those people here—that it had been another of my stupid ideas. But he had to know. I went back out in the kitchen.

"I think I made a . . . ," I began, and then my eye fell on the sixth set of shakers, sitting on the counter where Charmaine must have placed them as she helped clear the table.

". . . a pretty good dinner after all," I said.

"The best," Dad told me.

When Aunt Sally called later to see how the dinner had gone, Dad answered and I let him tell her about it. Somehow, sitting in the other room and listening to his version—the frozen turkey, the power saw and duct tape, the CCFO and the spill on the kitchen floor—made me realize just how wacky the day had been, and what a funny piece it would make for the school newspaper.

When I went to school the following Monday, I talked to Sara, the features editor, about my idea, and she said sure, write it up and they'd see if they could use it. So I did. I didn't bring in the CCFO, I just said we were having guests, and titled it "The Great Turkey Disaster." Sara and Nick liked it, and even though it appeared on the last page, at least twenty kids made a point of telling me how much they enjoyed it. Maybe my "Alice Time" was more valuable than I'd realized. I was finding out I was worth a lot more than I'd thought.

14
ELIZABETH'S SECRET

Seeing Patrick and Penny together at school was easier once I didn't feel that everyone was looking at me to see how I'd react. It was easier because I'd broken the ice with Patrick, and we always said "Hi" now when we passed in the halls.

Part of it, I suppose, was to preserve my pride. To snub Patrick or Penny would only make me look hurt and bitter, and even though that's the way I felt a lot of the time, I didn't exactly want the whole school to know.

But I had the drama club to go to, where we read plays aloud, and staff meetings for the school paper, and the Melody

Inn on Saturdays. I felt needed and appreciated, and that took some of the loneliness away.

And then, of course, there was Christmas, a plus and a minus both. I was used to thinking of Patrick at Christmas—of shopping for a gift for him, and knowing that he'd be over sometime during the holidays to bring one to me. Waiting for that extra-special Christmas kiss. And there was also New Year's Eve. Now, he was probably spending it with Penny.

But there was the house to decorate for Dad and Lester, and a gift to buy for Sylvia (Dad said we'd send them airmail express to make sure she got them in time), and presents for everyone else on my list.

"Al, the decorations look great!" Dad said on Saturday morning as I was draping tinsel, a strand at a time, over a wire strung above the shelves in the Gift Shoppe where we keep the Beethoven mugs and Scarlotti scarves and the Brahms T-shirts and the Liszt notepads (with CHOPIN LISZT printed at the top). I had arranged shiny gold and silver balls among the gift items, and the tinsel reflected the light and cast an icy, metallic shimmer over the merchandise.

"What are you giving Sylvia for Christmas?" Marilyn asked me later. She was looking pretty stunning herself in a red dress with little gold earrings in the form of a tree ornament at each ear.

I showed her the sterling silver pin I'd picked out for Sylvia from the gift wheel—the large revolving case next to the counter. You press a button, and the wheel begins to rotate. If a customer sees a ring or cuff links that interest her, she can press the button to stop the wheel, and then I open the case with a key and get it for her.

"Oh, Alice, it's just perfect for Sylvia!" Marilyn exclaimed, fingering the silver musical clef sign.

I was pleased that she thought so. "I decided that since it was the Messiah Sing-Along that brought her and Dad together, a clef sign would be a reminder of that, of something they have in common," I said.

"You're going to make a very thoughtful stepdaughter," Marilyn told me.

I beamed. "And she'll make the perfect stepmom."

The feature story that Sam Mayer and I had put together turned out well, though he thought his photographs should have been better. Sam is a little shorter than Patrick, and more stocky, but he's nice looking in his own way.

"They're too posed," he said. "I should have taken a few with their mouths open. Gesturing or something."

I folded up the issue of the school paper and stuck it in my notebook. "Are you always so hard on yourself?" I asked.

"You have to get used to criticism if you go into photo-journalism," he said.

"That's what it's going to be for you?"

"Yeah, I've decided."

"It must be nice to be sure," I said.

As we left Room 17, where we hold our staff meetings, we almost collided with a girl carrying a huge papier-mâché icicle, covered with glitter, on her way to the gym, where they were decorating for the Snow Ball. I had *really* been trying not to think of the Snow Ball. Didn't want to remember that Patrick and I had been dating for two years, and when the semiformal finally arrived in eighth grade, the one big dance we would attend, Patrick was sick and couldn't go. Now he would be dancing with Penny. She'd be wearing a glittering gown, he'd have his arms around her, and . . . "About ready for Christmas?" I asked quickly, refusing to dwell on it.

"Mom and I usually go to the movies on Christmas," Sam said.

I'd forgotten he was Jewish. "Oh. Right," I said.

"But this year I'll probably go over to Jennifer's for a while. Christmas is pretty big with her."

"Yeah. Us too," I said.

We said good-bye at the water cooler, and I went off to my locker, deciding to invite Elizabeth and Pamela for a sleepover the night of the Snow Ball. Neither of them was going, either. It seemed that not too many freshmen were going to be there. I guess we still all felt a little green, like we wanted to sit things out for a year and see how they were done.

Jill had been invited by a sophomore, though, and Brian was taking some girl from another school. But Karen was going to help serve at a holiday party her dad was giving, and Sam and Jennifer were going ice skating with Gwen and Legs, so I was glad to have Elizabeth and Pamela for company, and they were happy to have someplace to go. Dad and Lester had gone to a movie, and we had the house to ourselves. I have our old twelve-inch TV in my room, so we made some caramel corn in the microwave and took it upstairs.

There are times you really, truly appreciate your friends, and this was one of them. I think Elizabeth and Pamela were feeling it too. We'd been particularly close since Pamela had come back from Colorado, where she'd tried living with her mother and it hadn't worked. And whatever had been going on with Elizabeth last summer when she put herself on starvation rations only made us realize how vulnerable she was; how vulnerable we all were. Now it was my breakup with Patrick that bonded us closer still, and as I sprawled out on my bed beside Pamela, I actually felt I would rather be here with my best friends than anywhere else I could think of.

Elizabeth had heard all about our Thanksgiving with the three women from CCFO, but Pamela didn't know the details, so I filled her in. She was fascinated.

"I've never actually *seen* a prostitute," she said, reaching for a handful of popcorn and then her soda. "Not one I was sure of, anyway. How did she act, Alice? Did she try to put the moves on your dad or Les?"

"She *used* to be one, Pamela. Ginger was more flirtatious than Shirley, actually."

Pamela lay back on the bed in her black jeans and red sweater. "Can you even imagine it?" she said. "I mean, to stand on a street corner and get in a car with the first guy who stopped? Why, he could have AIDS! He could be a serial killer!"

We were quiet for a moment, wondering about it.

"Shirley said her mom got her into prostitution to help pay for her mom's drug habit—her *mom's*! And then Shirley started taking drugs just to get through the afternoons she had boys in her room," I said.

"In her pants, you mean. Imagine hating sex so much you'd have to drug yourself to do it," said Pamela.

Elizabeth was sitting over in the corner in my leopard-print chair, her knees drawn up to her chest, hugging them close to her body. "What I can't understand is how a mother could *do* that—*make* her daughter invite guys up to her room," she said. "Couldn't she even imagine how Shirley might have felt about it?"

"Ha!" said Pamela. "She probably didn't care! My mom sure doesn't care what happens to me! I could be in all kinds of trouble here, but as long as she's got Mr. Wonderful in Colorado, that's all that matters."

"She does care for you, Pamela. She's just all wrapped up in herself right now," I told her.

"Thank you, Alice, for your kind words, but she's all wrapped up in her NordicTrack instructor, that's what," Pamela said bitterly.

"I'll bet most prostitutes' mothers don't know what their daughters are doing. No one tells her mother *every*thing, you know. I can't imagine telling Sylvia every single thing I'm doing or thinking. Not that I'd be doing *that*!" I said.

"Even when we're little, we don't tell them everything,"

Pamela agreed. "I remember when I was five or six, I used to go to a playground and there was a girl who threw rocks at me. She said I couldn't come there unless she said so, and for a whole summer I stayed away and never told my parents why."

I was looking through the *TV Guide* and found a movie called *Dark Secret, Hidden Life*, about a girl who had a baby without anyone knowing. It would be on in ten minutes, so we decided to watch that.

"You keep hearing about girls being pregnant and no one knowing, but how is it possible?" I said. "Couldn't her mother tell? What about gym class?"

We tried to imagine how a girl could keep it hidden. "Maybe she just wore baggy clothes and never went to gym," Elizabeth said.

"But how can you keep a secret for nine whole months? Well, five, anyway, because that's when you'd really start to show if you were pregnant. How could a girl keep a secret like that from her mother for five months?" I asked.

"I can imagine keeping a secret from my mother, but I don't think I'd try to keep one from you guys," Pamela said. "When I think of all the times you've been here for me. . . ."

I nodded. "We can talk about things we'd never tell anyone else. All the embarrassing stuff! Remember when you were showing us that new bra, Pamela, and Mark sneaked up behind us and grabbed it out of your hands and took it to the top of the jungle gym?"

"And the time you lost your bikini bra in the ocean?" Elizabeth told her.

"How about you learning to use tampons at the pool?" Pamela said to Elizabeth. "And your first pelvic exam." She turned to me. "And the day at school when you found out Miss Summers was going to England for a year, and we followed you into the restroom. . . ."

"I don't know what we'd do without each other," I said to them both. "I hope we can still get together and talk like this when we're fifty."

"I don't think any of us could keep a pregnancy secret. We couldn't go for five *minutes* without telling someone, could we, Elizabeth?" said Pamela.

But Elizabeth didn't answer. The movie was on, and she came over to the bed where we were lying, and we all watched together. It was about a sixteen-year-old girl on trial for throwing her newborn baby in a Dumpster. Most of it was flashbacks, about how she'd lost her father as a little girl and missed him, but her mother had her hands full trying to support them and didn't give her the love she needed, so she threw herself at the first guy who came along.

It was a grade-B movie, actually, but the last part was really sad, when the judge sentenced her to thirty years, and when she stared at him in the courtroom, all she could see was her father. It had the three of us in tears.

"It didn't have to happen!" Elizabeth wept, blowing her nose. "If the mother had paid the slightest bit of attention, she would have seen what was going on."

"The mother had all kinds of problems herself, Liz," I said.

"Oh, I don't think the mother really cared," put in Pamela. "She was only concerned with her own pain."

"When you're a parent, it's your *job* to see how your kids are feeling," said Elizabeth, still choked up about the movie.

"What else could the mother have done?" I asked.

Elizabeth jerked angrily around and glared at me. "Look at the way she practically *encouraged* her daughter to go out with the guy. All she could think about was maybe he'd marry Marcie and take her off her hands. If she'd just once put her arms around her and asked how she really f-felt about the guy, and gave her a chance to . . . to . . ." And suddenly Elizabeth was sobbing. *Sobbing.*

I picked up the remote and muted the sound. Both Pamela and I scrambled to a sitting position and stared at Elizabeth, who had drawn up her knees and was lying there in the fetal position, crying huge, heaving sobs.

Pamela reached out and put her hand over Elizabeth's, and Elizabeth's fingers closed around it and held on as if she were drowning. All we could do was stare and keep repeating, "Liz, what *is* it? What *is* it?"

Elizabeth's cheeks were burning. "I . . . I . . . I've got to tell you something. I've kept a secret for seven *years*, and never told anyone before, not even the priest!"

This really got our attention.

"Okay," I said, wondering.

"Can you promise n-never to t-tell anyone? Especially my folks. Because if you can't"—she gulped—"I can't tell you."

Pamela promised right away, but I wasn't so sure.

"I don't know, Liz. If you're thinking of doing something terrible to yourself, I'm not going to keep it secret."

She rolled over and slowly sat up, her hair tangled, her nose clogged. I gave her a tissue. "It's something that's already happened, and nobody but you can ever know about it. *Ever!*" she said.

So I promised.

But all Elizabeth did was put her hands over her face and cry some more.

"What *was* it?" Pamela asked, reaching over to rub her back.

That seemed to give her courage. "A . . . a long time ago," she said, between sobs, her chin quivering, "a man . . . a man molested me."

"What?" Pamela said.

"*Who?*" I asked. I had this awful thought that maybe it was her father and she didn't want her mother to know. But it wasn't.

Elizabeth finally stopped crying and took a minute to blow her nose. "He was a . . . a family friend. Someone my folks had known in college. A biologist, I think. Sometimes he came to our house on holidays, or when he had a conference in D.C. That's where we were living then."

Neither Pamela nor I said a word. It was such a revelation— I mean, who would have expected this from *Elizabeth!*—that we didn't know what to say.

She took a deep breath and continued: "I think I was about seven, in second grade, because I can remember the dress I was wearing the first time it happened. A sundress. This man's wife had either died or they'd just divorced or something, and he'd come to Washington for a meeting—he lived out of state—and came a day early to visit us. We were living near Rock Creek Park, and he always brought a little present for me—a really nice gift—a puppet or a microscope or something. My folks thought he was wonderful. I did, too, at first. He was supposed to have done a lot for ghetto kids—got them scholarships and things . . ."

Elizabeth's voice was still shaky but it was getting stronger. "Well, on this one visit, he asked if I wanted to go on a 'secret nature walk,' just he and I, and my folks said, why, wouldn't that be fun. It was hot, and we went down into the park. And he showed me lots of 'secrets'—like the bugs and worms under a rock, moss growing on a tree, a cicada carcass—the kinds of things that interest a child."

She stopped and began to blush.

"You don't have to tell us anything if you don't want to," I said.

"Shut up, Alice. *I* want to hear!" said Pamela.

Elizabeth went on. "We came to this big rock—boulder, really—and he led me around behind it and told me to look real hard in a crevice in the rock where there were leaves and dirt, and see if I could find anything. He had . . . he was leaning on me from behind, his arms around me, his face against mine, like he was helping me look. And he brought his hands up under my dress in front and just . . . just casually rubbed my stomach, and then he . . . slipped one hand down inside my pants and"—she swallowed—"and stroked me between my legs."

"What did you *do*?" Pamela asked.

"That's the part I can't remember," Elizabeth said guiltily. "I *think* I squirmed away, and he just laughed and let me go. And on the way back to the house he said to remember that this was a secret walk, wasn't it, that he and I had a lot of secrets, and we wouldn't tell anyone about them, would we, because nobody else would understand."

"The creep!" Pamela said.

"And when we got back, my parents were doing the dishes, because I can remember a big white platter in my father's hands, and it looked like a big white eye staring at me. Mother asked what all we had seen and the man winked at me and said, oh, we couldn't tell, could we, but we'd seen all sorts of wonderful things. I just nodded yes. I really thought . . . for a long time I thought this . . . that my parents knew what he was going to do and had let me go because he was such a good friend."

"And he did it again?" I asked.

"I think there was just one other time. Maybe two, I'm not sure. But the time I remember, he brought me a little box full of drawers, and each drawer had a tiny carved wooden animal in it. It was a great present; I really loved it. He called it the 'secrets' chest. And when he asked if I wanted to go on another secret walk, I said okay, because my parents were smiling at me and I knew they expected me to go.

"He said we'd need a strainer, and Mom gave me one. This time I had on shorts and a T-shirt. And we went down in the park again, and this time we walked right along the rocks in the creek, and we tried to see what I could catch in the strainer— little water bugs and things. And then when we started home, he led me through some bushes and he was talking about how lonely he was, because his wife wasn't with him anymore, and he wondered if I would do something for him . . ."

Pamela let out her breath. We waited.

"And he . . . he asked me to stand very still and let him touch me. I let him lift me up to stand on a rock or something, and he pressed against me from behind and put his fingers down my pants again, and then we went home and he thanked me for helping him not to feel so lonely anymore."

"And your parents still didn't catch on?"

Elizabeth's face was all scrunched up again. "I still thought maybe they *knew*! That they wanted me to do this for him. He was one of their best friends, and I felt I should do whatever he said. It was only a couple years ago, in thinking about this, that I began to see they simply thought it was a game. It was all in fun, our walks. But I took their smiles to mean they knew what he was doing to me. How could I have been so dumb?"

"Elizabeth, you were only seven!" I said.

"Eight, by then. And when I got home that day and went to the bathroom, I found that my shorts and shirt were wet and sticky in back and I changed them, and rinsed them out under the faucet. When Mom asked why I'd changed my clothes, I told her I'd just got wet, and I guess she figured I'd slipped in the creek or something."

"It must have made perfect sense to them," Pamela said. "The walk to the creek . . . the strainer . . . the biologist . . . the trusted friend. Who would have thought?"

Elizabeth pressed the palms of her hands hard against her cheeks, sliding them up over her temples as though wanting to wipe the skin right off her forehead. "The thing is . . . the thing is . . . when he touched me, it . . . it felt good. I didn't think we should be doing that, but he wasn't hurting me, physically, and even later—years later—any time I thought of telling Mom about it, I couldn't, because I felt I was as guilty as he was. Because it had felt good . . . what he did."

So many things came to mind just then—the way Elizabeth had always reacted to talk about sex and bodies, the way she embarrassed so easily. All her emphasis on sin and confession— her mother never struck me as being that way particularly.

"Elizabeth," I said. "If a guy touches you without your permission and you get a ping out of it, it doesn't mean you did something wrong. When somebody touches the right button, you ping, that's all!"

She was thoughtful. "The next time he came, the next summer when I was nine, it was raining, and he didn't say anything about a secret walk. He and my folks were talking in the living room and I went down in the basement to play with this big Victorian dollhouse my dad had set up for me. After a while this man came down to see it. Dad and Mom came, too, and then the man sat down on a chair and he was sort of playing along with me, making silly things happen to the dolls. Dad and Mom stayed for a while, we were all laughing at him, and then they went upstairs and he stayed. For a while we were having fun. And then . . ."

I began to notice anger in Elizabeth's voice. "Then he said it was too bad we couldn't go for one of our walks, but did I want to *see* something secret? And he took one of my hands and . . . and put it on his pants. I could feel his penis underneath . . . and I pulled away from him and went upstairs to my room. I remember walking very deliberately; I didn't run or anything because I didn't want my parents to know I was walking out on him. I mean . . . believe it or not . . . it seemed so rude, and I just told Mom I was going to play in my room awhile."

"What'd the guy do? Follow you up there?" Pamela asked.

"No. He came up from the basement and played the piano awhile, and then he and Dad and Mom sat around talking the rest of the evening. When I got up the next morning, he'd already left for the conference."

"When did you see him again?" I asked.

"I didn't. About four months later he was killed in a car accident, a really freak accident, my dad always said. And . . . and it was like . . . like I'd made it happen."

"But you didn't!"

"I know, but the fact is I was *glad* when I heard it. Mom cried when we got the news, and Dad had tears in his eyes, but I wasn't sad at all, and they kept looking at me, like, what was wrong with me? This wonderful man who brought me presents and was respected in his field and had done so much for ghetto kids, and I wasn't even sad? And finally . . . finally . . . I made myself cry, not because I was sorry he died, but because my parents were so d-disappointed in me!"

Elizabeth broke down again, and I began to see how problems can get so complex, how all these different feelings could get mixed and matched in your head, and be so hard to get out later. I couldn't help but wonder about myself . . . a feeling I might have had, or still have, about my own mother when she died.

I don't know how Pamela and I knew what to do just then, but it seemed like we did the right thing: We hugged Elizabeth, Pamela on one side of her and I on the other, so that we were sort of a warm moist ball of arms and faces, and I think that without quite knowing it, we were making Elizabeth feel safe with us and protected. We just let her cry, and she cried softly, like a little mouse, until she was limp and drained. When we let her go, she sat there on the bed with her head on her knees.

"You know, Liz, you aren't going to be really free of this till you tell your folks," I said finally. "They really need to know."

"Why?" she asked, looking up at me, her face all streaked. "First, I'm not sure they'll believe me. They'll say I must have imagined it, or that it happened so long ago, I'm getting fact and fantasy mixed up. Or if it really happened, why didn't I tell them before? He was their best *friend*, Alice! Everyone loved him. Everyone but me."

"They need to know because they love you, and it's a part of you that's hurting," I told her.

"But I'm probably just as guilty as he was. I didn't try to stop him, except for that last time. He said 'stand still' so I did. I could have pushed him away."

"You were eight years old, Elizabeth! That's third grade!" I said. "And it wouldn't have made any difference if you were older, because he was the adult and you were the child. Look! We're considered minors till we're eighteen, right? Up until then, adults are supposed to know best and we're supposed to obey them, and that's exactly what you did."

"Well, I'm not telling Mom. It would just kill her. Let them remember him the way they think he was. But I feel better having told you," Elizabeth said.

We sat up another hour after that, talking. We heard Dad and Lester come in and go to bed, and when we finally turned out our light around one, Pamela and I in my double bed and Elizabeth on the cot under the window, I decided I was pretty sure what I wanted to do as a career. I truly did want to be a psychologist, someone who works with children before little problems become big ones. Someone who, maybe if she'd seen Elizabeth when she was eight or nine, could have helped her get the feelings out before they took up so much space in her life.

15
THE TEST

It turned out that Patrick and Penny hadn't gone to the Snow Ball, either, Jill told me. She stopped by the Melody Inn the next day to show me pictures of herself and the sophomore who had taken her to the dance. Jill had worn a white strapless dress, and her bosom was bulging over the top. If she'd sneezed, she would have popped right out.

I wondered what it meant that Patrick hadn't taken Penny, or whether it meant anything at all. But mostly I was thinking about Elizabeth. I couldn't get her out of my mind—what it must feel like to go five or six years hiding a secret like that and feeling guilty about it.

Nevertheless, I had work to do, and Marilyn and I spent the day restocking the display of Christmas CDs near the front of the store and making sure we were caught up on telephone orders. We left at the usual time, but Dad said he'd work another hour or two.

When I walked in the house, I could hear Lester rummaging about the kitchen, making dinner, but there was a message for me to call Karen, so I did.

"Alice," she said as soon as I dialed her number. "I didn't think I ought to call you at the Melody Inn. Is your dad home?"

"No. Why?"

"I just need to tell you something when he's not around, and I'm not even sure I should be telling you in the first place."

"What are you talking about?" I asked, puzzled.

"Well, I was at my dad's last night. I told you he was giving this party, and I was, like, helping out. Dad and Jim Sorringer are friends, you know. He bought that engagement ring for Miss Summers last February at Dad's jewelry store, remember? The ring she turned down? Anyway, Sorringer was there at the party, and at one point he was at the buffet table with his back to me—I was gathering up dirty glasses—and a woman asked him how he was going to spend the holidays, and I heard him say he was going to England. I . . . I just thought you should know."

At the first mention of Jim Sorringer I had felt a wave of cold rush over me, but now it felt as though I had swallowed an ice cube, and I wasn't even sure I could breathe.

"Alice . . . I . . . I didn't know if I should say anything . . ."

I tried not to sound worried. "Did he . . . say any more? Did he say he'd be going to Chester?"

"Yes. That's exactly where he said he'd be going. The woman said wouldn't Christmas in London be wonderful? And Jim said that actually he'd be spending it in Chester."

I wanted to throw up. "Well, there could be all kinds of explanations, I suppose," I managed to say. "There's no law that says he can't go to England."

"I suppose so. It probably doesn't mean anything at all. Maybe he's going with someone else and he's just stopping by to say hello to Miss Summers," Karen said quickly.

"Was he with anyone at the party?"

"No," she admitted. "He came alone."

"Well, thanks anyway, Karen," I said.

"Yeah, thanks for nothing," she said apologetically. "I just thought you should know, that's all."

After I hung up, I wondered if I was having a heart attack. If a fourteen-year-old girl could actually expire from anger and disappointment. And suddenly I lost it. I went stumbling out to the kitchen.

"I *hate* her!" I said, breaking into tears. "She's a liar and a cheat, and I *hate* her!"

"Who was that?" Lester asked.

"Karen."

"What did she do?"

"Not Karen. Miss Summers! Mr. Sorringer is going there for Christmas!"

Lester stopped chopping onions and stared at me. "When did you hear this?"

"Just now." In shaky fits and starts I told him about the party at Karen's dad's, and what Karen had heard Jim Sorringer say. "That's why she didn't want a diamond from Dad!" I wept. "That's why she didn't want any engagement ring at all! She didn't want to be wearing one when Jim came for Christmas! And she told Dad she'd be *traveling* during the holidays! Traveling with *Jim*, that's what!"

Lester put the knife down and leaned against the counter. I had expected him to say it wasn't any of our business. I expected him to say that this was between her and Dad, but this time he didn't. "How do you know Karen's telling the truth—that she isn't just stirring up trouble?" he asked.

"Well, what she told me before was true—about Jim Sorringer buying Sylvia a ring. I don't think she'd lie about this. She didn't sound as though she was trying to make trouble."

Les was thoughtful. "Well, there may not be anything to it," he said, "but this time, I think Dad ought to know. Maybe he already does. Maybe it's Sylvia's final good-bye to Jim or something—her way of making sure she's doing the right thing."

"How can you say that?" I shouted. "If she's not sure of Dad, then they shouldn't be engaged. Is she going to go on seeing Jim Sorringer for the rest of her life to make sure she did the right thing marrying Dad?"

"Well, let's not jump to conclusions. Let's tell Dad as calmly as we can and let him handle it in his own way."

But now the tears were really rolling. All my resolutions about not crying at every little thing . . . "It's two weeks before Christmas, Lester! Dad's been so happy. She'll break his heart. What I want to do is call Sylvia myself and tell her what she's doing to him."

"You'll do nothing of the kind. We're just going to tell Dad what you heard, and that's all. . . ."

The front door closed, and Dad's footsteps sounded in the hall. I froze. He walked straight into the kitchen and looked at me. "Well, what's all this?" he said jovially. "Has somebody called off Christmas?"

That made it even worse, because someone *had*, I wanted to say. Sylvia Summers, that's who, but I didn't trust myself to answer, so Lester answered for me.

"Al heard a disturbing piece of news just now, Dad. Karen was helping out at her father's Christmas party last night, and Jim Sorringer was one of the guests. Karen overheard him tell a woman that he would be spending Christmas in England. In Chester, to be exact."

Dad stared at us as though Lester were speaking Norwegian, as though Les weren't making a bit of sense. He reached out, opened the refrigerator, took out a bottle of cranberry juice, and set it on the counter. And two seconds later, just as mechanically, he put it back in again, his eyes unblinking. "Well, he'll find Sylvia gone. She'll be traveling," he said, but his face looked blank. Then he added, "It's possible that Jim's just doing some traveling himself. A coincidence, maybe."

We all knew the answer to that. London? Possibly. But, Chester? No.

"Was he going alone, do you happen to know?" Dad asked, looking at me. "Maybe he's traveling with a friend."

"I don't know. But Karen said he came to the party alone," I told him. And then I lost it again. "Dad, I'm so sorry," I wept. "I *hate* Sylvia!"

"Now, don't say that, Al. There could be a good explanation. We didn't hear all the facts," Dad said, but he didn't convince me.

"*Call* her!" I said. "Ask her what it's all about."

"No." Dad was firm. "I'll let her tell me herself without any prodding from me." And then he added, "She's supposed to call tonight, and she'll undoubtedly explain it then. Now, what are we having for dinner?"

I couldn't bear it. I couldn't stand the hurt in his eyes, his voice, his face . . . I blindly reached for the plates and set the table.

Dinner was a sober affair. I think we all ate the burritos without tasting. It looked as though our mouths were scarcely moving, as though we weren't even chewing.

"How are things at the store?" Lester asked finally. "Business has been nonstop at the shoe store."

"We sold two baby grands this week," Dad said. But his voice was flat, and the conversation died after that.

I did the dishes after dinner, and Lester and I went right on up to our rooms because we knew it was close to midnight in England, and Sylvia would be calling Dad any minute now. We wanted him to have the downstairs to himself so he could talk to her in private. I spread out my homework on my bed, but left the door ajar. When the phone rang and I heard Dad pick it up, I'll admit that I got up and went to my doorway.

"Oh, Sylvia, it's so good to hear your voice," Dad said. ". . . I know. I miss you, darling. . . ." There were murmurs, words I couldn't make out. Then I heard Dad telling her about work and the big pre-Christmas sale at the Melody Inn. I changed position and waited. "How I wish you could be in my arms at Christmas," Dad was saying now. "How will you spend the day, sweetheart?" He was fishing, I knew. Giving her every opportunity to tell him. More silence. Then, finally, "Oh . . . uh-huh . . . I see . . . well, that might be fun. . : . No, I won't try to reach you then, but you'll be calling me?"

She *wasn't* telling him! Whatever she said was a lie. I went back and sat on the edge of my bed, waiting for Dad to come up and tell us what she'd said. When we heard his footsteps on the stairs, both Les and I came to the doors of our rooms. Dad paused on the next to the top step, his hand on the banister.

"What did she say?" I asked.

"Well, she didn't mention Jim. I guess she plans to do her traveling just after Christmas, between Christmas and New Year's. I asked what she'd be doing Christmas Day, and she said that one of the teachers had invited her to have dinner with her family, and she'd be out most of the time, but she'd call me that evening."

"And you didn't ask her about Sorringer?" I wanted to know.

"No. . . . Whatever her reasons, she's keeping them to herself. But I trust her—"

"I can't believe you'd put up with that, Dad!" I cried. "If *you* had another woman coming *here* at Christmas . . . !"

"Al, cool it!" Lester said sternly.

Dad just sighed. "I've got to handle this in my own way, honey," he said, and walked slowly back to his room. He looked like an old, old man.

After I heard his door close and Lester closed his, I angrily wiped one arm across my eyes. *I* didn't have to trust Sylvia! *I* didn't have to excuse her! I rushed over to my dresser, grabbed the picture of Miss Summers off my mirror—the photo of her I'd always liked best, Sylvia in a filmy blue and green dress—and ripped the picture in half.

"There!" I cried, and ripped it a second time. "There! And there! And there!" And then I lay facedown on my bed and bawled some more.

As Christmas drew near, our house was like a morgue, and I began to feel that as much as I had loved Sylvia Summers in the past, I hated her now. I was glad we were busy at the store. I went in twice after school the week before vacation, just to help out. I'd bought Polartec gloves for both Dad and Lester, as well as their favorite candy. And I was going to make a chocolate cake for Christmas dinner, the best ever. But I knew that cake and gloves couldn't make Dad happy. I didn't have the power to do that for him, any more than he could make me forget Patrick. My anger at Sylvia was like a fever that wouldn't let up.

Elizabeth, however, seemed more relaxed these days somehow. I couldn't say she seemed happier, just thoughtful. Pamela and I didn't ask her any more about the episode with the biologist. To keep bringing the subject up would put more emphasis on it than it deserved. But when I saw her folks going in and out of their house, it bothered me that I knew something so basic about Elizabeth that they didn't.

On the last day of school, Sam Mayer wished me Merry Christmas, and I wished him Happy Hanukkah, and I was really surprised when Patrick called out, "Merry Christmas, Alice," as I was getting my coat out of my locker.

I took the chance to have a normal conversation. I smiled at him and said, "You too, Patrick. Doing anything special?"

"I'm going skiing with my folks in Vermont."

"Sounds good," I said. "Happy New Year, too."

"Same to you," he said, and smiled that funny little smile that wrinkled the bridge of his nose. I told myself I still saw a glint in his eye for me, imagined or not, because I needed every glint I could get this Christmas.

Elizabeth and I walked home from the bus stop together. I'd told her what Karen had said about Jim Sorringer. I had to, because Karen had already told some of the kids on the bus. Karen is one of those people who seems to be your really close friend, but you never know.

"Well, if it will make your Christmas any happier, Alice, I told my folks," Elizabeth said.

"About Miss Summers? Why would that . . . ?"

"No. About me. About what happened back in second grade."

I stopped and looked at her. "Good for you, Liz!" I said. I gave her a hug right there on the sidewalk, and repeated, "Good for you!"

"And you were right. I feel so much better."

"What did they say?"

"Well, they were stunned. It wasn't that they didn't believe me. They never said that maybe I imagined it, but they quizzed me in such detail that I could tell they wanted to make sure. And then Mom cried. I *knew* she'd do that. They both kept saying, 'Why didn't you tell us the first time?' That's the part they still can't understand. I can't, either. You just . . . when you're small, I think . . . you *accept* things about grown-ups, like whatever they do must be right because they're adults. There's so much they ask us to do anyway that we don't understand, so when this man told me I could help him not feel so lonely and asked me to stand still, well . . . it must be right, I figured, or my parents wouldn't have let me go on those walks."

"Kids can't reason like adults," I told her.

Elizabeth nodded. "What I feel worst about, though, is that . . . well, when I told my parents I thought they knew what their friend was doing to me, that's when Mom really cried. Dad even cried. But you know what? They hugged me. They both hugged me, just like you and Pamela did."

"You're lucky, Elizabeth, because you hear about girls telling their moms that their dads or stepdads are molesting them, and the mothers won't believe it. Don't *want* to believe."

204 • PHYLLIS REYNOLDS NAYLOR

"They made me promise that if anything like that ever happened again, I'd tell them. And best of all, they said I didn't have to tell the priest in confession unless I wanted. They said it was their friend who should have had to confess, not me. And it's like . . . like I'm twenty pounds lighter. I feel one hundred percent better."

"It must be a great feeling," I said, wishing I could feel the same about Sylvia Summers.

"The best! I don't even want to say the guy's name again. I'm going to call him *El Creepo*. Dad said that was fine with him."

We laughed a little.

"I did ask my parents, though, how a man who was supposedly loved by everyone and did such noble things could do something like that to a little girl, and they said that, unfortunately, a person can be mature in one way and infantile in another. He can be generous and selfish, both at the same time. And just because everyone seemed to love him didn't excuse what he did at all."

"I hope they also pointed out that a man who molests kids, no matter how wonderful he is, is breaking the law and, if he was still alive, would go to prison," I told her.

We got to Elizabeth's house and stopped. "The thing is," she said, "Mom's going to make an appointment with me to see a therapist. She wants to be sure I work out my feelings about El Creepo so that things won't bother me later on. I don't know how I feel about that."

"*I* think it's a great idea," I said. "I think it would make sense if we all had a head check once in a while."

* * *

We were halfway through dinner that night when the phone rang. Dad had just put a bite of pork chop in his mouth, and gestured for me to get it, so I scooted my chair out from the table and went down the hall.

It was Sylvia's voice on the line, and she sounded tense: "Alice, I need to talk to Ben," she said right off. "Is he there?"

"Yes," I said coldly. "I'll get him."

I clunked the telephone down on the hall table and hoped it hurt her ear. "It's Sylvia," I said in the kitchen. "She wants to talk to you."

Dad paused, his glass halfway to his lips. Then he hurriedly left the table, but I seethed.

Tell her this is the first year you've missed the Messiah Sing-Along, I wanted to say to Dad. *All because it would have reminded you of her. Tell her how she's ruined Christmas for us, the whole Christmas season. Tell her she's a cheat, and that I take back all the good things I ever said to her.* I speared a potato and angrily thrust it in my mouth.

"Chew, Al," Lester said, even though I knew he was listening too.

We both sat silently, trying to decipher what words we could hear of Dad's conversation.

"Sylvia? How *are* you?" Dad was asking.

There was a long silence. I heard the chair by the phone creak as he finally sat down. He still didn't say anything, and I could feel in my bones that this was good-bye. That she was going back to Jim Sorringer, and hadn't known how to tell him before.

"Swallow, Al," Lester said.

I swallowed the potato.

And then we heard Dad say, "Honey, I wouldn't have cared if you'd had dinner with him, but I think you handled it well." Lester and I looked at each other. "Of course! I can't help feeling sorry for the man." There was a long, long silence. Then, "I know. . . . I feel the same way. . . . You know I do. . . . Yes, beyond a doubt." And finally, so soft and gentle, we could hardly hear it, "I can't wait until you're in my arms again."

Lester and I looked across the table at each other and suddenly we began to grin and gave each other a high five, just as Dad came back in the kitchen.

"Al," he said, "Sylvia wants to talk to you." He was smiling. His cheeks were pink; his eyes sparkled.

"Me?" I slowly lowered my hand, and could feel my face redden. I had talked to her with ice in my voice and slammed the phone down on the table. I'd torn her *picture* in pieces, for heaven's sake!

"What . . . what'll I *say*?" I choked.

"How about *Merry Christmas*?" Dad said, smiling still.

I went down the hall and picked up the phone.

"Alice, I want you to know what's going on," she said. "There was a Christmas program at our school this afternoon, and when I got back to my flat, Jim Sorringer was waiting for me in the landlady's parlor." And then, as though she was talking with a friend—she *was* talking with a friend—she said, "That is *so* like him. Just up and decides he's going to do something, and . . . I had no idea he was coming. He evidently thought he could change my mind about things by surprising me here, but I explained to him that I am madly in love with your dad, and I think he finally got the message. He's on his way back to London, to spend Christmas there. I know how stories get around, though, and wanted you to know that I had nothing to do with his visit. Nothing has changed between me and your dad."

"Oh, Sylvia! I love you! I really, truly do!" I cried. "Merry Christmas!"

"Well, sweetheart, I love you, too," she said, and I could hear the smile in her voice. "And I hope you have the best Christmas ever!"

When she hung up, I walked slowly to the kitchen and gazed unblinking at my family.

"Helloooo!" Lester said, waving one hand in front of me.

I blinked. "Dad," I said. "You know that picture I like of Sylvia? The one you took of her in her blue-green dress?"

"Yes, I know the one," Dad said.

"Could you get me another print? Something happened to the one I had."

Dad studied me for a minute. Then he said, "I suppose that could be arranged. What size did you want, Al? Four by six? Five by seven?"

"Poster size?" I said, and gave him a sheepish grin.

Simply Alice

To the one and only Claudia Mills

Contents

1
THE SECOND HALF

The thing about the second semester of ninth grade is you're not so scared anymore. You know how everything works—your locker, the cafeteria line, the buses, grading points—and you don't go to school every day with your heart in your mouth, expecting to be humiliated half out of your mind.

Which, of course, makes it all the worse when it happens. Wearing an ankle-length beige skirt with a long-sleeved cotton T-shirt, I was coming out of the cafeteria with my two best friends, Elizabeth Price and Pamela Jones, heading for P.E. on the ground floor. I'd had a hugely busy morning, starting with a meeting of the newspaper staff before school, and I still hadn't had a chance to duck into a restroom. After the big glass of orange juice I'd drunk for breakfast, and now the can of Sprite for lunch, I was in agony.

"Hey, guys, I've really, *really* got to go," I said as we started toward the stairs. I could only walk in tiny, mincing steps.

"We'll be in the locker room in three minutes," Elizabeth said.

"I can't wait three minutes," I told her, looking around as we approached the stairs. "I thought there was a restroom on this floor, maybe just beyond . . ."

What happened next was like a home movie on fast-forward. We must have been closer to the top step than I thought, because I was still looking around when suddenly I felt my body plunging forward, my books flying out in front of me.

I heard Elizabeth scream, "Oh, Alice!" and someone else shout, "Grab her!" and I could see the guys on the lower level look our way, but I was tumbling down the stairs, trying to grasp the railing as I went, and came to a stop on the second from the last step.

"Oh, my gosh!" Pamela yelled. "Are you hurt?"

I was pretty shaken, but within a few seconds I knew I wasn't hurt, not seriously—just bumps and bruises. My pride, mostly. I'd cut one knee, and my cheekbone stung. What I *was* conscious of was that my underwear and thighs were soaked, and it just kept coming. It was like someone had pulled a plug and I couldn't stop.

A tall senior had one hand under my back and another

under my legs, and was lifting me to a standing position. "You okay?" he kept asking.

I wanted desperately for the earth to swallow me up, never to be seen again.

He must have felt the dampness because I saw him look behind me, like maybe I was broken and bleeding, and then he said gently, "My, my, my! That *did* scare the . . . uh . . . daylights out of you, didn't it?" He winked and walked away with the other guys, who didn't know what he was smiling about, and by that time Pamela and Elizabeth had reached the bottom of the stairs.

"Hide me," I choked.

"What? Are you all right? Are you hurt?" Elizabeth asked.

And then Pamela turned me around. "My gosh, Alice! You . . ." Trust Pamela to burst out laughing.

I backed up against the wall while kids stopped to pick up the pages of my three-ring notebook that were scattered all over the stairs. Then Pamela, walking ahead of me, and Elizabeth, walking behind, got me to the gym, and while the other girls played volleyball, I rinsed out my underwear and the back of my skirt, and held them under the blower to dry.

"Can anything be more humiliating than that?" I asked Elizabeth when we were showering later.

"You could have thrown up, too, while you were at it," she said.

At dinner that night, Dad said, "Al, what on earth happened to you?"

The left side of my face was bruised and swollen where I'd bumped against the stair rail. My real name is Alice Kathleen McKinley, but Dad and Lester, my twenty-two-year-old brother, call me Al.

"The most embarrassing thing that could possibly happen to a human being, that's all," I said, and launched into the whole dramatic story of how this handsome senior had knelt down to help me up and had felt my wet skirt. "Nothing in the world could be more awful than that," I repeated.

"Wrong," said Lester, passing the lentils and sausage, which, for anyone who cares to know, looks like mud. "He could have gathered you up in his arms, clutched your body to his, gazed into your eyes, and *then* you wet your pants."

"Well, believe it or not, there are some things in life worse than humiliation," said Dad. He, of course, means death and dying and wars and starvation, but it's sort of hard to think about those things when you're tumbling down a flight of stairs and losing control of your bladder at the same time.

I guess it's natural that my dad sees the serious side of life, because my mom died when I was in kindergarten, and I suppose you never get over something like that. But now he's engaged to my seventh-grade English teacher, Miss Summers, and he's the happiest I've ever known him to be, even though she's on a teacher-exchange program in England.

"So other than using the school stairs as a toilet, how was your day?" Lester asked me.

"Well, a nice thing *did* happen," I said. "Since I'm one of the freshman roving reporters for *The Edge*, and I'm also part of the stage crew for our spring musical, I'm supposed to write three articles on 'behind the scenes of a school production.' That should be fun."

"That's a great assignment," said Dad. "What musical?"

"*Fiddler on the Roof.*"

"Oh, I like that one. Wonderful music!" Dad said.

"So what do *you* do, Al? Pull the curtain?" asked Les.

"All sorts of stuff," I told him. "Scene changes, props, costumes—wherever I'm needed."

"I'm glad to see you expand yourself a little. This may turn out to be a good year for you after all," said Dad.

What he means, of course, is that I may not go to pieces or jump off a bridge or anything, just because Patrick and I broke up this last fall. Not that I would ever let somebody else make me so miserable that I'd do that. But it sure hadn't been an easy fall, watching Patrick and Penny, the "new girl in town," kissing around the school and doing all the things together that Patrick and I used to do.

But I'm trying to pay more attention to other people and not be so self-centered. So I turned to Lester and said, "How was *your* day?"

"Interesting," he said. "I had coffee with one of my philosophy instructors."

"The babe?" I said, knowing that one of his teachers was really attractive, or so he'd told me. "I thought faculty weren't supposed to date students."

"Did I say 'date'? I said 'coffee,' Al. We talked. . . . Besides, she's not actually a professor, just an adjunct instructor. She'd *like* to be a regular member of the faculty, though, and she's got the brains to do it."

"You flirted, I'll bet," I said.

"That's not a felony. It's not even a misdemeanor."

"So . . . how old is she?" I wanted to know.

"A year or two older than I am, I suppose."

"Watch it, Les," I said, and grinned.

Dad was smiling too. "Well, I had a letter from Sylvia today, and we're looking at July twenty-eighth to get married."

That was about the best news I'd had in two years. Two years of trying to connect the beautiful Sylvia Summers with my dad, and now they were really, truly, officially engaged, except that she didn't have a diamond or anything. Didn't even want one, Dad said.

"That's fabulous, Dad!" I said excitedly. "I hope she has ten bridesmaids and a symphony orchestra."

He laughed. "A simple little ceremony, Al, for family and friends. That's just the way we want it."

I guess, since it's their wedding, they can have whatever they want, but after working so hard to get them to fall in love, *I* thought we deserved an orchestra. A chamber quartet, anyway.

I was about as busy as I could imagine myself being, now that they were starting auditions for *Fiddler on the Roof*. The stage crew met three times a week after school, and it would be meeting daily when we got closer to production. Actually the stage crew was divided into lots of little crews, but most of us were on more than one—lighting, sound, sets, costumes, makeup, props, publicity. . . .

The real surprise came when Pamela told me she was dropping out of the drama club. I couldn't believe it. She's always talked about wanting to be an actress or a model, and she'd had the lead in our sixth-grade play.

"Why?" I asked when she told me.

"I didn't know it was going to be a musical, and I don't think my voice is good enough for a leading role," she said.

"But you could be in the chorus, Pam! Or you could work behind the scenes. There's always something you could do."

"I don't want the chorus and I don't want to work behind the scenes. If I try out and don't make it, Mr. Ellis will remember that when I audition next year or the year after that. When I try out for the first time, I want to knock his socks off, and I can tell I'm not that good yet. I don't want a second-rate part. I want a major role."

I couldn't understand the feeling, never having wanted to be the center of attention that much.

"So I'm going to take voice lessons," Pamela finished. "Dad's already found a teacher for me and signed me up. But listen! Elizabeth's got this great idea!"

We were on the bus going home, all squeezed together on one seat. Liz was by the window, I was in the middle, and Pam was on the end.

Pamela and Elizabeth were smiling. "Why don't the three of us sign up together as junior consultants for Tiddly Winks this spring!"

"Tiddly Winks?" I said in surprise. Tiddly Winks was an inexpensive earring store that had recently expanded to include accessories of all kinds—hair stuff, hats, scarves, belts, shawls, necklaces. . . . I tried to imagine myself a junior consultant. "What do you *do*?"

"It sounds really fun," Elizabeth assured me. "They're having a big promotion to advertise the new stuff in the store, and they want people to come in for a color and bone-structure analysis."

"*We're* supposed to do that?" I said. "What do I know about bone structure?"

"No, the professionals do that. Then they tell us what category the customer is in—like, she's a 'spring' or an 'autumn,' and 'angular' or 'round,' and then we show them all the colors and styles in her category."

"The thing is," Pamela continued, "we get points for every friend we bring in and points for every dollar each of our customers spends. When we get a certain number of points, we get free earrings or something."

"We're going to do it two evenings a week and on Sunday afternoons through the end of March," said Elizabeth. "We can all ride to the mall together."

I was beginning to feel squeezed in, and not just because I was sitting in the middle. "Hey, guys, I *can't*!" I said. "Between the Melody Inn on Saturdays and the newspaper and the stage crew, I'm stretched about as far as I can get already!"

"So give up the stage crew," said Pamela.

"*What?*"

"We joined the drama club together," she reminded me, "and now that I'm not going to try out, why don't you do Tiddly Winks with us? It's not as though you've got one of the major parts or anything. C'mon! Just tell them you don't want to do it, and sign up with Liz and me. We're going down tomorrow."

"I *can't!*" I croaked. "I already said I'd do it. I've been assigned to sets, props, and publicity."

"But that was when we thought we'd be going to rehearsals together," Pamela said. "Just tell them you changed your mind."

"But I *want* to do it!" I protested. "Just because you changed your mind doesn't mean *I* have to!"

Pamela seemed offended that I'd want to do something without her. "It's not as though you're the only one in school who can do the job, Alice. What's so important about being on the prop committee?" she asked.

"We could have so much fun together at Tiddly Winks!" Elizabeth said. "We'd have a blast. Of course, if you don't *want* to be with us . . ."

It did sound like it could be fun, but to tell the truth, the stage crew sounded better. I wasn't all that nuts about accessories. "I just can't," I said. "Don't be mad."

"Who's mad?" said Elizabeth, getting that look on her face. "I just thought it was *something* the three of us could do together—you're always so busy on the newspaper."

"*You* guys can still do it!" I said. "I'll come down and you can do a color analysis on me."

"Whatever," said Pamela.

They'll get over it, I told myself. After all, Elizabeth hadn't joined the drama club when Pamela and I signed up, and we hadn't made a fuss about it.

For the first time, I was doing things on my own and had made friends with another girl on the stage crew, a sophomore named Molly. She's shorter than I am, sort of squat, and wears overalls most of the time. Her hair is cut in a punk rock style, and she has the biggest, bluest eyes I've ever seen.

"So which of these things can you find?" Molly asked me the next day, after Mr. Ellis had distributed a list of all the different props we'd need.

"Not many," I said.

"Me either," said Molly. "It would help if one of us were Jewish, because all the characters in the musical are. Where are we going to find all this stuff?"

"We start asking, begging, pleading, borrowing, and hope we don't have to sell our bodies or resort to stealing," I joked.

There was one other girl who joined the stage crew, a junior. Her name was Faith, and she was tall, rail-thin, wore long, gauzy dresses of purple or black with beaded vests, black stockings, granny tie-up shoes with pointed toes, and lots of bracelets. Her hair was long and very straight, and she wore pale, almost white, face powder with her lips and eyes outlined in black.

We liked Faith a lot, but we didn't especially care for her boyfriend, Ron Blake. He'd hang around at the back of the room when we had meetings, and never let Faith out of his sight. She even told him when she was going to the restroom. When it was just the two of them in the cafeteria or out on the school steps, they cuddled a lot, and Ron gave her tender kisses. But when she was around other people—I don't know; Ron seemed jealous or something.

He was there again on Thursday when we met after school, slouched in a chair off to one side, while Faith and Molly and I were checking things off our lists.

Pretty soon I heard Ron say, "Hey! C'mere!"

I don't think Faith heard him, because we were busy deciding who was going to try to get vests for the guys in the cast if they didn't come up with any themselves.

"Hey!" Ron said again, more loudly.

Faith glanced around and held up one hand, as if to signal, *Wait a minute*, and went on talking to us.

Ron got up from his chair and strode over to her. Faith looked up. *"What?"* she asked.

"Let's head out," he said, as though Molly and I weren't even there.

"I've got to finish here first," Faith answered.

He looked at his watch. "We leave here at four," he told her, and left the room.

Four wasn't time enough to do all we had to do, because we

had each made a list of the props and clothes we were sure we could get, and those we still had to find. But this time when Ron came back he didn't call her name. He just walked up behind her, took hold of her long hair, and slowly tipped back her head until she was looking straight up at him.

"Owww!" she said, making a joke of it.

"Let's go," he said

"Just a minute, Ron," she said, trying to work her hair free.

"Now!" he said.

Faith stood up, and he let go of her hair. "If you find any more of this stuff, call me, okay?" she said to us.

We nodded and Faith left, with Ron steering her by one shoulder.

Molly and I looked at each other. "I think maybe Faith has problems," I said.

"And he's number one," said Molly.

What helped make the breakup with Patrick bearable was that we were still speaking. In that first week or two after we split, I hid whenever I saw him coming, especially if he had Penny with him. Or I'd turn and go in a different direction. But that can get exhausting after a while, and I decided I just wasn't going to live that way anymore. So I started speaking to him and he to me, and when our whole gang got together, we acted like old friends. We *were* friends. In fact, Penny was part of our crowd now, and it got so that I didn't mind very much that she was around.

Except I could still remember Patrick's kisses and the way he touched me, and it still hurt to think of him giving those same kisses to Penny. There was also a sort of affectionate politeness between Patrick and me. Sometimes even a look that passed between us, as though we understood things nobody else could. But that was all. He was in an accelerated program to graduate one year early, so he was busy, I was busy, and it wasn't "Alice and Patrick" anymore, simply "Alice."

One day at lunch I was eating my chicken salad and talking to Elizabeth and Pamela when I suddenly stopped chewing and said to Pamela, "That girl looks *so* familiar." She looked like me from behind, actually—her body, anyway. Maybe that was why.

Pamela and Elizabeth turned and looked in the direction I was staring. A pretty girl was in line at the pizza counter. She was about my size, same color hair, and was wearing white cords and a gray top. Her thick hair was blow-dried back away from her face in wave after glorious wave. She was talking animatedly to a couple of boys who obviously were hanging on to her every word.

"She does!" said Elizabeth. "Who *is* she?"

Pamela stared intently at the girl, then back at me. And suddenly we both said it together: "Charlene Verona!"

"Is it?" said Elizabeth. "Are you sure?"

Charlene Verona was in sixth grade with us. She had everything going for her: looks, talent, boyfriends, grades. . . . Everything good seemed to happen to Charlene Verona.

"Tell you what," said Pamela. "I'll go up and say, 'We've missed you,' and if she says, 'I know, everyone has,' it's Charlene."

We laughed.

"No," I said. "I'll go up to her and say, 'How do you get your hair so shiny?' and if she says, 'Beauty runs in my family,' we'll know it's Charlene."

But neither one of us went up to the girl in the white cords because it was undoubtedly true: Charlene Verona was back, and if there were wonderful things waiting to happen to anyone at all in the next few years of high school, you could be sure they'd happen to Charlene.

Elizabeth, though, didn't remember her as well as we did. "What's the matter with her?" she asked. "I used to jump rope with her on the playground. I didn't think she was so bad. Why don't you like her?"

Pamela and I looked at each other again.

"She's perfect," said Pamela.

"And she knows it," I said.

"Oh," said Elizabeth, and shrugged.

But people can change, I told myself. I was all prepared to hate Penny for making a play for Patrick—and getting him—but I still had to admit she was funny, wasn't stuck on herself, or phony. . . . How did I know Charlene hadn't changed?

"You know, Charlene might have changed a lot since we knew her," I said to Pamela as we left the cafeteria.

"I'm sure she has! For the worse," Pamela replied.

2
CAY

Elizabeth called me around the first of February.

"Where have you been?" she asked. "You weren't on the bus, and I've called you at least four times, but you weren't home yet."

"We had a staff meeting for the newspaper and then Molly and I had to pick up a tablecloth a woman is loaning us for the Sabbath."

"The *Sabbath*?"

"The Sabbath supper in *Fiddler on the Roof*. We're trying to make the scenes as authentic as possible, and a woman said her grandmother brought a tablecloth over from Russia."

"Who's Molly?" Elizabeth asked, a whine in her voice. She's

been going to a therapist to help her deal with her feelings about being molested when she was younger—by a family *friend*, no less—and lately she's been short-tempered. Hard to get along with sometimes.

"I've told you," I said. "I work with Molly and Faith getting props and things for the play. What's new with you?"

"Oh, nothing. The usual arguments with Mom. Why don't you come over after dinner?"

"I will," I said. "I thought you and Pamela were going to be down at Tiddly Winks for a while."

"That doesn't start till next week," she said.

It seemed I had less time for anyone anymore, myself included. When did I have a chance to cut my toenails? Write to Sylvia? Play cards with Dad? Go to a movie with Lester?

I walked across the street to Elizabeth's. She came to the door with Nathan in her arms. He's the one person who can always make Elizabeth smile these days. She'd been an only child until Nathan Paul was born about sixteen months ago, and now he's toddling all around the house and is into everything.

"I-yah!" he chortled when I came inside. That's what he calls me. I grabbed him from Elizabeth and swung him around, then blew on the side of his neck and he squealed happily, pulling away from me.

"He's a pill," Elizabeth declared. "Aren't you, Nate?" She kissed him.

Up in her room later, she was full of complaints. Her mom did this . . . her dad said that . . . no consideration . . . they never understood how she felt. I figured I didn't need to say anything, even if I'd known what to say, which I didn't. Maybe when you're seeing a therapist, all your angry feelings have to come out first before any positive ones can get through.

I was listening to what Elizabeth was saying, but what I was really looking at, or trying not to look at, was her chin, because right smack in the middle of it was a huge red pimple, and there was another on the left side of her forehead. She just had to feel awful about that—Elizabeth, who has always had skin like a china doll. I was lucky, I guess, because I usually got only a couple of pimples the week before my period, while Pamela had pimples on her forehead through most of middle school and still has some.

After a while I said, "Liz, you sound mad at the world. I hope you're not mad at me, too."

"Of course not," she said. "It's just, you're never around! At school you're always with kids we don't know."

"We eat lunch together, don't we?" I sighed sympathetically. "It's just the way things are going to be until the production is over. I promise I'll have you and Pam over soon."

"I'll believe it when it happens," Elizabeth said.

When I got home later and finished my homework, I checked my e-mail before I went to bed and found the usual messages from Karen and Jill and Pamela—one from Mark Stedmeister, even from my old boyfriend, Donald Sheavers, back in Takoma Park. And then, near the bottom of the list, was an e-mail address I'd never heard of, and when I clicked READ, it said:

Have been watching you. Curious?
Meet me at the statue outside the
auditorium tomorrow morning, 8:10.

I could feel the blood throbbing in my temples. Who was *this*? Of course I wouldn't go. Was he nuts? Was it even a he?

Still, I *was* curious. I thought about all those "How We Met" letters to Ann Landers. What if this turned out to be Mr. Wonderful, and years from now I'd write some columnist and say that my future husband had once sent me an anonymous e-mail. . . .

I called Pamela.

"Oh, my gosh! That is major romantic!" she said. "Alice, you've just got to go!"

"I don't think so," I said. "What if he's a rapist or something?"

"Inside the school, main entrance, just before the first bell? Are you crazy?"

"Well, why didn't he sign his name?"

"He's just making an adventure out of it, that's all. He's a romantic!" Pamela said. "Look, I'll even go with you. I'll stay back in the shadows and make sure you're all right."

"What if it's a grown man waiting there?"

"We'll report him to the office. Come on, Alice! It's probably someone you know."

"Well . . . okay. Just for the fun of it," I said.

She giggled. "Oh, Alice! What are you going to wear? Something sexy!"

"Pamela, you're out of your mind. I'm going to wear perfectly ordinary jeans and a sweater. And for Pete's sake, *promise* me you won't tell anybody. Not one word. I don't want an audience."

"Cross my heart," she said.

Of course, the first thing she did the next morning was tell Elizabeth, and Liz was hurt because I hadn't told her. But when she got over her snit, she said she wanted to come with us, too. So after we went to our lockers, we walked toward the auditorium.

"Okay, I've got it all figured out," Pamela said. "You know the kiosk at the top of the stairs? Elizabeth and I will hide behind that—actually, we'll just stand up there by the railing talking while you go down to the statue below, and we'll keep an eye on you. Make sure he isn't a serial killer."

I laughed. "This has got to be one of the stupidest things I've ever done."

"Huh-uh," said Liz. "Hiding Pamela up in your room last summer was the stupidest."

"No," said Pamela, "pulling my hair onstage in sixth grade was worse."

"Never mind," I said when we reached the kiosk. "Here I go."

Of course all three of us went to the stairs and looked down, but we didn't see anyone. The person could have been standing behind the statue, though.

"Good luck," said Elizabeth as I descended the steps in my best jeans, a white turtleneck, and my backpack. At the bottom,

I thrust my hands in the pockets of my jeans and looked around. Kids were coming through the doors from the buses, swarming around the statue, heading for their lockers.

No one seemed to be lingering.

"Hey, Alice, you're going the wrong way," someone called as she passed. I went over to one side and leaned back, one foot against the wall behind me, real casual, real cool. I felt that whoever the person was was watching me, but as the minutes ticked by and a couple kids looked at me as they passed, I could feel my face beginning to color. I glanced at my watch: 8:14. The note had definitely said 8:10. The bell would ring at 8:20.

I decided to give it one more minute. Out of the corner of my eye, I could see Pamela and Elizabeth looking over the railing in the hall above wondering the same thing I was: *Where the heck is he?*

At 8:15, I pushed away from the wall and quickly went back up the stairs. I knew my face was bright red, and wished like anything I'd never told Pamela, that I had suffered through this alone.

"Let's go," I murmured, taking big strides back down the hall.

"I wonder why he never showed," Elizabeth said, hurrying to catch up with me.

"I don't know, but whoever wrote the note I don't even *want* to meet. He was probably somewhere watching, laughing his head off."

At the corner I stopped. "Listen, if you two are my best

friends, you will never, ever, tell anyone else about this."

"Oh, we wouldn't!" said Elizabeth.

"Not a soul," said Pamela.

I checked my e-mail when I got home that day. Nothing. But when I checked it again just before going to bed, I found this:

> I'm really sorry about this morning if
> you were at the statue. Our bus had to
> go around the construction on Dale Drive
> and we were late. Would you give me
> one more chance? Meet me at the statue
> today at 12:35?
> CAY (Crazy About You)

I clicked DELETE and turned my computer off.

On Saturdays at the Melody Inn, I run the Gift Shoppe. It's under the stairs leading to the second floor, where instructors give music lessons in soundproof cubicles. Dad's the manager of the store, and Marilyn Rawley, one of Lester's former girlfriends, is assistant manager

We sell all kinds of stuff in the Gift Shoppe—from novelty items to useful things like guitar picks, batons, mouthpieces, and strings. Dad usually handles the instrument sales, Marilyn the sheet music, and I do the Gift Shoppe. There are other part-time clerks who help out on evenings and weekends.

In January, we have a big sale to get rid of the stuff we over-stocked for Christmas, and make room for new things. Salesmen come by with catalogs of new music boxes in the shape of violins, sweatshirts with keyboards on both sleeves, men's shorts with clef signs, scarves with the "Moonlight" Sonata printed on them, earrings in the shape of middle C, and all sorts of jewelry for the revolving glass case beside the counter.

"Hi, how you doing?" Marilyn said when I came in on Saturday. Her brown hair is straight and shoulder length, curled under at the ends, and she wears a lot of Indian prints. Today she had on a calf-length black wool skirt with a slit up the side, and a green silk blouse with embroidery on both sleeves. I always wished she and Les would get back together. I think Marilyn would in the blink of an eye, but I don't know about Lester.

"Busy," I told her. "That's the one word that describes high school—busy, hectic, tense. . . ."

"How about 'exciting, different, challenging'?" Marilyn said.

"Well, that, too," I told her.

She gave me a computer printout listing all the merchandise we had ordered for the Gift Shoppe within the last year.

"We'll be doing inventory next week," she said. "What we need you to do is cross out any item that we've sold out completely."

I set to work on the printout sheet and was halfway through when I heard someone say, "Excuse me, but there's no one in sheet music. Could you help me?"

I turned around to see Charlene Verona, The Girl Who Has Everything.

"Hey . . . aren't you . . . Alice McKinley?" she asked. "Weren't we in sixth grade together?"

"Yes," I said. "You're Charlene, aren't you?"

"Yes! Oh, it's great seeing all my old friends! We just moved back here the first of the year, and it's like I never left!"

What I wanted to say was, *Whoop-dee-do*. What I said was, "What do you need from sheet music?"

But she went bubbling on: "Dad was transferred to Illinois and I just *hated* it there. I mean, I had to start all over again and I didn't know anyone, but now we're back and he promises I can complete high school in Silver Spring, so here I am!"

"Here you are!" I repeated. "What can I get you?" *Why do I dislike her so much?* I wondered.

"I'm trying out for *Fiddler on the Roof* and I need to learn some songs. Do you have a songbook from the musical?"

"I think so," I said. I used my key to lock the cash register, then went over to sheet music. Both Dad and Marilyn were helping students in the instruments section, and the part-time clerk was on a rest break.

"I just love that musical," Charlene said as she followed me across the store. "I want to play Tevye's daughter Hodel. She sings that gorgeous song about wherever her lover is, that's home. Do you know it?"

I didn't, exactly, but I secretly hoped we were out of the music. At the same time, I made a mental note that we should order more songbooks immediately, because other kids were going to be coming in looking for them.

I went to the file cabinet marked MUSICALS and began looking through file folders in alphabetical order. There it was, only one copy left—the songbook for *Fiddler on the Roof*.

My first thought was to tell her it was already sold, then buy it myself, give it to Pamela, and urge her to learn the songs and try out. But then my mature self took over, and I knew that was Pamela's decision to make, not mine.

"Here you are," I said, and rang up the sale.

"How about you?" Charlene asked. "Aren't you going to try out?" And then her face froze and she said, "Oh, I'm sorry, Alice. I forgot you can't sing. Me and my big mouth."

She didn't have to put it that way. Of course I can sing. I just can't carry a tune, that's all. It's embarrassing enough without having to be the daughter of a man who manages a music store.

"Eighteen dollars and ninety cents," I told her.

She kept trying to make it up to me. "Oh, well. You must be horribly busy here. I'll bet it's fun to work in a music store."

"Out of twenty," I said stonily, taking the bill she handed me, and gave her the change.

"Thanks, Alice!" she said. "See you around school! Wish me luck!" And she was off.

"In a pig's eye," I muttered.

Marilyn came hurrying over. "Thanks. We're a little short-handed this morning. Did the girl get what she needed?"

"No," I said. "What she needed was a punch in the mouth, but she got *Fiddler on the Roof* instead. By the way, we need to rush order lots more of those songbooks."

Marilyn gave me a quizzical smile. "Friend?"

"The Girl We Love to Hate," I said. "The girl who gets everything she sets her heart on."

Marilyn studied Charlene as she left the store, and then me. "Nobody gets everything she wants, Alice. Trust me," she said, and I knew she was referring to Lester.

I told her then about the e-mail message from someone signing himself CAY. How I'd gone to the statue but no one was there, and about the follow-up apology.

"I sure wouldn't take it any further if I were you," Marilyn said. "Any guy who can't introduce himself isn't the kind you want to get involved with."

"That's about what I figured," I told her. What I didn't tell her, though, was how I kept looking at all the guys in my classes, wondering, *Was it him? Was it him?*

3
HEART OF GOLD

I don't wear a lot of jewelry—I like a simple look—but for my birthday last year, Aunt Sally in Chicago, Mom's older sister, gave me a small gold heart-shaped locket that used to belong to my mother, with a lock of Mom's hair in it. It was the same color as mine, strawberry blond.

I'm not sure how Aunt Sally came to have it in the first place—maybe Mom left all her jewelry to her sister when she died—but Aunt Sally felt I should have it. And maybe she'd saved it for my fourteenth birthday because she felt I'd be responsible enough by then to take good care of it.

In eighth grade I wore it a couple of times, but when I put it on over a navy blue sweater in ninth, I liked the look so much that I began to wear it often.

"It's nice, Alice," Elizabeth said once. "Who gave it to you?"

"It's something of Mom's," I answered.

That's one thing that bothers my dad, that I don't talk about Mom more. I don't think he realizes how little I remember of her. I was only five or so when she died, and they say kids don't remember much before the age of four. Combine this with the fact that Aunt Sally took care of us for a few years after Mom's death, so a lot of my memories are confused with Aunt Sally.

"Did you hear any more from Cay?" Pamela asked me at school one day. We started calling him—or her—Cay, because we didn't know how else to refer to him.

"Maybe he's a member of the faculty and he can't reveal himself," said Elizabeth. "Maybe all he can do is worship you from afar, Alice, and the day you graduate from high school, he'll profess his undying love, and you'll find out he was your algebra teacher or something."

"Maybe he's the custodian," said Pamela, grinning.

"Or the bus driver," said Elizabeth.

"The principal!" said Pamela.

"I'm not interested," I told them, "Somebody was obviously playing a joke to see if I'd fall for it."

Between fifth and sixth periods, I literally bumped into Patrick in the corridor, and we walked as far as my history class.

"How's it going?" he asked.

"Busy," I answered. "Exams in all my classes, inventory at the store, stage crew for *Fiddler on the Roof* . . . How about you?"

"I may graduate in three years, but they'll probably have to carry me across the stage," he said. "This semester's a lot worse than last."

"I'll bet!" I said. "Patrick, you always were a brain."

He just grinned. "See you," he said.

I'll admit I felt sort of down on Valentine's Day. What I tried not to think about was what Patrick was giving Penny as a present—that he was kissing her, stroking her hair. I wore my heart locket to school—sort of a talisman, I guess, against hurt. I couldn't help studying Penny in the cafeteria at lunchtime, trying to see if she was wearing anything Patrick might have given her. To her credit, she didn't mention either him or Valentine's Day. She could have rubbed my face in it, but she's not that kind of girl. I don't think Patrick would have fallen for her if she was.

I found myself listening for Penny's name over the speaker system, though. In our high school, I discovered, guys sometimes send flowers to their girls in care of the school office. Some of the teachers' husbands do it, too. Then the school secretary calls out those persons' names between classes, and they go down to the office and collect their bouquets.

My face felt hot just thinking about it. It was such a public declaration of love—wonderful if it happened to you, horrible if it happened to someone you envied. If Penny went around all day carrying flowers from Patrick, how could I stand it? But only a dozen or so girls got their names called, and we—The Forgotten Others—tried not to look daggers at them.

Faith, though, got a bouquet from Ron—*roses*, no less—and you just had to be glad for her. You'd think it was the most wonderful moment of her life, the way she brightened, and I figured Ron couldn't be all bad if he could make Faith that happy.

Penny's name was never called. At least, I didn't hear it if it was.

Maybe I was feeling especially low because not only did I not have a boyfriend, but I had the vague feeling that Elizabeth and Pamela and I weren't as close as we were at the beginning of ninth grade. They've been my two best friends since seventh, and I think they're still best friends with each other. Just not with me.

It's so subtle, though. Nothing I can put my finger on. I wouldn't even know how to bring it up. When I say, "Are you mad?" Liz says, "Of course not!" But they don't call me like they used to, and I think—I *know*—they do things together on weekends without even asking if I want to come. Of course I don't call them as often, either, but they know how busy I am right now. And they've been having a ball at Tiddly Winks. On the bus to school they're always showing the other girls what earrings they've got so far for being junior consultants.

Did I just imagine it, I wondered, or did Pamela show the pair of turquoise teardrops to everyone on the bus but me? Was I being oversensitive to the fact that Elizabeth invited four girls to come to Tiddly Winks on Friday night—promised they'd all go out for pizza afterward—and then, suddenly looking in my direction, seemed to invite me as an afterthought?

When they did talk to me, it sounded too polite, too forced—not the chummy, teasing way we used to be with each other. But how exactly do you accuse someone of being too polite? Too cold? I kept waiting for an opening—for something bigger to happen, so I could say, "What's wrong?" But I already knew. We were starting to grow away from one another, to look around at other friends, which is what you're supposed to do as you grow up, I guess, but all it made me want to do was cry. I'd thought we were going to be best friends forever.

Dad confided at dinner that he had sent a dozen roses to Sylvia Summers in Chester. Even my brother looked amazed.

"Well, *that* must have set you back big bucks!" he said.

"I won't even tell you how much," Dad said. "It was just something I wanted to do."

I stared at him over the spaghetti. Dad looked like a fuzzy teddy bear in his plaid flannel shirt and Docker pants—his scruffies, he calls them—the most comfortable clothes he can think of when he gets home from work. "You had a dozen roses flown to England?" I exclaimed.

Dad laughed. "No, hon. I called a florist here who takes international orders. He calls a florist in Chester, and that florist delivers the flowers."

Sylvia called Dad about seven. She'd found the roses when she got home from school, she told him, and even though it was midnight there, she and Dad were on the phone for a long time.

I spent the last hour before bed e-mailing some of my friends. Even though I doubted they'd answer, I told Pamela and Elizabeth about Dad sending roses to Sylvia, checked with Karen about the history assignment, and tried to find out from Jill if she'd gone to the Valentine Dance. What I really wanted to know was whether Penny and Patrick had been there, and they had. Just before I signed off, the red flag on my "You've Got Mail!" box went up, so I checked the incoming mail once more and found this message:

> Still watching, still admiring. Would
> you give me another chance?
> CAY

This time I e-mailed back:

> If you really want to meet me, you'll
> walk up and say Hi.

There was something creepy about this, but I sure wasn't going to tell Elizabeth or Pamela about it this time.

When I got home from the Melody Inn on Saturday, there was a message on the answering machine.

"Where *were* you?" came Elizabeth's voice, sharp and

brittle-sounding. "You could at least have let me know if you couldn't make it!"

I immediately dialed her number. "Liz? What are you talking about? Where was I *when*?"

"Last night! At Tiddly Winks. You said you'd come, and I'd invited four other girls for pizza afterward. We didn't know whether to wait for you or what."

"Oh, my gosh!" I said. "We had a meeting after school, and it dragged on, and when I got home I just heated leftovers for my dinner and stretched out on the couch. I completely forgot!"

"If we bring in five girls at once, we get bonus points and Tiddly Winks pays for the pizza afterward. Because I only had four girls, I lost the bonus points and had to pay for their dinner myself. If I'd known you weren't coming, I could have invited someone else."

"I'm really sorry! I guess I just conked out. Listen, I'll pay for the pizza, Liz."

"Oh, never mind," she said.

"No! Really!"

"Forget it," she said.

Mr. Ellis was holding tryouts for *Fiddler on the Roof*, and the big buzz was that Charlene Verona would get the part of Hodel. Every day after school the first two rows of the auditorium were filled with hopefuls, who were called up onstage one at a time and asked to sing a song from *Fiddler*. Any piece they wanted. Charlene did well with "Far From the Home I Love."

The stage crew attended just to be part of the general excitement. Each actor would be required to furnish his or her own costume, but we were supposed to help out and find anything that an actor couldn't. I'll admit, I wished I could sing. I wished I had the nerve to be up there all by myself, with Mr. Ellis and the others looking up at me, while I belted out a song un-self-consciously to the piano accompaniment.

Dad said that my mother used to sing—that she was tall, that she liked to wear slacks a lot, was a good swimmer, and always made him a pineapple upside-down cake on his birthday. And they loved each other a lot. Maybe Dad, being musical, loved her *especially* because she could sing. I wondered what went wrong in me.

I was sitting in the next to the last row in the auditorium with Faith and Molly when Charlene's turn came to audition a second time. The kids who were most likely to get a part were called back again; the others were thanked and told they could leave. If you didn't get a callback, you were either out, or were part of the chorus. This time Mr. Ellis had several girls go onstage together, singing different songs, saying the speaking parts, listening to the sounds of their voices and how they looked and sounded together.

"Charlene really wants to play Hodel," said Faith, propping one delicately booted foot on the back of the seat in front of her. "I heard she'd kill for the part."

"I don't know," I said. "That small girl in the tan shirt has a great voice too."

"Mr. Ellis has to look at all the parts—who's going to play Golde, who's going to play the other sisters—all of that," Molly told us. "I think Kurt Weinstein is going to get the part of Tevye. He's got a terrific voice."

He did, too. After Charlene sang a second time, Kurt went up onstage. He's a senior, a big guy—goes out for wrestling as well as choir—and as soon as we heard him, we knew he'd get the part. He not only sang, he gestured and strutted around the stage, and we clapped like crazy when he'd finished.

"Hey!" came a whisper, and I turned to see Ron Blake in the row behind us. He reached forward and stroked Faith's cheek and she responded by kissing his fingers.

Down in front, though, Mr. Ellis was asking another guy, who was also auditioning for Tevye, to come up and sing. He wanted to compare the two, and so did we. It was sort of hard to concentrate with all the cheek-stroking and finger-kissing going on beside me, but Ron, I guess, can only be kind for so long. I think he resents Faith doing anything that doesn't involve him.

"Hey, babe, let's go," he whispered.

"I want to stay long enough to hear this guy sing. See if he's as good as Kurt," Faith whispered back.

Ron especially doesn't like Faith paying attention to other guys, even to the way they sing.

"Well, I want to leave now," he told her.

It was all I could do to keep from saying, *Well, she doesn't, so get your big self out of here,* but I didn't.

Faith turned around again, facing the stage, and Molly and I sort of leaned toward her, helping pin her in to strengthen her resolve. The second guy went up onstage and sang "If I Were a Rich Man." Suddenly a big foot appeared beside my face, and I turned to see that Ron had stuck both his feet up on Faith's shoulders and was holding her head in a vice grip with his heavy boots.

She just gave a little laugh and went on watching the stage. When she didn't react, he clamped his boots tighter against her face and began rocking her head from side to side. Both Molly and I turned around and glared at him.

"Leave her alone," I said.

His eyes narrowed, and he studied me for a long moment as though he had designs on me, too. I'd seen him look at me like that before. Was he "the watcher," I wondered? Could he be CAY?

"Who asked your opinion?" he said.

"Nobody. You got it for free," I said.

"Oh, Alice!" Faith whispered.

"Quit being such a bully!" put in Molly.

Ron put his feet down and leaned forward, grabbing Faith's shoulder. "We're leaving," he said.

And to our dismay, Faith got up. "I've gotta go," she said, maneuvering past Molly's legs, and left the auditorium with Ron.

Molly slid over beside me. "He is really bad news," she whispered.

"I know. What does she see in him?"

"He gives her a lot of attention, all the wrong kind," Molly said.

Kurt got the lead. The names were posted on the bulletin board beside the orchestra room on Friday. Most of the cast were juniors and seniors, and Charlene lost out on Hodel but got the part of Tzeitel, the oldest daughter—a huge plus, considering she's only a freshman. But the other two girls chosen for daughters were smaller in size than Charlene and their voices were higher, even though they were seniors, so Mr. Ellis knew what he was doing, I guess. I decided that even if Pamela had tried out, she wouldn't have gotten a part, so maybe she was right to wait for her junior or senior year.

But there was no time to talk with her about it. I was going to e-mail her, but forgot, and when I finally sat down at the computer, I found there were two old e-mails from her I'd never answered. The fact was, I often had to go to school early for a meeting of the newspaper staff, and I stayed every day after school to work with the stage crew, and only rode the bus a few times a week.

When I got on one morning, Pam and Liz were laughing together at some private joke. I took the seat behind them, got up my nerve, and finally leaned over the back of their seat, trying to sound as friendly as I could. "What's up?" I asked.

"Nothing. What's with you?" said Elizabeth.

"Everything's going on at once," I said. "I feel I'm going around in circles."

"So we've noticed," said Pamela.

"You guys want to get together this weekend?" I asked. "Saturday night, maybe?"

"Busy," said Pamela.

"Sunday?"

"We've got Tiddly Winks then," said Elizabeth.

"Sunday night?" I offered.

"Sorry," said Elizabeth. "I've got something going on."

"Gosh, I'm not the only one who's crazy busy right now," I told them.

"Yeah," said Pamela, and turned to look out the window.

At lunchtime, when I got my tray in the cafeteria, I was heading to the table where I always sit when Molly, at a closer table, waved me over. I looked across at where the gang had gathered, and the only vacant spot was beside Pamela, across from Elizabeth. If the noontime conversation was going to be anything like it had been on the bus that morning, why put myself through it?

"What's up?" I said, sliding in beside Molly. And we chatted about the musical.

"What did you think of the casting?" she asked me, vigorously attacking her ham and cheese sandwich.

"Ecstatic that Kurt got the lead. He's perfect!" I said. "The choice for Golde was good, too."

"Tzeitel was a surprise, though. Charlene Verona's the only

freshman who got a part. Her voice is great, but a lot of girls in the chorus are jealous," Molly said.

She went back and got two ice-cream cups for us, and I was just finishing mine when Pamela and Elizabeth and Brian Brewster walked by, taking their trays to the counter.

"Hey, Al!" said Brian. "What's the matter? We're not good enough for you?"

I could tell he was joking, and I quickly tried to make a joke of it myself. "No, I'm just too popular, I guess," I said, laughing.

I saw Elizabeth and Pamela nudge each other as they walked on by. I put my head in my hands. Why did I say *that*? Why is it that sometimes your mouth says the very worst thing possible, like it's detached from your brain? I didn't want to live like this, having to be so careful! It was like walking on eggshells. I had to watch every single thing I did or said or somebody got mad.

"Headache?" Molly asked.

"Big time," I told her.

I decided I just couldn't afford to get upset right then. There was too much to do, and I had to turn in the first of my articles to the school paper, not to mention homework, which was piling up like mad. My first article would be about tryouts—the hopefuls, the feeling of being left out and stuff. I wouldn't use any names, of course. But I wanted to get inside the skin of every person who gets up onstage and sings, knowing afterward that you haven't done your best, that others were better than you, that the director's comments about your "nice" voice were just that, "nice," but not too exciting. And yet, it couldn't be a put-down of the kids who had ended up in chorus. I couldn't make them sound any less important.

So I wrote the piece from my own viewpoint—a girl who couldn't carry a tune, so she was content to work behind the scenes painting sets and gathering props and leaving the glory to others. I wrote it humorously, and was really surprised when Sara and Nick, the editors, put it on the third page of our four-page newspaper. First page is best, of course, but third is next best, because your eye falls on the third page when you open the paper.

I started out: *For a girl who can't carry a tune, being a member of the stage crew for the spring musical,* Fiddler on the Roof, *is as close as I'll ever get to glory . . . .* And I ended with: *. . . so here I stand, paintbrush in hand, while those braver than I, and certainly more talented, sing their hearts out onstage, knowing that while only a few of them get the coveted roles, the rest of us will provide the backup, the greasepaint, and the props to get this production off the ground.*

I was amazed at the response. Kids came up to me the next day and said, "Loved the article, Alice." And, "You really can't carry a tune?" Stuff like that. Patrick stopped me as I was coming out of gym and put one hand on my shoulder. "Enjoyed the article, Alice. Really funny."

Mr. Ellis liked it a lot. So did Faith and Molly.

"You said it for all of us," said Faith. "Except I really wouldn't want to be up there onstage. I like behind-the-scenes stuff."

"Really?"

"Yeah. You know what I'd like to do? Work for some repertoire company. Be one of the permanent stage crew that dresses all in black and comes onstage to change props between scenes."

"Maybe you will," I said. "Where would you go? New York?"

"Yeah, that would be best, but I'll probably end up going wherever Ron does," she said.

The two people who didn't mention the article at all were Elizabeth and Pamela. When I got on the bus that afternoon, they were so busy talking about Tiddly Winks that they had everyone's attention and ignored me completely. I asked them a question and they answered, but then they went right on talking, their voices unnaturally high and loud, and I knew they were putting on a show just to hurt me. I could hardly stand it. How could girls who liked each other as much as we did suddenly turn on one of their own this way? Couldn't they see that I was drowning in work right now, but it wouldn't always be this way?

I decided that when Elizabeth and I got off the bus together, I would confront her about it. But when we reached our stop and I stood to get off, Liz stayed where she was and I knew she was going on to Pamela's. I walked home alone, tears in my eyes.

Why does everything have to stay exactly as it is or somebody gets mad? I knew they resented Molly and Faith, but wasn't I allowed to have other friends? Did it have to be just "Alice, Elizabeth, and Pamela" forever? I wondered how I'd feel if Elizabeth joined a club I didn't belong to, and seemed to be spending all her time there. Or if Pamela got a new friend and did things with her that she didn't do with me. I probably wouldn't like it, either, but once *Fiddler on the Roof* was over, we could be closer again. I just had to ride it out, I decided.

I was still getting compliments about the article on Monday, and could feel my face flush with excitement when anyone praised my writing. Several teachers commented on it too. I ducked in the restroom once to see if my face looked as warm as it felt, and suddenly my heart seemed to be beating double time because the gold locket I'd put on that morning was gone. There was my face and the white expanse of my sweater beneath it, but no gold locket, not even the chain.

I panicked. My mother's gold locket! The only real piece of my mother I had left—her hair. I retraced my steps as fast as possible, all the way back to my last class, but couldn't find it. I checked my pockets, my backpack. Then, crying, I went to the school office to ask at Lost and Found.

"We'll let your homeroom teacher know if it's turned in," the school secretary said. I had to get a pass to my next class and went in, my eyes red.

There was a stage crew meeting again after school, so I was late going home. But when I got to my locker for my jacket, I found a piece of paper stuck in one of the narrow ventilation slots.

I think you dropped your locket leaving class today.
I tried to slip it through this slot, but the heart was

*too big to go through. If you'll meet me at the statue
at 8:10 tomorrow, I promise I'll be there and will
give it to you then.*
Crazy About You

4

BEHIND THE CURTAIN

I wanted my locket back.

Could CAY—the watcher, the stalker—possibly have unfastened it somehow? But even as I thought it, I remembered having trouble with the hook that morning when I put the locket on. Maybe it hadn't been fastened completely. The note said I'd dropped it when "leaving class today." Did that mean this person was in a class with me? Which one?

I didn't tell anyone about CAY this time. I couldn't have told Pamela or Elizabeth if I'd wanted to, because they didn't answer my e-mails anymore. We said "Hi" to each other in the halls, out of courtesy, but then they turned away or I turned away. As I sat staring out the bus window the next morning,

I wondered again how this could have happened to us in the space of a few weeks.

Deep inside, I knew that what I should do was go over to Elizabeth's house, invite myself in, and have a face-to-face talk with her. Apologize for anything I'd done wrong. But I was angry, too. I *hadn't* done anything except get involved in school activities that didn't include them. Make friends with girls they didn't know. Was this the way it had to be when you were best friends with someone—they controlled your life, who you could see, what you could do? Is that what was happening with Faith and Ron?

They're the ones who should apologize, I told myself, and so I just stared out the window and thought angry thoughts while Pamela and Elizabeth, sitting behind me, were probably doing the same—all three of us making ourselves miserable.

At school, I got off first and headed for the corridor where my locker was, but when I was sure they had gone to theirs, I backtracked and went down the stairs to the auditorium. Once again, no one was there—just kids coming from their buses, heading for class. If he stood me up again . . . !

I glanced at my watch. Nine minutes after eight. I turned slowly around, studying every person coming toward me, but they all went by. When I turned again, I was face-to-face with a familiar blond guy several inches taller than me, wearing an Eddie Bauer jacket, a backpack over one shoulder. He just smiled and held out an envelope. I took it. I could feel the shape of the locket inside.

"Thanks," I said. "I don't know where I dropped it."

He was in my biology class, and had thick blond eyebrows that formed a bridge over his nose, a mouth that turned slightly down at the corners when he smiled. He opened his mouth then, but nothing came out. Instead, he blinked his eyes a couple of times and finally he said, "O-O-On the floor in b-b-b-biology."

I kept looking at him. "Are you Cay?" I asked, then felt myself blush when I realized he wouldn't know I'd been referring to him by those initials. It was his turn to stare now, and then he got it. He grinned and nodded.

For some reason, we both laughed.

"You sit over by the window, don't you? Second table?" I asked.

"Yeah."

"I was afraid you were a stalker. Some creep who was going to follow me around school the rest of the year."

He laughed again. "N-Not to worry."

I looked at my watch again. "I've got English first period."

"Me t-too," he said. "Mr. Larson."

"Worrell," I told him, and we started walking together. I glanced over at him. "Do you always e-mail girls you want to meet?"

This time he didn't look at me, just smiled, his eyes straight ahead. "Just you."

I smiled back. "I don't bite."

He laughed then, and changed the subject. "That was a g-great p-p-p-piece in *The Edge*."

"Thanks," I said. "It was a lot of fun to write." We'd reached my class. "Thanks again for returning my locket. It was Mom's and it's all I really have of her. A lock of her hair, I mean."

He looked serious then. "She died?"

"Yeah. When I was five. My aunt gave me this locket of Mom's for my fourteenth birthday."

"I'm really sss-sorry," he said.

"But Dad's getting married again this summer. To my seventh-grade English teacher. It's really wild." I glanced inside the classroom. "Anyway, thanks . . . uh . . . Eric?"

"Yeah. Eric F-Fielding."

"I'll see you," I said.

"See you," he answered, and walked away. Smiling.

When I sat down in my chair, I opened the envelope. There was Mom's locket, and inside, the lock of her hair. No note. Just the locket, as he'd said.

I slipped it around my neck and made sure it was fastened right this time. He seemed nice. Sort of shy, maybe. Possibly because he stuttered. But at least I knew he wasn't some creep. Wait till I told Pamela! And then I remembered about Pamela and Elizabeth, and felt hollow inside.

This wasn't right! I told myself. I shouldn't have to feel guilty about making new friends. The problem was that Elizabeth was too wrapped up right now in her own troubles to take on anything else, and Pamela, who had always seemed self-confident to me, had gotten scared off by the competition in high school and wanted to return to the safe little threesome we used to be. In a way, I wanted that, too, but I also wanted more.

I told Dad and Lester about Eric at dinner that night. Before dinner, actually. Dad was cooking Chinese, and when he does that, Les and I have to get all the veggies chopped and ready to throw into the wok when he wants them.

"He seems really nice, just shy," I said. "And he stutters."

"You've got to watch out for shy, stuttering guys," said Les, dropping a handful of bean sprouts into the wok as Dad stirred them around in the oil.

"Why?"

"They'll grab a girl's heart every time because they seem so vulnerable."

"Oh, I don't know. Eric looks as though he could take care of himself very well," I said. "Were you ever shy?"

"Was I ever *shy*? Why, I'd flatten myself up against a wall so tight you'd think I was wallpaper," Lester said. "If a girl came up to me at a school dance, I'd be looking for the nearest exit."

"That I don't believe for one second."

"I *was*! *Timidus Extremus*, that was me."

"When did you decide to pull out of it?"

"I didn't. When I saw how popular it was making me, I milked it for all it was worth."

I gave him a look and turned to Dad. "How about you?"

"I was shy in grade school, maybe even high school, a little. By the time I got to college, though, I figured if I really wanted something, I had to go after it, and after that the shyness took care of itself."

"Well, I think Eric's nice, and not because he stutters or he's shy, but because he returned my locket."

"I'm glad you got it back, honey," said Dad. "Your mother would have enjoyed seeing it on you."

I checked my e-mail that night. There was a message from Eric:

> I'm glad we finally connected and you're
> convinced I'm not a stalker. You lost your
> Mom when you were five, and that's about the
> time I started stuttering. They're not the same,
> I know, but I guess we've got that much in
> common: a difficult five!
> Eric alias CAY

I e-mailed back:

> Hi, Eric alias CAY,
> Thanks for returning my locket.
> I owe you one.
> Alice

What happened the next day after school was so unexpected, so shocking, I couldn't believe it.

I'd heard some of the people on the stage crew talking about "earning your tattoo," and a few boys had joked about their own tattoos, but I figured it was a guy thing. Except for some extras who wander in from time to time, the stage crew for this production consisted of Molly and Faith and me, and four guys— Richard, Devon, Harry, and Ed. They're sort of a combination burly-funky-macho-artsy, and I think they've all got a body piercing somewhere. Friendly, though. Or so I thought.

When we met again the following week to start painting one of the backdrops for the outdoor scenes, I had just walked backstage with a paintbrush to ask where they wanted me to start, but I didn't see anyone there. Molly and Faith had gone to the home arts room to get the burlap pillow someone had stitched for us, but I was looking for Ed or Devon, who were doing the painting.

Suddenly the heavy black curtain at the back of the stage rippled, and then a couple of hands grabbed me, pulling me back behind it and down over somebody's knee. I was on my stomach, sprawled over a guy's leg.

"Hey, Alice, it's initiation time!" Ed said. "You gotta get your tattoo!"

My first thought was that it was a joke, but then I felt two hands tugging at my jeans, and my second thought was that I was about to be raped. Fingers were fumbling around in front, trying to unzip my fly because my jeans hardly budged, and when I started to kick and scream, I heard Devon's laugh, and a turpentine-smelling hand went over my mouth.

"Hey, hey, hey! Be good, now," Devon said.

I was struggling and trying to bite the fingers that were over my mouth, but somebody else appeared—Richard, I think—and they held me so tight, I couldn't move.

"Hey, guys, cut it out. She doesn't want it," came Harry's voice from the other side of the stage.

I was practically upside down, like a kid over her dad's knee, and my jeans and underpants were halfway down my bottom when somebody pressed something cold and hard against my right buttock, and then they let me go.

I tumbled to the floor, furious, and looked up at Ed and Devon and Richard, laughing at me and holding a rubber stamp belonging to the drama department, of the two Greek masks, comedy and tragedy, which they obviously had stamped on my butt.

"Are you out of your mind?" I yelled, scrambling to my feet and pulling my jeans back up. My face burned from both anger and humiliation. Molly appeared on the stage, Faith behind her, holding back the curtain. Molly stopped and stared at me, then at the guys.

"What were you *doing* to her?" Molly said.

"Initiation time, that's all!" Richard said. He was the tallest of the guys, lanky, and he didn't laugh, he leered.

"The Greek Tattoo!" Ed explained.

"Yeah? When they initiated me last year, they put it on my back. So where were you guys going to put it?" Molly said.

"*We* put it on her back!" Devon said innocently, and laughed.

I was pulling up my zipper as the side door of the stage

opened, and the custodian came in. "Somebody yelling in here?" he asked, looking around. "You people have business back here?"

And when Devon said, "Yeah, we're painting sets," I didn't say a word. Neither did Faith or Molly. It was supposed to be all in fun. It was supposed to be a way of making me "one of the boys."

"Just forget about it, Alice, that's the way guys are," Faith said as the boys moved to the far side of the stage and opened the paint cans.

"It's not the way all guys are," I told her, thinking of Patrick. Of Eric. "And the ones that are shouldn't be allowed to get away with it. That was humiliating."

"They only meant it as a joke," she said. "When I was a freshman they put mine on a breast. I just laughed it off."

"Why are you defending them?" I asked.

"Well, what are *you* going to do? You're not going to report them, are you?" she said.

"I don't know," I answered. What I *did* know was that I hadn't been a "good sport," and I guess I figured that was embarrassment enough. It was over, and they wouldn't try it again. On me, anyway. So I didn't say anything.

When I told Dad that evening, though, he was furious.

"If that's not molestation, I don't know what is," he said.

"Stupidity," said Les.

"Al, had any of you talked about this before? Had the guys joked with you about getting this tattoo?"

266 • PHYLLIS REYNOLDS NAYLOR

"No! I didn't even know what initiation they were talking about. They just grabbed me!"

"Well, I'm going to call the superintendent," said Dad. "A freshman girl should not have to worry about being accosted by seniors."

"No! Dad, please don't!" I pleaded in horror.

Then he got angry at me. "You want to let something like that pass? No one reports it, and it will keep on happening to all the girls who come along after you."

"Al's right, though, Dad. She should handle it, not you," said Lester.

"What I'd *like* to do is pull the pants off those three guys and throw them out the window. Let them go outside buck naked and get them," I said.

"Well, you know you won't do that, so what *are* you going to do?" asked Dad.

"I'll think of something," I told him.

5
OUT OF THE WOODWORK

I still hadn't decided what I was going to do about it when I stayed after school the next day for our weekly staff meeting for *The Edge*. A part of me wished I'd handled it better—even laughed when the guys stamped my bottom. It would have made me a lot more popular.

The other part of me said that it was just this reaction—going along with the joke, no matter how humiliating—that kept this sort of hazing going. Nobody complained, nobody told, so it happened to the next batch of freshmen and the next and the next.

I'd thought about going to Mr. Ellis himself, but with

all the other problems he was having getting the production off the ground, it was the last thing he wanted to hear. He'd probably say he'd take care of it, and nothing would happen. If I went to the student council, I'd be the poor little freshman telling on those big bad juniors and seniors, and if I went to the principal or superintendent, I'd have to make a formal compliant, they'd call in all the guys, and whatever happened, I'd be *persona non grata* on the stage crew. So I took it to the newspaper.

First I told Sara, our features editor, and before I'd even finished, she was rapping the table with her pen.

"Nick? Nick?" she kept saying till she got his attention. "You said we need more good lead stories, right? An exposé we can tie in with a good editorial? How about hazing?"

Nick looked a little pained. "Oh, come on, Sara."

"No, *you* come on!" she said. "We all know it happens, but Alice happens to know about it firsthand. Tell them, Alice."

So, in front of seven kids, I had to tell what happened to me behind the stage curtains the day before. A couple of the guys tried to hide a grin, but the girls were indignant. Nick, though, looked thoughtful.

"I'm thinking about the guy last year who got a tooth broken when they tried to force his head in the toilet—football initiation," he said. "The principal got involved, and we printed the new rules in the newspaper. That was supposed to stop the hazing, and obviously it hasn't. But how do we know this wasn't an isolated incident?"

Everybody started speaking at once. Each person there seemed to know of something that had happened to a friend.

"When I joined the girls' soccer team, they made me wear all my clothes inside out for a week," one of the sophomores said.

"That's not the kind of hazing we're talking about," said Sara.

We were all quiet for a moment.

"I know a guy in Arizona . . ." The boy who started the sentence didn't finish. We turned and looked at him.

Tom Cordona was playing with a paper clip between his fingers. He didn't look up. "It was some guys on the wrestling team who did it to him. The broom-handle initiation," he said quietly.

"Oh, good grief!" said Sara, burying her head in her hands. "See what I mean, Nick? See how disgusting and humiliating . . ."

"Oh, man!" said our senior sports editor.

"Okay, listen," said Nick. "I think there's a story here, a lead story, but I don't want to go out on a limb with it if it didn't actually happen in our school. I want you people to ask everyone you know and get the facts. It can't just be something they've heard about happening to someone else. We need names and dates and we'll promise not to print them, just report what went on, see if we can't light a fire!"

What it lit, it seemed, was a forest fire. Even before we met again the following week, we were comparing notes and found out it was a much bigger story than we'd thought. When kids knew we wouldn't use their names, we began hearing things we'd thought couldn't happen in our school. "Freshman initiation"—a group of guys circling a couple of freshmen girls in the parking lot, making them get down on their knees and unzip the boys' flies with their teeth; a boy who had to walk around all day with his fly open; a girl who had to crawl through a lineup of guys who paddled her; a boy who had to wear girls' underwear for a day; the girl who had to goose five guys.

We sat around the table in the journalism room and stared at one another when we realized what we had. These weren't just happening in Arizona or New York or Michigan or California, they were happening right here in Maryland in our school. To our students. And nobody, except the guy who had his tooth broken last year and whose dad had taken the incident to the school board, had complained. Everyone wanted to be a "good sport." We all had sort of swept it under the rug. No more.

"It's sexual and it's degrading, and I don't like the two put together," said Sara.

Miss Ames, our sponsor, agreed. She gave her okay to do a story on it. Taking all of the information we'd gathered, Nick and Sara wrote the lead article, but we used the names of the entire staff in the byline, because we'd all contributed something, and we wanted to show that we were all behind it.

It blew the roof off the school. The superintendent called us into his office and wanted details, names, and dates, but our adviser sided with us and said we didn't have to disclose them. It was a serious problem and had to be addressed now to stop future hazing.

The following week there was a school assembly, and the

principal announced a new set of rules. It was clear, he said, that some forms of hazing were all in fun and helped create a feeling of belonging in a group. Things like being sent out on a scavenger hunt to get weird stuff, or going around with your club's name printed on your forehead. But no hazing of any kind, anywhere, was allowed unless it was cleared first with a coach or sponsor. Unauthorized hazing would lead to expulsion.

We all felt great! We went to Starbucks after school and celebrated. Sam Mayer, one of the paper's photographers, gave me a hug. "Nice going, Alice," he said. Sara and Nick were pleased, too. I wasn't too happy about the fact that Sara kept referring to it as "her" idea, but I guess when you're a lowly freshman you have to pay your dues and let the big guns get the glory.

"That's the way to do it, kiddo! Take it to the newspaper!" Lester told me when I showed him the article in *The Edge*.

"Get an extra copy for me," said Dad. "I want to send it to Sylvia. No, get three. Let's send one to Sally and Milt, and one to your uncles in Tennessee."

Patrick complimented me on the article, and so did Penny. I was feeling so super-confident of myself that I found I could even talk to her as though we'd been friends forever. I didn't have to go around the rest of my life known as "Patrick's ex."

"I'll bet you guys on the newspaper have some interesting staff meetings," Penny said to me. "There are probably all sorts of things that go on in school you don't even put in the paper. Right?"

"Well, some," I said.

We were at lunch, and she had broken her giant-sized cookie in two and put half on my tray. Patrick never ate with us because he didn't have time for lunch. He grabbed a sandwich between classes. "You going to major in journalism?"

"I'm not sure yet."

"You'd be good at it," Penny said.

"I've been thinking about psychology."

"Really? I think I'm interested in advertising, and there's a lot of psychology in that," she said.

Gwen liked my article, too. She's the friend who's helped me with math and algebra more times than I can count. "Way to go, girl!" she said.

But the two people I would most like to have shared it with didn't say much of anything. Every time our eyes met, Liz and Pam were suddenly deep in conversation with each other, and it was all so phony. They laughed and joked with the other kids, but if the spotlight fell on me, they started giggling over their own little secrets.

I remembered a column in the *Washington Post* about problems that parents were having with their children, and one of the things it said was that sometimes when a child is behaving the worst, he's most in need of love. Maybe you didn't have to be a child. Maybe no matter how old you were, you needed love most when you were the most disagreeable, which was the way Pamela and Elizabeth had been acting toward me lately. And maybe it was up to me to make the first move.

On Friday night, when I saw a light up in Elizabeth's room at eight o'clock, I figured she was home for the evening, and took a chance.

I wrote a note and went over to her house. When her dad answered the door, I asked if he'd take the note up to Liz, and I'd wait. I could tell he was glad to see me, that he'd wondered what was wrong between us.

The note said:

> Liz, if I have done or said anything to hurt you,
> I'm sorry. I still like you best in the whole wide
> world, and really miss you. Can I come up?
> Alice

It took about two minutes, but finally her dad came back down and said it was okay for me to go up. When I got to her room, she was crying. I started to cry, too, and we stood in her doorway, crying and hugging. She had three pimples on her face now, and if ever she needed to be loved, it was then. What I didn't know was that Pamela was on her way over to spend the night with Liz, and she got there a few minutes later. I gave her the same type of note I'd given Liz, all ready to go in my pocket. She didn't cry but she hugged me, and we sat facing one another on Elizabeth's twin beds with the white ruffled spreads and canopies, and talked it out.

"Pamela, do you remember back in seventh grade, how you were always telling me I wasn't part of the 'seventh-grade experience' unless I joined some clubs, got active? I'm just taking your advice, that's all. Trying to get into things more. It always seemed easier for you than for me," I said.

"But you're doing so *many* things!" Elizabeth protested.

"I know. But Liz, remember when you were taking ballet and tap and piano and I don't know what all! I didn't shut you out. I've been a wallflower for so long, I'm just trying to make up for lost time," I said, wanting to make her laugh.

"Yes, but you . . . you don't have to be so stuck on yourself," Elizabeth said.

I was surprised. "Am I? Is that the way I seem? Because I don't think of myself like that at all. I'm just a lowly stagehand."

"Yeah, but that newspaper thing," said Pamela. "We've been friends a lot longer than you've been in ninth grade, remember. And when you say you'll show up and you don't, and you don't answer e-mails . . ."

I could see now how I must have appeared to them. "I know, and it's going to get worse from here until the production's over," I said. "Between the newspaper and *Fiddler on the Roof* and the Melody Inn and my homework on weekends, I'm going down for the third time, guys. Can't you see me through this? I really, really need you."

"Maybe it's a good thing you don't have a boyfriend this semester, Alice," said Elizabeth. "At least *we* can understand."

"But do you?" I said. "Things are going to be really awful for the next few weeks, but we could get together over spring vacation and do something. Easter comes early this year."

"All right," said Pamela. "But it's got to be something really wild."

"Something we've never done before!" said Elizabeth bravely.

"Right!" I said. We all laughed.

"Oh, guys, it's so good to be back again," I told them. "I needed you so bad a couple of weeks ago. I wanted to call you, but I was afraid you wouldn't talk to me."

"What happened?" they both asked together.

If there is one thing that makes your girlfriends sympathetic, it's something bad happening to you, I've decided. "I was back-stage getting ready to paint one of the sets," I said, "when some of the guys grabbed me, turned me over, and pulled down my jeans."

Elizabeth almost went catatonic. "They *didn't*!" she gasped.

"You mean . . . that story in the newspaper . . . about putting a rubber stamp on your bottom, was *you*?"

I felt embarrassed all over again. In answer, I stood up, turned around, and pulled my jeans halfway down. The stamp mark with the two masks had faded some, but the permanent ink was still visible.

When I sat down again, they were both speechless.

"You mean . . . ?" Pamela said finally. "You mean they actually held you down and pulled your jeans completely off?"

"No, just down far enough to put the stamp."

"Exactly how far was that?" Elizabeth said. "Turn around again."

"Now, Liz . . ."

"What were you wearing underneath?"

"Underpants, of course!"

"See-through?" asked Elizabeth. She has to know the details.

"My gosh, what does it matter?" said Pamela. "The underwear went down, too! Alice, I'd be furious!"

"Well, I was."

"But . . . what if . . . what if you'd been having your period and were wearing a pad!" Elizabeth went on in horror. "What if you had pimples on your butt or . . . ?"

Leave it to Elizabeth. If you don't provide enough details, she'll offer some of her own.

"Exactly," I said. "But even if I'd been wearing French underwear and looked like a million bucks, no one had the right to embarrass me like that."

"What did you do?" asked Pamela.

"Everything I could think of. I yelled and kicked and bit, but it didn't do any good. There were three of them. Harry was the only one who didn't take part, but he didn't make them stop, either." I was surprised to find my mouth sagging down at the corner. "I wanted so bad to call you guys that night. . . ."

We all hugged again.

"You know," I said. "Being best friends means we've got to be there for each other when things are going good, too. It's easy to comfort someone when they're down, but sometimes when we're up, we need to know we haven't lost our best friends. Listen, Pamela, you may not believe me, but your voice is every bit as good as some of the girls who tried out. Next year you might get a starring role. Wouldn't you want Liz and me there, cheering you on?"

"If that ever happens, sure, I would," she said. "Listen, Alice. I'm sorry. I've been a toad, and I know it."

"Me too," said Elizabeth.

"A toad?" I said, laughing. "A *toad*?"

"Totally Obnoxious Anytime Dame," Pamela explained, laughing.

"Okay, you want to know a secret?" I said. They were all ears. "I found out who CAY is."

"Who?" they cried.

"A guy in my biology class. Eric Fielding."

They each tried to remember.

"Blond?" asked Pamela. I nodded.

"He's cute, but he stutters, doesn't he?"

"So?"

"Gosh, he never says two words to anyone!" said Elizabeth. "He's in my history class. Did you meet him at the statue or what?"

I told them about Mom's locket and how he had found it on the floor.

"It takes him forever and a day to say anything," said Elizabeth. "The teacher hardly ever calls on him because it's so painful to listen to him. He's worse in class."

"A lot more painful for him, I imagine," I said.

"So did he talk? Did he say anything?" asked Pamela.

"Of course. He walked me to my next class."

"Are you going out with him?" Pamela asked.

"We're just friends," I said. "So what's happening with you guys? Tell me everything."

"Have you got all night?" asked Elizabeth.

"Well, actually, yes. Yes, I do."

"Why don't you stay over, then? Pamela is."

"I haven't got any stuff with me."

"Use ours," said Pamela. "Don't go home, and we'll see what we can dig up for you."

I laughed. "Okay," I said. "Let me call Dad."

They rounded up toothpaste and deodorant and a comb and pj's for me, and we hunkered down on Elizabeth's twin beds. Pamela told me how her voice lessons were going and how her dad's dating a nurse. Elizabeth said she was feeling mad at her therapist lately, but her therapist says it's normal, and at least she's getting along better with her folks now.

Then Nathan toddled into the room in his jammies to kiss Elizabeth good night, and we made him kiss us all. We got down on the floor and growled at him and chased him around the beds on our knees, watching his short little legs churn across the floor and listening to his excited squeals, till Mrs. Price came in to rescue him.

"You'll have him so worked up, he'll never go to sleep," she said, laughing. "Are you staying all night, Alice? I could bring up the cot."

"Tonight we're going to push the two beds together and all sleep in one big bed." Elizabeth said.

"We've got a lot to talk about," said Pamela.

***

Another person who had a lot to talk about was Aunt Sally. I should have known what would happen if Dad sent her a copy of *The Edge* with that article on hazing in it. I was quietly eating some chocolate grahams one day after school when Aunt Sally called from Chicago.

"Alice, I am *shocked*! Simply *shocked*!" she said. "I want you taken out of that school and enrolled in a private academy, and your Uncle Milt and I have the money to pay for it if necessary."

"Uh . . . Aunt Sally—" I began.

"If Marie knew that her little Alice was going to a school where girls have to get down on their knees in the parking lot and unzip boys' pants with their *teeth* . . . ! The *humiliation*, not to mention what it does to teeth! I could hardly sleep last night from worrying about you."

"I'm sure that—"

"And that poor girl who had her pants pulled down in front of a gang of leering boys. She'll be traumatized for life. She'll probably never marry because of it and, if she does, she'll be one of those women who undresses in the closet."

"What?" I said. Once in a while I actually learn something from Aunt Sally. And then, playing innocent, I asked, "Is that what it means to 'come out of the closet'?"

"No, no, no," Aunt Sally said hastily. "I'm speaking about the misguided souls who are too shy to undress in front of their husbands even after fifty years."

"Well, I happen to know the girl who had her jeans pulled

down, Aunt Sally, and she was pretty upset for a while, but she's getting over it," I said. "It was largely on account of her that we published the article."

"You never know about these things, though," said Aunt Sally. "A girl could experience something like that and the effects might not show up for five or ten years." I thought of Elizabeth and how that was probably true. "The best thing you can do for your friend, Alice, is encourage her to get her feelings out, even if they're irrational and against all men in general. She shouldn't just sit around and let them fester."

"I'll remember to tell her that, Aunt Sally," I said. "But meanwhile, the principal has gotten real strict about enforcing the rules, and anyone who does any unauthorized hazing could get expelled."

"I should hope so!" she said. "But anytime you feel you want to change schools, dear, Uncle Milt and I could help out."

"I really appreciate it," I said.

"And keep an eye on that girlfriend," she added.

Lester came home just then, and lumbered out to the kitchen for a beer. As he leaned over to get one out of the fridge, I reached out with my foot and gave him a little kick on the behind.

He reared up. "What was *that* for?"

"For mankind in general," I said.

"*Why?*"

"So I don't sit around and fester," I told him.

6
SPRING SURPRISES

Probably because I hadn't scrubbed the bathroom or kitchen for three weeks, Dad suddenly noticed how grimy our house had become. No one had hassled me because they knew I had to stay at school late most afternoons, if not for the stage crew, then for the newspaper. Consequently I was excused from all cleaning and cooking until *Fiddler on the Roof* was over. But because the bathroom and kitchen were so dirty, Dad and Les had sort of let the vacuuming and dusting go, too, and the fact was, our house was filthy.

"I can't let Sylvia move into this place looking the way it

does," Dad said the week before spring break. "We've got to do something."

"We could start with a wrecking crew," said Les, stuffing the last third of a doughnut into his mouth as he finished his coffee.

"A constructive suggestion, please," said Dad.

"A fumigation company? Dust-Busters?"

Dad ignored him. "The drapes have to be taken down and cleaned, the bathroom and kitchen repainted—I should really have my bedroom redecorated. It looks like a hermit's been living in there."

"A hermit has," I said fondly.

"Hey, Dad, leave a little something for Sylvia to do. She'll probably want to change things around, anyway," said Les.

"Well, the place has to be clean, at least," Dad said.

"I can help out over spring vacation," I promised.

"What about closets?" asked Dad. "Are we supposed to clean closets, too? I can't remember that Marie ever did."

"Let's don't go overboard now," Les told him.

"And the inside of the oven. Now I know you're supposed to clean that."

"Why?" said Les. "Just turn it on to five hundred degrees, and the heat will kill all the germs."

"What else do you clean?" asked Dad, looking at me. "Are you supposed to clean the inside of the dryer? The dishwasher? How is a man supposed to know all this stuff?"

"You could always call Aunt Sally," I chirped helpfully.

"No!" Dad and Lester bellowed together. We all knew that

one phone call to Chicago and Aunt Sally would be on the next plane, broom and bucket in hand. And she'd probably start by making us clean the broom and the bucket.

I'd begun sitting by Eric in biology. We can sit wherever we like, but once we start a project with someone, we have to stay at that particular table till it's finished.

"You want t-to d-do something Friday nnnn-night—celebrate a week of vacation?" he asked.

"Sure," I said. "What would you like to do?"

"Sail around the world, for one," he said.

"Sounds good to me," I told him, and he laughed. I noticed that sometimes he stuttered and sometimes he didn't. Or he would repeat the first letter of a word one time and drag it out another. It was always worse, it seemed, when he first began a conversation. After he got into it, he often didn't. He also seemed to stutter on particular letters, like P and B. But after awhile I wasn't listening to his stutter. I was listening to what he had to say. To a person who stutters, though, I suppose he thinks we only focus on the stutter.

"Would you like to see a movie at Wheaten P-Plaza? The new T-Tom Hanks movie?" he asked.

"That sounds fun," I said. I knew, from the first note he'd sent me, that he lived out by Dale Drive, and we lived in exactly the opposite direction. "Want me to meet you there?"

"Okay. But I'll t-take you home," he said. "If you d-don't mind the b-b-b-b-bus."

"Sure. What time?"

"I'll e-mail you," he said.

One thing I had discovered about Eric: he never called me on the phone.

Meanwhile, Elizabeth, Pamela, and I were trying to think of something we could do over spring break to "express ourselves," as Liz had put it. "Something that is really, truly us."

The question, of course, was what we really, truly were. Not only were the three of us different from each other, but we changed from day to day, and so did our moods. One of us might be up and the other two down, or vice versa.

"Maybe we could get jobs as go-go girls for the week," said Pamela. "Dance on customers' tables." She grinned at me, noticing Elizabeth's change of expression. "Or we could even get hired as lap dancers."

"As what?" said Elizabeth.

"You dance in customer's laps," I told her.

"*What?* You actually stand up on a man's legs and—"

"You sit," said Pamela, grinning. "You sit facing him on his lap with your legs on either side of him,"

Elizabeth looked from Pamela to me.

"And wiggle around," I explained.

A look of horror crossed Elizabeth's face. "That's obscene!"

"That's the point," said Pamela.

We decided not to apply as go-go dancers. We thought of taking a moonlight cruise—just the three of us—on a dinner boat on the Potomac, but that cost more than any of us wanted to spend.

It was Elizabeth, finally, who came up with something wacky, if not entirely wild. She saw a notice on the community bulletin board at the library that high school students were invited to dress up as their favorite storybook characters and read to groups of children at the Martin Luther King Library between nine and five during spring vacation.

"Let's do it!" said Pamela. "I want to dress up like Scarlett O'Hara."

"And read *Gone with the Wind* to preschoolers?" I said.

We finally decided on Huck Finn for me, a monster from *Where the Wild Things Are* for Elizabeth, and *Amelia Bedelia* for Pamela. So in addition to having to find props for *Fiddler on the Roof*, finishing my last "behind-the-scenes" article for *The Edge*, doing school assignments, working on Saturday at the Melody Inn, helping Dad clean the house, and going out with Eric, I had to put together a costume. I thought my head would pop off.

I think we were all glad for a week's break before the production. We'd have three weeks after we got back to do the final rehearsals and get things shipshape, but for now we needed a rest.

I told Dad I was meeting Eric at the cinema at Wheaton Plaza.

"Just make sure he sees you home," he said. "I don't want you coming home after dark by yourself."

I took the bus to Wheaton Plaza, and Eric was waiting for me at the box office. He had our tickets.

"I was afraid you m-might stand me up to p-pay me back for that first t-time," he said, grinning at me as we went inside.

And there, standing right in front of the refreshment stand, were Patrick and Penny, buying an extra-large tub of popcorn.

"Hey, Eric! How's it going?" Patrick said. And then he saw me. "Alice!"

"Hi, Patrick. Hi, Penny," I said. "Everybody's out celebrating our week of freedom, huh?"

"Looks that way," said Penny.

They went on inside, and Eric bought popcorn and drinks for us. I was glad he didn't suggest sitting with Patrick and Penny. We sat halfway down on one side. Eric put the popcorn between us, and when the tub was gone and our eyes were on the screen, he casually put his arm around the back of my seat and I noticed that when something really funny happened, he'd squeeze my shoulder when he laughed.

I felt comfortable with Eric, just as I had with Patrick, and discovered that was one thing I looked for in a guy: I wanted to feel comfortable with him, know that I could be myself. That I didn't have to worry about what he might do or say next.

When it was over, he suggested we go to the Pizza Hut, so we did. I told him we'd split the check, and we got a table along one side where it wasn't too noisy, and just talked over Coke and a couple slices of pizza, triple cheese.

"We're moving in June," he said.

"You *are*?"

"Yeah. Dad's with IBM, and they're mmm-moving us to Dallas."

"Darn!" I said. "Just when I start liking a guy, he up and moves away." I surprised even myself. I guess I felt I could say it because he'd be leaving anyway.

I could tell it pleased him, though. He reached across and put his hand over mine. "I g-guess that n-note I sent you was pretty c-c-c-c-"

It seemed as though the word just wouldn't come out. If I knew what he was trying to say, I might have said it for him. But his face was beginning to color, his eyes began blinking faster, and he jerked his head slightly as though trying to shake the word from his mouth.

Finally I smiled at him and said, "Need help?"

"N-N-No," he said. "C-Crazy. That's the word. I g-guess you thought that n-note was pretty crazy."

"Well, it had me wondering," I said. "I'll admit it was different, and it certainly got my attention."

He still had hold of my hand. "Thanks," he said.

"For what?"

"For not finishing the sentence for me b-back there. P-People always do that. They think they're helping, but it just mmm-makes me feel like I'm five years old."

"You're welcome," I said, and smiled back.

"So n-now that we broke the ice, c-can we get together again b-before I move?"

"Of course," I said.

We took the bus back to my house. Les was out for the evening, but Dad was home, and he invited Eric in and talked a little bit about the kind of work his dad did. He offered to drive Eric home, but Eric said he'd rather take the bus.

I walked him back out on the porch, and he kissed me. A light, friendly, platonic kind of kiss, and then, because I smiled at him, maybe, he kissed me again, not quite so platonic this time.

"This was a good way to begin vacation," I told him, "I had a great time."

He squeezed my arm. "So did I," he said.

Elizabeth called the Martin Luther King Library in the District, and they gave us the ten-to-two time slot. Elizabeth would read *Where the Wild Things Are* to groups of preschoolers, Pamela would read one of the *Amelia Bedelia* books to the first through third graders, and I would read something from *Tom Sawyer* or *Huckleberry Finn* to fourth and fifth graders. And we each had to perform four times.

The fun part was that Mrs. Price drove us to the Metro each morning, and we rode the subway downtown in costume. What was really wild was that Washington, D.C., is full of tourists around Easter, and when we'd get on the subway in Silver Spring, there would be loads of kids and their parents going down to the Smithsonian museums, and suddenly kids would start shouting, "Mom! Look! A monster!" Or, "There's Amelia Bedelia!" Or, "Hi, Huck. How ya doin'?"

We were having a blast. Pamela had on a plain blue dress and a white apron; a hat, with her hair fashioned into bangs peeking out beneath the brim; and black shoes. A. BEDELIA was embroidered on her apron, just so kids would know.

Elizabeth looked great in a fleece costume her mom had made for her, with long claws in the pads of the hands and feet, large eyes resting above her own eyes, and fangs. It was really a teen-sized sleeper with a zipper front, and because she couldn't do anything with her hands, we had to get a fare card for her, hold a tissue so she could blow her nose, and help her get the costume off when she had to go to the bathroom. Once, when Huck Finn was blowing the monster's nose, people started snapping our picture. As we were heading for the library after we'd left the Metro, a photographer for the *Post* happened to be driving by, and he stopped his car and took our picture. It was on the first page of the Metro section the next day.

Going back home that first day, we realized we were more effective if we acted the parts. We'd get on the Metro and while Huck Finn slouched down in his seat with his straw hat at a tipsy angle, and corncob pipe in his mouth, Amelia Bedelia sat prim and proper with her hands in her lap, while the monster had a ball going up and down the aisle, showing her claws and roaring her terrible roar, while kids laughed and shrieked and hid behind their mothers. I think some of the tourists thought we were hired by the Metro to provide entertainment during spring vacation.

***

"It was great!" I told Dad and Lester that night. "I never saw Elizabeth cut loose like that. I guess it was because she could hide behind that monster suit."

"And how were the audiences?" Dad asked. I was trying to read Dad's mood, to see if he was even listening to me, because Sylvia was supposed to have called him the night before and she didn't. She'd be traveling around England during Easter vacation, she'd told us, and he wanted to know how she had liked Bath, the place she was to visit first.

"The audiences were terrific!" I told him. "It's nice to be having fun and doing something useful at the same time."

It was a good thing Les brought home Thai food that night, because I was too tired to help cook, and Dad had just taken down all our drapes and curtains and sent them to the cleaners. I put on a pair of leggings and an old shirt and would have eaten whatever was on the table, I was so tired, and Dad was in his sweats. But we were all feeling mellow—Dad, because he'd made a dent in spring cleaning; Les, because he was going to a concert with his philosophy instructor later in the week; and me, because it had been a really fun day, and Liz and Pam and I were friends again.

Dad had just stood up to get the ice cream from the fridge when the doorbell rang. *Eric?* I thought, and hoped it wasn't him, because I was too tired to see anyone except my family.

"I'll get it," Dad said.

"There were some boys from a football team out selling raffle tickets, Dad," Les called. "Why don't you just not answer?"

But Dad's never been able to do that, so he padded to the door in his stocking feet, taking the mint chocolate chip with him.

I heard the door open, and then what sounded like a cry from Dad, followed by, "Sylvia!"

"Oh, Ben!"

Les and I scooted out from the table and peered down the hall. My father had his arms around Sylvia Summers. All I could see of her was her light brown hair against Dad's face, her black slacks and turquoise sweater, because her lips were probably against Dad's, her arms were around his neck, and he was hugging her close to him, while a cab pulled away out front.

I quietly tiptoed out into the hall, rescued the mint chocolate chip from where it had fallen beside Sylvia's suitcase, and took it back to the kitchen.

7
CONVERSATION

Les and I both finished our ice cream before Dad came up for air. We just sat at the kitchen table grinning at each other, and finally Dad and Sylvia walked into the kitchen. She looked flushed and girlish, and Dad had the look of a little boy in love, lipstick on his chin.

"So . . . are you going to elope?" Les asked, and that made us all laugh.

"I really intended to spend spring vacation traveling around England," Sylvia explained, sitting down at the table, "but as I was packing I thought, *I don't want to do this without Ben; I don't want to see all these places until I can share them with him. And* suddenly I knew that what I wanted most was to spend my two weeks back here. I called the airline, and they said a plane was leaving in three hours. I never packed so fast in my life. And here I am."

"Oh, Sylvia!" I said, jumping up and hugging her.

All I could think of, of course, was where she was going to sleep. And then Dad said, "Let me take a quick shower and I'll drive you over."

While Dad was upstairs, Sylvia explained that the woman who had been renting her house had decided to go to Syracuse the month before. "I'm anxious to see my place, drive my car, see how my plants survived the winter. . . ." She looked at me and smiled. "I guess I was just plain homesick. For Ben. For all of you."

"Are you going to stay?" I asked.

"Oh, no. I've got to go back. A contract is a contract. But July will be here before we know it. I can hardly wait."

"Neither can I!" I said happily.

"I don't know if I'm ready for all that hullabaloo," Les joked. "The ribbons, the flowers, the invitations, the clothes, the photographers, the . . ."

"How do *you* know, Les? You've never been married," I said.

"I've been best man at too many weddings. I know," he said. "Besides, weddings are like infections. They're contagious. Once Dad gets caught up in it, we'll all be caught up in it." And then he said, "Seriously, Sylvia, we're all glad you're back. He's a new man when you're around."

"He's the same old Ben to me," she said, and smiled some more.

She ate ice cream with us while we told her all our news and she told us more about Chester. And then Dad came down in a fresh shirt, his hair washed and combed, and as he threw on his jacket he said, "I don't know just when I'll be back. Carry on!" And, with his arm around Sylvia, they went out to his car.

I looked at Les.

"Shut up," he said.

"*What?* All I was going to say was—"

"Don't even go there," said Les.

I grinned. "I think we should have given Dad a curfew."

Les smiled back. "It wouldn't have done one bit of good."

Of course I had to go right to the phone and call Elizabeth, then Pamela.

"Where is she going to sleep?" asked Elizabeth. She sounded just like me.

"Dad's driving her back to her place."

"Oh, Alice! Isn't this exciting! In four more months you'll be calling her 'Mother.' You never guessed, did you, when you walked in her English class back in seventh grade that someday she'd be marrying your father?"

"No. And Dad never guessed it, either. Boy, he was so lonely back then, Liz. Isn't it amazing how fast your life can turn around?"

* * *

I stayed up late to watch an old *ER* rerun with Lester, and then I conked out. Around eleven thirty I felt someone shaking my shoulder and opened my eyes to see that I had fallen across Lester's lap, one arm on the couch cushion, one dangling on the floor, my feet at an awkward angle on the rug.

"Hey, Al, go to bed," he told me. He'd turned the TV off, and I realized I must have been asleep for a while, because my neck was stiff. I slowly unwound my feet and sat up.

"Is Dad home yet?" I asked, flopping back against the cushions.

"Not yet."

"I just had the weirdest dream, Les! I"—I yawned, then snapped my jaws together—"I dreamed that there were all these people—I don't know where I was, but we were in this big crowd, and you were chasing me, only I don't know why, and Dad and Sylvia were there but they didn't try to stop you, and I realized I knew how to fly. I climbed up this tall ladder . . . no, maybe it was a tower . . . and I got to the top and was so sure that if I just put my arms straight out and flapped them up and down, I would fly. I just knew it. And you got to the top of the tower and I said I was going to jump off and you said no, wait, and all the people were looking up and I jumped . . . and then I woke up. I wanted to see if I could do it, but I woke up! I was so sure!"

I yawned again and hugged myself with my arms, my eyes half closed. "Why were you chasing me?" I asked.

"How the heck should I know? It was *your* dream."

"What do you think it meant?"

"Aha!" Lester stroked his chin and took on the voice of a Viennese psychiatrist. "Und vat ver you vearing?"

"Uh . . . shorts, I think. And a T-shirt; I'm not sure."

"Un vat vass *I* vearing?"

"I don't know. Jeans, maybe."

"Vat iss your first azzoziation to my chazing you?"

I thought about it. "I don't think I was scared. I just wanted to show you I could fly."

"Aha!" said Lester. And then, in his normal voice, "Obviously, you've got a crush on your older brother and—"

"I do *not*!" I said.

"And to gain his approval, you wanted to show that you could do something extraordinary. In this case, that you could fly."

"I thought dreams were supposed to be predictions of things to come."

"You want predictions? Okay. You are going to do something scary that you have never done before. How's that?"

"And? What happens, Les?"

"You fall flat on your face."

"*Les*-ter!"

"So go to bed, Al," he said. "I'm tired." He got up and began turning off lights.

"You're going to leave one on for Dad, aren't you?" I said.

"Oh. Right." He left a light on by the phone in the hallway, and we both went upstairs. I put on my pajamas and fell into bed. I slept soundly till about two fifteen. I was desperately thirsty from all the corn chips Les and I had eaten, so I got up to get a drink. The light was still on downstairs. I glanced at Dad's room. The door was open, his bed untouched.

I was in my Huck Finn costume the next morning and just getting ready to leave when Dad came downstairs in his robe, looking very sleepy. Les glanced up from his coffee and raised one eyebrow at Dad, smiling.

"Guess I overslept," Dad said, reaching for a mug from the cupboard, trying to keep his eyes open and look more awake than he was.

"And . . . uh . . . what time did *you* get in last night?" Les said.

"Pretty late, I'm afraid. We had a lot to talk about."

"Uh-huh," I said.

"She sure took us by surprise, didn't she?" said Dad.

Les cleared his throat and looked at me. "I don't know, Al. Do you think we should have some rules around here? A curfew, maybe?"

"I don't think that eleven o'clock would be at all unreasonable," I said.

"And of course we need to know where you'll be, Dad, and who you're with," Les continued.

"And you have to promise to call if you see you're going to be late," I said.

Dad just chuckled. "Go ahead," he said. "Have your fun. But you can't get a rise out of me, because I'm mellow."

"Cool, you mean," said Lester.

"Yes," said Dad, smiling still. "Very cool indeed."

The Metro was really crowded the next day. Some big event was going on in Washington, and there was standing room only. It wasn't too difficult for Pamela and me to maneuver in our costumes, but Elizabeth, in her monster suit, with footpads and claws, didn't have such an easy time of it. Half the stuff on her costume was attached by Velcro, and she didn't want to lose any of it. Of course, she could have carried it in a bag and put it on once we got to the library, but that would have ruined the fun.

We had to squeeze to make sure we all got on the same car, and when the train stopped at the next station, everyone had to move back even more. The closer we got to downtown Washington, though, the more people got off, and when there was space enough to breathe again, I looked at Elizabeth and said, "Liz, your goggle eyes are missing."

"What?" She reached up and felt the space above her own eyes where the huge goggle eyes of the monster were supposed to be. They were gone.

We immediately started looking all around as people smiled at us and children pointed, and then Pam said, "Oh, look!"

A very dignified man in a gray pinstripe suit had a briefcase in one hand, and was holding on to the handrail overhead with the other. He was standing near the front of the car, and the band of Velcro with the goggle eyes on it was stuck to the bottom of his suit coat.

"Pamela!" Elizabeth gasped.

"Go get them!" I said. "The next stop is Metro Center, and half the car will be getting off."

Someone moved forward in the aisle, brushing past the man in the pinstripe suit, and now the goggle eyes had slipped down to the dignified man's pants and seemed glued to his bottom. A little boy saw them and began laughing.

"Liz, go!" I said again.

Elizabeth lurched forward as the train began to slow, her footpads flopping on the floor of the car, and when she reached the gentleman she said, "Excuse me, sir, but I believe my eyes are on the seat of your pants." And she bent down and peeled them off while he stared at her incredulously. Two rows of people who were watching burst into laughter, and then the man laughed, too.

He turned and looked at Pamela and me, and then Elizabeth again. "You look like something out of a book I used to read to my son when he was little," he said. "'The night Max wore his wolf suit and made mischief of one kind or another, his mother called him wild thing. . . .'" He winked at us. "Maurice Sendak, I think," he said, and as the door opened, he stepped out onto the platform and into the crowd.

Sylvia and I went shopping the last day of spring vacation. Dad didn't feel he could take any more time away from the store, and Sylvia needed some things she couldn't find in England, so she asked if I would like to go to White Flint with her. When I got home from the library and changed clothes, she drove over from Kensington and picked me up, and we went to Bloomingdale's and Lord and Taylor's. I would have followed her wherever she went, lost in a trail of her wonderful perfume.

White Flint Mall is a fancier kind of mall than Wheaton Plaza, and it was having a strolling fashion show. Models walked around all three levels in clothes I wouldn't wear in a million years, and there were strolling musicians and a photographer taking people's pictures.

We had just bought some panty hose and a white jacket for Sylvia, and a couple of shirts for me, and were having tea and scones at a little table outside a restaurant on the top level when the musicians came over to play for us. One was playing an accordion and the other a violin, and they smiled at us—at Sylvia, mostly—as they played. And while we were listening, a photographer snapped our picture and gave Sylvia a number and an address in case she wanted to order a copy.

"I'm glad I came back over spring vacation," she said when he'd gone.

"I'm glad you came, too," I said. "I've never seen Dad so happy."

"And *I've* never *felt* so happy," she said. "I can't believe I'm so lucky to get a ready-made family. You know what it felt like today, shopping with you? As though I were with my sister again."

"She's out west, isn't she?"

"Yes. I almost feel guilty not going out there while I'm back, but I'll see her in just a few months when she comes for the wedding. We used to do everything together when we were growing up, and I miss that sometimes."

"What all did you do?" I asked.

"Well"—Sylvia took another sip of her tea—"Let's see. She's a couple years younger than I am. I wheeled her around in my doll buggy once. I remember that because I accidentally tipped it, and over she went. I taught her to play hopscotch. We sang duets together. We curled each other's hair. I don't know. . . . Some girls fight with their sisters, but we were really close."

"It's good you remember so much," I told her.

"What do you remember of your mother?"

"Not very much. But I think she and Dad loved each other a lot." I wondered suddenly if I should have said that. Or *why* I'd said that. Why did my brain think of what might upset someone the most and then direct my mouth to say it? But it didn't seem to bother her a bit. If anything, she liked to hear it.

"That's a good sign," she said. "I don't think I would be comfortable marrying a man who had been miserable in a marriage. This means he liked being married, and knows it will probably make him happy again."

"But don't . . . don't you want him to forget about Mom when he's with you?" I asked.

Sylvia cocked her head and looked at me with her blue-green eyes. "Why on earth would I expect that of him, Alice? Marie was such a big part of his life. There were some men in my life who I like to think about now and then. Little things that

302 • PHYLLIS REYNOLDS NAYLOR

remind me of them. Ben and I like to share these memories with each other."

"What?" I said. "You actually *tell* each other you're thinking of someone else?"

She laughed. "Why not? There's a lot of difference between just thinking about a person and actually going out and *being* with another person—in a close, intimate way, I mean. That kind of relationship is reserved for your dad."

I sighed. "It sounds very adult to me. I'm not sure I could ever feel that mature about things. I mean, that I wouldn't mind if a guy I was with was thinking about another girl. To tell the truth, I don't understand a lot about love."

Sylvia chuckled and divided the last scone between us. "To tell the truth, I don't either. But we don't have to, you know. All we need to do is enjoy it."

She went back two days before her school reopened after spring break. I thought Dad would be really down, but he wasn't. He seemed just as happy as he was before, as though her love would keep him going for the next few months until she was in his arms again. I was almost jealous of her—that she could make him feel that good.

When I kissed him that night, I played our little game. "Like me?" I asked, rubbing his nose with mine.

"Hm?" he asked.

I tried again. "Like me?"

"Rivers." He grinned.

"Love me?"

As I said the words, however, the phone rang and he sprang up to answer. It was someone collecting used clothes for Purple Heart. When he came back to the sofa, he said, "I thought it might be Sylvia saying that her flight was canceled or something."

I repeated the phrase. "Love me?"

"Of course," he said.

"No, Dad! You're supposed to say *'oceans'*!" I told him.

"Of course. Oceans," he said. But he *could* have put a little more feeling into it.

8

PRODUCTION

We had three weeks after we returned from spring vacation to get the musical in shape. The cast worked to master their lines, the orchestra to fine-tune the music, the stage crew to get all the props and costumes. The production was to run for four nights—Friday and Saturday of one week, and Friday and Saturday the next. Dad gave me both Saturdays off from the Melody Inn, and a couple of the teachers even gave us an extra week to do our assignments.

The stage crew was down to the nitty-gritty now—no goofing off. Because I was matter-of-fact with the three guys who had "tattooed" me, they began to treat me okay. Harry, in fact—

the fourth guy on the stage crew—apologized for not stopping the other boys when they'd pulled my jeans down. "Next time I see something like that," he said, "I'll do more than just tell them to stop."

"Let's hope there's no next time for anybody," I said.

A week before the first performance, Mr. Ellis told us that the entire cast and crew were invited to the home of Kurt Weinstein, the guy who was playing Tevye, to observe the Sabbath. At first they said only the cast members were to go, then they said everyone was invited, that the Weinsteins had a big house. Some of the kids couldn't make it, but the rest of us, maybe thirty in all, sat or stood around the Weinsteins' family room on a Friday night, meeting the parents and grandparents who spent the Sabbath with them every week, as well as the ninety-eight-year-old great-grandfather.

We shared stories and listened to the grandfather's hesitant account of a grammar-school production he was in after his family came over from Russia.

"And because I did not still know the English well, I was given no lines to say, but was to play the part of the mule," he told us, and we laughed.

Kurt's father studied his watch and, at sundown, signaled that the Sabbath candles were to be lit. We all squeezed into the living and dining rooms, where two long tables had been placed end to end, extending from one room into the other. The meal had been cooked, and the heavy silver candelabrum polished. Kurt's mother, wearing a beautiful silk blouse, lit two candles, and Mr. Weinstein explained that they were symbols of peace, freedom, and light, which the Sabbath brings to the human soul. Copies of the blessings had been given to each of us, and we watched in fascination as the candlelight flickered and the prayers were said.

The Weinsteins and some of the cast sang "Shalom Aleichem," which Mrs. Weinstein explained means "Peace Be Unto You," and after that Kurt's dad filled a silver cup with wine and recited the Kiddush. Finally, after lifting the challah bread in the air and reciting a blessing, he cut off a piece for everyone, explaining that the blade of the knife should always tip inward, toward the table, not outward, toward the guests.

Then we ate—roast chicken, gefilte fish, chicken soup, kugel. . . . There were more Sabbath prayers and hymns as the evening went on, ending with "Ein K'Elokenu"—"None Is Like Our Lord." As our parting gift to the Weinsteins, the cast sang one of the songs from *Fiddler*, the "Sabbath Prayer," and I had to blink and swallow, it was so moving.

The great-grandfather, in a voice we could hardly hear, said his Friday nights would never be the same after that. Neither would ours. Sharing the Sabbath with a family who truly understood the traditions would help us make *Fiddler on the Roof* all the more convincing.

The night of the first performance was gorgeous. Soft April-smelling breezes blew over the parking lot, and a half moon illuminated the cast members who ran into the building, holding their costumes over their arms, calling out to one another. The whole place was a buzz of excitement.

I loved the energy of it. Faith and I set about checking every prop to make sure it was in place—every chair, every pitcher, every bottle or basket or barrel just exactly where it was supposed to be, so there would be no surprises for the cast once the curtain rose. Molly and the guys were checking the lights, the microphones, the speakers—testing, retesting—and I fell right in beside them, helping out, forcing Richard to look at me so he could see I had survived my humiliation. I can't say he was exactly chummy, but that was okay with me.

The orchestra members were filling in, and now and then an instrument would tune up, then two or three at a time, making an awful racket. Faith and I peeked out from behind the curtain as the auditorium filled, families with young children in tow, parents carrying cameras for picture-taking afterward, friends of cast members coming in groups and sitting down near the front, everyone talking and calling out to one another, changing seats, long-legged guys stepping over the backs of one row to get to another.

Backstage, one of the girls had ripped her skirt, and Molly and I were desperately trying to find enough safety pins to make a new seam. Tevye had a headache, one of the cossacks had the flu, someone had taken the menorah off to be polished and it wasn't where it was supposed to be, one of the microphones was whistling, and Charlene Verona was being a pill. She had discovered herself. Again.

Just as Molly and I were trying to get our hands inside the skirt without making the girl take it off, Charlene appeared at our elbows, all aglow, and said, "Isn't mauve the perfect eye shadow for me?"

I looked at her and then at Molly as I took another safety pin from my mouth, but Molly couldn't help herself. "Charlene," she said, "did you ever hear of Galileo?"

Charlene looked at her nonplussed. "What?"

"How the earth's not the center of the universe?" Molly continued.

"Of course!" Charlene's brow wrinkled even more.

"Well, neither are you," said Molly. "We've got a hundred problems here. Be helpful. If you can't be helpful, could you at least be quiet?"

Charlene flounced off, but I don't think I could have said that in a million years. The menorah reappeared, polished, the skirt got pinned, somebody gave Tevye a Tylenol, an understudy took the cossack's part, and we all gathered in the wings.

"Break a leg," cast members whispered laughingly to one another—the good-luck blessing among actors.

I decided to focus my second article for *The Edge* on the tension backstage before the curtain rises—the assorted worries running through people's heads: *Are all the props in place? Do I need a cough drop? Is my fly zipped? Can I remember the words to the second verse?*

The Orchestra director took his place in the pit and was

going through the official tune-up now. It looked to us as though almost all the seats were filled. Then Harry got the signal to dim the house lights, the audience quieted down, and at last we heard the familiar strains of the lone violin.

The scene onstage was an open view of Tevye and Golde's hut, their yard to one side, and a backdrop of trees and other small huts in the village. There would be nine scene changes in act one and eight in act two, so the stage crew really had to hustle. When the lights onstage went off completely, we had to help the actors get to their places without falling over anything, so that when the lights came on again, there they were, the village was going about its business, and Tevye launched into the opening song, "Tradition."

When he sang "If I Were a Rich Man," the audience began clapping along to the rhythm halfway through, and that seemed to make him strut even more. I realized then how the audience takes part in a production—how they react to what's onstage and the cast responds to their reaction. I'd remember to put that in one of my articles. And when he ended at last on the phrase ". . . If I were a wealthy man," it brought down the house. Later, when the rousing "To Life" was sung by all the guys, the audience really got into it and clapped in time much of the way through. Backstage we all smiled at each other, relieved that it was going so well.

There were some glitches, of course, and we just hoped the audience didn't notice. A boy's beard came unglued and dangled off one side of his face, and another guy's pillow had slid so far down his abdomen, we were afraid it would slip out the bottom of his tunic.

"Grab that guy the minute he comes offstage and fix that pillow," Faith whispered to me, and I was able to get it tied in place again.

Tevye's daughters sang beautifully, even Charlene, I had to admit. We were eager to see how the audience would react to the ghost scene, where Lazar Wolf's dead wife supposedly speaks to Tevye in a dream. Some of the cast, dressed in white sheets, came moaning and keening down the aisle toward the stage, while the ghost of the dead wife shrieked out her warning, seated high in the opening of the projection booth at the back.

The audience did just what we wanted them to do—turned and gasped—and that song got great applause, too. In all, the first night went off just as it should. Everyone whistled and clapped and cheered when it was over, loudest of all for Tevye. After the cast took their bow, the stage crew was called out, so we linked hands and sort of line-danced our way across the stage in our black jeans and T-shirts. Then the orchestra took the applause and, last of all, the director. One performance down, three to go.

Dad and Lester came the second night. They were sitting in the second row off to one side. I was watching from behind the curtain when Tevye and Golde were singing "Sunrise, Sunset," and was surprised to see my father furtively wipe tears off his cheek. *Was he thinking about how he would feel when I married?* I wondered. Or was he thinking of Sylvia? Of Mom? I saw Eric there too, sitting on the other side of the auditorium, and he came around afterward long enough to tell me we'd done a good job on the scenery and props.

"You think you cccc-can squeeze me in some w-w-weekend when this is over?" he asked.

I smiled. "I'll ask my secretary," I joked. "It can probably be arranged."

One of the cast members drove me home, and Dad and Lester were still up, making grilled cheese sandwiches.

"How did you like it?" I asked eagerly. "You had good seats."

"So close, we got spittle on us all through 'If I Were a Rich Man,'" Lester said.

"Orchestra was terrific, Al! And everyone sang with such enthusiasm. It was great!" Dad said.

"I especially liked the part where a stagehand came out to move a bench between scenes—one of the girls, I think, about your size, actually—and when she bent over we noticed a rip in her pants," said Lester.

"What?" I cried.

"Relax," said Dad. "It never happened."

I gave Lester a look, and after he went to bed I said, "Are you disappointed in me, Dad, because I can't sing? I really wish I could have been out there onstage, in the chorus, even."

"If you could carry a tune, you wouldn't be you now, would you? And I wouldn't change you for the world," he said.

How is it that fathers can word things exactly right?

"Well, I wouldn't change you for the world, either," I said, and gave him a hug. "Maybe in another life I'll come back as a canary. Or maybe I'll sing at the Met."

"I'll settle for whatever you do in this one," Dad said.

The whole gang came the fourth night of the production. Charlene, of course, went around backstage before the performance, hugging everyone, getting ready for her bawl when it was finally over, I guess. We noticed that friends of cast members in the audience came carrying single roses and bouquets to give to them afterward, and someone rushed backstage to say that all the programs were gone. We had a full house.

I suppose the final performance is always difficult because you know you're doing it for the last time. The audience was even more enthusiastic, and every actor seemed to be adding little flourishes to his performance. We were missing three understudies, including Charlene's—the flu was making the rounds—but the original cast onstage seemed healthy, and we had only this last night to finish.

During intermission, though, Charlene, in her usual "watch me" mode, was using backstage as a dance floor. Her face set in concentration as though she wasn't aware that Mr. Ellis was about and that people were watching her, she folded her arms across her chest and went whirling around and around, her full skirt twirling about her. Then, using every ballet step she knew, she went leaping from one end to the other, but when she turned to go back, she danced too close to a ladder lying on the floor and caught her foot behind a rung. She stumbled, twisting her leg, and fell to the floor.

I knew she had been trying to show Mr. Ellis that she could not only sing, she could dance. But I hadn't expected this!

She howled, and Ed and Devon ran to pick her up, but she was really in pain and somebody joked, "Hey, Charlene, when I said, 'Break a leg,' I didn't mean it!"

Mr. Ellis came over then and examined her ankle, which was beginning to swell.

"It's okay," Charlene kept saying, clenching her teeth. "I can go on, Mr. E."

But when she tried to stand up and put her weight on it, she couldn't. Suddenly Mr. Ellis grabbed my arm. "Alice, you're going to have to be Tzeitel in the second act," he said. "Charlene's understudy is sick."

"What?" I cried.

"You've got her hair, her build. You've been here enough, you know what to do."

"Mr. Ellis, I can't sing!" I croaked.

"You don't have to. She doesn't have any songs in the second act, and you can lip-synch along with the chorus. If you don't know what to do, fake it."

Charlene started to cry, and I almost cried with her. I had to admit that of everyone else on stage, I probably looked most like Charlene, and yes, I knew where she stood and what she did, which wasn't much in the second act. But . . .

There was no time for buts. We were already late with Act

Two. Charlene cried all the while she took off her costume, and *really* sobbed as she handed it to me. I was numb with terror. One of her friends handed her a robe we kept backstage, and another located her parents in the audience. Ten minutes later, Charlene was on her way to Holy Cross Hospital, and I was tying her kerchief under my hair in back, and smoothing my apron over the long gingham skirt, wondering if I was going to throw up.

The guy who played Tevye came over and put one arm around me. "Don't worry," he said. "We'll guide you around the stage. Just act like you belong there and no one will know the difference."

I would swear that when the curtain rose for Act Two, I heard Pamela gasp, "That's *Alice!*"

I think I went through the whole second act in a trance. I could see the scenes in my mind, and could sort of place where Tzeitel stood, the few places where she had a line to say. Once, when I missed it, somebody else said it for me and it didn't really matter. I was never, ever, so glad to hear the final chorus, "Anatevka," and suddenly I began to feel loose and relaxed, and lip-synched my way through it as though I were singing my heart out. I could see Elizabeth and Pamela and Mark and Brian and Penny and Patrick staring at me in amazement from the fourth row. And then I realized that at least part of Lester's interpretation of my dream had come true: I *had* done something scary I'd never done before, but I didn't fall flat on my face.

To make the whole thing worse for Charlene, I got the bouquets intended for her, and when Tevye's three daughters held hands and came forward for their own special bow, my friends went crazy and cheered and clapped as though I'd been the star, which was almost embarrassing, but of course everyone else had friends there cheering for them, too. Molly and Faith grabbed me after the final curtain and gave me a hug. "You looked half scared to death, but with the villagers being scattered to the four winds, that was exactly right," Faith said, and we laughed.

When the gang gathered backstage, I had to explain how it had happened, and how I'd lip-synched along with the chorus, and then we went out into the hall where parents and friends were taking pictures and cast members were autographing programs. When people came up to me for my autograph, I had no choice but to write "Tzeitel" beside Charlene's name, and only one of them asked if I was the same girl who played it in Act One. Worse yet for Charlene, Sam was there taking pictures of the cast for the yearbook, and we all went back onstage and posed for a couple of scenes. My name would appear under the stage crew listing, of course, but my picture would appear over Charlene's name.

Mr. E. said the stage crew would be expected to come back to school the next day and strike the set, but that we were all going to enjoy the cast party that night. I took off Charlene's costume because I wanted to go in my black jeans and T-shirt as part of the stage crew. We all piled in the cars of the juniors and seniors and drove to the home of the girl who played Golde, where her parents had prepared refreshments.

It was loud and noisy and fun, and there were a lot of silly awards given out—the person who came late to rehearsals most times, the person who took longest to learn his lines—and I was delighted to receive an award for "Most Grace Under Pressure," for filling in for Charlene. We laughed at all the things that had gone wrong, the last-minute changes the audience didn't know about, and then we presented Mr. E. with a miniature gold-plated fiddle that I had ordered specially through the Melody Inn.

It was one of the best times I'd ever had, and it wasn't until the end, when the cast sang "Sunrise, Sunset," as our final tribute to our director, that I realized Faith hadn't come to the party, and I would have bet my last dollar that it was Ron who had kept her away.

9
CLEARING THE AIR

I woke up the next morning smiling at the mementos I saw strewn about my room: the black T-shirt with FIDDLER on the back. A bunch of flowers. A program. A poster. A black balloon from the party. I wandered around in my pajamas pinning things to my bulletin board, taping the poster to the wall. When I went down to breakfast, Lester had gone to play volleyball with some of his buddies, and Dad was looking up painters in the yellow pages because he wanted to have the inside of the house done before Sylvia came back in June.

"Have a nice time at the cast party?" he asked.

"Yes! I've made a whole new bunch of friends," I said. "A lot more people I can say hi to in the halls."

"It's nice to see you bloom, Al," Dad said.

"Huh?"

"Bloom. Blossom. Spread your wings."

Fathers are so strange sometimes. With Dad I'm either a flower or a bird.

"I'm going back to school today and help strike the set. I'll take the city bus," I told him.

"Okay, hon. It's just you and me for dinner tonight. Les will be out. Why don't we go somewhere? What appeals?"

"Let's try something we've never had before," I suggested.

"Okay. You pick the restaurant," said Dad.

When I got to the high school, most of the crew were there, and it was like another party, but less rowdy. Mr. E. had brought pizza and Cokes for us, and while the guys dismantled the sets, the girls were packing up props, sorting out things from the school's storeroom, boxing up the things we had borrowed from other people. Even Richard and Devon were more friendly toward me.

Mr. E. stayed until the backdrops were down and dismantled, and asked if we could finish on our own, which, of course, we could.

"Hey, Faith, missed you at the party," Harry called over. "You should have come."

"Yeah, I'm sorry I couldn't make it," Faith said, and sounded wistful.

"What could be more important than a cast party?" Molly called from the other side of the stage, where she was wrapping up electrical cord.

"Oh, Ron had other plans for us," Faith said.

Molly and I exchanged glances.

We were just finishing the last of the pizza and were going to stack the scenery and take all the stuff to the storage room when we saw Ron walk in though a side door. He stood for a minute with his hands in his pockets, a toothpick between his lips. One of the guys had been teasing Faith, making her laugh, and Ron didn't look too happy about that. He sauntered over, coming up behind Faith, and clapped one hand over her shoulder. "Hey, babe," he said. "Let's go."

Faith had just picked up a piece of pizza and opened a Coke. She turned around. "We've still got a lot of stuff to do," she said.

"Like what? Having a picnic? You said you'd be through by one."

"I know, but there's a lot of stuff that has to be packed up," Faith told him. By now, everyone had stopped talking and was watching the little drama.

"They can finish up. C'mon." We could see his fingers clamp more tightly on her shoulder.

"Let me eat this, then I will," said Faith.

"I'm parked in the custodian's place. C'mon," he said, and jiggled her shoulder so hard that the Coke spilled out of the can and onto her jeans.

I stared at Faith, at the way her face flushed. She'd seemed to be having so much fun before.

Suddenly Harry stood up and took a step forward. "She said she wants to finish her lunch. Maybe you didn't hear," he told Ron. Ron looked up.

And then, to my surprise, Richard and Devon stood up, too. "This is a cast party," Devon said. "You can wait outside if you want."

"Hey, this is between Faith and me. It's none of your business," Ron said.

"Wrong, buddy. Faith's our friend, and you treating her like dirt is our business. She'll leave when she's good and ready. Right now, she's not ready," Harry said.

Ron's jaw clenched. He stared down at Faith. "You coming?"

She kept her eyes on her lap. "No."

"What?" said Ron, anger in his voice. "I didn't hear you."

"She said *no*," said Harry. "She's staying, and we'll see that she gets home."

Ron glared around the stage, then turned suddenly and left, and the rest of us broke into applause. I couldn't tell what Faith was feeling, embarrassment or relief or what.

"Good for you, Faith! You finally stood up for yourself," Molly told her.

I handed Faith a paper napkin to blot up the Coke on her jeans. "He's going to be really mad," I told her, wondering if we'd only made it harder for her. "He won't . . . he won't hurt you, will he?"

"Oh, gosh, no, he's just the jealous type. He means well."

"Wrong," said Harry. "He's a control freak, and you deserve better."

We awkwardly changed the subject then, as Faith silently finished her lunch. I didn't know if what had happened was enough to turn the tide or not. Maybe it meant a lot to her to have us all in her corner. Or maybe she just decided on her own that it was time. But as we finished packing up, I noticed that her color returned to normal, she was a little more talkative than usual, and Harry, true to his word, drove her home.

I was thinking about her on the bus later. Now that the production was over, it would be too easy to go back to our old clique again and forget about Faith. But this was when she needed new friends the most, yet I was afraid if I called her, she wouldn't want to do anything with me—a freshman trying to hang out with a junior. But I called her anyway when I got home and asked if she wanted to see a movie with Pamela and Elizabeth and me the next day.

"Thanks for asking, Alice, but I'm going somewhere with Molly," she said.

Well, that was good, too.

Charlene called me when I got home.

"It wasn't broken after all," she said. "Just a really bad sprain. How did it go, Alice?"

I knew that the only possible answer that would satisfy her would be to say that I fell on my face. "Well, I guess you'd have to ask someone else. I was too scared to think, almost," I said truthfully. "But the other kids covered for me. I don't think too many people noticed." She *definitely* did not want to hear that. "The show had to go on, and your understudy was sick. What else could we do?"

"They could have sat me in a chair or something," she said, and her nose sounded clogged, as though she'd been crying. "Mother was wondering if I got any flowers. I mean, I'm home now, of course, but I have to stay off my foot and wear this bandage, and . . . I *did* get flowers, didn't I?"

"We sort of divided them up among the whole cast and crew so that everyone got flowers," I said. "But I'll be glad to bring some over if you give me your address."

I called Elizabeth and Pamela and asked if they wanted to go on a mission of mercy.

"To where?" asked Pamela. "Who are we being merciful to?"

"Charlene Verona," I said.

"Are you nuts?"

"Probably. But she deserves her flowers. Les said he'd drive us over."

Liz and Pam have had a crush on Lester almost since the day we moved in, so they said they'd go. I'd just stuck the flowers I'd gotten at the performance in one of Lester's beer steins (*Remember to buy a vase before Sylvia comes to live with us,* I told myself), so I took some plastic wrap to wind around the stems and when Elizabeth and Pamela came over, we all crawled in the backseat of Lester's car.

"Dad and I are eating out tonight, Les," I said. "Where are you going?"

"Heavy date," he said as he backed out of the drive.

"Heavy as in fat?" asked Elizabeth.

"No. I'd say, maybe a hundred and thirty pounds, nicely stacked," he replied.

"Heavy as in *serious*?" asked Pamela.

"Heavy as in 'interest,'" said Lester. "Lauren's a very attractive, intelligent woman. Anything else you want to know?"

He left himself wide open on that one.

"Sure!" said Pamela. "How *intimate* are you with this woman, Les?"

"Pamela!" said Elizabeth, but I'll bet she was curious, too.

"Intimate as in 'soul mates'?" said Lester. "Intimate as in 'philosophically in tune'? Intimate as in—"

"Never mind," I said, knowing he'd never tell us anyway. I checked the address Charlene had given me. "Turn right at the next light, Lester, then left at the second stop sign."

"So who is this woman, Lester? Your fave girl?" asked Elizabeth.

"Your latest conquest?" asked Pamela.

"Latest victim?" I put in.

"She happens to be one of my philosophy instructors at the U of Maryland," Lester told us.

"Isn't that against the law? Dating a student?" asked Elizabeth.

"She could go to jail for corrupting the morals of a minor," said Pamela.

"Ha!" I said.

Lester just smiled at us in the rearview mirror and pulled up to a gray brick house. "Here you are, ladies. Take your inquiring minds with you, please. How are you getting home, Al?"

"We'll catch a bus," I told him.

"Good-bye, sweetheart," said Pam, getting out.

"Have a good day, luv," said Elizabeth.

Charlene's mother met us at the door. She was a thin redhead who looked as though she could have been a dancer in her day.

"You're the girl who filled in for Charlene," she guessed when she saw the flowers. And when I nodded, she said, "She's in here," and led us to the living room, where Charlene sat with her foot propped on a hassock.

"Here are the flowers, Charlene," I said. "I'm sorry about your foot."

She hardly even looked at the flowers, just gave them to her mother to put in a vase. She seemed so much smaller—more vulnerable, maybe—hunched down in the chair in her pajamas. I was beginning to have mixed feelings about Charlene. She was pretty even in her pajamas with a bandage on her foot—naturally pretty. She'd been *born* pretty. And somehow I was holding that against her. That, and all her talent; she could sing like anything.

"So how did it go?" asked Mrs. Verona. "We went right to the emergency room and didn't get to see any of the second act. Such a disappointment! Charlene worked so hard!"

"Oh, it went great!" said Pamela. "Everyone said the final performance was the best!" I couldn't stop her. I wondered if Pam was jealous of her too.

"But how did you manage?" her mother asked, turning to me. "Charlene said you can't even sing!"

Elizabeth answered, "I don't think anyone even knew there was a change," and Mrs. Verona looked stricken.

"At least you were there for the first act, and that's the one that counted," I told Charlene quickly.

Mrs. Verona turned to her daughter: "Well, honey, it's only your freshman year. You have three more years to be in the productions. I wasn't in a musical till I was in *college*!" Then, to us, "Usually these roles go to the seniors. We were just so pleased to find out that Charlene got a major part. But she's so talented."

I started to say something nice, like, "Yes, she was very lucky," or something. After all, we were guests in their home. But Pamela piped up with, "Oh, and they took pictures for the yearbook afterward. Won't that be a hoot, Alice?"

"For the *yearbook*?" Charlene wailed.

"Don't worry. I gave your name, not mine," I assured her. "It's only fair that you get the credit."

"But it won't be Charlene's picture!" cried her mother. "I simply don't know why they had to wait till the final night to take pictures. I so wanted to have copies made and to send them out with our cards next Christmas! I had the whole thing planned, and now *this*!"

All the while her mother was talking, Charlene seemed to be

sinking lower and lower in the chair, eyes on her mom, feeling worse, it seemed, that she'd let her down. I don't know if she'd leveled with her mother or not about how she had hurt her foot, but if I had a pushy mom like that, maybe I'd feel like whirling myself around and around—right off the end of the stage, in fact—anything to let off some steam.

"Well," I said quickly. "We just stopped in, Charlene. I really hope you'll be better soon. The kids'll fill you in on everything when you get back."

Her mother thanked us for coming over and took us to the door. We were never so glad to get out.

"Whew!" said Elizabeth.

"I guess it's hard not to think of yourself as the center of the universe if your mom believes that you are," I said.

"They make me sick," said Elizabeth. "Charlene with her perfect face, perfect skin, perfect everything. Her mother just wants her to be what *she* was. Or never was, one or the other."

"Charlene *did* look sort of pathetic," I said.

"You're *sorry* for her?" Pamela exclaimed. "Ha! It couldn't have happened to a better person. All she wants is to be the star."

That sure sounded familiar. We *were* jealous, all three of us! Pamela was accusing Charlene of wanting exactly the same thing she did. And wasn't it curious that Elizabeth, who had been fighting acne lately, happened to mention Charlene's perfect skin? As for me, hadn't I wished a few weeks ago that I could get up on a stage and belt out a song like the others did at the audition, Charlene included?

"Well," I said, "she *is* stuck on herself, and she is obnoxious at times, but if she were homely, we wouldn't be talking about her like this. Right?"

"If she were homely, she wouldn't be stuck on herself," said Pamela.

But Elizabeth can see a moral a mile away, and you can make her feel guilty about almost anything. Maybe jealousy is a sin. "So we can dislike her for being conceited, but we can't dislike her for being pretty and talented and loved and coddled?" she said.

I nudged her in the ribs. "Hey, Elizabeth, *you're* pretty and talented and loved and coddled, and we don't hate *you*!" I grinned.

She just elbowed me back.

"Listen," I said. "Dad and I are going out for dinner tonight. Someplace we've never been before. You guys want to come?" I knew he wouldn't mind.

"Sure," said Elizabeth.

"If it's okay with him," said Pamela.

We went to an Afghanistan restaurant and had little deep-fried *sambosas* for an appetizer, and *quabill palow* for main course—lamb and saffron rice with carrots and almonds and raisins. And somehow, after a great dinner in good company, we began to feel that we could make it through three more years of high school with Charlene Verona if we really worked at it.

My last article for *The Edge* was about the production as a community—the actors, the orchestra, the director, all the different stage crews—and how it takes all of us to bring a musical to life. All of us deserve the applause. I described the cast party afterward, how we'd been through something big together, and felt sort of like family.

Nick and Sara said it was the best writing I'd done so far, and that made me feel really good. Things were suddenly going well for me again—I'd made new friends, was back on track with my old ones, Patrick and I were pals, Gwen was helping me with algebra when I needed it. I was fine, Dad and Sylvia were fine. Lester and Lauren were . . .

"So how was *your* evening?" I asked Lester at breakfast the next morning as I buttered my English muffin.

"Well, I'm seeing her again next weekend, if that answers your question," said Les, who doesn't usually care much for early-morning conversation.

"You're getting an A in her course, I presume?" I chirped.

"My course work and our relationship have nothing to do with each other," said Les. "There's no law against an instructor and a student having intellectual discussions and enjoying cultural events together. This is college, after all, not high school."

"Be careful, Les," said Dad.

On Monday, in the middle of the morning, I got a pain. It was somewhere down around my navel, but I started getting these sharp little stabbing pains that turned into a steady throb by lunchtime. I wasn't sure if I was going to throw up or not, so I didn't eat anything.

"What's the matter?" asked Gwen.

"I don't know. I've got this pain in my abdomen."

"Cramps?"

"No. I had my period just a week ago."

"Then it's probably not ovulation, either," said Gwen.

"Ovulation gives you a bellyache?"

"Sometimes—when the egg breaks out of the ovary. Does it feel like a stomachache?"

"Not exactly. Just sort of a throbbing, burning pain."

"You ought to go see the nurse—have it checked out," she said.

I made a little face. "Probably something I ate," I said.

"I don't think so," she said. "You didn't eat anything for lunch, right?"

By fourth period, the pain was unmistakably worse. I asked for a pass and went to see the nurse. She asked me the same things about my period and had me lie down on the cot. Then she bent over me and gently prodded my abdomen. When she got about halfway between my navel and my hipbone on the right side, I gave a yelp.

She put a thermometer in my mouth, and when she came back and checked it, she said, "I'm no doctor, Alice, but my guess is you've got appendicitis. I think we ought to call your dad."

"Is that—?"

"It's not serious, but I rather think you're going to have your appendix taken out."

"An operation?" I gasped. And the next thing I knew, I felt the room going around, and I blacked out.

10
THE GIRL IN WHITE

When I came to, I heard the nurse talking on the phone to my dad. She must have been sitting beside my cot, stroking the side of my face with one hand and holding the phone to her ear with the other.

"Alice? Alice?" she said as I struggled to open my eyes. And then, to my dad, "She's coming to now, Mr. McKinley. She's going to be fine. . . . Yes, I'll tell her you're on your way."

I felt as though I were down in a deep, deep well. I could hear what was going on and feel the nurse's fingers on my cheek, but I didn't have the energy even to open my eyes.

The nurse grasped my fingers. "Alice," she said, "if you can hear me, squeeze my hand."

Somehow I managed to do that, and then I opened my eyes.

"I think that was a bit of a shock, and I could be completely wrong about that pain in your tummy, but if I'm not, it's about the most common operation you could imagine. It's really not a big deal," she said.

I just looked at her. It was *my* abdomen we were talking about, not hers.

"Your dad's on his way over, so you just lie there and rest a little," she said.

I didn't say anything because I was afraid if I opened my mouth, I might vomit.

A girl came in with a sore throat, and a guy who had hurt his thumb in gym. They could probably see my legs and feet sticking out from behind the curtain, I realized, and I turned my face toward the wall.

The pain was pretty constant now. It throbbed like a finger when you get a cut on it. Finally I heard my dad's voice out in the hall, then coming through the door, and next, right beside me.

"Al, honey?" he said. "Think you can sit up?"

Wincing, I sat up and he crouched down beside me. I put my arms around his neck and started to cry. "I don't *want* an operation!" I sobbed.

He stroked my back. "Now let's don't jump to conclusions. Dr. Beverly said he'd see you as soon as I brought you in, so let's let him have a look at you." He reached down to get my

332 • PHYLLIS REYNOLDS NAYLOR

shoes off the floor and helped put them on my feet.

"She has a temperature of a hundred and one," the nurse said. "And the pain's definitely in the right place."

"Thanks for taking care of her," Dad said. And then, to me, "My car's right outside. Just take it slow and easy."

Of course the bell had to ring just as we moved out into the hall, and as kids passed, staring at Dad with his arm around me and the way I was walking, sort of bent over and holding my stomach, they parted to make room for us. I felt like Moses parting the waters of the Red Sea.

Eric passed us, then suddenly jerked around and stared at me. "Alice?" he said.

"Hi, Eric," I said, but some kids pushed between us just then, and Dad and I turned and went out the door.

I cried all the way to Dr. Beverly's. "I don't *want* an operation," I wept again. "I don't want an ugly scar on my belly. I want to wear a bikini, and I'm *scared*!"

"Al, there are a lot worse things than a scar on your abdomen," he said.

I knew there were, but I didn't want to hear about them.

Dr. Beverly took me right in when we got there, and it was a good thing, because I threw up in his wastebasket.

"Oh!" he said, and rang for the nurse, who wiped my face and left with the wastebasket. Then I promptly threw up on the floor.

I figured the nurse would come in this time with a mop.

SIMPLY ALICE • 333

She did, but she also gave me a basin to hold on my lap, and just staring down into it, knowing what it was for, made me upchuck again.

Dr. Beverly wanted to know which came first, the pain or the nausea. The fever or the tenderness in the abdomen. This time when I was being examined, I shrank away when he got even close to the place where it hurt. He took my temperature again, and this time it had gone up half a degree.

"Appendicitis," he told Dad. He made a few calls, then told Dad to take me over to Suburban Hospital in Bethesda, that the surgeon on call said he could take me within the hour.

By now the pain was relentless, and I didn't think about the operation much, I just wanted the pain to stop. Dad got me admitted to Suburban and waited outside my room while the attendant helped me get my clothes off and put on a hideous white cotton robe that tied in the back. Then she rolled me over onto a stretcher. Dad sat with me while I waited to go to the operating room. He held my hand and patted my shoulder till they wheeled me in.

I hated the strangeness of the operating room. The big metal mirror and the instruments and lights. The surgeon came in and had to poke me again just to make sure I'd yell, I guess. I started crying.

"What if I d-don't wake up?" I mewed.

Dr. Salinas smiled. "Well, I've only done about a hundred and sixty of these, and I've never failed to have one wake up yet," he said. He bent over me.

"Wait!" I gasped. "What if I wake up too soon while you're still operating?"

"Won't happen," he said. "I guarantee it."

A nurse moved in. "Wait!" I cried. "What if . . . what if you leave something in me before you sew me up?" I thought of all the cartoons I'd seen of doctors leaving sponges and things in patients. "What if you leave a pair of scissors?"

"That won't happen, either," he said, his eyes smiling above his mask. "We need every pair of scissors we can get."

Why hadn't they put my robe on with the opening in front? I wondered. Now they would have to roll me over and untie the robe and roll me back again.

"Wait!" I cried as the nurse put something in my arm. I wanted to explain about the fading tattoo on my bottom but then I felt myself beginning to sink deliciously into sleep, the noises around me grew fainter, and I felt my arms relax.

I couldn't tell how long I had been out. My first thought was that I must have fainted again, and as my eyelids fluttered, I saw that I was in a bed with metal sides.

"Al?" came Dad's voice. "You're doing fine, honey."

I think I drifted off again. Then Lester's voice: "We could always fill a bedpan and dump it on her."

I opened my eyes and saw him standing over me.

"Don't . . . you . . . dare," I managed to say.

He grinned. "She's awake."

"How do you feel, sweetheart?" asked Dad, and I realized

he was standing on the other side of me.

I felt my tummy. There was a bandage. "Is it over?" I asked, surprised.

"All done. You came through with flying colors."

The nurse walked in. "Well, look who's awake," she said, and adjusted something in my arm, then cranked the head of my bed up a little.

I realized I was feeling quite good, actually. Sort of foggy and fuzzy. My belly was sore, but the throbbing pain was gone.

When the nurse had checked on me and taken Dad out in the hall to direct him to a restroom, Lester handed me something wrapped in tinfoil and tied with string. "A little present," he said.

I slowly untied the ribbon. Everything about me seemed to function in slow motion. My fingers felt all thumbs. Inside the foil wrap was a small jar, and inside the jar . . . I couldn't figure out what it was.

"Appendix," said Lester. "The surgeon thought you'd want to keep it."

"Oh, gross!" I said, looking at it curiously. About the size of a pinkie, it was thin and white and shriveled, sort of lumpy at one end. "What am I supposed to do with *this*, Les?"

He shrugged. "Wear it on a chain around your neck, give it to an admirer, feed it to a pet . . . I don't know."

I went home the next day. Dad took off work to take care of me until he was sure I could manage on my own. I was still a little wobbly, and had to keep the bandage dry, but by the day after that I was perfectly able to be by myself, and the doctor said I could go back to school the following Monday, but couldn't take gym for a while. Dad sort of let me take over the living room and gave me all kinds of little projects to do to keep me occupied and to help us get ready for Sylvia—a box of unmatched socks to sort through; the same with a box of shoelaces; pictures to put in albums; clothes to be mended . . .

Pamela and Elizabeth came to see me, of course; Karen dropped by with Gwen, and a lot of people called.

"Oh, my gosh, was it awful?" Pamela asked. "Alice, you're the first one of us who ever had an operation."

"You don't feel a thing," I told her.

"Do you have to be completely naked?" Elizabeth wondered.

"I have no idea. I was unconscious, you know."

"If I ever have an operation, I'll have a local anesthetic," Elizabeth declared. "I want to know absolutely everything that's going on."

It was when I was checking my e-mail later that I found a note from Eric.

> Hey, what happened? Someone said you
> were sick.
> CAY

I e-mailed back:

> Just a little appendicitis, is all. I'll be
> back in school on Monday.

It was time, I decided, that Eric meet the rest of my friends. So when I got a second message from him, *Can I come over? Sunday afternoon, maybe?* I e-mailed back, *Sure,* and invited Pamela and Elizabeth and Mark and Brian and whoever else wanted to come, too. I said we'd have a nachos party, and I put on my soulful, sick-little-girl look for Lester. It actually worked. He went out and brought home a large order of nachos and some sodas, which was a good thing because Karen and Jill and Justin showed up, too, and later, Patrick. I was wearing my best sweats and just socks on my feet, and felt perfectly comfortable.

Eric was surprised to find a room full of people when he came to the door, but I grasped his arm and pulled him inside. "Eric, you probably know most of these people," I said. "Eric Fielding, everybody."

Patrick had been telling a story of something that had happened on the last band trip out of town, and we were all listening to that, so it gave Eric a chance to settle down in a corner with a plate of nachos, and he's most relaxed when he's not the center of attention.

"So three guys sneaked out to bring back some beer, and the rest of us locked the door on them," Patrick said.

"Where were you, a motel?" asked Mark.

"No, a dorm, in Towson. They'd really been a pain, spouting off the whole trip about how, when we got to Towson, they were going to do this and they were going to do that, but we had a big competition coming up the next morning. So after they left we locked our room door, and evidently the custodian locked the front door too. When they got back with four six-packs, they couldn't get in, and they didn't know what room we were in, what window was ours."

We all started to laugh.

Patrick was laughing, too. "So they decided to hide the beer first, then figure out how to wake us up, then come back and get the booze. They made two mistakes: They threw gravel at a window and it happened to be the band director's, and later, when they went down to get the beer, after he'd let them in, the unlocked car they'd put it in had driven away."

We hooted.

"Eric, are you in the band?" asked Mark.

Everyone turned to Eric.

"N-N-No," Eric said, his face coloring a little.

Brian grinned. "I take it that's a n-n-no?"

All faces turned from Eric to Brian. I couldn't believe he'd said something so insensitive.

"Brian!" Elizabeth murmured disapprovingly.

But Eric, strangely, smiled too. "Y-Y-Yes," he said, smiling, and this time it seemed he was stuttering on purpose. "That was a n-n-no."

We all laughed then, and I thought how well he'd handled it.

"Eric's on the track team with me," Patrick explained.

"We t-teamed up in the rrr-relays," said Eric.

"Came in second, too!" said Patrick.

The gang stayed for a couple of hours. Of course, we had to pass around the jar with my appendix in it.

"Oh, get it *out* of here!" said Karen.

"It looks like a finger," said Jill.

"A uvula," said Gwen.

"A what?"

"That little thing that hangs down the back of your throat between your tonsils," she said.

Mark studied the jar. "Looks more like a part of the private anatomy of a male monkey," he said, and we all laughed. I had to be careful of my stitches when I laughed.

Patrick, however, held the jar in his hands, turning it this way and that, and finally he said, "You know what this is, Alice? A piece of white asparagus."

"What?" I said.

He unscrewed the lid and sniffed. "Preserved in vinegar," he told us.

"*What?*" I shrieked again. Then, "Lester!" as I caught sight of him out in the hall.

He poked his head in the doorway. "You called?"

"That's not my appendix, it's asparagus," I said.

"Is that a fact?" He grinned. "Well, you can't blame me for trying. I was in the Safeway and wondered what I could pick up for you. Balloons and flowers cost too much, but the produce man let me have a stalk of white asparagus for nothing, slightly wilted at the ends. But with a little imagination you can see it's a decaying remnant of the large intestine, a little gangrenous there in the middle with . . . Say. Anyone got an appetite for more nachos?"

When everyone left about four, Eric stayed a while longer. He looked around at all my half-finished projects for Dad and picked up the box of assorted shoelaces. "Starting a c-cottage industry?" he joked.

"Dad's put me to work cleaning out drawers and stuff, getting ready for his wedding this summer," I said, and told him the story of Miss Summers and how they'd met at the Messiah Sing-Along.

All the while I was talking, I noticed that Eric was playing around with the shoelaces, and then I realized he wasn't exactly playing. He was idly tying intricate knots. "What are you, a sailor?" I asked, and he grinned.

"N-Not exactly. I was a SSSS-Scout once, and had to learn a zillion knots," he said.

I went over and sat beside him, and he showed me how to tie a figure eight, a fisherman's knot, a stopper knot . . .

"Congratulations," he said. "Remind me to send you my camping badge when I get home."

The phone rang. It was Pamela.

"I'll call you later," I said. "Eric's here."

"He's still there? Oh, definitely! Call me back!" she said.

Eric and I talked about movies and favorite vacations and sharks and what food we would miss most if we were stranded on a desert island. Eric said what he would really miss was his CD player, and then we talked about our favorite songs and I told him how much I liked the music from *Fiddler on the Roof.*

"I liked those articles you wrote for *The Edge*," he said. "Especially the one about how you felt watching the others s-sing, and you can't carry a t-tune."

"Yeah," I said. "It always looks so *easy* for them. How do they *know* they're singing the right notes? I've always wondered, and Dad says they can just hear it. Well, I can 'hear' myself, of course, but I can't tell if I'm on the right note or not. It seems so magical to me, that others just *know*."

Eric smiled ruefully. "That's how I feel," he said. "T-Talking always looks so easy for everyone else."

"Just to open your mouth and say the words?" I asked.

"Yeah. Instead of all this sss-stopping and ssss-starting."

"And practice doesn't help?"

He laughed. "I can ssss-stand up on a stage in an empty auditorium and recite the P-Pledge of Allegiance without a hitch, b-but let one p-person come in, and I ssss-start ssss-stuttering again. I discovered that from experience."

"Then it doesn't sound like something you were b-born with," I said, and suddenly stared at him. "I just stuttered!"

He laughed. "So it's catching!" Then he put two fingers under my chin, turned my head toward him, and kissed me.

I liked being surprised that way; I didn't have to worry about it in advance. I blinked and just looked up at him when he let me go. And then he kissed me again.

We both smiled at each other afterward. So I laughed and said, "What was the second kiss for?"

"For k-keeping your mouth shut after the first one," he said.

I leaned back against his arm. "Well, if you don't practice not stuttering, what does your therapist have you do?" I asked.

"More s-stuttering."

"What?"

"He says the more I c-can do it openly and easily, the m-more I'll relax. And when I don't try so hard to fight it, I won't k-keep my tongue or my jaw or throat muscles so tense. And everyone else will feel more comfortable, too."

I sighed. "I wish it was the same for singing. No matter *how* relaxed I am, nobody wants to listen. I was practically banned from singing 'Happy Birthday' at parties when I was little."

Eric laughed out loud.

"In fact, when I was in grade school, and all the other kids were singing, the teacher gave me the triangle to play instead."

We both laughed that time. Eric kissed me again. "I like you b-better with your mouth closed," he said.

"See?" I told him. "Even *you* think so!"

When I called Pamela later, she asked, "How long did he stay?"

"I don't know. Another hour, anyway."

"He really *is* crazy about you, Alice!"

"Well, that's nice to know," I said.

"So, what are you going to do?"

"What do you mean?"

"I mean, he likes you, but he's a stutterer!"

"No, he's a guy who happens to stutter, along with a whole lot of other stuff he does very well, Pamela."

"Like what?"

"Like kissing," I told her, and we laughed.

11

THE COLOR PURPLE

Lester was in love.

Again.

Well, he didn't use the word "love," and he said it was an intense, intellectual relationship, but I know Lester, and he was more nuts over this woman than he'd been over someone in a long time. I figured any woman was better than his last girlfriend, Eva, a walking clothes hanger, who criticized everything he did. Several nights a week at the dinner table, Les told us about his conversations with Lauren that he said were helping to sharpen his mind.

"So what did we learn at school today?" I asked him brightly over the chili.

"Actually," said Lester, spearing a piece of broccoli, "we're comparing John Stuart Mills's distinction between higher and lower pleasures with Aristotle's Nicomachean Ethics."

I was sorry I'd asked. What I really wanted to know was what Lauren had said to him before or after class and what he'd said to Lauren. "What about lunch?" I asked. "Did you eat with her again?"

"Usually she eats in the faculty dining room, but sometimes I can persuade her to eat with me out on the grass, if the weather's nice. That's where we have our best discussions. Mills's approach, see, is that some pleasures are different and superior to others, and he chooses the higher pleasures, those of the mind versus those of the body."

"And you're for the pleasures of the body, of course," I said.

"Well, that's what we're discussing. Mills says that anyone who says the lower pleasures are better isn't qualified to judge, that you need to be trained and educated to appreciate the higher things. And while there may be some truth to that, I say that maybe the intellectual has lost the capacity to enjoy some of the lower pleasures."

"All work and no play makes Jack a dull boy?" I said helpfully, trying to condense the argument.

"You might say that, yes!" Lester said, and looked at me appreciatively as though I had actually said something important.

"And Lauren's view?" asked Dad.

"Well, right now we're discussing the fact that not *all* intellectuals have lost the capacity to enjoy the lower pleasures."

"You, for one," I said.

"Darned right." Lester sprinkled cheese over his chili and took another bite.

"These discussions over lunch," said Dad. "I assume that anyone can join in? Anyone passing by you out on the grass?"

Lester shrugged and thought about it a minute. "I suppose. We don't exactly put out a welcome sign, but if anyone came along and wanted to join in, we wouldn't stop them. We're just so intent on the conversation, we don't like to be disturbed."

Dad didn't say anything more. If anybody was disturbed, I'd say it was Dad.

Les and Lauren may have been intellectual buddies, but the fact that he wanted to bring her by the house to meet us obviously meant something, so I put on my best jeans and a clean shirt to look halfway decent.

My scar had almost healed—it hardly showed—and I was able to take gym again. I was so happy to be back in the World of Well that I felt I was ready for anything. Operations don't sound like much when they happen to someone else, but when they happen to you, when it's *your* mind that's going to sleep, and *your* body that's going to be cut open, it's not so casual anymore.

I ran the sweeper over the carpet and wiped out the bathroom sink. I also made a pitcher of iced tea and a quick-mix coffee cake. About four o'clock on Sunday, Les pulled up in front of the house, came around to the passenger side, and opened the door for the brown-haired woman in a blue short-sleeved sweater and slacks, wearing tiny pearl earrings and a floating pearl necklace. She was about the same height as Lester, with a small waist and broad hips—nice looking—more hand-some, I'd say, than beautiful.

Lester gallantly held one hand under her elbow as he guided her up the steps.

"Lauren, this is Alice, and my dad, Ben," he said, and we politely shook hands all around before we moved into the living room and I set about slicing the cake.

She had an interesting-looking face, but I think she was a little uneasy with us. There was a sort of forced self-confidence about her that made her begin each sentence louder than it ended up, as though she was trying to convince herself that she was still the instructor here, oblivious of the lovesick puppy look on Lester's face.

"How are you liking the University of Maryland?" Dad asked her, handing her a glass of iced tea.

"Well, I got my degree from Ohio State," she said, "and Maryland seems a bit more personal, more manageable. This is my first teaching job, and I was very lucky to get it, even though it's just adjunct instructor."

"She got the job because she's smart, period," Les said proudly.

Lauren gave him a fond, admonishing look. "And Les is one of my best students. He's the only graduate student taking my course, actually, but he needs it for his degree."

The coffee cake was pretty awful. I thought maybe I had taken it out of the oven too soon, because the center was gummy, and we all sort of ate around it, mauling our slices just enough to show we'd tried.

"Is the pay comparable with other universities?" Dad asked.

"I suppose so," said Lauren. "It's not a lot, but"—she stopped and smiled at Lester—"Les had been so good at showing me around—the least expensive restaurants, all the things there are to do on campus. He's been a great guide."

Obviously. Les never seemed to be home anymore. He was on campus every night. There, I'd guess, or Lauren's apartment, and I suspected the apartment.

She was originally from Tennessee, Lauren said, and Dad told her he was from Tennessee, too. They talked about Nashville and Memphis, while I poured more iced tea for everyone and had to keep running to the bathroom. I threw out the rest of the cake.

Nothing Lauren said indicated that Lester was more than a friend to her. But once, when I came back in the living room and Dad was out in the kitchen getting more ice, I noticed that Les was rubbing his thumb over her hand.

Eric invited me to a coffeehouse one evening. It was held in a church basement, where small tables had been set up with red-and-white-checked tablecloths, and a candle in the middle of each. Eric said there would be music and poetry and stuff.

"Are you going to read something?" I asked.

"No. Just listen over a c-cappuccino," he said.

Probably most of the people there were high-school seniors or college age, but we seemed to fit right in. I guess the coffeehouse was run by a singles group at the church, who served as waiters, and I ordered a mocha, which arrived under a heap of whipped cream and a cinnamon stick.

"So is this where you hang out?" I asked him.

"N-Not exactly," he said.

"But do you come here a lot?"

"Not exactly," Eric said, smiling.

I gave him a quizzical look. "Have you *ever* been here before?" I asked curiously.

"Nope," he said, and we both laughed. "I just w-wanted sssss-something different."

The first person to read was a man with a beard who read several far-out poems in a sort of dry, distant voice, and twice Eric rolled his eyes at me, asking if I wanted to leave, I guess. But after that a girl stood up and read a funny monologue about some of her fantasies when she rides the Metro. Then a guy played the guitar and sang, and by the end of the evening, though I could hear liquid sloshing around in my stomach whenever I changed position, we decided it had been fun.

Eric walked me home—all fourteen blocks—because it was a gorgeous spring night. We held hands, and I was thinking I could really get to like this guy, if only he were sticking around.

"Your moving to Dallas is definite then?" I asked.

"'Fraid so."

"Do you have any brothers or sisters? How do they feel about it?"

"A mm-married sister in Missouri, so it d-doesn't affect her."

"What does your mom think?"

"She's all fff-for it, because that's where she's from. We've g-got relatives all over T-Texas."

"Oh. So it's not like you're moving to a distant land or anything."

"N-No. In fact, I've g-got a ccccc-cousin who says she's going to ggg-give me a pppp-party when I get there. She sss-says I'll have girls swarming all over me."

I laughed. "Lucky you," I said.

"Lucky me," said Eric. Then he said. "I'd g-give it all to be with you."

"Ah!" I said. "What a great line, Eric! It sounds like the last line of a poem."

"Hmmm," said Eric, starting to smile as we walked along. Then he began, "'I wandered lonely as a cloud . . .'"

"'When all at once I saw a crowd . . .'" I put in, teasing, realizing that his class must be studying Wordsworth, too.

"No, no, that's the third line," Eric said. "It's 'That floats on high o'er vales and hills . . .'" He nodded at me to join in then, and we both said together, "'When all at once I saw a crowd, A host of golden daffodils.'"

Eric was grinning now. "Though Dallas beauties do await . . ."

I made up the next line: "Um . . . beneath a sky of azure blue . . ." We were really into it now, and I discovered that he didn't stutter when he was reciting something.

"And rosy lips shall be my fate . . . ," said Eric.

Together we ended with, "I'd give it all to be with you."

We gave each other a high five.

"Hey, we're really good!" I crowed. "Do you think we should read it at the coffeehouse sometime?" We both laughed. "I didn't know you liked poetry," I told him.

"I d-don't, exactly. Well, that's not true. Mom always read t-to us, so I like it, but I go mmm-more for the adventurous poems—'The Cremation of Sam Magee' and stuff."

I let my head rest on his shoulder. "Tonight was a lot of fun, Eric," I said. "I'm going to miss you."

He looked down at me. "There's e-mail, rrrr-remember?"

"Yes," I said. "How could I forget?"

We stopped and kissed then, a long, long kiss that would have been embarrassing it was so long if I'd thought he didn't mean it. It wasn't like Patrick's kisses. Eric's were a little more intense, maybe—sort of a signature kiss, all his own.

If I felt bad that Eric was leaving, the one thing I felt good about was that I didn't see Faith and Ron together anymore. They ate at separate tables in the cafeteria, and though I couldn't say that Faith looked happy, at least she wasn't being ordered around by "The Corporal," as we called Ron.

Pamela and Elizabeth had gone to the auditorium over

lunch one day to watch a fashion show put on by the home arts department, but I slipped outdoors to enjoy ten minutes of spring sunshine, and found Faith sitting on the school steps, hugging her knees, her eyes closed, face tilted toward the sun.

I sat down beside her. "You, too?" I said.

She opened her eyes. "Yeah. It feels so good. I'm always cold."

"Maybe you should take up basketball—get the blood circulating." I said. She didn't answer, so I added, "How are things?"

"Between Ron and me?" she asked.

"Well, that, too."

"I hear he's not dating anyone," she said.

"Surprise, surprise!" I said. "After the way he treated you, who would have him?"

"You only saw one side of him, Alice. I saw his tender side. Some guys hide part of themselves when they're around other people, you know? But when it was just the two of us, he was so incredibly loving."

I didn't know what to say. Finally I asked, "Did you ever wonder, though, why he felt the need to treat you like that in public?"

"Yes." She laughed a little. "It was just his defense. He's really an old softie inside."

"But . . . doesn't it bother you that he had to be so controlling, Faith? I mean, it was as though he didn't want you to have any friends except him."

"It's just that he needed me so much, Alice." She shrugged. "And sometimes it's nice to be needed."

"Oh, Faith, you've got so much going for you! You've got a whole lifetime ahead of you and . . ." I sounded like Aunt Sally.

"I know, I know. I'm just reliving old memories. Just a slight case of sunstroke, that's all," she said.

"I would hope so," I told her, and laughed.

The most difficult part of my freshman year was not the course work (except for algebra) or finding my way around. It was juggling all the different parts of my life. And I didn't even have a boyfriend. Not officially, anyway. Eric may have been seeing other girls, for all I knew, and he never asked if I was seeing anyone else. We didn't go out every weekend or anything like that, and he never called. We were just friends. Erotically-charged friends, I supposed Les would say.

It helped that *Fiddler on the Roof* was over, but there was still my work on the newspaper, my assignments, my Saturday job at the Melody Inn, my friends and family, the housework. I was very careful to do something each week with Elizabeth and Pamela, but Dad seemed to be asking me to do more and more around the house to get it ready for Sylvia, and there just weren't enough hours in the day to do everything.

I was complaining about it to Marilyn at work on Saturday. "I'm only one person!" I cried. "I have only two arms and two legs."

Marilyn was sorting though mail orders to see which had

been filled and which were still waiting for supplies to come in. "Doesn't Les help out?" she asked.

"He's so crazy over this new girlfriend that he—" I stopped.

"It's okay, Alice," she said.

But I knew it wasn't okay. It would never be okay as far as Marilyn was concerned, because I didn't think she'd ever gotten over him.

"So tell me about her. What's she like? I promise not to cry," she said.

"She's a new philosophy instructor at the U, and I don't think Dad's too happy about it."

"If she's faculty, then she should know better than to date a student," Marilyn said.

"I guess there's no reasoning with a woman in love," I said. I paused, realizing suddenly that Marilyn did *not* look especially sad, did *not* have tears in her eyes. In fact, she was taking it very well. "So what's new with you?" I asked.

"I'm dating again," she said.

"The trombone teacher?" I said, thinking of all the men who gave music lessons in the practice cubicles upstairs.

"No. He's a guitarist who plays with a group in Baltimore. A friend introduced us."

"That's great!" I said. "How long have you been seeing him?"

"About a month now."

"No wonder you look so sparkly!" I told her, and she laughed.

***

Dad had gotten up early Sunday morning to make waffles, and left the batter for Les and me. I was making a second waffle when he stumbled into the kitchen in his T-shirt and boxer shorts. It was one of the pairs we'd given him for his birthday, with a lipstick pattern all over it, red ruby lips half parted for a sensuous kiss.

"You want this waffle?" I asked. "If you want it, it's yours."

"Never look a gift horse in the mouth," said Les. "Sure."

"What does a horse have to do with anything?" I asked.

"Never mind," said Les. He poured himself some coffee and sat down at the table.

I slid the waffle toward him, then the butter and syrup, and sat down across the table. I knew he and Lauren had gone to a concert the evening before. "Have a good time last night?" I asked.

"The best."

"Good concert?"

"Passable. But the company was excellent." Lauren, he meant.

There was something about the satisfied look on his face that made me study him a little more intently, and then I saw a large hickey mark on the side of his neck. That *really* made me worry. Just how intimate were they? I wondered. What if he got Lauren pregnant? What if she lost her job? What if Lester suddenly found himself a husband and father and he wasn't even though grad school yet? What if he grew to resent her and reject the baby, and Dad and Sylvia and I would have to take the baby in, and I'd be the aunt who raised this little child who . . . ?

"Lester, you *are* using birth control, aren't you?" I gasped.

The fork fell out of his hand. "What?"

"You're so in love with her, and—"

"Al, can it! I'm more than seven years older than you, and I don't ask if *you* use birth control, do I?"

"I don't."

"What?" he said again. "Meaning . . . ?"

Dad came back in the kitchen to refill his coffee cup. "What are we talking about?" he asked.

"I'm not sure," said Lester.

"Birth control," I said.

"*What?*" cried Dad.

"What" was the favorite word at breakfast that morning, it seemed.

"If Les and Lauren aren't using any kind of birth control, Dad, I think we ought to decide right now if we can accept the responsibility of a little baby in our house while Lester finishes school so he won't abandon his wife and child," I said.

"*What?*" yelled Lester. "I thought we were talking about you, Al."

Dad's head swiveled from one of us to the other. He decided to focus on me. Almost in a panic, he said, "If you're thinking of having sex at the age of fourteen, Al, forget it. But if you decide to have sex anyway, I hope you will go to Dr. Beverly and discuss it confidentially."

"None of the above," I said. "It's Les I'm worried about."

"Well, then, I wish you'd stop," said Lester. "Lauren and I are both adults, and I can handle myself just fine."

"I hope you're right," Dad said, and had to sit down right then to get his bearings.

Elizabeth was having another fight with her folks. She called and asked if she could spend the night, and I told her to come over in about an hour. Gwen was there helping me with algebra, and I couldn't take on Elizabeth's problems until I'd solved my own.

Gwen had told me once she wanted to be a singer. "You should be a teacher," I said. "I can't make sense of algebra in class, but when you explain it, I can catch on enough to squeak by."

"Lack of self-confidence, girl. That's your problem," she said.

"Huh-uh. Lack of intelligence."

"What's with Elizabeth?"

"She's coming over to spend the night. Problems with her folks again."

"Looks like you're running some kind of shelter here," Gwen said, smiling.

"For wayward girls," I told her. "You want to stay?"

"Can't. Told my grandfather I'd be home in time to play him a game of cards," she said, and grinned.

What I couldn't figure was that Elizabeth got mad at her parents over every little thing these days. She'd been in therapy now for about four or five months, and though I think she was feeling better about herself, her parents were feeling worse. I could see that she might be mad at them for not having suspected that their friend had been molesting her when she was younger, but it seemed as though she was going to hold it against them forever. I even began to wonder if she hadn't already worked this through and was just using it as an excuse to rebel against any other thing she didn't like about them. Elizabeth had been such a dutiful daughter for so long that, now that she'd had a taste of what it felt like to rebel, she couldn't get enough of it, it seemed. Pamela and Gwen and I just wondered how far she'd go.

"Elizabeth's coming over to spend the night," I told Dad. "And she's upset."

"Man the lifeboats," said Lester.

"Do her parents know she'll be here?" Dad asked, not wanting a replay of what had happened last summer when Pamela once spent the night.

"They know," I said. "At this point they're probably glad to get rid of her."

I was at least half right, because Elizabeth walked in dressed in purple from head to toe. She had tinted her hair purple, was wearing purple eye shadow, mascara, lipstick, and nail polish, and had on a long, granny-style purple dress with a purple stole.

Now what? I wondered.

Once in my room, she whirled around and faced me. "I *like* it, okay?" she snapped.

"Did I say anything?" I asked. "You can paint your behind purple for all I care, Liz. Don't jump on me!"

"Sorry." She dropped her bag on the floor and stood with her arms folded, staring out the window. "No matter what I do, they're against it!" she complained. "Every little thing."

I smiled a little and studied her some more. "Sure you're not just trying to get a rise out of them?"

"I *like* purple!"

"So, fine! You look good in it! Just come up for air occasionally, will you?"

"You know what, Alice? I don't know who I am," she said ruefully.

"You're Elizabeth," I told her. "Take a seat and stay awhile."

"Hey, Al!" said Lester. "You've got a birthday coming up. The big ol' one five!"

"Yeah?" I said. "What's the proper gift for a fifteenth birthday, Lester? Rubies? Emeralds? Sapphires?"

"Plastic," said Les.

"Les-ter!"

"No, seriously. I thought of something else. I told Lauren I wanted to do something special for your birthday, and she suggested taking you to a show in Baltimore—a play, actually—a spoof on Italian weddings called *Tony 'n' Tina's Wedding*."

"Oh, Les! Really? I've heard kids talk about it."

"You seemed to have such a good time with *Fiddler on the Roof*. I could get tickets for us next Friday night, the day before your birthday. They were sold out on Saturday."

I threw my arms around him. Going somewhere with Les was always special. Then I wondered if I had to share him with Lauren.

"Is Lauren coming too?" I asked.

SIMPLY ALICE • 359

"No, she has something else going on."

Good! I thought. "How should I dress?"

"Like you're going to a wedding, I suppose. The audience is part of it, I think."

I wish he'd said I could bring some friends, but knowing how expensive tickets were these days, I knew he was already spending far over his budget.

"We could go Dutch," I said. "I've got some money saved."

"Hey, kiddo. It's your birthday. It's on me," he said. "Just don't do anything to embarrass me, okay?"

12
TONY AND TINA

Aunt Sally and Uncle Milt had sent me a check for my birthday, and I splurged on a dress I really loved. Marilyn went with me on a lunch hour at the Melody Inn to buy it. It looked sort of like a slip—just a short, backless, cream-colored sheath that covered the front of me, but was completely bare in back from the waist up except for the halter strap around the neck and two thin strings that tied below it.

I giggled when I saw myself in the mirror. So did Marilyn.

"Lester will have a spaz," she said, "but it's good for his heart. He needs to exercise it a bit." We giggled some more.

"Now shoes," said Marilyn. "You need something light."

"I have a pair of beige flats with thin cross-straps over the top," I told her.

"Perfect," she said.

"But what do I do for a bra?" I wondered, checking the dress again.

Marilyn put her hand to my ear. "You don't wear one," she said.

"But . . . my *nipples*!"

"So you have two little points down there. It's not against the law."

"But, Dad—"

"I know. Better not let your dad see you in it at all."

"Oh, Marilyn, I love this dress, but do you think I should?" I asked her.

"Be adventurous," she said. "And blame it on me."

Fortunately, the night we were to go to *Tony 'n' Tina's Wedding*, Dad was going to a chamber music concert with the clarinet instructor from the store and his wife, and they left before we did. I waited till he was out the door and down the drive before I put on my new dress and came downstairs, where Lester, in his good sport coat and pants, was reading the paper.

"I'm ready," I said.

"Good for you! Right on time," he said, looking at his watch. "Never keep a date waiting if you can help it." He looked me over. "Nice dress."

"Thank you," I said.

"Except for your . . . uh . . . mammary glands," he said.

"Can't you sort of walk round-shouldered so they're not so prominent?"

"Don't be ridiculous, Les," I said, and started for the door.

"Al!" he gasped. "You're naked back there!"

I tried not to laugh. "I am not. There are strings—"

"What if some guy reached out and pulled them?"

"They'd untie, I suppose," I said. "But there's still the halter strap."

"But . . . there's nothing at the sides! A guy could slip his hand in there!"

"Not with you here to protect me," I said. "You sound like Aunt Sally, Lester. Don't tell me you wouldn't be delighted if Lauren wore a dress like this."

"You're not Lauren, Al. You're fourteen years old."

"Fifteen tomorrow," I said.

"In that dress, you're jailbait."

I just smiled sweetly. "Shall we go?"

One of the things I like about my brother is that when he offers to take me someplace, he treats me like a grown-up. He's not patronizing, doesn't act as though he can't wait for the evening to be over. It *was* my birthday present, after all.

So we headed toward the beltway and the road that would take us to Baltimore, and I had to keep reminding myself that I was dressed. I'll admit, though, I felt as naked as Lester thought I looked. I wasn't used to feeling the back of the car seat against my bare shoulder blades, but I looked, well, *sexy* in front, the shape of my thighs under the thin fabric of my dress, no slip underneath.

"Am I dressed appropriately for the occasion, Les?" I asked. "I mean, do I look as though I'm going to a wedding?"

"No, you look as though you're going to work in a strip joint."

"Les-ter!"

"A *nice* strip joint, I mean."

"*Les*-ter!"

"A really classy dump."

"Lester, I don't care what you say, I am going to Tony and Tina's wedding in this dress and I think I look ravishing."

"So you do. That's why I worry."

Lester pulled up to the address that was on our tickets, and after we'd parked, we went inside and up the stairs, where a crowd of people were milling about a lobby outside a makeshift chapel. Immediately a grandmotherly-looking woman in a navy blue dress came up to me and said, "It's been ages! Oh, you look so good, and you should see Tina! She's absolutely beautiful."

While I was still staring, an elderly man grabbed Lester by the arm and kept shaking his hand up and down, saying, "So glad you could come! So glad! I've got another grandchild since I saw you last. Look here at little Anna." And he pulled out a worn plastic picture folder with photos of people we had never seen before, and I guess we were supposed to play along, because Les said, "And look at little Teddy there. He's the spittin' image of you, Gramps!" The man laughed and slapped Les on the shoulder, and ambled off to show his pictures to someone else. I grinned at Lester, and he grinned back. This was going to be fun.

"You want a 7UP or something?" he asked.

"Sure."

We had to stop by a desk to turn in our tickets and were given our table number for the reception. The woman sitting there was obviously doubling as a bridesmaid. Two men in tuxedos were arguing loudly nearby as to which one had dated the bride most recently, and everyone was watching and laughing. It was as though we were all onstage, and none of us knew our lines, but it didn't really matter. We were just part of the chorus. As long as I didn't have to sing, I didn't really care *what* happened.

While Les was at the bar getting my soft drink, a third man in a tuxedo sidled up to me and said how much he liked my dress. "An extraordinary dress," he said, examining it from all angles.

Les moved in. "Excuse me, she's with me," he said.

The tuxedoed man put up his hands. "Hey, hey! No offense! Just looking, no touching."

Then a large guy wearing shades, who looked like a member of the Mafia, stepped up on a chair and bellowed, "Okay now, all youse who came to celebrate the marriage of my buddy Tony to his dame shoulda got your table assignments by now, and you can put your drinks down where you can find 'em later and go in the chapel there. No fair takin' somebody else's drink when you come out, either, if you're too cheap to buy your own."

We laughed and headed toward a door with fake stained glass, and found ourselves in a small chapel with flowers in front. Les and I sat down next to the aisle because I wanted to see the bride when she came in. The old grandfather was the first relative to come in, though, and he was still stopping along the aisle to show off pictures of his grandchildren. Then the father of the groom came in with his new trophy wife in a very low-cut red dress with black fishnet stockings, and finally the mother of the bride, who had greeted us when we first arrived.

The recorded organ music began, and an actor in priest's robes stood up in front along with a nun who was supposed to be a relative of the bride.

It was a funny ceremony, with the grandfather having to go to the bathroom in the middle of it, the nun leading the congregation in a rousing hymn she'd written herself, then the wedding procession, with one of the bridesmaids obviously pregnant and chewing gum.

Tony, the groom, was too laid back to suit the priest, and Tina, a beautiful actress, was annoyed with him because he kept forgetting what to do. But at last they were "married," and we all went to a large room for the reception and dinner.

Les and I were seated at a table where we could see both the wedding party at their table and the dance floor, and there was something going on every minute. Having taken part in the school production, I could appreciate all that the actors and actresses had to do, because they had to improvise a lot, and they doubled as waiters and waitresses, wheeling out the steam tables, dishing up the food, and organizing the buffet line.

We never knew what was going to happen next because the actors kept mixing with the audience, coming by and pretending they knew everyone, as though we were all relatives. Of course one of the bridesmaids got a little "drunk," and somebody's aunt "fainted." Tony and Tina themselves got into an argument because she thought he had insulted her mother, but toasts were made, then there was dancing, and when one of the ushers invited me out on the dance floor, Les just smiled and shrugged. "Enjoy," he said.

While we were dancing, though, the actor kept peering around at the back of my dress, making the audience laugh, and then he began fumbling with the strings as though he were going to untie them. Tina, who was dancing with her "father," reached over and slapped his hands, and everyone laughed again, including me. When he took me back to our table, Les grinned, and I admitted I'd actually enjoyed being out there on the dance floor, like I was one of the performers myself. It was fun going along with the act.

Then the father of the groom insulted the mother of the bride, the father's new wife climbed up on a table and began dancing, the nun kept trying to lead the audience in song, and the tipsy bridesmaid came over to our table and invited Les to dance. "C'mon, honey," she said. "I've had my eye on you all evening."

Wanting to be a good sport, he got up and escorted her out on the floor with some other couples.

For the first few minutes they danced like everyone else, the tipsy bridesmaid smiling at him and flirting. Les rolled his eyes at me as they waltzed by our table, and I laughed. But then the bridesmaid began leaning more and more heavily against Les, as though she were barely able to stand up straight, and he struggled more and more to hold her up. She put her head on his shoulder, one arm draped around his neck, and when they danced by a second time, I saw that her other hand was tightly clutching the seat of his pants.

There were a lot of other crazy things going on around the room, but the people in the audience who were sitting nearest me saw the little drama going on between Lester and the bridesmaid. More and more people began watching, laughing and pointing, and I could tell that the bridesmaid was not about to stop and let him go. In fact, when she wasn't scrunching up his pants, she was drumming a tattoo on Lester's behind.

For one of the few times I could remember, I saw Lester blush. His neck, his cheeks, his forehead were pink, and he was good-naturedly trying to extricate himself from the woman, but she wasn't about to let him go. The more he tried to edge her back to a table, the more she clung to him, and Lester, his face really red now, resigned, kept on gallantly moving her around the floor while she played with his bottom.

I don't know how I had the nerve—emboldened maybe by being Charlene's substitute in *Fiddler*, or the fact that the audience was supposed to play along with the story, or maybe because I knew that no matter how outrageously I behaved, I'd never see any of these people again. But I suddenly got up from the table and, taking my 7UP glass with me to look more sophisticated—it was in a wine goblet—I edged out onto the dance floor and over to Lester and the bridesmaid. I couldn't tell if Les was more relieved or alarmed, but I tapped the bridesmaid on her broad back and said, "Excuse me, I'm cutting in."

I saw some of the other actors glance around, amused.

The bridesmaid never got out of character for a moment. She opened one eye to look at me sideways and, in a slurred voice, said, "Yeah? You and who else?"

"You're dancing with my fiancé," I told her.

"Well, sweetie, I think your fi-an-say fancies *me*, if I say so myself," she said, and plunked her head on Lester's shoulder again.

I was really in the spirit of things now, and everyone was looking at us and smiling. It was all a big joke, I knew, and they were playing for laughs, but there was a slight edge of anger roiling up inside me, too. I had to save my brother!

I tapped her again. "I want him back," I said.

She kept her head next to his, her lips an inch away from his face, and said, "She wants you back. Imagine that. Well, she can't have you, luv, 'cause you're mine. Alllllll mine!"

Les was beet red now.

She turned her body so that she and Les were dancing away from me. I simply held out my hand and poured my 7UP right down her back.

Everyone gasped, but the other actors and actresses were laughing, and a couple of them even applauded.

The bridesmaid instantly let go of Les and stared at me. And then, actress that she was—and mindful that I was a paying customer—said, "Well don't have a hissy fit, sweetheart. He's all yours!" and she huffily left the floor, the large dark stain spreading out over the back of her dress.

I set my empty glass on the nearest table, smiled sweetly at Lester, and put one hand on his shoulder as he danced me around the floor. Everyone was smiling at us.

"Hey, babe, I didn't know you had it in you," he said, looking slightly stunned.

"Neither did I," I said, and gazed at him with fake adoration. It was so much fun. Everyone figured we were a couple. So this was what it felt like to be one of Lester's girlfriends, I thought; this was the way it was for Crystal and Marilyn and Eva when they danced with him. For Lauren, too, maybe. Except they were in love with him, and I simply loved him as a brother.

I lifted my head and looked into his eyes again. "Les, do you remember the time you took me out to a club on my thirteenth birthday and while you were in the restroom this guy came on to me, and you rescued me?"

"Yeah. How could I forget?"

"So now we're even," I said.

"Thanks," said Lester.

The bridesmaid came back with a big towel stuffed down the back of her dress, and that made it all the funnier. Every time she passed our table she hissed at me and gave me dirty looks, but I could tell she was enjoying herself as much as anyone.

I guess when you put on the same play night after night, you hope something spontaneous will happen to liven things up. You want the audience to react and keep you going—anything to help your performance.

As soon as the wedding cake was cut and served, Les said. "You ready to call it a night, Al? Should we duck out?"

"I'm ready," I told him. "We've got to drive back to Silver Spring." We moved over to the door where some of the wedding party were saying good-bye to guests. The bridesmaid was at the end of the line, and when I got to her, she smiled and gave me a quick kiss on the cheek. "No hard feelings, luv," she said, and gave me the rose in her hair as a memento. As we started up the stairs, however, she reached out and gave Lester a pinch on the behind.

I'd forgotten that Dad would be home before we would, but when I saw him, I burst into the living room, full of our evening, wanting to tell him everything.

"Al!" he said, before I'd got a whole sentence out. "Where's your dress?"

I looked down quickly, afraid it had somehow fallen off. "What?"

"Uh . . . that *is* her dress," Lester said, throwing his suit coat over the back of a chair.

Dad was horrified. "It's just a slip!"

I decided I might as well get this over with, so I struck a modeling pose and turned slowly around.

For a moment, Dad was speechless. He stared first at me, then at Lester. "You let her *go* like that?"

"Well, Pops, she *is* fifteen. And I was along to see that nothing happened."

"And you're going to go along every time she wears that dress?" Dad asked.

"Dad, backless dresses are *in* now! You should see what the prom dresses look like this year!" I told him.

Dad leaned back against the sofa and shook his head. "I don't think I'm ready for this, Al," he said.

"Marilyn thought I looked great in it, and so did . . ." I started to say "all the men at *Tony 'n' Tina's Wedding*" but I knew that would send Dad over the edge. "So did Lester," I finished.

"Well, it *is* a nice-looking dress," Lester admitted.

"Come here," Dad said to me, and when I walked over, he sat me on one knee. I laughed.

"I can remember," he said, "when you were only a year old, in a little pink playsuit, and I'd bounce you on my foot."

"I don't remember that at all," I said.

"Of course. You were too young, And when you were three . . .

four . . . wearing your OshKosh overalls, you'd sit in my lap and snuggle back against me while I read *Goodnight, Moon* or *Little Bear's Visit*. And now here you are, almost all grown up, attracting the glances of admiring men. . . ." He smiled at me and patted my hand. "I wish I could put you in a protective bubble, hon, and keep you safe forever, but I know I can't."

"She'd miss all the fun," said Lester.

"I know," said Dad.

"I'd never meet anybody," I told him.

"I know," said Dad.

"I'd probably grow up to be neurotic as anything."

"I know," Dad said again.

"And I'd never marry or get a job, and I'd be on your and Lester's hands for the rest of my life," I added, leaning over to kiss his forehead.

"Whoa! No plastic bubble for her, Dad!" cried Lester. "Zip, zero, zed!"

13
THE INSTRUCTOR FLAP

Elizabeth and Pamela had already given me earrings for my birthday, and Eric sent balloons, but the next day, my official birthday, Dad gave me time off from the Melody Inn to go to the movies with Molly—her present to me. We'd gotten there early and bought a large tub of popcorn to share between us. I told her about *Tony 'n' Tina's Wedding* and how I'd had to rescue Lester.

"I wish I'd been there to see that," Molly said. "You just reached out and poured your drink down her dress?"

"It was all I could think of to do." I giggled. "She wasn't about to let go, and she looked like she was trying to give Les a wedgie." We laughed some more. "What's surprising to me is that I actually enjoyed myself, everyone looking at me. I didn't think I'd have the nerve."

"I *know* I wouldn't!" Molly said.

"Maybe I'll try out for the senior play when the time comes," I said. "I probably wouldn't get a part, but—"

"Nothing ventured, nothing gained," Molly finished for me.

We heard a familiar voice several rows back.

"I thought you said 'buttered,'" came a girl's voice.

Then a guy's: "I said *un*buttered. Salt, no butter."

"So?"

"So go get me salt, no butter."

"Oh, Ron—"

We turned to see Faith getting up, setting the unwanted popcorn on her seat and heading up the aisle again as Ron put his feet on the back of the seat in front of him. Incredibly, he took a big handful of the popcorn he'd said he didn't want.

Molly and I stared at each other. "She went *back* to him?" I said in disbelief.

"Looks that way."

"Why?"

"A glutton for punishment, I guess," said Molly.

After the movie we went to the restroom and Faith was there, waiting in line.

"Faith, what happened? I thought you broke up with Ron," I said. Tactful, that's me.

She shrugged self-consciously and gave a little laugh.

"Who can explain love?" she said, and ducked into a cubicle.

Molly and I went to a Starbucks afterward and sat at a little table, still musing about Faith.

"That's not love, that's an addiction," Molly said.

"That's why I want to be a psychologist," I said. "I want to know why. No, I want to stop it before it begins."

"Good luck," said Molly.

When I got home, a small, flat package was waiting for me from Sylvia. I opened it and found the framed photo of her and me that was taken at White Flint Mall over spring vacation. I had sort of a weird smile on my face in the picture, but it wasn't bad. It looked like a mother and daughter having lunch together, and I wondered if I really would get used to calling her Mom.

Of course I had to call Elizabeth and Pamela and tell them about *Tony 'n' Tina's Wedding*, and they laughed at the way the bridesmaid had danced with Lester.

"The next time we come over, we each should pinch him on the buns," said Pamela. "I'd do it just to see Lester blush."

"Well, it takes a lot to embarrass Lester," I told her.

We call May the Mad Month at school because it's so frantic. There's statewide testing, for one, and all big assignments are due. The seniors who have applied for colleges know where they've been accepted, and while they might feel they can slide through till graduation, the freshmen and sophomores and juniors aren't so lucky.

Eric and I went for ice cream after lunch one day, and sauntered back to school, cones in hand.

"I ggg-guess we're g-going to b-b-be moving n-next
m-month," Eric said, and I'd never heard him stutter so much
in one sentence. But he didn't seem at all upset by it.

"Does your dad have a house already?" I asked.

"Yeah. It's about the ssss-size of the one we've gggg-got
nnnn-now." He was smiling at me.

I smiled back quizzically. "You aren't doing that on purpose,
are you?"

"D-Doing w-what? M-Moving?"

"Stuttering."

He laughed. "You guessed."

"Why?"

"It's an assignment. D-Desensitizing myself, so I won't freak
out when I sss-stutter. I'll get so used to stuttering more in public, I won't fight it."

"I don't know anything about stuttering," I said, "but that
makes sense. The more you try to keep from doing something,
the more scared you are it'll happen."

"I'm learning to just let it c-come," he said.

"Okay b-by m-me," I said, and we laughed.

Dad and I were sharing a supper of baked beans, corn bread,
and tomatoes when he said, "You know, Al, if you want to work
full time at the store this summer, we can use you, but I don't
know if this is good for you or not."

"What do you mean?"

"Well, it's the same thing you've been doing, working for your dad. You're not getting out and exploring the world."

"I'm not exactly climbing Mount Everest, no," I said. "But if you'd like to send me to Paris . . ."

"I thought what might be an ideal arrangement would be for you to work for me part of the summer, but take a few weeks, at least, to do something else."

"Dad, who's going to hire me for only a few weeks?"

He handed me the Style section of the *Washington Post*, where he'd checkmarked an article on summer camps for children and, in a side column, a few camps that ran for only a few weeks and needed assistant counselors, fourteen years of age or older.

I tried to think about what Dad was really saying. It was true I wasn't getting a lot of experience just working for him all summer. But I wondered if part of it wasn't his need to be alone more with Sylvia before the wedding—just have her here getting used to our house, making suggestions for redecorating, cooking together, all the little domestic things they'd be doing after they were married—without me around putting in my two cents' worth.

"I'll think about it," I told him.

I called Gwen to see if she was interested, and she said maybe. I called Elizabeth. "I'll be willing," she said. "Let's do an overnight camp if we can get it. Mom and I need to be apart for a while before we kill each other."

I would never in a million years have believed that Elizabeth would say something like that; she was always so close to her mom. But maybe the fact that she could bring out negative feelings like this, even jokingly, was a good sign. Maybe she'd just never felt before that she could.

I called Pam next, and she said almost the same thing. "Dad got a letter from Mom. She wants to come back," she said.

"What?"

"She walked out on the NordicTrack instructor and moved in with another guy, and he left her, and now she wants to come home. Dad says no way. If she does come back and they start fighting again, I'm going to move out, I swear it. See if you can get a camp that runs all summer, Alice."

You know what's weird? Life. All these years, it seems, I've been looking for a mom, and now that I'm about to get one, I'm planning on going away. And Pamela and Elizabeth, who've had one all their lives, want nothing more than to get away from theirs. Once Dad and Sylvia marry, though, I think she'll be the kind of mom I want to be around always. She's never been a mother, of course, but she's been a teacher, and it can't be that much different, can it?

I called all the camps listed in the *Post* to find out more about them. The only one that sounded just about right was Camp Overlook, near Cumberland, Maryland: three weeks, from June 18 to July 10. The director said she'd need to interview all four of us, but she was impressed when I told her that Gwen and I had volunteered last summer to work in a hospital, and that

Elizabeth and Pamela and I had spent some of spring vacation reading to kids at the Martin Luther King Library.

When the forms came, we each filled one out. Had we ever been arrested for driving while intoxicated? Had we ever used illegal drugs? Had we ever been arrested for abusing children? Shoplifting? I wondered if they were going to take our fingerprints, too.

The last day of school, when classes were officially over, we went to the interview together in Rockville. Pamela's dad drove us over, and Lester said he'd pick us up.

Our interview was in the county office building, and Camp Overlook, we found out, was run by the county specifically for underprivileged children in foster homes.

Miss Martinez looked us in the eye. "You're going to get a lot of sad-faced youngsters in need of far more than what three weeks at camp could possibly give them. Some will come with a chip on their shoulder, angry at life and angry at you, and all of them come with a certain amount of emotional baggage. The most we can hope for in that short a time is to give them a break from the kinds of lives they've lived and get them to smile. We're not miracle workers, though we do see miracles now and then."

I think all four of us were wondering if we could do this, but Miss Martinez looked thoughtful. "These kids are all going to come back to the very same problems they've had before, but perhaps a little better equipped to deal with them. We do try to set aside some time each day for our counselors to unwind and socialize with one another, but basically you will be on call twenty-four hours a day. A kid may need you in the middle of the night. He may be scared or angry or confused or sick or home-sick or all of the above. Many of them have never even been in the woods before, or seen a lake. This is your chance to make a difference, even a small one. If you don't think you can take their constant need for attention, then this job isn't for you."

She smiled at us and waited. "There's no disgrace in saying you can't handle it, you know. But we'd rather find out now than after you get there. Your room and meals, of course, are free."

Elizabeth and Pamela and Gwen and I sat mutely mulling it over.

"I think I can do it," said Gwen.

"It doesn't sound easy, but I want to try," said Elizabeth.

"Me too," said Pamela and I nodded.

"Okay," Miss Martinez said. "If you change your minds, please don't wait till the last minute to tell me. You'll each be getting more information in the mail about what to bring with you, and it will tell you a lot more about the camp. Any other questions?" We shook hands as though we were mature adult women, and felt very grown up as we sat out on the steps wait-ing for Lester.

"What I *really* wanted to ask was whether any guys had signed up for assistant counselors, but I was afraid I'd jinx my application," said Pamela.

"Do you think we can really stand three weeks of constant 'neediness'?" I asked.

"It'll give me a break from being on call at home," Gwen smiled. "There's always an aunt or a grandmother wanting something."

Elizabeth said, "I asked myself if I could stand a whole cabin full of kids acting like Nathan at his crankiest, but these are older kids, six to ten, so I think I can deal with that. At least they can say what's wrong, not just fuss."

Lester drove up and my three friends piled in back. I sat up front with him. "Home, James!" I said grandly.

"So? How did it go?" he asked.

"We're hired!" Elizabeth said. "You'll be rid of us for three whole weeks this summer, Lester. What will you do without us?"

"Celebrate," he said.

We all trooped inside for a while, eager to talk about what we'd take to camp. Les said he was going upstairs to study, could we please keep our shouts and groans and giggles to sixty decibels?

"Sure, Les," Pamela said and, as he started up the steps, she reached out and pinched his buns.

After dinner that night, Lester got a phone call from Lauren. He answered on the phone in the downstairs hall but, after talking a few minutes, he said to me as I passed, "Al, I'm going to take this call upstairs. Would you hang up down here?"

"Sure," I said.

I held the phone to my ear while Les went upstairs. When I heard him pick up, I lowered the phone, but not before I'd heard him say, "Lauren, there's got to be a way around this."

I put the handset back in the cradle and wondered what he was talking about. Then I sat on the couch waiting for him to come back down. My first thought, of course, was that Lauren was pregnant, except I wasn't at all sure they'd been sleeping together. Or maybe she belonged to a strict religion and wasn't supposed to marry outside the faith. Or maybe she was taking a job in Alaska.

Dad was trying out some new sheet music at the piano, and then he just set it aside and played one of his favorite Beethoven sonatas, one that Sylvia especially liked, and smiled as he played.

I didn't want to ruin the piece, but as soon as he finished, I asked, "What's going on with Les and Lauren?"

Dad shrugged. "Is something going on?"

"That was Lauren on the phone. They've been talking for twenty-five minutes."

"You've been known to go for an hour or more," he said.

"I know, but he seemed so serious."

"Well, if he wants to tell us, he will," Dad said.

The phone rang again around nine, Jill wanting to know about an assignment. I realized then that Les and Lauren's conversation was over, but he hadn't come back downstairs.

When he hadn't come down by eleven, though, I went on up, washed my face, and put on my pajamas. When I came out of the bathroom, I saw that Lester's door was open and his room was empty. Then I heard him and Dad talking down in the kitchen.

I knew I shouldn't eavesdrop. In fact, I felt sure now that Les had been waiting for me to go to bed so he could talk to Dad. But I felt I had to know. If my brother was in trouble, it was my business, too, wasn't it? I was part of the family, too.

I made my way downstairs one step at a time until I could hear most of what they said.

"I hate to say I told you so, Les, but I think you knew this was a possibility," Dad was saying.

"I know, I know. I just didn't think they'd come down on her so hard. She's certainly allowed to have friends. I think she's overreacting to a few remarks people may have made. She admits that no one came right out and said she couldn't go on seeing me. . . ."

"What's at stake here is her impartiality, Les," said Dad. "She wasn't just dating a student, she was dating one of *her* students. You've been getting excellent grades in her class—deserved, I've no doubt—but it would be hard to prove that she wasn't favoring you."

"But we could still see each other off campus! I don't have any more courses with her, so how could it hurt? Why do we have to break it off completely?"

So that was it! For only the second time in his life, maybe, Les had been dumped. There was a quiver in his voice, and it always scares me when Dad or Lester is in pain.

"Maybe she was just plain scared and wants to rectify a

foolish mistake. She'd undoubtedly like to become a professor, and doesn't want to jeopardize that," said Dad.

"But if I could just talk with her face-to-face . . . ! We . . . we love each other, Dad."

There was silence in the kitchen. Finally Dad said, "Are you sure of that now?"

"Well, I love her, and I thought . . . You think she's using this as an excuse to break up with me? Is that it?"

"I don't know. All I'm saying is that if she sees a way around it and wants to renew the relationship, I'm sure she'll let you know. Maybe she needs time to think it over."

There was real anguish in Lester's voice now, and I could hardly bear listening to him: "I can't just let her go! She owes me a better explanation than this!"

Dad's voice rose. "Les, be reasonable. I know this hurts, but she owes you nothing. She was new in town, you were a ready and willing guide—a friend—and I'm sure she valued your friendship. But is it possible you read more into the relationship than what was there?"

"Don't tell *me* what was in our relationship and what wasn't! What do *you* know about it!" Les snapped.

"I don't, although—"

"Well, then, butt out, Dad! You don't know anything about it; we were a lot closer than you think."

"In that case, this relationship can only lead to more trouble for her, Les, and if you care for her, you won't put her in harm's way," Dad shot back.

I wanted so much to go down and put my arms around Lester, but I went back up the stairs, instead, and into his room. I left a note on his pillow.

> *Luv you, Les.*
> *Me*

It wasn't the same, I knew, and it wouldn't help much, but there are times I think people need every little bit of love they can get.

14
CHANGES

I guess if I had to sum up my freshman year in one word, it would be "changes." I came out of my shell and got "involved," as Pamela was always telling me to do, while Pam and Liz sort of took a time-out. I made new friends and almost lost Elizabeth and Pamela because of it, and Les, in a strange turn of events, got dropped by a girl instead of being the dropper. It seemed as though the only person whose life wasn't on a roller coaster was Dad, and if anybody deserved some happiness, Dad was the one.

Frankly, I couldn't understand why Les and Lauren couldn't at least date over the summer, and hang out where no one could see them. But Lauren would be teaching some summer courses, and Les would be on campus taking a course, so it would still be a faculty-student no-no, and Les was taking it hard.

The first day of summer vacation, I gave myself the pleasure of eating breakfast in my pajamas. Les was already up, getting ready for his part-time job in a shoe store. He wasn't eating his usual bagel, though, just staring down into his coffee cup. Dad had already left for the Melody Inn.

I thought of how often Lester had been there for me when I'd had problems, and wished I could do the same for him.

"Les, I'm really sorry about you and Lauren," I said, opening a new box of Wheat Chex and pouring some into a bowl.

"So what do you know about it?" he rasped.

"I happened to hear you and Dad talking last night."

"'Happened' to, my eye. You were eavesdropping."

"Well, I'm worried about you," I said. "Do you want to talk about it?"

"No."

I got milk from the fridge, poured it over my cereal, and started to eat. After a minute or two, when Les still didn't speak, I said, "Am I chewing too loud for you?"

"Yeah. I can hear you breathing, too. Stop chewing and breathing and I'll be fine." He took another sip of coffee and stared morosely out the window.

"The course of true love never did run smooth," I said helpfully.

Les didn't answer. When that didn't seem to help, I said,

"Every cloud has a silver lining, Les." And when he still didn't say anything, I said, "Whenever a door closes, you know, a window opens."

"Will you stifle it, please?" he growled. "What are you? The Book of Proverbs?"

"I'm just trying to make you feel better, after all the times you've been there for me."

That seemed to soften him a little. He got up and refilled his cup, then stood leaning against the counter, still staring out the window.

"I just thought we had a good thing going," he said at last. "I was even starting to feel I might have found the right woman for me and then, just like that, I get the brush-off."

"Yeah, she was about a thousand times better than Eva," I said.

"That's for sure," said Les.

"Maybe she'll teach at another college here, and then you can date all you want," I said.

"I don't think so," Lester said. "She's hoping she'll be hired again next year, and if she's asked, she won't have much use for me."

I hated to see my brother look so sad. There *had* to be a way around it if they were really in love, regardless of what Dad said.

"Then what you've got to do, Les, is have a secret courtship until *you've* got *your* Ph.D., and then you won't be a student anymore."

"A three-year secret courtship?" he sneered.

"If she's the love of your life, it's worth it," I said.

"So what do you suggest, doctor? She has Caller ID and doesn't answer my phone calls. She won't answer my e-mails, either. Maybe she thinks they've got her place bugged, I don't know."

"You've just got to do something wild and reckless, Lester! She still sees you as a student. Be a take-charge man! Do something so romantic, so full of animal magnetism that she can't resist."

"Like what? Grab her by the hair as she comes out of the faculty dining room and drag her off to my den?"

"No, but if you were to climb through her window at night with a bouquet of flowers or something—oh, Les, she'd just melt in your arms."

Lester was looking at me strangely, and I realized I had his attention.

"Where does she live, Lester?"

"An apartment off-campus."

"What floor?"

"It's a garden apartment. Ground floor."

"Perfect! It's destiny, Lester! You'd knock her socks off if you showed you cared that much about her."

Les continued staring at me for another fifteen seconds. Then he put his cup down. "You're nuts, Al," he said, and left the kitchen.

A few days later, Eric came over and we went for a long walk, holding hands like Patrick and I used to do. In fact, I found us walking around the same block, down the same sidewalks that

Patrick and I had walked the night we broke up. Were these streets endings and beginnings? I wondered, now that Eric was leaving.

"SSSS-So, what are you thinking?" he asked.

"About endings and beginnings," I said.

"And?"

"It's just been a really wild year. Relationships, I mean. Like half the time I'm not even sure what's going on."

"M-maybe you d-don't have to figure it all out. Maybe you sss-shouldn't even try. Just let things b-be; see what happens."

I figured he was talking about us right then. I knew he'd be dating others girls down in Texas, and I'd be seeing other guys back here. It just felt as though there was a huge question mark hanging over my head. But maybe he was right: I tried to control things too much.

"Okay," I said suddenly. "New resolution: Live one day at a time. Just go with the flow and don't try to guess what will happen next."

He grabbed me then and gave me a real movie-star kiss, bending me backward under the new shade of a box elder, then lifting me back to a standing position.

"What was *that*?" I gasped.

"Didn't you r-recognize it?" he said. "That was what happened next."

A week later, the phone rang, and at first I thought no one was there.

"Hello?" I kept saying. "Hello?" I thought I heard someone breathing on the other end of the line, and for a moment I figured it was an obscene call and was about to hang up.

Then a voice said, "A-Alice?" and I realized it was the first time Eric had ever called me on the phone.

"Eric?" I said.

"Yeah, I just c-called to say g-g-good-bye," he said. "We've g-got a six o'clock flight."

"Oh, Eric!" I said. "I hope things turn out great for you."

"Right n-now all I'm thinking about is g-getting my d-driver's license while I'm down there. And mm-missing you."

"Well, good luck on that and everything else," I told him. And then, "It's wonderful you could call me."

"Yeah. P-Progress. Will you write?" he asked.

"Sure, if you'll answer."

"Of course I will," he said.

"Okay. I'll look for that first letter."

"I m-might surprise you. I might even c-call."

"Even better," I told him.

That's what I mean about change.

I'd no sooner hung up when the phone rang again. I figured Eric had something else he wanted to tell me. But this time it was Karen. "Did you hear?" she asked.

"Hear what?"

"Patrick and Penny. They broke up!"

I was getting dual images in my brain right then of Patrick

on one side, Eric on the other. "Really?" I said. "What about?"

"I'm not sure. Penny told Jill it was mutual—that they just didn't seem to have time for each other. I thought you should be the first to know."

"Why?"

"Well, you have a shot at him again," she said.

"Karen, I'm not on a safari," I told her.

"Yeah, but he was yours in the first place, Alice," she argued.

"I don't think anyone ever gave me a title to him," I said.

"You're letting a great opportunity slip by," she said, and hung up.

I'll admit, I waited to see if Patrick would call me that night. If he wanted to get back together. But he didn't, and I didn't call him. And though a part of me would have been glad to have him tell me that all the while he was dating Penny, he was really thinking of me and couldn't live without me, another part was liking this freedom to just explore and see what was around the next corner. To concentrate on who I was, for a change, without a boyfriend as an appendage. In a way it was nice to be simply "Alice" again, not "Alice and Patrick," or "Alice and Eric." I think I was feeling better about myself than I could ever remember.

Lester was going out for the evening, and Dad had a season ticket to the National Symphony, so I invited Pamela and Elizabeth for the night. When we get together now, it's usually at my place, because what with Elizabeth's grudge against her parents, and Pamela's dad dating again, and her never quite knowing what's going on between her folks, it's just simpler to have the girls here. I'd hoped Gwen could come over, too, so we could plan some more about camp, but she was going somewhere with a brother.

To take, Elizabeth had written down on a sheet of paper. "Toilet paper," she said.

"What?" I said.

"Camps never have enough toilet paper. I'm bringing my own supply. Tampons, too. And a huge jar of Noxzema."

"Sunscreen," said Pamela. "Write that down."

"M&M's, for the middle of the night if I get hungry," I said. "They're also great bribes if we have discipline problems."

"Boys," said Pamela. "Add those to the list. Big and brawny and cute."

I was just about to get out a frozen pizza when the phone rang. Who could be calling at ten o'clock at night? I wondered. Patrick? I went out in the hall and picked up the phone outside my room.

"Al," came Lester's voice. "Dad there?"

"No. He's at the symphony, remember?"

Lester muttered something I couldn't understand. Then he added, "I forgot."

"What's wrong?"

"Listen. Write this down because I only get one call," he told me. I motioned to Liz to bring me her pad and pencil.

"Okay," I said. "I'm ready."

"I'm at the police station in College Park, and as soon as Dad gets home, ask him to come over here and get me out."

"What?" I cried. "What happened?"

"They took me in for breaking and entering, Al, and I don't know if they're going to set bail or what. Just tell Dad to come over here as soon as he can." He gave me the address and phone number and said he had to go.

"Oh, Les. Did you . . . did Lauren . . . ?"

"Let's just say she didn't think it was all that romantic," Lester said, and hung up.

Pamela and Elizabeth were standing in my doorway, staring at me.

"Lester's been arrested!" I gasped. "For breaking and entering his girlfriend's apartment, and it's all my fault!" I told them about the breakup and what I'd suggested.

"Alice, we've got to get him out!" said Elizabeth. "Your dad may not be home for another hour or two, and Les could be beaten up by then! He could be locked up with murderers and stranglers and . . ."

I was already scared enough, and didn't need that, but Pamela was all fired up too. "Let's pool our money and take a cab!" she said. "We'll all be character witnesses for Lester, and he'll be indebted to us for life."

I did feel responsible, and I wanted to get him out before Dad got home. So Pamela called a cab and I left a note on the kitchen table for Dad in case he got home before we did, saying I'd be back soon. When the cab pulled up, all three of us crowded in the backseat and asked the driver to take us to the College Park police station.

We could see him studying us in his rearview mirror. "Any . . . uh . . . particular reason you girls are going to the police station?" he asked.

"A mission of mercy," said Elizabeth, and off we went.

"My gosh, can you *believe* this?" Pamela kept whispering as the cab sped along the beltway toward College Park. "Did you ever think that *we'd* be rescuing *Lester*?"

"He's going to be so glad to see us!" exclaimed Elizabeth.

When the driver pulled up outside police headquarters, he asked, "You want me to wait outside?"

I thought a minute. "Yes, I guess you'd better. I'll come out and let you know."

"Okay, but you're up to eleven dollars now," he said.

I swallowed, and we went inside. A sergeant sat at a desk and was talking with two other officers standing near the back. They all three stopped talking when they saw us.

"Can I help you?" the man at the desk said.

"Yes. I'd like to see my brother, Lester McKinley," I told him.

"Al?" came Lester's voice from somewhere down the hall.

"Lester?" I called back.

And suddenly Elizabeth cried, "Please let him go! We've known him all his life, practically, and he wouldn't hurt anyone, and—"

"Couldn't you just release him to our custody and we'll promise to bring him back for the trial?" Pamela put in.

"Al!" yelled Lester again, and I wondered if inmates were beating him up already.

"Don't let anyone hurt him!" I pleaded. "Just put him in solitary confinement if you won't let him out."

"Uh . . . sister . . . your brother's just getting his things together. The lady refuses to press charges. He's free to go," the sergeant told me.

"What?" I said.

Just then Lester came down the hall, and all three of us rushed over and threw our arms around him. I was crying because this all had happened on account of me.

Lester shook us loose and fumbled around in his pocket for his car keys. "Damnation!" he said. "My car's back at her apartment." He turned to the officers. "Now that you got me out here, how about a ride back?"

"Sorry, buddy. The lady called 911, and we responded. We were just doing our job. One-way transportation only."

"It's okay, Lester, I've got a cab waiting," I told him.

He stared at me. "What?"

"It's all arranged," I said. "The cab will drive you back to get your car, and we'll go with you."

We went outside and the three of us crawled in the taxi again while Lester got in front with the driver. The cabbie looked at him warily, and Lester gave him Lauren's address.

"It's okay," I told the driver. "He's not violent or anything."

"Al!" said Lester.

"Only when he's being studly," Elizabeth said, giggling.

"And then he's wild! Pure animal energy!" purred Pamela.

Les turned around. "Will you *stop*?"

We all got out at Lauren's apartment building, paid the cab driver, and climbed in Lester's car. The windows in the ground-floor apartment were dark. I figured she had probably turned out the lights and was watching from a window.

Lester didn't even glance toward the building. He pulled away from the curb with a screech of tires, and headed back toward Silver Spring.

"Who wants to be dropped off first?" he asked.

"No such luck, Les. They're spending the night," I said.

He groaned. "Listen," he said. "I would really appreciate it if you guys wouldn't tell Dad any of this."

"Okay, but you have to tell us what really happened, then," I said, eager to bargain.

"Oh, good grief!" Lester said. He was quiet for a minute or two, but finally said, "Lauren had asked me days ago to return her house key, so . . . I was returning the key. I just happened to let myself in first, and was sitting at her kitchen table waiting for her when she walked in. With a new boyfriend, it so happens, a professor in the physics department. I was only going to plead my case, but she never gave me the chance. She pretended I was a student obsessed with her, and called 911 to make it convincing."

"Maybe you should have brought flowers," I said.

"It wouldn't have helped," Les said bitterly. "She obviously hadn't told her new boyfriend about me, and especially didn't want him to know she'd given me her key. That really teed me off, so I was standing there shouting at her when the police arrived. . . . All this time she's just been using me to get acquainted, find her way around. . . ."

"Oh, poor Les," said Pamela. "There are other fish in the ocean, you know."

"It's always darkest before the light," said Elizabeth.

"It may seem awful now, Lester, but tonight's the first night of the rest of your life," I told him.

"Are they offering a course now in platitudes at your school? *Bartlett's Quotations*?" Lester said. "Just forget it, will you? It's over. I'm lucky to have found out now. But remember, not a word to Dad. I don't want to worry him. He's too happy these days."

I agreed.

Dad was already home when we got there, standing in the kitchen, puzzling over my note.

"Well!" he said, as we all trooped in. "Where have you been?"

"Out with Lester for a night on the town," I said.

"Oh?" Dad looked pleased. Pleased, I guess, that Lester was getting over his breakup so soon.

"A little reality contact, that's all," Lester said.

"I'm glad to hear it," Dad told him. "I had a great evening, too. All Schubert and Mendelssohn. A real treat."

"Then everybody's happy!" I said, and led the girls back up to my room. Les had paid the cab fare for us, so we weren't out anything.

We lay on my bed a long time discussing the evening—Lester's breakup and all.

"You know what that means, don't you?" said Elizabeth.

"What *what* means?"

"His having the key to her apartment," said Elizabeth. "It means they were having sex. When you give a man a key to your apartment, it's his invitation. You know . . . the guy is the key, and the woman's the keyhole, and—"

"You *were* dropped on your head as a baby," I said. "Maybe she let him have a key so he could study there, where it was quiet. How do you know?"

"Yeah, and maybe they just liked to get together and play Tiddly Winks," said Pamela. "Anyone who believes they were just friends, please raise you hand."

"Okay, maybe. But this keyhole business—"

"It is, it is! Everything's symbolic!" said Elizabeth, warming to the subject. "Pistons and cylinders, candles and holders—"

"Plugs and sockets," said Pamela.

There was a tap on the door, and Lester opened it a crack. "Everyone decent?" he called.

"No, Les, we're all lying here naked," Pamela called. "Come on in and join the party."

We giggled.

Les opened the door tentatively, and finally all the way.

"See?" said Pamela. "That didn't stop him one bit."

"Just wanted to say thanks, Al," Lester said. "It was a comedy of errors from the get-go. At least she had enough decency not to press charges, but I'm still steamed."

"Well, don't do anything rash, Lester," I said.

"Don't worry. I'm off women for the duration."

"The duration of what?" I asked. "The next three years at the U? Till you get your Ph.D.? What?"

"I didn't say I'm a eunuch, Al. The duration of the summer, anyway."

He said good night and went back to his room.

"You know what that means . . . ," said Elizabeth.

"What *what* means?" I said.

"That he's not going to be a eunuch. A eunuch can't have intercourse, you know, so if Lester's *not* going to be a eunuch, then it can only mean that—"

"Good night, Elizabeth," I said. "Sweet dreams." And I turned out the light.

15

SYLVIA

Dad was in a cleaning frenzy. I thought we had already done spring cleaning, but he said we'd hardly begun. Sylvia was coming exactly two days before I left for my three weeks as an assistant camp counselor, and Dad wanted the house to be perfect. When a house has been as imperfect as ours has been for all the years we've lived here, it's sort of a lost cause, I think. Lester and I considered moving to the Y for the week, but we wanted to do what we could to make Sylvia feel welcome. So I finally called Aunt Sally in Chicago.

"Alice, sweetheart, it's been so long since I've heard your voice!" she said. "How *are* you?"

For a moment I was tempted to tell her that Lester had been in jail, because I knew she would catch the next plane to Maryland if I did, and then, as long as she was here, she would clean the house from top to bottom and save us the trouble. Not only clean the house, but bake a couple of pies while she was at it.

"Is anything wrong, Alice?" Aunt Sally said, and sounded worried.

"Not at all, we're just fine!" I said. "Except that Miss Summers is due back from England in a week, and Dad wants the house to be perfect. I don't know where to begin."

There was a long moment of silence, and I was afraid I'd already said too much—that Aunt Sally was even then looking up the number for United Airlines in the yellow pages. But finally she said, "If there are still any clothes of your mother's around, Alice, don't let her wear them."

"What?" I said, wondering how we got from cleaning to clothes.

"Out of respect for Marie," she said.

"Aunt Sally, I really don't think Sylvia wants Mom's clothes. Trust me," I said.

"I mean, how would you feel if you were dead and your husband brought home a new wife?" Aunt Sally continued.

Sometimes it's best to not even try to answer.

"Well," she said, "as far as housecleaning, Sylvia's not moving in right away, is she? When is the wedding?"

"July twenty-eighth," I said.

"Then I'd let her worry about the cleaning. She'll have two

whole months to clean the house herself. Unless, of course, she's moving in *before* they're married, which I trust is not the case, not with you and Lester there."

I had to smile. "No, I don't think so, Aunt Sally. She has a house of her own, you know."

"Good. Then here's all you have to remember, Alice. *Susie Dances Very Well.*"

"Huh?" I said.

"That's what my mother taught me: SDVW—Susie Dances Very Well. S stands for 'Scrub sinks, tub, and floor'; D stands for 'Dust all flat surfaces'; V stands for 'Vacuum carpets and rugs'; and W stands for 'Wash windows, towels, and bedding.' If you can remember that, the house will be clean enough when Sylvia gets there, and you don't have to worry about doing anything more."

"Thanks, Aunt Sally," I said uncertainly.

"And Alice, if she *does* move in before they're married, tell her I disapprove."

Dad didn't pay the least bit of attention to *Susie Dances Very Well*. You would think our house had termites, vermin, bats' nests, and mold, the way he got us up early Sunday morning and made us attack the windows, the woodwork, the floors, and rugs. Every finger mark disappeared from the walls, every smudge on a window, every spot on a rug. Lester rented a rug cleaner from the supermart, and we vacuumed and laundered; we dusted and scrubbed. We stripped the beds and washed the blankets, aired the pillows, and cleaned the closets.

By seven that evening, Dad was asleep on the couch, Lester lay sprawled on his back on the living room rug, and I was curled up in my beanbag chair, too tired to move.

I guess none of us heard the doorbell. Dad was snoring, Les was snoring, even I was snoring, probably, when I was vaguely conscious of the doorbell, the footsteps, then Marilyn standing over me, saying, "Alice? Alice? Is everything all right here?"

Dad stirred, Les raised his head and plunked it down again, and I heard Marilyn say, "Thank goodness! When no one answered the door, I looked through the window and thought you were all overcome by carbon monoxide or something." Then she saw the buckets and brooms and mops. "Wow!" she said. *"House Beautiful!"*

"I'd get up and ask you to sit down, Marilyn, but I don't think I can move," said Dad.

"I won't even try," murmured Lester.

I just sat up and rubbed my eyes.

"I brought over the inventory you asked for, Mr. M. I worked up some figures at home," Marilyn said. "I thought you might want them."

"Just put them there on the table, will you?" said Dad, his lips barely moving.

Marilyn looked around at us. "Have you eaten?"

"Too tired to cook," said Dad.

And suddenly Marilyn became Mother Superior. She went to the phone and ordered antipasti and veal scallopini to be delivered, with an order of cannoli for dessert. Then she set the table, lit some candles, and when the food was delivered, paid for it herself, which finally brought Dad to his feet so he could reimburse her.

By then, the smell of the food had revived us, we managed to get ourselves to the table, and invited Marilyn to eat with us.

"Well done, Marilyn," Dad said. "Hiring you was one of the best things I ever did."

"Now's your chance, Mar," Lester joked. "Ask for a raise." We all laughed.

"As a matter of fact," Dad went on, "she got a raise just last week, and she's worth every penny of it."

Marilyn beamed.

I watched Les watching Marilyn, Marilyn watching Dad, and Dad eating his scallopini, and thought what a great, happy family we'd be if Les would just marry Marilyn in a double-ring ceremony with Dad and Sylvia. We could all live here together, and . . .

"I can't stay any longer," Marilyn said, before she had dessert. "Jack's coming over a little later, and I want to be there."

"Big date, huh?" Les said.

"Yes. He's pretty special," Marilyn said, and smiled. "Well, thanks for letting me stay, Mr. M. Glad you enjoyed the dinner. Double glad you weren't all dead! Scared me to death for a minute there."

And then she was gone.

It could have been so perfect—Les could have fallen in love with Marilyn again, and proposed over the cannoli. He could have forgotten all about Lauren and being in jail and . . . Life isn't like that, I guess. Sometimes change *isn't* for the better.

I was afraid he'd really be depressed now. Not only had Lauren dumped him, but his old reliable girlfriend was seeing someone new. Lester, though, looked refreshed and relieved. Maybe he was feeling the same way I was now: free to enjoy being unattached for a while.

"Thank you, you two," Dad said to us later as he walked through the living room, the clean scent of Lemon Pledge and Windex wafting through the house. "Sylvia's going to be impressed."

"I think Sylvia will have eyes only for you, Dad, and all this work won't matter," Les told him.

We decided that we'd all go to the airport to meet her. We wanted to welcome her back as a family, so she would feel really glad about moving into our house and taking Mom's place. Les and I wanted to show that we loved her, too.

So the three of us stood at the gate at Dulles when her flight was due, knowing she'd be coming through customs, that she'd be tired from the long flight, but we were ready to give her and Dad space once we got home. Les, in fact, was going to take me to the movies.

All these months, Dad had been the patient one, the calm one, the man who could put his dreams on hold till his love was in his arms again. And now, waiting for Sylvia, he was as jumpy as I'd ever seen him, like a horse at the starting gate. He'd be talking with Lester and me one minute, then striding over to the window to see if a shuttle was coming yet from the far terminal. And as each shuttle arrived and disgorged its passengers, he watched every face, hoping for a first glimpse of her. Checking his watch, raising himself up on his toes to see over the crowd, crossing his arms, then uncrossing them again.

And then, coming out of a fourth shuttle, there she was—the light brown hair, the beautifully shaped brows, the wispy green silk scarf on top of her blouse, her smile. She was as beautiful as ever, but more tired looking than I'd ever seen her. Her eyes, of course, were on Dad, but they lit up, too, when they saw Les and me, and she put down her carry-on bag and opened her arms to embrace us all at once.

But Dad got to her first and couldn't help himself. He lifted her a few inches off the floor and spun around with her as though he were twenty years old, and what happened next came so fast we could hardly believe it: Sylvia suddenly pushed away from him, stepped backward, and threw up on the floor. On Dad's shoes, in fact, splattering the cuffs of his pants as well.

"Darling!" cried Dad.

She only gagged again and vomited a second time. People around us averted their eyes and gave us a wide berth as they passed, and an airline employee phoned for a janitor.

"Oh, I'm so sorry, Ben!" Sylvia said, wiping her mouth, the front of her blouse stained.

"Sweetheart, you're sick!" Dad cried, putting an arm around her.

"Just airsick. There was such turbulence, and . . ." She clamped her mouth shut, afraid she would vomit again, but I was already heading for a restroom behind us to get some wet paper towels.

I was back almost immediately, and Dad took them from me. Gently, lovingly, he wiped her face, a spot on her scarf, her blouse, and only when she had been escorted to a chair did he tend to his own pants and shoes. A man with a mop and pail was coming down the corridor, and we moved away to sit with Sylvia.

"How embarrassing!" she said, smiling at us wanly.

"For a grand entrance, Sylvia, I'd say you win the prize," Les joked, and she laughed.

So it happens to the best and the beautiful, too, I was thinking. All the embarrassing, ridiculous, gross, humiliating things that had happened to me in my fifteen years happened to other people as well, even grown-up career women who were madly in love. It was comforting in a way to know that I wasn't alone, but terrifying to think that these things go on forever. The only thing that changes, I guess, is the way we react to them.

"We're not going out to the car until you're feeling better," Dad said, leaning over her and kissing her forehead.

"Hard to believe, but I'm feeling *much* better, now that I'm off the plane," Sylvia said. "I guess the only thing that would have been worse is if I'd been sick on my seatmates." She turned to Lester and me. "Well, you *know* how *I* am. How are *you*?"

"Glad to see you, that's what," I said. "I can't believe you're here to stay."

"Neither can I," said Sylvia, smiling at Dad. For a long minute their eyes feasted on each other, like their eyes were doing all the talking. And finally, when the color had returned to Sylvia's face and she seemed herself again, she said, "Let's go home."

Les and I stayed at the house for only a half hour or so, and then we headed for the movies. We got there twenty minutes early, but felt we should give Dad and Sylvia as much time alone as we could. So we ate most of our popcorn ahead of time and drank half our drinks as well.

"That's what I want." I sighed, thinking of Dad and Sylvia again. "Did you see the gentle way he wiped her face, Lester? I'll bet some men would have been disgusted at a woman throwing up in public, especially all over his shoes. But it was as though Dad didn't even notice. All he cared about was her. When I think about marrying, I'm going to look for someone like that."

"So what are you going to do? Give each potential husband the barf test?" he asked. "Puke on his shoes and see what happens?"

"No, just pay attention to how he treats me when I'm sick. Like, when we can't go somewhere we'd planned because I'm having cramps or have a bad cold. Or when I'm feeling really upset and depressed, if he can talk to me about it, or whether he just wants me to get over it."

I was thinking of Faith and Ron right then, and the way Ron never seemed to care what *she* was feeling. The way he got his jollies, it seemed, was by ordering Faith around.

"It works both ways, you know," Les said. "Some girls—and I've known a few—want to be catered to like princesses. Like the guy is her servant, and it's *her* feelings, *her* moods that are important. She never stops to consider what kind of a day *he* might have had, or how little money's in his pocket."

I remembered the time Patrick got on the school bus and threw up in the aisle, how embarrassing it was for him. And how the next day the kids wanted to tease him about it, but I was the only one who wouldn't go along with the joke. I felt pretty good just then to know that I could consider a boy's feelings, and at the same time, I felt a sudden rush of missing Patrick.

"Neither one of us has a love life right now, Les. Do you realize that?" I asked.

He stopped chewing, unsure of what I was going to suggest, I guess. "So?"

"So, are we depressed, or what?"

"I don't know. Are we Siamese twins sharing the same brain?"

"It's just that I'm not always sure *how* I'm feeling. I've had a great year, actually. . . ."

"So go with the great year! Quit thinking about what you're *supposed* to feel, *supposed* to have, *supposed* to be—just enjoy the moment, Al."

"What about you? What about *your* year?" I asked him.

"I had a great time with Lauren, but now it's over, and *I'm* enjoying the present. That's enough."

I leaned over and gazed dramatically into his eyes. "*Are* you enjoying this moment, Lester—sitting in the theater beside your sister?"

"Get your hand out of the popcorn, Al, and I'll enjoy it a whole lot more," he said.

Patiently Alice

Contents

1
LEAVING HOME

The summer between ninth and tenth grades, I learned that life doesn't always follow your agenda.

I had signed up to be assistant counselor at a camp for disadvantaged kids. Somehow I had the idea that at the end of three weeks I could get the little girls in my cabin feeling like one big happy family. First, though, I had to talk myself into going.

I was sitting at the breakfast table watching Dad pour half-and-half in his coffee, and I decided that was a metaphor for my feelings. Half of me wanted to go to camp the following morning, and half of me wanted to stay home and be in on the excitement of Dad's marriage to Sylvia two weeks after I got back.

I wanted *some*thing to happen. I wanted at least one thing to be resolved. Everything seemed up in the air these days—Dad's engagement to Sylvia, Pamela's mother leaving the family, Elizabeth's quarrels with her parents, Lester's on-again off-again relationships with women, Patrick and I breaking up. My life in general, you might say.

"Are you eating that toast or just mauling it?" asked Lester, my twenty-something brother, who was leaving soon for his summer class at the U of Maryland. "That's the last of the bread, and if you don't want it, I do."

I slid my plate toward him. "I can't decide whether to go to camp or stay here and be helpful," I said.

"Be helpful," said Lester. "Go to camp."

I turned toward Dad, hoping he might beg me to stay.

"I can't think of a single reason why you shouldn't go, Alice," he said. "Sylvia's got everything under control."

That's what I was afraid of. Not that she shouldn't be in control. It was her wedding, not mine. But Sylvia had just gotten back from England, where she'd been teaching for a year, the wedding was about six weeks off, and if they had done any planning, I hadn't heard about it.

"I thought you were supposed to start planning a wedding a year in advance," I said.

"We're just having a simple ceremony for friends and family," Dad said, turning the page of his newspaper and folding it over. He looked like a cozy teddy bear in his white summer robe with floppy sleeves, and for a moment I felt like going over and sitting in his lap. He's lost a little weight, though, on purpose. I know he wants to look handsome and svelte for the wedding, but he'll always look like a teddy bear to me.

I lifted my glass of orange juice and took a sip. "You're not just driving over to the courthouse to be married by a justice of the peace, are you?" I asked suspiciously. Maybe it was going to be even simpler than simple. I felt I couldn't stand it if Sylvia didn't wear a white gown with all the trimmings. She had already told Dad she didn't want a diamond engagement ring, and that, according to Pamela Jones, was sacrilege. "How can it be forever if you don't have a diamond?" she'd said.

"Of course we're not getting married in a courthouse," said Dad, and told me they were still planning to have the wedding at the church on Cedar Lane in Bethesda. That was perfect, because it was sort of where they'd met.

Miss Summers was my seventh-grade English teacher at the time, and—because Mom died when I was in kindergarten—I've been looking for a new mom ever since. A role model, anyway. And Sylvia, with her blue eyes and light brown hair, her wonderful smile and wonderful scent, seemed the perfect model for me and the perfect wife for Dad. All I had to do was get them together, so I'd invited her to the Messiah Sing-Along at Cedar Lane, and the rest is history.

Well, not quite. It's taken all this time to make it stick. But she finally gave up her old boyfriend, our junior high assistant principal, Jim Sorringer, for Dad. And now the wedding is set for July 28, and I wanted *details*. It had seemed impolite to start asking Sylvia questions the minute she got off the plane.

"Long gown and veil?" I asked Dad.

"No, he's wearing a suit," said Lester.

"Is *Sylvia* wearing a long dress?" I asked.

Dad smiled. "I haven't seen it yet."

"Orchestra?"

"A piano trio of a good friend of mine, Martin Small," said Dad.

"Three *pianos*?"

"Piano, violin, and cello," Dad said.

"You want him to fill out a questionnaire, Al?" Les asked. My full name is Alice Kathleen McKinley, but Dad and Lester call me Al.

"Something like that," I said, and grinned. Then I said it aloud: "I just want to feel needed, Dad. I want to make absolutely sure this wedding takes place. Maybe I ought to stay home and help out."

"If you want to feel needed, hon, you could hardly find a better place than Camp Overlook—all those kids needing attention like you wouldn't believe."

That was true, and I knew I couldn't back out anyway. Pamela Jones, Elizabeth Price, and Gwen Wheeler were going to be assistant counselors along with me. We'd been interviewed, received our instructions, gone through a day of orientation and training, and tomorrow we'd get on one of the buses taking the kids up into the Appalachian Mountains.

The phone rang for the fourth time that morning.

"I'm outta here," said Lester, scooting back from the table and picking up his books. "See you, Dad." Lester himself was looking pretty svelte these days. He has thick brown hair—on the sides, anyway. It's a little thin on top. He's taller than Dad, but I'll bet he looks a lot like Dad did when he was Lester's age. Handsome as anything. All my girlfriends are nuts about him.

I went to the phone in the hallway and picked it up. "Hello?"

"Toilet paper," came Elizabeth's voice.

"What?"

"We'd better bring our own. No telling what kind they have at camp," she said. "And tampons."

"I've already thought of that," I said. "But I still need to buy a sports bra."

"And I need a baseball cap to keep the sun out of my eyes," said Elizabeth. "You want to run over to the shops on Georgia Avenue?"

"I'll meet you outside," I said.

Elizabeth lives just across the street, and we were on our way in five minutes. We were trying to think of things we may have forgotten.

"Breath mints," said Liz.

"Mosquito repellent," I suggested.

"Imodium, in case we get the runs," she went on.

I glanced over at her, beautiful Elizabeth with her long dark hair and thick eyelashes, who was studying the list in her hand, covering every conceivable thing that might cause her embarrassment while off in the wilderness. She was wearing jeans and a white T-shirt, and was beginning to look more filled out again after a season of skinniness that had worried not only Pamela and me, but her folks as well.

"Watch out," I said, steering her away from a signpost. Gwen and Pamela and I joke sometimes that we never have to worry about anything, because Elizabeth will do our worrying for us. Which isn't exactly true, of course. We just worry about different things.

We got the bra and the cap and stopped at the drugstore for the rest. I was heading for the checkout counter with my mosquito repellent when Elizabeth called, "One more thing, Alice."

I went back to find her looking at men's hair tonic and shaving cream.

"Now what?" I asked.

"Just a minute," was all she said.

I leaned against the shelves behind me and noticed how hair products for men took only half the space of hair stuff for women. *Maybe because women have twice as much hair*, I thought, smiling to myself. I'm letting my hair grow long now. It's almost as long as Elizabeth's, but Pamela still wears hers short, and looks more sophisticated.

I was anxious to get home and finish packing, so when I saw Elizabeth moving slowly along the display a second time, I said, "What are you looking for? Let me help." Maybe she was supposed to buy something for her dad.

"Oh . . . something," said Elizabeth.

"*What?* I want to get home."

"Alice, I promised myself I wouldn't leave this store until I found them," she said. And then, looking quickly around, she whispered, "Condoms."

"*Condoms?*" I yelped. I couldn't help myself.

Elizabeth clapped one hand over my mouth, but there was no one in our aisle to hear. I jerked her hand away.

"Are you nuts?" I said. "Who for?"

"*Anyone,*" Elizabeth said determinedly. And then she added, "Well, for Pamela, mostly. Just in case."

"*Pamela?*"

"Well, you know how moody she's been lately."

"In case of *what?* She's moody so she needs condoms?"

"Her mother and everything."

"Her *mother* needs condoms?"

"Oh, Alice, when someone's as upset as Pamela, she could do all sorts of things you wouldn't expect. We don't know who she's going to meet or what the guys are like, and she'll be away from home. . . ."

"So will *we!*" I said.

"Look," she told me, "I was reading this article—'If He *Won't,* Then *You Should*'—and it said that especially when a girl is away from home, she should have back-up protection in case she's in a situation she can't control."

I don't know where Elizabeth finds this stuff.

"If she can control it enough to get a guy to put on a condom, I'd think she could also get herself out of there," I said.

"Okay, but we *don't* know what's going to happen at camp, right?"

"Hardly *that!*" I said.

"But just in case, I'll have condoms for anyone who needs them," she told me.

I sighed. Elizabeth has been trying so hard to be cool lately that she's getting bizarre. But right then she looked like a little Mother Superior trying to protect us all, and it struck me as pretty funny.

"Maybe condoms are in the plumbing section," I said.

"What?" She turned and looked at me.

I tried not to laugh. "You know . . . you put them on a man's . . . uh . . . faucet."

She gave me a sardonic smile. "Be serious."

"Toy counter? When you want to *play?*" I suggested. "Automotive needs? In case you do it in the backseat of a car?"

"Alice!"

"How about over with the school supplies? No, I've got it! In men's wear!"

She ignored me. "I wonder if we need a prescription."

"Let's go home," I told her.

"No!"

A clerk appeared at the end of our aisle with a box of deodorants and began shelving them. I pushed Elizabeth forward. "Go ask him," I said.

The man looked up. "Can I help you?" he asked. He was a plump guy of about thirty, friendly and businesslike.

"Yes," Elizabeth said, her words coming in a rush, cheeks pink, "I wonder if you could tell me where I could find men's condoms."

The clerk paused only a moment, then said, in the same businesslike manner, "Aisle eight, next to women's sanitary products."

Now Elizabeth's face turned crimson. The clerk immediately returned to his deodorants, and I pushed Elizabeth around the corner into the next aisle, where we collapsed against each other, trying not to laugh out loud.

"I was so *embarrassed!*" she gasped. "If anyone *heard* . . . !" And then, as though afraid she might lose her nerve, she propelled herself toward aisle eight. The next thing I knew we were standing in front of a row of little boxes, with pictures of men and women in romantic poses, walking along the beach at sunset or dancing among palm trees.

Elizabeth grabbed a box of Trojans and was off toward the cash register, her face still peppermint pink. I tagged gleefully along as she surveyed the three lines. Two of the cashiers were men in their twenties. Elizabeth took the line with a middle-aged woman at the register.

Standing behind her, I rested my chin on her shoulder. "She's probably going to ask if you have a permission slip from your mother," I whispered.

"Shut up," Elizabeth murmured.

"Maybe you have to be eighteen. Maybe she'll call the manager," I went on.

"Alice!"

We were next in line. I plunked down my mosquito repellent, and Elizabeth put down a package of breath mints, another of Imodium, and the condoms. We put our money on the counter as the woman rang up the items, but when she picked up the box of condoms, she couldn't find a price sticker. And then, while we cringed, the grandmotherly looking lady held them up and called out in a gravel-truck voice, "Frank, do you know how much these are?"

The thin-faced man at the next register said, "What are they? Regular?"

And the woman said, "No. Lubricated tip."

Now both our faces were burning.

The man gave a price, the clerk rang them up, and the minute Elizabeth had the sack in her hand, we headed for the exit.

"That's another store I can never enter for the rest of my natural life," said Elizabeth.

I'd been home only ten minutes when the phone rang.

"Alice, do you have any good mysteries? I want something to read in case I'm bored out of my skull," came Pamela's voice.

"Elizabeth doesn't think that will happen," I said. "She's bringing condoms."

"*Elizabeth?*" cried Pamela.

"For you," I added.

There were three seconds of silence, and then we both burst out laughing.

"She sure must think I lead an exciting life," Pamela said.

"I think she's more afraid that you *will*!" I told her.

"Can you see Elizabeth going into a drugstore and asking for condoms? I mean, can you even imagine that?" Pamela asked me.

"Now I can," I told her. "I was there."

Sylvia came for dinner that night. "Well, are you excited, Alice?" she asked.

"Are *you* excited?" I countered. "Your wedding's next month!"

"Yes, but I'm so busy, I hardly have time to think," she said.

As soon as she had walked in, she and Dad embraced, and I looked away. I mean, it's such a private moment. I guess the other reason I look away, though, is because their kisses are reminders of Patrick and me—the way we used to kiss. And though I'm supposed to be over him now—we broke up last fall—I guess you never quite forget your first real boyfriend. It helps, of course, that we're still friends, but it's hard to think of someone as just another buddy when you've been as close as we were.

"I've got a list of things to do for each of the five weeks, and first on my list, while I can catch you, Alice, is to ask if you'll be my bridesmaid," Sylvia said. And before I could even squeal out my delight, she said, "My sister's coming from Albuquerque to be maid of honor."

"Of course I'll be a bridesmaid!" I said. "How many are you going to have?"

"Just you and Nancy. I have so many friends at the school that if I picked any one of them, the others would get upset. So I'm going to choose only the two women closest to me."

Women! She had called me a *woman!* I could almost feel my breasts expanding inside my 32B bra.

"Oh, Sylvia!" I said.

"I've got a dressmaker who says she can whip up two dresses in time, and I got my gown off the rack, so if you'll choose the dress you like, I'll have it made while you're at camp," Sylvia said.

Dad and Lester were busy making beef Burgundy for dinner, so Sylvia and I took over the dining room table and she put three different dress patterns in front of me. Her color scheme, she said, was teal and royal blue. I couldn't imagine it until I saw the two colors together, and they worked really well. Her sister was going to be in royal blue, so I got to be in teal. That pleased me because my hair is strawberry blond. In some lights it looks blond, in some it looks red, and at night it even looks brown, but blue green is definitely good on me.

The gowns were all very simple in design. One was straight across the front with spaghetti straps and a long narrow skirt; one had a scoop neckline and short sleeves, and the third had a V neck with straps that crossed in back.

"I can choose any one of them?" I asked.

"Yes," said Sylvia. "Nancy's already chosen the one she likes best, but I'm not going to tell you which it is. You should have the gown you like best. I'm not one of those people who believes bridesmaids should look like identical twins."

"I like the one with the spaghetti straps," I said.

"That's exactly the one Nancy chose," she said, and hugged me. "Excellent taste, Alice. As soon as we have dinner, I'll take your measurements."

"Oh, her measurements are simple," Les said from the doorway. "Thirty . . . thirty . . . thirty."

"Lester!" I said.

Sylvia just laughed. "Don't you believe it, Alice. You've got a great figure."

Sylvia Summers is the only one who could ever lie and get away with it. I'm more like thirty-two, twenty-five, thirty-four, but what I was really wondering right then was if my bra and underpants had holes in them and whether I'd have to take off everything to be measured.

At the table Lester asked Sylvia, "Do you actually enjoy this? The photographer, the cake, the flowers, the rings, the candles, the music, the . . ."

"I love it," said Sylvia.

"Actually," said Dad, "we've sort of divided up the work. She's taking care of the wedding details, and I'm arranging the honeymoon."

"Sounds fair," said Les.

I was able to slip away before dinner was over and change my bra, which had old elastic in back, and by the time Sylvia came upstairs with the measuring tape, I was in my robe.

She's very efficient and acted as though this were what she

did every day of her life: measured girls in their underwear. I knew I shouldn't have minded—she was almost my stepmother—but I was glad when I could put on my robe again.

"Well, someday, Alice, it will probably be you and me in a room together taking measurements for your *wedding* dress," she said, smiling.

I smiled back and said flippantly, "And having that intimate conversation for the bride-to-be."

She laughed and I laughed, and then, because my joke had gone over so well, I took it a step further: "But now *you're* the bride, so if there's anything you need to know, Sylvia, just ask me."

"Well," she said, "nothing I can think of at the moment. Is there anything you would like to ask *me*?"

I could feel myself blushing. Had I been that obvious? Had she seen right through me? What I really wanted to know, of course, was whether she and Dad had already made love, but it was none of my business and I wouldn't ask it in a zillion years.

"No," I said, "but if I think of something, I will."

"Good," said Sylvia. "I want to keep things open and honest between us. I know we won't get along perfectly all the time— no one does, not even Ben and me. But I'd like it if we could promise each other that when something upsets us, we'll talk it out. There's nothing worse than people going around holding grudges and never talking about them and nobody quite know- ing who's mad about what. Agree?"

"Yeah, that's pretty awful," I said, thinking of the time Elizabeth and Pamela had turned against me for a while and nobody would come right out and say what was wrong.

"Is that the way you and Dad solve problems? Talk them out?"

"We're working on it," she said.

I got one more call before I went to bed that night. It was Gwen.

"You all packed, girl?" she asked.

"All except the small stuff," I said. "You know what I wish? I wish we were going to a camp where we wouldn't need a hair dryer, conditioner, nail file, lip gloss. . . ."

"It's called Girl Scout Camp," she told me. "We've been there, done that. Those kinds of camps, I mean."

"So it's all about guys, isn't it? Who we might meet?" I said.

"You could say that," said Gwen. I thought of her perfect eyebrows, her short but shapely legs, her skin the color of cocoa. I'll bet she's had a different boyfriend for every year of her life, though she and Leo—Legs is his nickname—have been going together for eighteen months.

"So what's up?" I asked her.

"Legs and I had a fight," she said.

"You broke up?"

"Not exactly. He said he was going to drive out and visit sometime during the three weeks we're at camp, and I said I didn't want him to. I think he's been seeing another girl when I'm out of the picture, and I guess I just want to be free to fool around myself if I meet somebody."

"Fool around . . . meaning . . . ?" I asked.

She laughed. "Hang out with . . . kiss . . ."

I couldn't help myself: "Elizabeth's bringing condoms," I said.

I heard the expected gasp at the other end of the line. *"Elizabeth?"*

"For Pamela. Just in case. She says anything could happen."

She laughed. "She goes around thinking like that, anything might. Anyway, I just wanted to tell you that if Legs calls asking for directions to that camp, don't give them to him. Okay?"

"Got'cha," I told her.

I had just gone to bed when the last call came. Dad tapped lightly on my door. "Al? Hate to disturb you, but it's your Aunt Sally. Shall I tell her you've gone to bed, or do you want to talk with her? It's only ten o'clock Chicago time."

"I'll take it," I said groggily, and padded out to the upstairs phone in the hallway. If I didn't talk to her now, I knew she'd call again the next morning when I was trying to get out the door.

"Oh, Alice, dear, I just want to wish you a very happy time at Camp Overlook," Aunt Sally said. She's Mom's older sister and looked after our family for a while after Mom died. She and Uncle Milt have a daughter named Carol, a few years older than Les.

"Thanks, Aunt Sally," I said. "I'm an assistant counselor, you know. I'm not going as a camper."

"I know that, dear. Counselors have a lot of responsibility, and little children look up to them."

I wondered why Aunt Sally didn't give her sermons from a pulpit every Sunday.

"Meaning . . . ?" I said, knowing very well that Aunt Sally didn't call just to wish me happy camping.

"Why, nothing, dear! I think it's wonderful that you are going to be a role model for all those little children. They'll want to imitate everything you do."

"Thank you," I said

There was a brief silence, and then Aunt Sally said, "Your father tells me it's a coed camp."

Here it comes, I thought. "Yes," I told her.

"So there will be male counselors as well as female?"

"That's what 'coed' means, all right," I said.

"Well, as I said to your Uncle Milt, you're Marie's daughter, and I know you would want her to be proud of you. Of course, this is the first time you've been away from home for any length of time, and there are all those woods and hills and valleys and—"

"Aunt Sally," I interrupted, trying not to laugh, "are you afraid I'll get lost?"

"Oh, no," she said.

"Are you afraid I'll drown?"

"Not really."

"Are you afraid I'll go off in the woods in a fit of passion?"

"Why, whatever made you say that?" Aunt Sally choked.

"Because I can read you like a book," I said gently. "Actually, I doubt there's anything you could worry about that Elizabeth Price hasn't thought of first. But I appreciate your call, and I will really try to have a most magnificent summer, role model and all."

2
INTO THE WILDS

Gwen's mother was to pick us all up the following morning. I gave Dad and Lester a hug and went over to Elizabeth's to wait.

Liz was not only looking more normal these days—she wasn't putting purple in her hair any longer—but she seemed more relaxed, if you can ever call Elizabeth relaxed. She saved her hugs and kisses for her little year-and-a-half-old brother, though—just a quick "Bye-bye" to her parents, and that must have hurt. Both Elizabeth and Pamela were having parent problems, and I was glad it was Gwen's mom driving us to the recreation center, where we would board the buses.

Pamela was with the Wheelers when they drove up, and all

four of us—Gwen and Liz and Pamela and me—were in shorts and tank tops. Elizabeth's legs actually looked good again; you wouldn't mistake her for a prisoner of war, with sticklike things and knobby knees.

Mrs. Wheeler was on the short side, like Gwen, and wore her hair in a well-shaped Afro. "Off you go, into the wilds," she said, smiling. "Please don't break any bones, Gwen."

Gwen's mom is a lawyer who works at the Justice Department. Even though it was Saturday, she looked smart in her linen shirt and pants, while we looked like we were going to dig potatoes or something. "Your father wants you to call home every weekend," she said. I saw Gwen roll her eyes. "Humor him, please."

"And I suppose I should call Granny," Gwen said.

"That would be nice."

I think we all envied Gwen's extended family. She seemed to have aunts and uncles and cousins and grandparents all over the place. The closest relatives I've got are Dad's brothers, Uncle Howard and Uncle Harold—twins—down in Tennessee, though I don't see them as often as I see Aunt Sally in Chicago.

So one minute we were taking our bags out of the trunk of Mrs. Wheeler's car, and the next we were walking up the sidewalk toward the recreation center, where about eighty kids were milling about, yelling and chasing each other, swinging their duffel bags at friends, teasing, laughing, jumping, and spinning, all except a dozen or so who had grown tearful and were clinging to a relative or caretaker.

The full counselors were already at work comforting the weepers, and after pointing out the buses we'd be riding on, they gave us clipboards with names of campers on them. We were each responsible for locating the kids on our list and showing them where to line up.

I had just started towards a group of girls sitting on the steps of the building when I heard Pamela say, "Whoa!" Coming out the door of the center were two guys, *very* good-looking guys, also holding clipboards. They noticed us about the same time and came over.

"Name, please?" one of them said to Pamela jokingly, looking over his list. "Age? Marital status?"

We smiled.

"Craig Kimball," he said to all of us. "Nice to meet you."

"Andy Simms," said his friend, a tall African American wearing an Orioles T-shirt.

"I'm Pamela. This is Elizabeth and Alice and Gwen," Pamela told them.

"You have your cabin assignments yet?" asked Craig. "It's there on top of your clipboards."

We checked. Gwen and I discovered we were in the same cabin, number six. Elizabeth was in eight, and Pamela was in twelve.

"Darn!" said Craig. "They did it again, Andy. Girls on one side of the camp, guys on the other."

We laughed, but there were kids to be rounded up, so off we went.

***

Gwen and I were to be in charge of six girls, ages seven to ten. One was a little Korean girl, Kim, who sat tearfully on the steps clinging to a grown woman.

It was Gwen who knew how to handle that. She reached in her duffel bag and pulled out a little black box, the hinged kind that jewelry comes in. She simply sat down on the steps next to the little girl and, without a word, opened the box. Inside was a butterfly, perfectly preserved under a plastic bubble. Its wings were a shimmering pattern of brown and yellow with orange spots.

Gwen held it out for Kim to see.

"It's beautiful," said the woman, and introduced herself as Kim's aunt.

"Can I touch it?" asked Kim.

"No, because it would crumble," Gwen said. "I collect them. But not till after they die."

Then she let Kim try on her watch and rings, and by the time we were to get on the bus, Kim had attached herself to Gwen, and I herded the other five girls on board.

The youngest was a chubby African-American girl of seven named Ruby, but the smallest child, who was eight, was Josephine. I swear I could have carried her about in one arm. She and her older sister, Mary, were the only white kids in the bunch. Then there was Estelle, who was Latina, and Latisha, the oldest of the six girls, also black. We decided it was no accident that each cabin was a miniature melting pot.

When we finally had our girls settled and their belongings accounted for, and Craig and Andy had done the same with their campers, our bus pulled away. Gwen looked at me and said, "Well, our lives are about to change!"

For the worse, it seemed, because a boy at the back of the bus started singing "Ninety-nine Bottles of Beer on the Wall," only his friend changed the lyrics to "Ninety-nine bottles of snot on the wall." As the song progressed, the word became "pee," then "poop," and each new word brought yelps of laughter from the boys and at least half the girls. The other girls covered their ears and pretended to look offended.

I glanced across the aisle at Pamela and Elizabeth and shouted, "Do you think you can stand this for three weeks?"

But Elizabeth was looking toward the front of the bus and smiling, and when I followed her gaze, I saw Craig and Andy looking back at us.

"Oh, yes!" Elizabeth said in answer. "I think I can stand this very well."

We decided that Camp Overlook must have been built for munchkins, because there were two facing rows of small cabins, twelve in all, odd numbers on one side of camp, even on the other. Each was crammed with four bunk beds but no facilities— just two small dressers with drawers, some shelves, and eight coat hooks. We'd read that it was owned by a church, which donated the camp to the county's social services for three weeks each summer to provide summer camp for poor kids. It was run on a shoestring, and none of us expected more than the basics. The basics were all we got.

Each cabin had either one counselor and seven campers or two assistant counselors and six campers. Each cabin was to choose a name for itself. Our girls chose the Coyotes, which should have told us something right there.

The first hurdle we faced was the sleeping arrangements. Mary, we discovered, did all the talking for her sister. "Josie can't sleep on the top," she announced. "She has to sleep on the bottom."

"Okay," I said. "Mary will sleep on the top bunk of this bed, and Josephine will sleep on the bottom."

Mary surveyed the sloping roof of the cabin with a wary eye. "I can't sleep on the top either because of spiders," she said, which just about cooked the top bunk for anyone else, and Gwen and I knew where *we'd* be sleeping.

But seven-year-old Ruby was our salvation. "Yeah, but if you sleep on the bottom bunk, there's bears!" she said knowingly.

"And snakes!" said Estelle.

Now everybody wanted a top bunk.

We decided at last that Gwen and I, Josephine, and Kim would all have lower beds. Mary would sleep above her sister; Ruby would sleep above me; Estelle would sleep above Kim; and Latisha would sleep above Gwen. That settled, we assigned drawers and shelf space for our belongings, and the last order of business was to confiscate every piece of candy, bag of chips, or box of cookies in or out of sight. Each child had been instructed not to bring food or anything that would attract wildlife, but as pockets and bags were inspected, out fell Snickers bars, cheese twists, animal crackers, and pretzels.

Each child solemnly turned in her supply, all but Josephine, who had two Hershey's Kisses squeezed tightly in her tiny fist.

"She doesn't want to let go," said Mary, reporting the obvious.

We explained about mice and rats and raccoons and squirrels, and how we would keep all our treasures in this big metal box that came with each cabin, but Josephine's fist remained closed.

"She likes Hershey's Kisses," said Mary.

We knew this was going to be a contest of wills, and while it was important that we show who was in control, we didn't want a major scene over two Hershey's Kisses.

"Tell you what," said Gwen. "I'm going to close my eyes and hold out my hand, and when I count to three, Josephine will drop one of the kisses in my hand. Okay?"

The other girls gathered around to watch this strange proceeding. Josephine stared at Gwen out of her small, narrow face.

Gwen closed her eyes and held out her hands.

"One . . . two . . . three," she said.

Plop. It was like magic.

"Thank you," said Gwen. "We'll just put this in the box, and you can have it after lunch. Now I'll close my eyes again and count to three, and you give me the other one. One . . . two . . . three."

Nothing happened.

"She doesn't want to do it," said Mary.

"You can have them both after lunch," said Gwen.

Josephine shook her head. The Hershey's Kiss, what was left of it, was beginning to melt in the warmth of Josie's hand, and chocolate oozed out from between her fingers.

I snuggled up close to Josephine on the bottom bunk and put my arm around her. "How about if I trade you a real, live kiss for that ooey, gooey chocolate in your hand?" I said. "Okay?"

Josephine just looked at me. I learned over, took her face in my hands, and gave her a big fat kiss on the cheek, grinning at her. I got the chocolate, and we all set off for lunch in the dining hall. Following along behind the girls, Gwen and I gave each other a high five.

Pamela and Elizabeth were just going ahead of us with their groups when we got there, and as we went through the door I heard Pamela say, "Oh, my gosh! They're gorgeous!"

Coming through the door on the other side of the hall were Andy and Craig and a couple more guys. I don't know if it was because they were brawny and tanned (some of them, anyway) or because we were feeling rather desperate for male company, but they sure looked good to us. One of them had an acne-scarred face, but his smile was warm, he was cute, and his little charges were hanging all over him. If there's one thing that's attractive to a girl, it's a guy who seems to get along well with kids.

"I get the one in the sweatshirt," Elizabeth murmured.

"There are two in sweatshirts, Liz," Pamela said. "I want the one in the red shorts."

"That's the one I meant!" Elizabeth told her.

"Sorry, he's taken," Pamela joked.

As they directed their boys to one of the long wooden tables Craig asked us, "So what name did you pick for yourselves? Andy and I got the Buzzards."

"Coyotes," I told him.

"Bunnies," said Elizabeth.

"Mermaids," said Pamela.

"Hey guys," Andy said to the little boys hanging on his arm. He motioned toward Pamela's girls. "Meet the Mermaids."

"Yuck!" said one of his boys, who immediately grabbed a bench at the table, spreading out his arms and legs the length of it. "Don't let the girls sit here," he warned his fellow campers, and the game was an instant success: Never let the girls sit at a boys' table. As though they would have. The Coyotes chose a table as far from the Buzzards as they could get, while the Bunnies and Mermaids all turned their backs on the boys at the next table.

"Welcome, campers!"

The camp director for Camp Overlook was not the woman who had interviewed us back home, but a short curly-haired woman in jeans and a CAMP OVERLOOK T-shirt. Connie Kendrick's voice was loud for so small a woman, but she absolutely radiated cheerfulness. You had the feeling that if the dining hall were sliding down the mountain, she would still be smiling.

"I am *so* glad to have you here for three weeks at Camp Overlook!" she said.

"And the very first thing we need to do, before we *eat*, even, which is the *next* most important thing we do, is learn the Camp Overlook cheer. And here it is:

> *'Clap your hands!*
> *Stamp your feet!*
> *Our Camp Overlook*
> *Can't be beat!'*

"Everybody, now! Say it with me!"

The dining hall resounded with the sound of hands clapping, the wooden floor rocked with the vibration of stamping feet, and all the kids shouted the cheer together.

Then each table assigned a designated runner to go to the kitchen and return with platters of hot dogs, french fries, sliced tomatoes and cucumbers, and large squares of chocolate brownies for dessert. The way some kids ate, I wondered if this was the first full meal they'd had that week.

"Here comes five pounds, easy!" Gwen moaned, but we were hungry already, and when we'd polished off a hot dog, we each took a brownie.

After lunch the assistant director, Jack Harrigan, introduced all the full counselors and assistant counselors. I noticed that the guy both Pamela and Elizabeth had their eyes on was Ross Mueller. The cute guy with the acne was Richard Harrigan, Jack's son. Connie Kendrick went over the camp rules, and then there was a guided tour of the whole place. This gave the assistant counselors a chance to hang back and talk with each other while the kids trooped on ahead of us, following Connie and Jack.

"So where you girls from?" Ross asked Elizabeth as we headed down to the river. He was one of the blondest guys I'd ever seen. His skin was tanned, and this made the hair on his arms and legs, his eyebrows, even, seem blonder still. Even Pamela's short hair was not as light as his.

"Silver Spring," she told him, smiling. "What about you?"

"Philly," he said.

"You came all the way here from Pennsylvania?" Pamela asked in surprise.

"Yeah. I'm going to major in P.E. Figure 'assistant counselor' will look pretty good on a college application." He grinned at her. "So what brought *you* here? The scenery? The kids? The food? The river?"

We laughed, because Camp Overlook is to camps in general what Motel 6 is to hotels, what Budget is to rental cars. No frills. Part of the river front was sectioned off for swimming. Next to that were a couple of rowboats and, farther on, a bunch of canoes. That was the extent of water sports.

"Not the river, that's for sure," Pamela said.

"Not the food," added Elizabeth.

"The company," said Gwen, eyeing another assistant counselor, almost as short as Gwen but probably the most muscular guy in the camp. I figured she was going to forget Legs in a hurry.

"Ah, yes! The company!" said Ross, and grinned at Elizabeth this time.

We kidded around all the way to the baseball diamond, but when Connie got to the edge of the field where the woods began, with various paths leading off into the trees, she faced the young campers. "You are *never* to go on any of these trails without the permission of your counselor, and you are never to go alone. Some of these paths go on for miles, folks. It's easy to get lost. We're going to follow one right now, though, to the overlook, for which the camp is named."

We went to the overlook then, Gwen and I elbowing each other at the way Elizabeth and Pamela were both competing for Ross's attention. Elizabeth's voice gets higher when she talks to a guy she likes, while Pamela's gets more sultry. Sophisticated Pamela acts a little too blasé, as though she could hardly care less, while Elizabeth is all enthusiasm.

"When you become a psychiatrist," Gwen whispered to me, "they're your first case study."

"Psychologist," I said. "No med school for me."

The overlook was probably the only—and certainly the most—spectacular thing about Camp Overlook. On a natural promontory, protected by a chest-high stone wall, we could see far out over the valley and the mountains beyond—layer upon layer of gray blue.

One of Andy's boys tried to climb up on the four-foot wall, and Andy was after him in a second. It wasn't a sheer drop-off—if he'd fallen, he would have rolled—but it was a lesson to all of us just how alert we had to be.

Maybe it was a good thing that the boys' cabins were on one side of the clearing and the girls' on the other, I thought as we went back to camp for quiet time. The way Pamela and Elizabeth were watching Ross, half our girls could have run off before they'd notice.

3

AROUND THE CAMPFIRE

We spent the "quiet hour" not very quiet at all, settling some disputes about whose stuff was taking more shelf space and whose sneakers were smelling up the place.

Gwen and I began to see a pattern: Ruby and Kim were the clingiest. When either of us sat down on the edge of our bunk, one or both of those girls were right beside us, leaning against us, stroking our arms, toying with our hair. Estelle was a trouble-maker; Latisha, the oldest, the aloof one. Josephine was used to playing the "baby" role, with Mary, her sister, her appointed nursemaid and caretaker.

Did I know what I was in for? I wondered as I got up to get

some Kleenex from my bag, and instantly Ruby and Kim rose up on either side like appendages and moved with me across the floor.

I could have been swimming at Mark Stedmeister's pool. I could have been going to the movies with Lester or ordering Chinese to eat at home with Dad. But I told myself it was only three weeks out of my life, and it would give Dad and Sylvia a chance to be alone. Besides, Lester would appreciate me all the more when I got back. Maybe.

"I'm tired already," Gwen confided when the Coyotes settled down at last to trade stick-on tattoos, which most had brought along. Gwen and I simply stretched out on our bunks to rest up for whatever lay ahead. We were too tired to even sit up.

Dinner that night was chicken and noodles and a tossed salad. Josephine wouldn't eat it.

"She only eats fried chicken," Mary explained.

"Well, that's too bad, Josephine, because this is all we've got," I told her. "If you don't like the chicken, eat the noodles."

"They look like worms," said Josephine, which was about the first intelligible thing she'd said since she'd got here, and I wanted to throttle her.

"Eeuw!" said Estelle and Ruby.

"Worms!" said Latisha.

"And they're absolutely delicious. Eat!" Gwen commanded.

Everyone ate but Josephine.

The afternoon had been exhausting. After quiet time we'd

had a relay race, followed by a volleyball game, followed by a swim, but most of the kids claimed the water was too cold. So the dining hall smelled not only of chicken and noodles and disinfectant, but of hot sweaty bodies and stringy hair.

"Okay, campers, listen up!" said Connie when the cherry Jell-O dessert had been served. "At Camp Overlook we take our showers *before* we go to bed, not when we get up in the morning. The sheets are changed only once a week, and we want to be kind to our bunk mates and not stink up the cabins."

All the kids laughed and pointed at each other.

"So here's the plan," Connie continued. "After dinner you are to shower, then put on your pj's. Did everyone bring pajamas as the instructions told you to do? And then I want you—softly, silently, like deer in the moonlight—to follow your counselors to the campfire." Her voice got very low. "I want you to come so quietly that, just like deer, no one will hear you coming. The others will turn around and there you are, just like that."

At first there was a lot of hooting and snickering at even the word "pajamas," because pajamas are too much like underwear, and all you have to say to this crowd is "underpants," and they practically roll on the floor in laughter. But the "silently, like deer in the moonlight" phrase made them pause, and we noticed that they were quiet already, just leaving the dining hall.

Because the showers could hold only so many girls at once, two cabins were to go at a time, and when our girls were through, we were to knock on the doors of the next two cabins till everyone had a turn. Later, after the kids were clean and back in the cabins, the counselors got to shower, half of them at a time, while the others took charge.

Once inside the wooden walls of the shower house, though, our little campers hesitated, their towels wrapped tightly around them.

"C'mon, before the water gets cold," I called, testing it with one hand. I didn't want to tell them it was barely warm to begin with. "Last one in is a rotten egg!" I couldn't help smiling to myself, because I could remember when Elizabeth and Pamela and I used that line, only then we said, "Last one in is a virgin" and felt so sophisticated!

The younger girls gave in first—Ruby, then Josephine, and finally Kim. But the older girls hung back. We noticed the same reluctance from the girls in Elizabeth's cabin. We tried to be casual about it and sat down on a bench at one end. Tommie Lohman, Elizabeth's cabin mate, was a tall thin girl with light brown hair and very long legs. She had an easy, languid way about her that gave the impression she was in no hurry to see what the next day or month or year would bring.

At last all the Coyotes and Bunnies were standing in a line under the showers, hitting the soap dispensers with the palms of their hands and lathering up, eyeing each other furtively while they scrubbed.

Gwen and Elizabeth and I were listening to Tommie's funny account of all the things she'd forgotten to bring, when suddenly Latisha yelled, "She's lookin' at me!" and pointed to a girl in Elizabeth's cabin.

"Tend to your own bathing, Marcie," Elizabeth told the freckled girl.

But a moment later Latisha complained, "Now she's lookin' at me back *there!*"

"Latisha, your body's no different from anyone else's, so cool it," Gwen said.

"What if the boys come in?" asked Estelle warily.

"The boys have their own showers on the other side of camp," I told her.

"But what if they peek?" asked Ruby.

"Then we'll dunk their heads in the toilet," said Gwen, and the girls screeched with laughter.

At some point Josephine got Ruby's washcloth by mistake, and when they traded back again, Estelle jeered to Josie, "Ha-ha! Now you got nigger water on you!"

"Estelle!" I said, surprised, and the other girls covered their mouths in shock. They all turned to see what we would do.

"You watch your mouth, girl," Latisha warned Estelle, her eyes menacing.

Choose your battles, our counselor's handbook had said. *Some issues are worth addressing immediately, and some can be saved for later*. I decided not to make a big issue of it on our first night here in camp.

"I hope I won't hear that word again, Estelle," I told her. Gwen said nothing, and I knew she was waiting for the right time and place too.

When the girls were clean and back in the cabin, we counselors bathed alone, in record time. By then there was no hot water at all, and I was grateful for my flannel pajamas. It's *cold* in the mountains! Then, when the path to the showers had grown quiet, we heard a soft bell announcing the campfire. We all put on our sneakers and jackets and—just as Connie said—like deer coming out to cross the meadow in the moonlight, we walked silently out in the field, where logs had been placed in ever widening circles, and there was the smell of smoke in the air.

I had thought that this would be the highlight of the day. I had thought that these city kids, some of whom had never even heard a cricket chirp, would really go for the brightness of the stars, the sound of frogs and hoot owls and katydids.

Wrong. They were terrified half out of their minds. These kids, who were used to shouts and sirens, were petrified by the stillness of night in the mountains. This time not only did Ruby and Kim cling to us like Velcro, but Mary frantically reached for my hand, Josephine attached herself to Gwen's pajamas, and even the indomitable Estelle stayed as close to us as she could get. Only Latisha walked on ahead, but she leaped whenever something rustled or croaked.

The boys weren't quite as obvious in their terrors, but I could tell by their silence that they were awed. One little kid, sitting between Andy's knees, had his head tipped back about as far as it would go, one finger pointing toward the sky, trying to count the stars. But his other arm was wrapped around Andy's thigh in a death grip.

Connie Kendrick was sitting on a log with a blanket around

her shoulders, and when everyone was seated, she just started singing very softly, and one by one, those of us who knew the song joined in: "Kum ba yah, my Lord, Kum ba yah . . ."

When the song was over, Jack Harrigan—as tall as Connie was short—told an Indian legend about the Big Dipper, but I noticed that nobody suggested ghost stories around the fire.

Then a little boy's plaintive cry broke the spell: "I wanna go home," followed by a sob.

Now, a sob around a campfire on the first night away from home, we discovered, is like smallpox in a crowded tent. The cry was immediately followed by a whimper somewhere else, and then I heard Kim give a tearful gulp.

But Connie was ready. "Okay, campers," she called in a loud voice. "What's the Overlook cheer?" And everybody began to yell:

> *"Clap your hands!*
> *Stamp your feet!*
> *Our Camp Overlook*
> *Can't be beat!"*

"What?" said Connie. "I can hardly hear you. Is that the best you can do?"

> **"Clap your hands!**
> **Stamp your feet!**
> **Our Camp Overlook**
> **Can't be beat!"**

we all shouted, the children loudest of all, as much to drive the homesickness away as to frighten any creatures that might be lurking around.

We sang funny songs next—"Do Your Ears Hang Low"— and then Jack did an imitation of a clown who keeps trying to open an umbrella and hold his pants up at the same time. The kids shrieked out their laughter. Even Kim was giggling in my lap. She was fingering a lock of my hair, twisting it around and around, and I could feel her body shake when she laughed.

I noticed Richard Harrigan smiling at me across the campfire, and suddenly I felt very self-conscious. My hair was wet, my pajamas wrinkled, my Reeboks untied, and a new guy was smiling at me in a warm sort of way. I smiled back. Then I realized he was smiling at all of us, not me alone. Maybe he was feeling the same way I was, that it was just nice to be with friends. Or maybe I was fooling myself and missing Patrick more than I liked to admit. The cool star-filled night—I could almost feel Patrick's arm around me, the way I'd snuggle up against his shoulder. I found myself still missing him at odd moments, wondering where he was and what he was doing. But then it passed, and here I was, cozy in my pajamas and jacket, sharing a campfire in a new place with new people.

Jack went over the schedule for the following day. Then Connie sang a lullaby that she said Native American mothers sometimes sang to their children, and she told us to go softly back to our cabins and that a bell the next morning would announce breakfast.

Quietly we retraced our steps and, after one more trip to the toilets, crawled into bed by the light from our flashlights. We didn't want to turn on the overhead light because it would break the mood.

We had no sooner got everyone in her bunk than Josephine said she had to go to the bathroom again. I put on my shoes and we went to the toilets.

Ten minutes after I got her in bed the second time, she said she had to go again. I figured this was a bid for attention. "I guess the next time you have to go the bathroom, Josephine, Mary will have to take you," I said.

"Josephine, shut up and go to sleep," came Mary's voice in the darkness.

After that the cabin grew quiet.

Tired as I was, I couldn't fall asleep right away. There were too many things to think about: Dad and Sylvia back home; Estelle's remark in the showers; homesickness for Lester, for the gang; my self-doubt about how good an assistant counselor I would be; Elizabeth and Pamela both liking the same guy; not being in the same cabin with either of them; Richard's smile . . .

I decided that what I really wanted to happen at camp—in the romance department—was nothing. I wanted a time-out from wondering what guys were thinking about me, from fussing with my hair, using mouthwash in case a guy was going to kiss me. I would like one summer of just being friends with people. Smiling at guys and feeling a certain electric charge, but no blinking lights, no bells, no whistles. . . . Just liking each other without having to get involved. That would be nice.

"Hey, girlfriend," Gwen whispered, sneaking over to my bunk. "You awake?"

"Yeah."

"Me too. You think we're going to make it?"

"I don't know." I scooted over to make room for her, and she sat down on the edge. "Think what the full counselors go through. They've each got seven kids to handle all by themselves. It's all we can do to keep six kids in line between the two of us."

"You know who I miss?" said Gwen.

"Legs?"

"No. Granny."

"Your grandmother?"

"Yeah. She's always lived with us. As long as I can remember, I went in and kissed her before I went to bed. If I was going out for the evening, I'd kiss her before I went out. Isn't that weird? Fifteen years old and still missing my granny?"

"You want my blankie?" I asked, and we giggled. Then I asked, "Really, though, you're not thinking about Legs at all?"

"Not much," she said. "I finally realized he's not right for me, and there's a big wide world out there. . . ."

"Of guys," I added.

"Guys and everything else. Jobs! College! You know what I think? I think Legs was my 'blankie.' The *Boyfriend*, you know? Just to say I had one?"

"He really liked you, though, Gwen."

"Maybe. But we're so different. Isn't it strange how you can go with someone who hardly shares any of your interests and convince yourself he's The One?"

"Love's strange."

"It wasn't love."

"Well, relationships are strange, then," I said. "That's why I want to be totally free for now. The No-Boyfriend Summer."

We sat for a few minutes listening to the crickets through the screen.

"Well, if you want my permission to go call your granny, you've got it," I said finally.

Gwen laughed softly and stood up. "No, I just needed a heart-to-heart talk with my counselor. G'night, girl. Sleep tight."

I heard the springs squeak as she got into her bunk. And then a voice from somewhere above said, "I could hear everything you said!" and I knew that Estelle had been listening the whole time.

"Watch it, girl-baby," Gwen said.

4
WET

The next morning I couldn't believe it was time to get up already. I wanted to sleep twice as long and could tell that Gwen felt the same way. Even the girls were awake before us. I had no idea that working with kids could be so exhausting. It wasn't just that hiking was followed by rowing, and volleyball was followed by swimming; about thirty times a day we found ourselves mentally counting heads to be sure nobody had wandered off or drowned or fallen off Point Overlook.

"I've never been so tired in my life," Elizabeth said to us the third evening. "I'm even more tired than when I baby-sit Nathan all day."

"It's the responsibility," said Gwen. "And the fact that we have to stay one step ahead of the girls all the time."

"We've got a girl who cries for her foster mother and keeps begging to call home," said Elizabeth.

"I've got a girl who wets the bed when she gets upset," said Doris Bolden.

A bunch of us were sitting around Pamela and Doris's cabin, putting Band-Aids on our feet and witch hazel on our mosquito bites. If Gwen was the color of cocoa, Doris was the color of nutmeg, and I realized that my mind was once again focused on food. I'd eaten more the first day I'd been there than I eat in two days at home, but I needed every ounce of energy I could get.

The kids were up in the dining hall watching a movie, and the full counselors were supervising so we could have some time off. We'd talked about going swimming in the river, but nobody was making a move in that direction.

Pamela came in from the toilets just then. "Hey!" she said. "I just found out that the guys are skinny-dipping and left their clothes on the bank."

You never saw six girls come alive as fast as we did. Suddenly we weren't as tired as we'd thought. We piled out of the cabin and headed, giggling, toward the river.

There were twelve assistant counselors at camp—six for girls, six for boys. Gwen and Pamela and Elizabeth and I, plus Tommie Lohman and Doris Bolden, made up the assistant counselors in the girls' cabins. Andy Simms, Craig Kimball, Ross

Mueller, and Richard Harrigan were assistant counselors on the boys' side, plus a guy we called G. E. and the guy Gwen had her eye on, Joe Ortega.

We went down the path single file. The moon was half full, and the sky was cloudless. We could hear muffled laughter and talk from the guys as they splashed about in the water, and when we came through the trees, we could see their clothes in little heaps there on the ground.

Elizabeth grinned as she went over and sat on top of somebody's jeans and T-shirt. Then the rest of us chose our own little pile, where we sat cross-legged, like pieces on a chessboard, and it wasn't more than a few seconds before the guys saw us.

"Hey, c'mon in! Water's fine!" Ross called.

"No, thanks! We're just looking," Pamela called back, and we laughed.

"Just browsing," called Doris.

"The view from here is great," I told the guys.

They laughed and splashed some more, not rising above waist level, I noticed.

"Oh, this is heaven!" said Gwen. "I think I'll just sit here the rest of the evening."

"Yeah, it's so nice of you guys to leave your clothes for us to sit on," said Tommie. One of the boys splashed water on her, and she just laughed but wouldn't get up.

The guys did all sorts of stunts, like swimming along underwater, then popping up farther on. We felt so powerful sitting on their clothes, in complete control, none of us willing to leave so they could come out. The movie, we knew, was an hour and a half long. There would be snacks after that, so we had maybe forty minutes left.

"Hey!" Richard Harrigan called finally. "Somebody toss me my pants? Somebody with a good aim, please?"

"Which ones are yours?" called Pamela.

He pointed to the pile that Gwen was sitting on.

"Sorry," Gwen called. "You'll have to come get them."

Now we really hooted. Because Richard was the assistant director's son, we knew that alone would keep him from squealing on us. It's the same with a teacher's or preacher's kid, I think. He goes out of his way to prove he's one of the gang.

The boys laughed too and splashed us some more, but not too much because their clothes, after all, were getting wet. We could tell that there was a lot of whispering going on out there in the water. We couldn't see their faces, but the way they clumped together told us we had them stumped.

"They must be getting cold," Elizabeth said. "The river's cold even in the daytime." She grinned.

"They've been in for at least twenty minutes," said Doris. "I don't think I could stand it for more than ten. Not at night."

"Hey, c'mon, girls. You can keep our boxers if you really want them, but could we just have our jeans?" called Andy.

"How are you going to put them on in the water?" I asked.

"There's a bank over there. We'll swim to the other side so as not to offend your delicate sensibilities," said Craig.

We held a conference. They held a conference.

"Nope!" I said. "We like it here just fine. Most comfortable we've been all day."

We figured they'd swim downriver a ways, climb out in the dark, and go back to their cabins to put on something else. We began debating as to what we'd do with their clothes. String their underwear up the flagpole, maybe? Or decorate the trees and bushes with their clothes and be back in the dining hall before they could catch us?

But suddenly there was a great splashing of water, and here the guys came, charging up the riverbank, all six of them buck naked.

We gave a little scream and grabbed on to the guys' clothes so they'd have to wrestle us to get them back, but they didn't even bother with their clothes. I don't know who picked me up—Joe, I think—but each boy grabbed a girl and either dragged or carried her to the water and threw her in.

We gasped and gagged, shocked at this sudden reversal of fortune. And then the boys were in the water with us. We were all laughing and splashing each other with the palms of our hands.

"Hey, girls, you'd swim a lot easier if you didn't have anything on," Ross called.

Pamela giggled. So did Gwen and Tommie.

"Yeah, if anybody wants her shorts unzipped, I'm the man," said Craig, and we laughed some more.

But none of us girls took him up on his offer. We just floated around, watching each other in the moonlight, knowing the boys were totally naked under the water, and now and then colliding with a hairy leg. If Aunt Sally knew what her "little Alice" was doing right now, she'd probably pass out. It was exciting as anything, and Elizabeth looked positively in shock. Delightedly so.

"Hey, next time we go swimming, let's make it coed," said Andy. "Next time you girls have to take it all off."

"Ha! What next time?" said Doris.

"Next movie night. Deal?" said Ross.

"Deal!" said Pamela.

"Pamela!" Elizabeth and I said together, but we laughed, too.

We talked about ourselves then, just the basics—where we were from, what year we were in school. Craig and Richard, at seventeen, were the only ones who had been assistant counselors at Camp Overlook before.

"What's the hardest part of camp for you?" I asked Andy.

"Trying to keep my boys from sneaking over to peek in the girls' showers," he said, and the others grinned.

"Trying to keep *himself* from sneaking a peek, you mean," said Craig.

"Then my girls are right to worry," I told him. "It's the main topic of conversation in the showers."

Richard told us that the full counselors got Saturday nights off, and the assistant counselors got Friday nights. He said we had from six to midnight to go into town if we wanted, as long as we had one of the older counselors drive.

"Think we could get the camp minibus for the evening?" Craig asked.

"I don't know. Dad might let us. I'll see what I can do,"

Richard promised, and that was something to look forward to.

We could just make out the dining hall from where we were floating about in the water, and when the lights came on we knew the movie was over and the kids would be having their snack. We needed to be back there in ten minutes.

So we girls pulled ourselves out of the water, our clothes heavy and clinging, our sneakers squishing with every step we took. We stood on the bank a minute, squeezing water from our shorts, then told the guys good night and hurried back to our cabins to change.

"That was fun!" Elizabeth said breathlessly. "You didn't know where the guys were going to be in the water, and I'm pretty sure my foot touched somebody's . . . well . . . *you* know!"

"No, I *don't* know," Pamela said mischievously. "His what? His ear? His arm?"

But Elizabeth only said, "*You* know" again, and we smiled.

I was thinking back to the time when Elizabeth confessed to me that she had never seen a man naked. I guess her dad never walks between the bedroom and bathroom in his birthday suit, and she hadn't had a little brother yet. So, to help out, I'd gone through a pile of old *National Geographic* magazines looking for naked men, but there always seemed to be a spear or a shield in front of the very places Elizabeth would want to see most.

I had hardly got into a pair of dry shorts when the Coyotes trooped in, looking for us. Mary and Josephine were in the lead, Mary holding Josephine's hand, and were followed by Latisha, looking as belligerent as ever, then Estelle and Ruby and Kim.

Kim was near tears because we hadn't been there in the dining hall to escort them back to the cabin and they'd had to set out on their own. Kim clung to Gwen when she came in.

"Where *was* you?" Latisha demanded. "You're our counselors, and I'll bet you been swimming!"

"Right!" I said. "As a matter of fact, I got thrown into the water, and I'm just now drying off."

That shut them up in a hurry. They looked at us wide-eyed.

"Who threw you in?" asked Mary.

"Some of the guys," I told her.

"You gonna tell?" asked Ruby.

"No." Gwen laughed. "It was all in fun."

Kim still seemed on the verge of tears. "I don't want anybody to throw me in," she said.

"I won't let anyone do that to you, girl-baby," Gwen purred. "And if somebody did, I'd be right there to pull you out, so don't you worry." She put both arms around Kim and held her close, and that just seemed to be the opening bell, because all the other girls edged in for a hug. Even Estelle. But Latisha watched with a jaundiced eye.

"Bet one of 'em's your boyfriend," Latisha said to Gwen.

"Yeah? Which one?" Gwen said.

"I don't know. Andy somebody?"

"Nice guy," said Gwen. "But what about Joe?"

"Ohhhh! Jooooe!" the girls chorused.

Latisha gave a hoot. "They're gonna go off behind the cabins and kiiisss!" she said.

Gwen just smiled at her and looked mysterious, but the girls were still giggling and grinning.

"Well, *are* you?" Estelle asked.

And when Gwen raised an eyebrow, Estelle said, in a hoity-toity voice, "Are you going to go behind the cabins and *make love*?"

Now the girls really hooted.

"Joe is just a friend of mine, like all the other guys here are friends. We just met," said Gwen.

"She going to!" Latisha stage-whispered and the girls went laughing and giggling to the showers.

There was an incident Wednesday night that almost got Pamela's cabin mate, Doris Bolden, dismissed from camp.

She and Pamela had a particularly difficult girl in their cabin, a nine-year-old named Virginia, who was living in her third foster home, and had a vocabulary that would have shocked a sailor. When somebody displeased her, her first reaction was to clobber them on the head or the back, or make a quick jab with her elbow.

Doris had warned her that there would be consequences if she physically attacked another child again, but that night in the showers she knocked a girl down for using her towel, and when Doris grabbed her, she'd yelled, "Get your hands off me, nigger."

Pamela and Doris's girls had come down early and showered with us, as the girls in cabins eight and ten had cleanup duty in the dining hall that evening. So Gwen and I saw the whole thing. Punishment had to be swift and sure.

"Get dressed, Virginia," Doris had said. "You and I are going for a walk."

Gwen and I didn't think much about it. I thought that Pamela would probably get the other girls to bed, and then Doris would take Virginia for a "cool down" and discuss what had happened in the showers.

Back in our own cabin we went through the nightly ritual of confiscating the food that Ruby and Mary—the usual culprits—had sneaked out of the dining hall in fists or pockets, promising that if they got hungry, the food would be right there in our metal lockbox waiting for them. They didn't have to steal, only ask.

Mary insisted that Josephine say her prayers at night, and Ruby and Estelle said theirs as well. I asked the other girls to keep a respectful silence while they prayed.

Then we had a few stories while lying in our beds with the light off—made-up stories and tales about what had gone on during the day—when suddenly there came the most terrible far-off scream . . . then another and another, followed by loud sobbing.

I think the entire camp was on alert. If we heard a disturbance, out first duty, we'd been told, was to check for fire, and if there was no fire, we were to keep the girls in our cabins until there was word over the sound system as to what we should do in an emergency.

Gwen and I were on our feet instantly, staring through the screen door, but there was no smell of smoke or hint of fire. There was, however, the sound of running feet and a flashlight coming from the direction of the camp director's cabin, another coming from Jack Harrigan's.

The screams came again, then we heard Doris Bolden saying, "Hey, be quiet now," and finally, as we all gawked, our girls gathering behind us at the cabin door and windows, we saw Doris and Virginia and Connie and Jack all coming back from the campfire circle, Virginia crying loudly. They dropped Virginia off at Pamela's cabin, but Doris was escorted to the camp office.

When we'd gotten our girls settled down again at last, Gwen and I whispered together outside our cabin, trying to figure out what could have happened.

"You don't think Doris would hit her, do you?" Gwen whispered.

I shook my head.

Obviously, however, something terrifying had happened. It wasn't until the next day that we found out. Pamela told us.

As punishment for pushing a girl down in the shower, Doris had taken Virginia out to the campfire circle. She'd told Virginia that she was to sit alone on a log and think about how she could control her temper in the future and that Doris would be back for her later.

Doris had not actually left. She had gone back in the trees to keep watch over her, but Virginia had panicked, terrified at being alone at night. She would have preferred "getting smacked," she'd told Connie between sobs.

In Connie's office Doris had been lectured and almost let go. The whole idea of camp, Connie had said, was to get city kids in tune with nature, not to scare them with it, and with that punishment she had set Virginia back even further than she'd been when she came.

But because Doris was well liked by the other little girls and had not actually left the child alone, it was decided that she would stay here on probation and apologize to Virginia, which she did. She had gone back to their cabin, Pamela reported, where Virginia was still sniffling and, in front of the other girls, had told Virginia that she had made a serious mistake in making her think she was alone out there in the dark, that she would never have left her alone unwatched.

Doris assured her that it would not happen again but that if Virginia continued to hit other girls, she would have to sit in the director's office for a long time-out and would miss the next movie as well.

That seemed a fair punishment all around. Doris kept her job and her dignity, Virginia received the apology and the warning she deserved, and the rest of the assistant counselors got a lesson in discipline.

"It's like walking a tightrope," Tommie said. "One step to the left, you've gone too far. One step to the right, you haven't been assertive enough."

"It'll take every single bit of patience I've got," said Gwen.

"And you'd better not have your mind on anything else, because you need to concentrate totally on your girls," said Pamela. She sighed. "Maybe that's a good thing. It'll keep me from worrying about Mom and what *she's* up to."

Nobody spoke for a moment. Then I asked, "So what's going to keep us going for the next two weeks?"

This time Elizabeth and Pamela both grinned. "Friday night," said Pamela. "Assistant counselors' night out!"

5
GERALD

Gwen and I tried not to have favorites among the Coyotes because they were each needy in a different way. Kim needed all the reassurance she could get, and Ruby seemed to sail through the week without any particular problems as long as she got hugs now and then. But Latisha was mad at the world and took it out verbally on anyone who was handy.

"What you looking at, girl?" had been her first comment to Estelle the day we arrived, and of course Estelle had issues before Latisha even opened her mouth.

"Not you, that's for sure," Estelle had said, and the way Latisha bristled, we were prepared for flare-ups between the two.

But Mary and Josephine were my own little case study, as Gwen put it. I couldn't figure out why Mary felt so responsible for her sister—doing things for her that Josephine could probably do herself. At our first staff session I talked to Connie Kendrick about putting one of the sisters in another cabin.

"Better not," Connie said. "We had to pull a lot of strings to get them here in the first place, and they finally came on the condition that they not be separated. We take what we can get, and these two kids really needed a break from home." She winked at me. "Of course, they don't have to stick together like Siamese twins. There's no reason you can't be creative."

So at breakfast on Thursday, as Mary led Josephine to our table, I said, "I can't decide which of you two girls I want to sit beside most. So I'm just going to have to sit between you, and then I'll have one of you on each side. Lucky me!"

Mary paused a moment, then smiled and, letting go of her sister's hand, allowed me to slide between them on the bench.

"Mission accomplished," murmured Gwen, and I caught her smile from across the table.

Later that morning, as Jack Harrigan led the kids on a nature hike and the assistant counselors tagged along, G. E. came up beside me. His real name, he'd told us, was Gerald Eggers, but his friends all called him G. E. And I wondered sympathetically if that was because he was shaped like a hanging lightbulb, smaller at the top than the bottom—narrow chest and shoulders, heavy legs. He had a terrific voice, though. If you closed your eyes and listened to him, it was only his voice that was important.

"So how's it going?" he asked. "This your first time being a counselor?"

"Assistant counselor," I answered, and nodded. "You almost need a degree in psychology to know what's going on with these kids."

He chuckled. "First time for me too. But you seem a natural with the kids. Thinking about teaching somewhere down the line?"

"No. Psychology, actually."

"Yeah? I'd like to work with children. I was thinking about pediatrics, but I doubt I could get into med school. So I suppose I'll go into teaching."

Elizabeth and Pamela moved up behind us then, and G. E. went on ahead to walk with Ross and Craig.

"Guess who Gwen's pairing off with," Pamela said. "Joe."

"What do you mean, pairing off?" I asked.

"He had his arm around her back there."

I gave a quick glance behind me. Joe Ortega was giving Gwen a shoulder massage. "Good for Gwen," I said, grinning.

"Where do you suppose we'll go tomorrow night? What's in town?" asked Elizabeth.

"Richard says there's a place that has line dancing and a lot of the counselors hang out there on their night off," Pamela told us.

"I'm ready for a break," said Elizabeth.

"A Ross break," said Pamela.

"I saw him first," said Elizabeth

"No, you didn't," said Pamela. "He's mine!"

***

There was an hour of music after the hike. Whenever there's a special program, the assistant counselors get some time off, seeing as how we don't get paid. It's a chance to wash our underwear or call home or just nap. But I decided to go for a walk by myself. I wanted to take in the scents and sounds of the woods without a bunch of chattering kids around me, so I set out for the overlook.

I was halfway down the path when I heard someone say, "Mind if I join you?"

I turned to see Gerald walking briskly up behind me.

I really didn't want him along. I didn't want anyone along, actually.

"Or did you want to be alone?" he asked, looking at me uncertainly.

I didn't have the heart to tell him to go back.

"Oh, I was just trying to get away from the noise of camp— give my ears a rest," I said.

"I know what you mean." And then, unsure of himself, he said, "But if you'd rather I didn't come . . ."

Oh, for Pete's sake, don't be so wishy-washy! I thought. "Of course not," I said, and walked on. He gave a little skip to catch up.

Isn't it strange how just the slightest mannerism can turn you off? That little skip, and I knew for certain I could not feel romantic about Gerald Eggers in a million years.

"Penny for your thoughts," said Gerald.

I sighed and closed my eyes. He wasn't just in my face, he was in my head.

"Thinking about this summer, that's all. This'll be the longest I've ever been away from home," I said.

"Homesick?"

"Not really, I'm just hoping I can hold out another two weeks. Kids can sure be exhausting. I can't imagine what it's like to be a mother and be around little children all day."

"I think you'd make a great mother," said Gerald.

"That's a long way off," I said. I was beginning to get bad vibes.

"I had a cousin who married at eighteen, and she's really happy," said Gerald. "She's a great mother, too."

"Good for her," I said.

"I guess that's the first thing I look for in a girl," Gerald went on. "How she gets along with kids tells me what kind of mother she'd make."

I stared straight ahead. Was this a test? *Oh, brother.* Was this guy looking for wife material at the grand age of fifteen? If I said I loved children, would he propose? Ask me to wait for him while he worked his way through grad school?

I found myself suddenly babbling on about school and how I'd be entering tenth grade in the fall and how long I'd been on the newspaper staff and what had happened during our production of *Fiddler on the Roof* and how my dad was marrying my seventh-grade English teacher—anything to change the subject—and then I realized it might sound as though I were trying to impress him, show him I was the kind of girl he wanted to marry. My jaw snapped shut.

He glanced over at me. "Get a bug in your mouth?" he asked.

"No, my foot," I said. He gave me a quizzical smile.

We'd reached the end of the path and were facing the low stone wall, the overlook beyond. It was a gorgeous day, and the taller trees were spreading their shadows out over the ones below. All the assorted greens of summer were stretching before us, and beyond the trees the blue and purple layers of hills grew fainter and fainter in the distance. If I couldn't be alone, why couldn't Richard have followed me up here, or Andy or Craig?

And then I felt an arm around my waist as Gerald edged in closer to my side. Yikes! He was going to propose! He'd get down on one knee and pull a gold-plated ring out of his pocket—one size fits all—and . . . I moved away and went over to lean my elbows on the stone wall.

"Sorry," said G. E. "I guess I moved a little too fast."

The third reason not to like him. I swallowed. "I'm really not looking for romance this summer, Gerald," I said.

I heard him sigh. "Let me guess," he said. "You're about to give me that 'I like you as a friend, but . . .' line."

"And?"

"Well, you aren't the first girl who's said it."

"Maybe you come on a little too strong too fast," I said.

"So if I slow down, do I have a chance?"

It just seemed that everything Gerald said made it worse. He seemed so desperate, as though he had to pin down the rest of his life—his love life, anyway—in case he never got another chance.

"Maybe sometimes it's better to make a girl worry a little that you *won't* like her," I said.

He gave a small laugh. "That'll be the day."

I wanted to get back to camp. Even sitting on my bunk flossing my teeth seemed more exciting than continuing this conversation with Gerald. I started back along the path. "Sometimes it's nice just to be friends, G. E. You don't have to make it anything special," I said. "Okay?"

"The story of my life," Gerald said morosely. He put his hands in his pockets, and we walked along in silence for a while.

I thought of a girl I knew back in junior high who didn't have a lot of friends and finally stood in front of a train. It *didn't* exactly help to tell someone just to forget about having somebody special. There wasn't anyone special in my life just then, but I felt pretty sure there would be someday. Why was Gerald worrying about that now?

"Well, thanks for being honest with me," he said when we got close to camp again.

And that's where I lost it. "G. E., *listen* to yourself! We've not even been here a week, I hardly know you, and you tell me you're looking for a girl who's good with children. I'm not thinking that far ahead! I've got a lot of living to do, and so do you. Be a radio announcer or something. Be a singer!"

"I am a singer," said Gerald. "How did you know?"

I was so relieved to have something else to talk about that

I actually smiled. "Because you've got a great voice. You've got the best-sounding voice of any guy here. I'll bet you sing bass."

He grinned a little. "I do. I sing with the madrigals at our school."

"See?" I said. "You just need to get reacquainted with your good points. G. E., meet Gerald. Gerald . . . G. E." He laughed, and so, finally, did I.

When I got back to our cabin, I faced a drama of a different sort. The Coyotes were back from the music program, and Gwen was having a face-off with Estelle. Gwen's voice was loud: "I don't care what you thought Latisha was saying about you, girl! If you've got any complaints, you bring them to me. You don't go dumping someone else's stuff on the floor."

"She got my shoes!" Latisha was shouting. "She done something with my shoes!"

"Have you got Latisha's shoes, Estelle?" Gwen demanded.

Estelle was just begging for a fight, I could tell. Tossing her long black hair behind her, she thrust her face forward, scrunched up her eyes and nose, and said, in a mocking voice, "No, I don't have her stinking shoes, smelling up the place." And then she muttered, "Those nigger-smelling feet."

It took both Gwen and me to pull Latisha off her and get the girls separated.

"She think niggers smell, she ought to smell her own shit," shouted Latisha. "Her shit smells worse'n anybody's, all that dog food she eats."

Now it was Estelle lunging for Latisha. This time I took hold of Estelle and kept her back. Kim was cowering on her bunk, about as far away as she could get, and Mary had Josephine on her lap and was rocking her back and forth. Ruby simply watched from a top bunk, swinging her legs.

Don't get stuck on the language here, I told myself, remembering the advice in our handbook. *Focus on the feelings behind the words*. Estelle had prejudice, Latisha had attitude, and Latisha most of all wanted her shoes back.

I gripped Estelle by the shoulders and looked her square in the eyes. "Where are Latisha's shoes?"

Estelle tossed her head again. "Out there."

"Out where?"

She pointed and I went to the door to look. Latisha's sneakers, the laces tied together, had been tossed up over a sign strung above the road outside the cabins. An arrow pointed up the hill toward the dining hall. Latisha's sneakers hung down over the "c" in "office."

Gwen and I looked at each other. "Why did you do that?" she asked Estelle.

"I *told* you why!" Estelle countered. "Latisha's always leaving them for me to stumble over, and they stink!"

"No worse'n yours do!" Latisha shouted.

"And Latisha's always bossing us around, telling people what to do," said Estelle.

"Yeah? She bossier than *me*. She thinks she's white, too!" said Latisha. "*She's* colored too, ain't she, Alice? You got taco blood in you, you're colored."

"Okay, here's the deal," said Gwen. "We've got two girls who have to learn to get along with each other and a pair of sneakers dangling over the wire out there. You've got till three o'clock this afternoon to figure out a way to get them down, and you have to do it together. You can't ask anyone else to do it for you. If you're still enemies but you get them down, you get one point. If you get them down and you're not enemies anymore, you get two points. And if you get them down and decide to be *friends* the rest of the time we're here, you get three points."

"So what do we get with the points?" asked Latisha.

"One point, you get an extra bag of popcorn at the movie Saturday night. Two points, you get two bags of popcorn and a Milky Way. Three points . . ."

"Three points you have to kiss Joe Ortega in front of us!" said Estelle.

The cabin suddenly erupted in laughter, Latisha and Estelle both hooting together.

"You got it!" said Gwen, looking a little unnerved. "You get the shoes down and figure out how to be friends, and Joe and I will kiss right here in the doorway for all to see."

The Coyotes squealed and carried on, hands over their mouths, eyes wide with delight. We herded them to the dining hall for lunch.

Afterward it took some doing, but Estelle and Latisha finally borrowed a stepladder from the caretaker, carried it down to the cabin, and set it up, under Gwen's supervision. Estelle got an oar from the boathouse, climbed halfway up, with Latisha holding the ladder steady, and managed to knock the sneakers off the sign. They fell to the ground with a thud.

Estelle looked at Latisha uncertainly, but there was devilment in her eyes. "Okay, we're friends," she said.

"Really?" I asked.

Latisha gave a shrug. "Yeah," she said.

"Is this a promise that you'll really try?" asked Gwen.

Now Latisha was grinning. "Yeah. Now you got to go get Joe."

After Estelle climbed down and the ladder was returned, Gwen went in search of Joe Ortega and brought him grinning to the door of the cabin, the boys from his own cabin trailing curiously behind.

"Okay, girls, get ready," Joe said. He glanced up toward the office. "Nobody looking, are they? You want to see me kiss this lady?"

"Yessssssss!" all the girls chorused, and kids from other cabins gathered too.

Joe Ortega put one arm around Gwen's waist, the other under her shoulders, and dramatically swooped her backward, giving her a movie-star kiss. All the little campers clapped and screeched hysterically.

And suddenly I looked up to see Legs coming down the hill from the parking lot.

6
A LITTLE LESSON IN GROWING UP

It was like a movie. One minute we were watching Gwen and Joe in their movie-star embrace, accompanied by all the squealing kids, and the next we were watching long-legged Leo coming down the hill toward us, taking in the whole scene.

"Uh . . . Gwen," I said. "Company."

Joe brought her back to a standing position, then said to the little group from his own cabin, "And *that's* the way you kiss a lady." Then he saw Legs right in front of him, and I heard Gwen gasp.

I guess the next scene in a movie would be Legs punching Joe in the mouth, but that didn't happen. Legs looked at Joe a moment, then at Gwen, and said, "Well, hello."

"You drove all the way up here?" Gwen asked. We could see Jack Harrigan coming down the hill from the office.

"I didn't fly," Legs said in answer. "Just wanted to see how you're doing. Looks to me like you're having a pretty good time."

"Legs, this is Joe, my friend here at camp. Joe, this is Leo, from school," said Gwen.

Jack came up to us then. "Hello?" he said to Legs, a question mark in his voice. He put out his hand and Legs shook it.

"Leo Green," Legs said. "I'm a friend of Gwen's."

"We're glad to have you drop in, but all visitors have to register first at the office," Jack said cordially. "Our counselors are on twenty-four-hour duty here, so . . . I hope you understand. We generally limit visitors to Sunday."

In the movies Legs probably would have turned and pasted the assistant director in the mouth too, but that didn't happen either.

"Well, I work Sundays, and this is the only time I could get off. I just want to talk with Gwen for a few minutes," Legs said.

"Sure. You want to come up to the dining hall?" Jack waited. I'll bet he could smell trouble at fifty paces.

"I'll be right back," Gwen said to the rest of us, and, turning to Estelle and Latisha, she said, "Okay, girls. You did good! Now keep it up, hear?"

The kids only gawked.

Legs and Gwen went up toward the dining hall, Jack walking about ten feet behind them. Joe nodded in their direction and looked at me. "Is Leo bad news?" he asked.

"I don't know," I said honestly. It was really Gwen's story to tell, not mine.

It was time for the canoe lesson, so we guided the campers down to the river.

Connie was on the bank giving instructions through a bullhorn, starting with the safety talk about the right way to get in and out of a canoe while Tommie gave a demonstration. Then Ross took a canoe out into the water to show the kids the correct way to hold a paddle and a few of the basic strokes.

"Everyone will have a chance to go out in a canoe," Connie said. "Some of you will get to paddle, and some of you will just go along for the ride. But before camp is over, we want everyone who would like to learn to paddle to have a chance."

We lined the kids up in pairs, an older and a younger camper, and put life jackets on them. They reminded me of Chinese wontons, their heads the lumps in the middle, and they laughed and hooted at the sight of themselves.

It was when we actually tried to get them in the canoes that the trouble started. Kim was terrified, and one of Elizabeth's charges clung to her and wouldn't let go. Mary, of course, insisted that Josephine go in the same canoe with her.

Each fearful camper got the personal attention of a counselor, and I had to admire the way G. E. calmed Kim. He simply took her by both hands till she stopped trembling, and then, each taking a step sideways, G. E. counting all the while, "*one* banana, *two* banana . . . ," they moved together toward the water and he got her to sit in the middle of a canoe.

We held the canoes steady while the kids got in. After each of the dozen or so canoes received its passengers, the counselor in the stern moved it out into the water. The rest of the campers waited their turn on the bank.

As each counselor gave directions to the older camper in the bow of his canoe, the campers awkwardly brandished their paddles, while the younger passenger in the middle dangled his or her arms over the sides, prepared to enjoy the adventure, or sat frozen, as though the very act of breathing might overturn them all. But after about ten minutes of slowly moving out over the water, even the fearful ones, Kim included, looked as though they could enjoy it.

Once the kids got the hang of it, Connie called out instructions for the C stroke and the J stroke, so that they were turning this way and that, and Jack Harrigan came back from the dining hall to patrol the perimeter in his own canoe.

From where I stood on the bank with the campers still waiting their turn, I saw Gwen coming down the hill. Elizabeth looked over too, searching her face, and then Gwen gave us the okay sign. Not only that, but she was smiling. From somewhere back by the parking lot, we could hear the sound of a car pulling out and heading off down the mountain road. Gwen silently lifted a fist in the air and mouthed, *Yes!* When we saw Joe looking at her, we all laughed.

I couldn't say that the canoe lesson went especially well, but for kids who had never been on a river before, I think they did a pretty fair job. The canoes were going in circles, some more jerkily than others, but the counselors kept them far enough apart that they didn't bump into each other, and every child who wanted to try—and even some who didn't—had a chance to sit in front and paddle. In fact, I didn't do so bad either. Andy let me sit in the bow of his canoe, and though I managed to drop my paddle in the water and we had to chase it down—the kids jeering—it felt good to learn something I'd never done before.

"At the end of our third week, campers, we're going to have a canoe race, and we'll see which of our cabins wins," Connie told them. And the air was filled with shouts of *"We will!"* "No, *we're* gonna win!"

At one point, when the kids took a lemonade break, Pamela, Elizabeth, and I crowded around Gwen.

"What happened?" I asked.

"Legs came all the way up here to tell me that our trip to Baltimore is off when I get back, because his grandma is sick, and he's going to be spending all that time in Baltimore with her," Gwen said, grinning. "I just happen to know that the girl I've heard he's seeing on the side told her friends that she's going to Baltimore that exact same week. Not only that, but Legs's grandma lives in Frederick. I told him that if there was one thing I couldn't stand it was a cheatin' man and that he was crossed off my list as of yesterday. You should have seen the relief on his face!" She laughed some more.

It was a good day at Camp Overlook.

Except that when the canoes went out and came in a second time with another batch of kids, Mary didn't wait for us to help her out. My back was turned momentarily as I helped Estelle make the jump to the bank. When I turned around, Mary and Josephine were starting to climb out of their canoe by themselves. Josephine stumbled climbing over the side, and because the girls were holding hands, both went into the water.

Camp Overlook's philosophy is to let campers experience the consequences of their actions unless it's a question of safety, and neither girl, of course, went under. They bobbed about on the surface in their life jackets, holding hands no longer, and the surprise in Josephine's tiny face soon gave way to delight when she discovered she could not sink if she tried. In fact, she could maneuver any way she wanted.

It was Mary who went bananas, even though the water wasn't over their heads.

"Josie!" she screamed. "Josie, grab my hand! Paddle over here!"

But the more she yelled, the more Josephine grinned and dog-paddled away. Gwen and I were both ready to jump in after them—Ross was already in the water—but we caught Jack Harrigan shaking his head. He motioned for Ross to just circle the girls and let them get the feel of moving about in the water and staying afloat.

"Alice!" Mary screamed. "Gwen! You come get us!"

"Your sister seems to be doing okay, Mary," Jack called. "Can you see why we wanted you to get out of the canoe one at a time?"

"She's going to drown!" she kept bawling, horrified to see

Josephine moving farther and farther away from her in the water, with no one going after her. It was painful to listen to the terror in her voice.

Ross corralled Josephine at last and brought her in, and we got the girls back to our cabin and into dry clothes, Gwen set about combing Josephine's matted hair and I motioned Mary to join me for a private walk. I wasn't sure what I was going to say, but all the assistant counselors were told to squeeze in as many one-on-one walks as we could, and the kids adored it. It was a sign that the chosen boy or girl was special.

I held Mary's hand.

"I guess that was pretty scary," I said.

"I almost drowned! So did Josephine, and you would've let her!" she declared.

I gave her hand a playful tug. "Do you really believe that, Mary? You knew we were right there, and Josie showed us she was okay."

Mary just shook her head. "She could've drowned, though. She's not ever going to grow up right."

"Why not?"

"She's too little," Mary said. "She was born too soon. Mama said."

"Really?"

Mary let go of my hand to demonstrate. "Mama says she was only *this* big!" She held her hands about eight inches apart, then grabbed hold of mine again.

"Boy, that *is* little!" I said. "Look how much she's grown!"

"She's still too little. When she came home from the hospital, we had to watch to see that she didn't stop breathing. Well . . . I don't remember that, but my uncle says so. Everything Josephine does, I have to watch she doesn't hurt herself."

I looked down at the top of Mary's head—only two years older than her sister's—and wondered just what Mary would do with herself if she didn't have Josephine to watch over. I was beginning to get a handle on the problem.

"Well, you sure must have done a good job, Mary, because look at all Josie can do!" I said. "And guess what? When she's a grown girl, she can tell her friends that her big sister showed her how to do everything herself."

Mary continued walking, her round face in a frown. I hoped I knew what I was talking about. "The more you let Josephine do for herself, the more you're teaching her how to grow up."

"She makes a lot of mistakes!" said Mary, rolling her eyes.

"So do I!" I said. "But that's the way I learn. And I'll bet you'll be a very good teacher."

Friday evening we gathered in Elizabeth and Tommie's cabin to get ready for our big night out. Gwen, sitting on the edge of a bunk, was replaiting one of her cornrows. I noticed her black bra.

"Black! Hmm!" I smiled.

"Hey! You put on a white bra and I don't make any comment," she teased.

"It's not the same and you know it," said Pamela. "Not if it's lace, it's not!"

"She's not going to keep it on long, anyway," Tommie said, and we laughed.

"It's her underpants I'm worried about," I said. I tugged at Gwen's jeans. "Let's see your undies, Gwen. Is there lace on those, too?" She playfully pushed me away.

And then Elizabeth, her face slightly flushed, dropped something on Gwen's lap. "Just in case," she said.

Gwen looked down at the box of Trojans resting on her thighs. "Get *outta* here, girl!" she cried, as we all burst into laughter.

"You just might need them," Elizabeth said.

"Get *out!*" Gwen repeated.

Pamela grabbed the Trojans from Gwen and examined the package. "*'Ribbed'? 'Prelubricated'? 'For maximum pleasure'?* Aha! What do *you* know about these kinds of things, Liz?"

Elizabeth's face was fiery red in spite of herself. "I . . . I just grabbed the first package I saw," she said. Then, looking around at us, she said, "Why? Didn't I get the right kind?"

Tommie took the box next and examined it. Without cracking a smile, she said, "Are you sure they're the right size?"

Elizabeth's face fell. "There are . . . sizes?"

We all tried to keep a straight face.

"Of course!" said Tommie. "Extra small, small, average, large, extra large, super stud . . . ." She tossed the box back to Gwen.

I thought my face was going to explode, I was trying so hard not to laugh.

"But how do you *know*?" Elizabeth asked in bewilderment.

"You have to *measure*, Elizabeth!" said Pamela. "You have to carry several different sizes with you and bring a ruler and—"

Elizabeth suddenly caught on, and when we burst into laughter, she said, "Oh . . . you . . . guys!" and laughed a little too.

"Listen," said Doris, "I really want to know. Did you actually buy these yourself?"

"She *did*!" I volunteered.

"Yes, but I couldn't find them at first," Elizabeth continued, "and then a clerk asked if he could help. I was so *embarrassed*!"

"So what did you tell him?" Tommie asked. "That you wanted some ribbed condoms with a lubricated tip?"

"No! I just said I wanted some men's condoms."

"*Men's* condoms?" Pamela shrieked, and we were off again.

Elizabeth sat helplessly down on her bunk bed. "He sent me over to women's sanitary products, and right beside them were all these little boxes with pictures of a man and woman doing romantic stuff."

"So why did you choose this kind?" Gwen asked.

"I liked the sunset," Elizabeth said, and we doubled over. She told the rest of the story then: the lines at the checkout counter, the price check . . .

"Liz, it could only happen to you," said Pamela.

"Yeah, but why are you giving them to me?" Gwen said to Elizabeth. "You think the first time I go out with a guy I'm going to get naked?"

"Don't get mad," said Elizabeth. "I just don't want any of us to get into trouble."

"If you don't want them, Gwen, I'll take them," Pamela offered, plucking the box from Gwen's hand. "If Ross and I hook up . . ."

"I didn't buy them for you and Ross!" said Elizabeth hotly.

"Don't tell me we're going to have a catfight right here," said Tommie. She grabbed the condoms out of Pamela's hand and turned to Doris.

"You take them," she said.

"I'm in enough hot water as it is," Doris said. "I'm lucky I didn't get kicked out of camp. Nope. I don't plan to worry about this stuff till I'm married."

"We could give them to Gerald," said Tommie.

"G. E.?" we all asked in surprise.

"Yeah. He's been following me around all afternoon telling me how he's turned on by girls who get along with kids—how it means they'd make good wives and mothers."

I stared. "That's what he told *me* this morning! The very same thing."

We all looked at each other. "Now there's a guy who wants to fall in love," said Gwen. "So who's going to put him out of his misery?"

"Don't look at me," said Doris.

We all turned toward Elizabeth.

"Let's tell him Elizabeth loves her little brother," Pamela said.

"Yeah, let's say that she *adores* kids and that her greatest wish in life is to be a faithful wife and mother," said Gwen.

"Hey, guys!" said Elizabeth.

496 • PHYLLIS REYNOLDS NAYLOR

"I'll say she lets them snuggle up to her in bed," said Tommie.

"Oh, stop it!" Elizabeth said, swatting at us.

We finished getting ready and probably looked the best we had since we'd come. We'd showered, blow-dried our hair, put on lip gloss and mascara. Two of the paid counselors, Phil and Sue, were going to take us to a restaurant called the White Rooster, and after the mandatory lecture from Jack about none of us going into the bar section, nobody leaving the building and going off alone, we set off in the camp's minibus.

It felt good to get away for the evening. Everything seemed dark and mysterious on the winding dirt road with no lights other than those on the minibus.

Sue had the radio going, and when we weren't chattering away, we were humming along with the music—everyone but me, of course. I won't even hum in public; clearly, I was the only counselor at Camp Overlook who couldn't carry a tune.

Suddenly Elizabeth leaned against my shoulder and whispered, "So who has them, do you know?"

"Has what?" I whispered back.

"The condoms. Nobody gave them back."

"I don't know," I told her. "The last person who had them was Tommie, I think. Or was it Pamela?"

I felt Elizabeth stiffen beside me, but then the lights of the White Rooster came into view, and we soon piled out of the car.

7
NIGHT OUT

"C'mon," Phil said, and led us over to a table by the dance floor in the restaurant. It was a big high-ceilinged room with bare rafters overhead and old signs decorating the walls—signs advertising Burma-Shave and Ivory Flakes and twenty-five-cent chili dogs. We ordered sodas, and they were brought to our table with a big bowl of peanuts. The band was playing a country song, and couples in western dress were already whirling around out on the floor.

"So how goes it?" Phil asked us over the music. "Think you can stick it out for two more weeks?"

"As long as we get Fridays off," Ross said.

"Can the *kids* hold out? That's the question," said Tommie.

"I think only a couple of kids have been sent home in the past few years," said Sue. "Most kids are pretty tough."

"Besides, they'll all want to go on the Kelpie Hunt," said Phil, grinning mysteriously.

"Yeah, what *is* that?" I asked. "I've seen it on the schedule."

"The Kelpie Hunt," Phil said, "is what we do on the last night. It's like a ghost walk. We'll get them psyched up for this two weeks in advance, so they can work up their nerve. Nobody wants to admit he's scared, so they all stick it out."

"What's a kelpie?" I asked.

Richard faked surprise. "You never heard of a kelpie?" I saw him wink at Phil. "Well," he said. "I guess you'll have to stick around and find out."

"Yeah," said Craig. "We'll give the girls a sneak preview."

Sue laughed. "They always do this," she told us. "A camp tradition."

Something else to look forward to. I was really beginning to like Camp Overlook. I liked sitting here at a table with a bunch of new friends—old friends, too.

When the music stopped, we saw people getting into position for line dancing. I'd never done any—I don't know that Elizabeth or Pamela had either—but Elizabeth's taken all kinds of dance lessons, and she can pick up almost any step. So there we were in three rows in the middle of the floor, side-stepping along and tapping our heels on the beat.

To tell the truth, I never did figure out for sure what we were doing. I managed to pick up a simple step, which I repeated over and over as we moved across the floor. But half the fun was coming in a second late on the scuff or the stomp or the hop or the jump and laughing along with the others. When we finished one sequence, I found we'd turned and were facing a different direction.

The seasoned line dancers put up with us good-naturedly, and when one of the fiddle players called out to me that I was doing fine, I knew immediately that I wasn't. But I didn't care, because some of the guys weren't doing so hot either, and we cast each other funny, sympathetic glances. As the music went from "Whatcha Gonna Do with a Cowboy" to "I Feel Lucky," and the dance changed from Cowboy Motion to the Freeze, I discovered that it didn't much matter what I did as long as I could keep from bumping into someone. I was having a great time.

G. E. had positioned himself next to Elizabeth, I noticed, and kept giving her a special smile whenever she looked in his direction. When the music stopped a second time and we took a break, he put one hand on her waist as they left the floor, guiding her back to our table, and I almost laughed out loud.

All us girls trooped to the restroom then, and as soon as we got inside, Elizabeth said, "Somebody else has to dance next to Gerald next time."

"What'd he do? Paw you?" asked Doris.

"No. He's a clinger. Pamela, you dance next to him. He'll be scared of you."

"Why?"

"Just act normal. Make a pass at him. I'll bet he'll run for his life," Elizabeth said.

"I'll bet he won't."

"Extra-large Coke?" said Tommie. "I'm betting he will too. I'll bet he's the kind of guy who would be scared to death if a girl made the first move."

"Okay. If he doesn't, what do I do?" said Pamela. "Who can I pass him off on?"

"We'll think of something," said Doris.

I began to feel sorry for G. E. Did guys think the same thing about girls who seemed as desperate? I wondered how I'd feel if a guy made a pass at me and I found out later it was on a dare. Still, Gerald did act like a dork at times, and if anybody could discourage him, it was Pamela.

We got back to the table and saw that Phil and Sue were holding hands. And for the first time I noticed Sue wearing an engagement ring. They were our most senior counselors, next to Connie and Jack, and I wondered if they'd met here—if love had blossomed at Camp Overlook. I could see how it could happen.

There was definitely something exciting about being away from home overnight, even for me, the Girl Who Wasn't Looking for Romance. Just being up here in the mountains with six available guys around, I guess, gave me the feeling that maybe we'd go a little further than we ordinarily would.

When we got back out on the floor for the second set, Ross was dancing between Pamela and Elizabeth, Gerald on the other side of Pamela. The dancing was even more vigorous this time, and I stumbled over my feet a lot. I felt as though everyone else was wearing tap shoes and I was wearing clogs. But when the number was over, Pamela suddenly threw her arms around Gerald's neck and kissed him, a long hard kiss on the lips, like a dramatic flourish to the end of the dance.

Gerald didn't move away. He held his hands tentatively on Pamela's waist, but he didn't try to prolong the kiss, either. There was an embarrassed, fake smile on his face, and I think we all cringed when we realized that Gerald wasn't enough of a dork not to know that this was a put-up job.

What Pamela didn't see, though, was that when she moved away from Ross on one side of her for that dramatic kiss with Gerald, Ross missed it entirely, because he had turned toward Elizabeth, lifted her hair up off the nape of her neck, and was gently blowing on her to cool her down.

Hey, hey! I thought.

Elizabeth looked absolutely radiant.

It was a good night. For everyone but Gerald, I guess. On the way back to camp Richard and Craig taught us a bawdy song the counselors had made up one year, sung to the tune of "Oh, Susannah."

> *Oh, she came from south of Overlook,*
> *A virgin tried and true,*
> *She'd saved herself for Billy Boy,*
> *Back in Timbuktu.*

But Billy Boy was feeling sad,
And found himself a sheep,
The virgin up in Overlook,
Cried herself to sleep.

Oh, Susannah,
Oh, don't you cry no more,
The fellas up in Overlook
Will even up the score.

We laughed, and even in the dark of the van I could see the puzzled look on Elizabeth's face and wondered if I'd have to explain it to her later.

"Too bad we don't have any sheep up here," said Joe.

"Yeah," said Ross. "Even a motherly goat would do."

"A chicken, even," said Andy.

"A *chicken*?" the guys all said, and we laughed.

Elizabeth gave me a questioning look.

"Don't ask," I whispered.

The minibus came out of the woods on an open stretch, and Phil suddenly pulled over to the side of the road. "Look at the stars!" he said.

We all piled out. For five or six minutes we stood leaning against the bus, looking up, Sue leaning back against Phil, his arms around her.

"This is where we should come in August when the Perseid meteor shower comes along," said Sue. "I don't think I've ever seen a sky so bright. There must not be any cloud cover at all."

I don't know what made me say what I did or why I was the one to break the silence then, but I heard myself saying, "I wonder if Dad and Sylvia are looking at these stars."

There was another moment of silence, and then Andy said, "Who?"

"My dad's getting married next month," I said.

"Ah!" said Phil.

"To her seventh-grade English teacher," Elizabeth explained. "They've been an item for several years, and it's been quite a romance. With a little help from Alice."

Then I had to tell them about how I'd invited Sylvia Summers to the Messiah Sing-Along without Dad knowing and how he'd won her away from our vice principal, Jim Sorringer, by writing such wonderful love letters when she went to England on a teacher-exchange program.

We talked about love all the way back to camp, about how it must feel to be married to the same person for forty or fifty years.

"I don't know," Phil said, turning to smile at Sue. "I think I could stand that quite well."

I realized that Pamela hadn't said anything for a long time, and I could have kicked myself for bringing up a subject that reminded her of her folks.

And then the bus was pulling into the wooded drive of Camp Overlook, and it was time to go back to our cabins.

When Gwen and I went inside ours to relieve Marsha,

another full counselor who was taking over till we got back, we found the Coyotes still awake.

When Marsha had gone, Estelle asked, "So did you kiss?"

"Kiss? Kiss who?" asked Gwen.

"Anybody!" said Estelle. "Did you kiss any boys?"

"Only frogs," Gwen teased. "Did *you*?"

"Kiss *boys*?" Mary asked. And immediately the cabin was filled with cries of denial and disgust.

"So what *did* you do?" I asked.

"Saw a movie and had an ice-cream party," said Kim.

"And Josephine threw up," Mary announced.

"On your bed," Ruby added, looking at me.

Great! I thought as I pulled off the cover and threw it into the corner. Gwen and I took off our clothes in the dark, but I can always sense the girls watching. Latisha noticed the black underwear.

"Why you got on those pants?" she asked Gwen.

"'Cause I felt like it," Gwen said.

It was like living on stage each night, undressing in front of those girls. Even in the dark.

I don't know what it was—whether it was because all the junior counselors had gone out the night before so that the usual bedtime ritual was different or what—but Latisha was out of sorts all weekend. Despite the truce they'd made, the promise of friendship, she and Estelle fought constantly, and if Latisha wasn't arguing with Estelle, then it was anyone who got in her way. Kim seemed afraid of her and kept close to Gwen and me. My idea of having a group of close-knit girls was evaporating day by day.

"Latisha, knock it off!" I scolded her at dinner on Sunday when she kept bumping her arm against Ruby's, insisting that Ruby was taking up too much room.

"Okay," Latisha said, and promptly knocked Ruby's plastic water glass to the floor.

We studied her. "The mop is in the kitchen. Go get it," Gwen said.

Latisha simply folded her arms over her chest and sat with her lower lip protruding, glaring at us both.

"The mop, Latisha," I said.

She shook her head and refused. Ruby was all for going to get the mop herself for harmony's sake, but we wouldn't let her. Ruby would lie down on the floor and let people walk on her if we allowed it. Don't-Rock-the-Boat Ruby, we called her in our twice-weekly staff sessions.

When we got back to the cabin later, we held a conference to decide what Latisha's punishment should be.

"I think she ought to get her black ass whipped," said Estelle.

Latisha turned her glare on her.

"She shouldn't have any breakfast," said Mary.

"Shut your mouth," said Latisha.

It was obvious that anything we told Latisha she had to do, she would refuse, so we decided that for the remainder of the week, the evening server at the dining table would go to the kitchen to bring back food for everyone but Latisha. She would have to go to the kitchen and get her own unless she apologized to Ruby.

Latisha only shrugged. "So what?" she said.

But by the next night, as food was passed around the table to all but her, she was clearly getting angrier and angrier.

We brought it up at staff session.

"Seems to me you're handling it okay," Jack said. "You can't let her behavior go without consequences."

But on Tuesday night, when the girls were taking their showers, we realized that Latisha was missing.

"Who was the last one in here tonight?" I asked the other girls. "Mary, did Latisha follow you and Josephine to the showers?"

"I think so," said Mary.

"Can't you remember?"

"She was behind us when we left the cabin. I don't know if she came inside or not."

"Latisha?" I called over the rush of the water. "Latisha?" I called up at the high open window above.

No answer.

"I'll go," I told Gwen. Quickly retracing my steps to the cabin, I half expected to find Latisha sitting defiantly on her bunk, refusing to shower with the rest of the girls. But the cabin was empty.

I immediately headed for the dining hall and the office. Connie was standing in the doorway talking to Richard and his dad.

"I can't find Latisha," I said breathlessly, my hair damp

on my forehead. I told them how long we thought she'd been missing.

A missing camper at Camp Overlook is a red alert. Jack immediately set out for the overlook with a search lantern and gave another to Richard and me, instructing us to go to the river. Connie said she would check the cabins one by one and get more counselors searching if we didn't find Latisha right away.

"I'm scared," I confided to Richard as we headed down to the river. "I just can't see how she could slip away like that. I'm sure she was with us before we left for the showers." My voice was shaking.

"She upset about anything?" Richard asked. He's tall and lanky, very much like his dad. Probably got the longest neck of any boy I ever knew.

"Latisha's always upset about something. Her nose has been out of joint ever since we went into town the other night and someone else was in charge of our cabin. Then she was punished for knocking Ruby's glass on the floor in the dining hall. All you have to do is look at Latisha cross-eyed and she's mad."

"Well, we always check the river and the overlook first," Richard said. "We've found that the kids usually go to someplace familiar. She's not likely to go off in the woods by herself, but you never know. My guess is that she's hiding out in someone's cabin. It's too scary to go very far alone. Unless . . ." He stopped.

"Unless what?"

"Oh . . . unless she's suicidal or something, which I doubt."

He grabbed my hand in the darkness because the path was rough, but I'm sure he knew that my heart was in my mouth. The lanterns they use at night in camp are really strong, and we could make out the riverfront even before we got there.

"No matter what I do for her, it's never enough," I said, my words coming fast. "And punishing her the other night must have seemed like proof positive that we don't like her."

"We've got a kid like that in our cabin," Richard said. "Kids who grow up without love—well, they can't get enough, you know? Sometimes I think every kid should have a dog. A dog'll love you no matter what."

We walked along the riverbank, up and down, but there was no sign of Latisha, either sitting under a tree or floating in the water. That much, I guess, was fortunate.

"If anything's happened to her . . . ," I said, feeling more and more responsible. Then, "You don't think someone would come into camp and kidnap her, do you? Grab one of the kids?"

"Very unlikely," Richard said, and gripped my hand all the harder.

When we got back to camp, Connie hadn't found Latisha either, and the whole camp went on a "missing person alert." The outdoor lights came on, and all the children were instructed to stay on their bunks and be accounted for. Every full counselor and assistant counselor was given an area to check.

Gwen and I searched the picnic area.

"Do you think she's trying to walk back home?" I asked finally.

"Don't go off the deep end, Alice," Gwen said. "She's as clever as she is angry. We'll find her." We'd been looking now for twenty minutes, however, and no one had found her yet. We went back to our cabin more frightened than ever.

And then Mary and Josephine had to go to the bathroom, and they were the ones who made the discovery.

"Latisha!" the girls bellowed together, and Gwen and I came running.

Josephine would use only the stall that didn't have a lock on it because she was afraid she might not be able to get out. When she'd swung the door open, she told us, there was Latisha, standing up on the toilet seat, hidden behind the door. We could have looked, *should* have looked, not just taken a cursory glance under each door, looking for feet.

All I could do was put my arms around Latisha and hug her to me. I didn't have any voice to scold. And strangely enough, this time Latisha hugged back.

8
NEWS FROM SILVER SPRING

The next morning dawned dark and gloomy, and we had crafts in the big dining hall, while rain pattered down outside, spilling out the rainspouts and drumming on the roof. All the doors and windows were open, so the humid air brought with it the faint odor of mustiness and mildew, typical summer camp. The kids were working on making little baskets out of twigs, which they could then fill with small treasures found here at Overlook— pine cones and such—and take them with them when they left for home.

Mary had told me that Josephine was sick, so I'd taken her to the camp nurse, but it turned out that her temperature was normal, and the sickness seemed to be a figment of Mary's imagination. When I got Josephine back to the dining hall, Gwen had a second project in progress.

One of the tables was covered with newspaper, and Gwen had about six different colors of paint in little containers in the center of the table. They were various shades of white, brown, black, yellow, orange, and red.

Each girl, Gwen said, was to take some of the paint and put it on her saucer. She was to keep mixing different colors until she matched the color of her own skin.

"Huh?" said Estelle. "I'm white. You're black."

"Really?" said Gwen, sitting down beside her. "Let's see."

Gwen put some black paint on her saucer, then smeared some on her arm. There was a great contrast between the pecan brown color of her skin and the paint.

"Now let's try you," she said, and put white on Estelle's saucer. Estelle smeared white on her arm, and of course it didn't match at all.

The Coyotes were engrossed in the project, and each began experimenting. Latisha and Ruby started out with brown paint, but it was much too dark. Mary and Josephine and Estelle started out with white paint, and it was much too white. Kim, strangely, chose orange as her color, but it didn't match any better that the others. Just to be different, I took red.

"You look like a ghost!" Latisha said to Estelle.

Silently, Estelle mixed some yellow into the white paint on her saucer, then tried that on her arm. No match.

"You've gotta add some of *that*!" Kim said, pointing to the brown. Estelle mixed in a bit of brown. Better. She mixed in some more. Better still.

"Hey, look! I'm an Indian!" said Mary, making red stripes on her arm.

Several kids from a nearby table came over to watch. I looked at Gwen in admiration. She hadn't said a word. She had merely put out the paints, and every girl at the table learned that each of us is made up of a lot of different colors.

Connie was impressed. "Did you think this one up on your own, Gwen?" she asked.

"No. It's a project we did at summer Bible school," said Gwen.

"Well, I'm going to remember this one with my next load of campers," Connie told her. "I'm glad you're on board, Gwen."

So was I.

We lost the war with Latisha, though. Because lunch was served buffet style, everyone helped himself, and by evening we were back to our usual dinner routine, one runner serving the whole table, Latisha included. Gwen and I were too tired to carry it further. We knew we hadn't handled it well, but we didn't want her disappearing again.

"We can't win them all, and we can't reach them all, either," Gwen told me. "If we do a good job with the others, we'll just have to accept that five out of six isn't bad."

A farm nearby allowed Camp Overlook to bring the children over a few times each summer to ride horses. So we marched the kids over there Wednesday afternoon, hiking across a high, breezy pasture, the campers exclaiming and jumping over cow pies, but I was surprised at the number who declared they'd never get on a horse. What surprised me even more was my own reluctance.

I'd never been on horseback, never been on a farm, really. Horses were something I saw from a distance. But suddenly here we were, standing at a fence, as six or seven horses were led out of a barn and saddled up. Richard rode one over to the fence and it seemed far larger than I had expected. When it rolled its eyes and snorted and chomped down on the bit, Josie gave a cry and dived behind my legs, and even Latisha vowed she wouldn't ride.

Connie walked alongside the horse as it moved down the line of campers. She told them its name—Soldier—and held up some of the braver children to stroke its side, but all it took was a toss of the head from Soldier and the kids cowered again. Only a dozen or so said they were willing to get on.

"It doesn't matter if you've never been on a horse," said Connie to the kids. She looked around at the assistant counselors. "Where's an assistant counselor who has never been on a horse. Doris? Tommie?"

I raised my hand, thinking I would be in the majority, and was suddenly horrified to discover I was the only one. No! They had to be lying! How could it be that I'd reached the age of fifteen and was the only one here who hadn't been on horseback? I quickly lowered my hand. Did ponies count? Ponies at a fairground? But I wasn't even sure I'd done that. A merry-go-round! Yes! I'd ridden a merry-go-round!

But then I heard Connie say, "Okay, Alice. Come right in here. We're going to start you out with Richard." I shrank back, shaking my head, and then I heard Estelle say, "Just tell her you're not gonna do it, Alice. You don't have to!" And then I knew I had to.

The farmer opened the gate so I could get through. I was trying to smile and swallow at the same time. He walked me over to Soldier, who lifted one hoof impatiently and put it down again with another toss of his head. What if he bit me? What if he kicked?

"The kids will feel safer if they can ride along with someone," Connie said, "so we're going to put you up there with Richard and show them how it's done."

Richard smiled down at me and moved back a little in the saddle. He slipped one foot out of the stirrup so I could use it to hoist myself up.

"Here you go," the farmer said, and I awkwardly swung my other leg over the horse, almost hitting Richard in the chest. Then I was in the saddle in front of him, and his arms were on either side of me, holding the reins.

"Just relax," Richard said as we moved forward. "He's really very gentle."

Connie was giving instructions, explaining how you tell a horse to go, to stop, to turn, to trot. I focused on Soldier's ears, the way they raised, they flattened, then twitched, as though he could understand everything we said. *How do you tell a horse that you're scared half out of your mind? To be merciful?*

Just as I was getting used to the feel of the horse beneath me, the heat of its body soaking into my thighs and calves, I could feel Richard make some slight movement and Soldier began to trot.

"Oh!" I said, startled.

"It's okay," Richard said into my hair. "Just hold on to the saddle."

But my fingers dug into his thighs like claws, and I was afraid to let go. My spine felt so stiff against Richard's chest, I was afraid I'd push him backward, but I couldn't help myself.

"Trust me," came his voice. It was all that was left to do. I held on as we went once around the paddock, and then the horse slowed to a walk, and it was someone else's turn to feel their insides turn to jelly. Richard brought Soldier to the gate again, and I slid off. Other campers stepped forward, and other horses were put into use.

"You did good, Alice!" Ruby said.

"Yeah! I thought he was going to buck!" said Mary.

"Was it fun?" asked Latisha.

"It was an adventure," I said, perspiration trickling down from my armpits.

"Well, maybe I'll go next week," Latisha told us.

We were coming back from the baseball diamond on Friday when I saw Lester outside the office, talking with Connie, hands in his pockets. Actually, Pamela saw him first.

"Studly!" she cried. That's what Pamela calls every guy who looks sexy to her.

Actually, he looked as though he'd been digging ditches, because he was windblown and sweat-stained. Handsome, nonetheless.

"Gwen, can you take over for me?" I asked.

"Tell him to stick around so we can see him too," said Pamela.

Lester pulled one hand out of his jeans' pocket and waved when he saw us, smiling at me as I crossed the clearing, Kim sticking to my side.

"Who's that? Your boyfriend?" Estelle asked.

"My brother," I said.

Latisha gave a little whistle. "He good-looking, all right," she said, making Mary and Ruby laugh.

"This is a surprise!" I told Lester as Connie smiled and went back in the office, but my pulse was speeding up. Why had he driven all the way up here? Why hadn't he just called? There must have been something about my face that told him how anxious I was, because Lester held up one hand to stop me. "Hey! Nobody died," he said, which only told me that *something* had happened.

Gwen herded the Coyotes on by, practically peeling Kim away from me, and Pamela and Elizabeth took their own girls into the dining hall for their afternoon popcorn and lemonade.

I gave Lester a hug but studied his eyes when I backed off. "So?" I said.

"Relax, will you? I've been mountain biking. Met some buddies up here yesterday, and we rented a cabin and some bikes. Figured I was so close, I might as well drop by the camp and check it out on the way home."

"Spy on me, you mean." I laughed, steering him over to a bench under an oak tree. I fanned myself with the hem of my T-shirt. "We just finished a baseball game. Let me cool off, and then I'll show you around. So what's happening back home?"

"Well, there *is* a bit of disappointing news. Sylvia . . ."

I stopped fanning. *"What?"*

"Sylvia . . ."

"She *didn't*! She broke their engagement?"

"No, Al!"

"She's been in an accident?"

"Al, will you please shut up for five seconds? Her sister is very ill in Albuquerque, and Sylvia's flying out there. The wedding's been postponed."

"Oh, Lester! *No!"*

"I'm afraid so. Dad's pretty disappointed, as you can guess, but he agrees there's nothing else to do. Nancy was in the hospital for a bowel operation, and she's developed septicemia. Blood poisoning. It can be really serious."

"How can she be having a bowel operation? She's supposed to be Sylvia's maid of honor!"

"Tell that to her bowels. She didn't plan it, Al."

"But how long will Sylvia be gone?"

"Till her sister's out of danger and recovering, I imagine."

"But . . . but that could be a long time! Sylvia and Dad could have the wedding, and *then* she could go to Albuquerque! Lester, she and Dad were *this close* to getting married! First she goes to England. Now she's going to Albuquerque. Doesn't she care anything about Dad's feelings? Doesn't she—"

"Al," Les said sternly, "grow up."

I stopped cold. "What?"

"You're talking like an eight-year-old."

"But it's *true*! Dad will be so hurt! If it's going to take a long time for her sister to get better, they could get married and go on their honeymoon, and *then* Sylvia could take care of her!"

"Her sister could die."

I stared at Lester. "It's . . . it's that serious?"

He nodded. "And what kind of honeymoon do you think they would have with Sylvia worried constantly about Nancy?"

"What kind of wedding will they have if Nancy *dies*?" I countered. My shoulders slumped and I sat with my legs apart, arms dangling between my knees. "I was all set to be her bridesmaid. She took my measurements and everything!"

"So is this about your feelings or Sylvia's?"

I felt like crying, but I saw Craig and Ross glance at me from across the clearing, and Lester's admonition to grow up kept the tears back, I guess.

I sighed instead. "Is there anything I can do? Does Dad want me to come home now?"

"No, not at all. He's driving Sylvia to the airport this afternoon, and I told him I'd look in on you while I was up here—make sure the guys were treating you with respect."

I kicked his foot and we laughed. It felt good to laugh about *something*.

"They're really nice," I said. "The assistant counselor's part is hard, though. It's *work* keeping track of the kids, but the guys are fun."

"*How* much fun?" Lester said, raising one eyebrow.

"Well," I teased, "for one thing, we went swimming one night, and the guys were naked."

"Whoa!" Lester said, and looked at me hard.

"The girls had their clothes on, though."

"Yeah? Paint me a picture," Les said.

So I told him how we had sat on the boys' clothes and how the guys had come out and thrown us in. I wanted to tell him just enough to make him nervous but not enough to make him worry. Then Elizabeth and Pamela came out of the dining hall and sauntered over.

"Hi, handsome," Pamela said, sitting down next to Lester so that their thighs touched. She's shameless.

"Hey! How's it going?" he asked her.

"Great!" said Elizabeth. "The boys are terrific!"

"Yeah?" said Les.

"We went to a bar the other night," Pamela told him.

"A *restaurant*," I corrected. "We didn't drink, Lester, and an older counselor drove. It was pure, wholesome fun."

"I'll bet," said Lester.

"You don't have to worry about a thing," said Pamela. "Besides, Elizabeth brought condoms."

"Pamela!" Elizabeth yelled.

Lester looked at her, then at me.

"They're for Pamela," I said.

"Alice!" cried Pamela.

Lester looked around. "I take it there *is* adult supervision up here?"

"Yes, Lester. We're perfectly fine." I turned to Pamela and Elizabeth. "Sylvia's sister is sick and the wedding's been postponed. She's flying to Albuquerque this afternoon."

"Oh, Alice!" they said together.

"It's not the end of the world," I told them, trying to summon a little maturity. "I guess it will be a fall wedding. Whenever Nancy gets better, that is. . . ."

"So, are you going to show me around?" Les asked.

"Sure." I jumped up and grabbed his arm. The kids were all in the dining hall now having their snacks, so Pamela and Elizabeth went with us. We showed Lester the river and the canoes, the paths in the woods, and then Pamela and Elizabeth went back to the dining hall while Les and I walked to the overlook.

It was a really gorgeous afternoon—not too hot—and we could see layers of mountains, fading as clouds moved by, then coming into focus again. Les put his arm around me, and this time I felt the tears coming.

"I . . . f-feel so sorry for Dad," I gulped.

"So do I. But it will all work out, Al. When you've got somebody to share your troubles, it's a lot easier. He still has Sylvia, you know." And then, realizing that I didn't have a boyfriend, he said, "And even if you *don't* have somebody special, you—"

"Cool it, Lester. I'm not about to jump off the overlook because Sylvia postponed the wedding," I said.

He laughed and gave my waist a little tug. "Okay. Let's talk about you. What's the deal about the condoms?"

"Elizabeth brought some," I said. And added, laughing, "A ribbed Trojan with a lubricated tip."

Lester choked. *"Elizabeth?"*

I grinned. "She said they're for Pamela, except she gave them to Gwen, and I don't know who has them now."

"You're not sharing *condoms*, are you?"

"Les, I'm not even having sex. Relax."

"Whew!" he said. "Okay. I'm relaxed. It is a nice place up here. I hope you're having a good time."

"I am. I'm glad I came."

We walked back and I introduced him to a few of the guys. Then Les talked a few minutes with Jack Harrigan, and finally he drove away.

There's mail call every day at three o'clock, and I went up to the office to see if I got something. I didn't. There was an envelope for Pamela, though. If any one of the assistant counselors needed a letter, I thought, it was Pamela. First her mom got everyone upset by leaving the family, and then she got them upset by saying she wanted to come back. Pamela seemed not to even want to think about it.

"Hey, Pamela! For you!" I said, waving the letter, and sat down beside her on the steps. As soon as she saw the postmark, though, her face clouded up. I looked the other way while she read it.

"Guess who's coming to town," Pamela said, crumpling up the letter into a tight little ball, then angrily squeezing it again for good measure.

"I don't know," I said, hesitating.

"Mom."

I studied her for a moment. "She really is, then! She wrote you from Colorado? How did she get the address up here?"

"Who knows? She finds out everything."

"When is she coming?"

"She doesn't say. I don't want to be around when she shows up," Pamela said determinedly. "Let me stay at your place or something when she does, Alice! There'll probably be a big scene, and I just don't think I could take it. I can't understand why she'd even want to come back if Dad doesn't love her anymore."

"You don't think . . . maybe . . . they could work things out?"

"It's too late for that. It's been too long. Dad hates her."

We were both quiet for a minute or two.

"What do you *want* to happen?" I asked finally.

"I just want it *over*, one way or another. I hate this waiting around, wondering what will happen next. I either want them together or I want them apart."

I thought how often I'd felt something like that for the past couple of years about Dad and Sylvia. Except I'd never wanted them apart. I'd *always* wanted them to be together.

9
GOING COED

That night, *our* night, none of the older counselors was available to drive us into town, so the six of us girls decided to sneak down to the river early and go skinny-dipping, just to say that we had. Doris, who felt she was on the verge of a cold, didn't want to go in but said she'd be our lookout.

"We'll just take a short swim before the guys start looking for us," Pamela said with a giggle. But we were all secretly hoping that the guys would find out where we'd gone and . . . Well, who knows what we were hoping. Just for something exciting to happen, I guess.

We weren't foolish enough to leave our clothes on the bank,

though. We wadded them up and stuck them in the fork of a low tree. When we got down to our underpants, we wore them to the water's edge, then gave them to Doris to put in the tree for us, and dived in. Elizabeth refused to take off either her underpants or her bra, so there we were: one girl on the bank fully clothed; one girl in the water in her underwear; and four girls in the river naked.

We swam quietly, giggling to each other, feeling very risqué. When the guys didn't come down right away, I noticed, none of us suggested we get out, even though the water was frigid and I could feel my teeth chattering. We just kept swimming around, watching the path to the dining hall. I noticed Pamela's voice getting a little louder, just in case the guys were within earshot. And soon, down the path they came—all six of the male assistant counselors.

What we did, of course, was shriek and duck down under the water, swimming a little downriver to pretend we weren't there, which was ridiculous. And then *they* were in the water, all their clothes on the bank, and after we got over being semi-embarrassed and silly, we just swam around and talked, and it seemed to me we were pretty grown-up, Gerald included.

"Was that your boyfriend or your brother I saw you with this afternoon?" Craig asked me.

"My brother. Les. My dad's wedding's been postponed because my new mom's sister is sick," I explained.

"Tough luck," said Craig.

"I'm going to feel so much better when they're finally married," I told him. "Dad's been waiting a long time."

"Yeah, sure," I heard Joe murmur, and the others laughed.

I didn't say any more about Dad and Sylvia. I didn't want people guessing about their private lives when they didn't even know them. So I just dog-paddled around, thinking how strange and exciting it felt to be swimming at night. The sky was cloudy, though, and we couldn't see much of anything except a ball of white somewhere back on the bank, which I realized, finally, was our ball of underwear in the fork of the tree.

Both Elizabeth and Pamela were swimming around Ross like sharks, I thought. Gwen and Joe were nuzzling off by themselves, G. E. was talking with Doris, who was sitting on an overturned canoe, and the rest of us were just floating about, enjoying a free swim without the little kids.

As I watched Gwen and Joe, though, who were now kissing, their lips and who knows what else locked together, I began to wonder if the directors of this camp knew what they were doing. We were running on hormones, everyone said, and here we were, away from home, totally naked, in the dark, and . . . Maybe they figured there was safety in numbers. G. E. slid into the water next.

There was a sudden rustling in the bushes, the quick thud of feet, and suddenly, with a loud "Hi-*yah!*" Jack Harrigan did a cannonball into the river, splashing everyone within ten yards. He was the only one besides Elizabeth and Doris *not* naked. Maybe the directors *did* know what they were doing.

"So how's the fishing?" he asked, and his voice held a grin.

"Not so good," Andy joked. "The babes aren't biting."

"Speak for yourself," came Joe's voice, and I heard Gwen laugh.

"Maybe you're using the wrong bait," said Richard's dad.

"Hey, we've got a river, a breeze, a night, a moon . . . ," said Ross.

"No moon," said Andy.

"Okay, skip the moon. But . . ."

With the guys talking to Richard's father, we girls felt it was safe to swim downstream, sneak out, and get our clothes. Doris had retrieved our bundle of underwear from the tree and brought it down to a row of bushes, then went back to get the rest of our pants and shirts. We climbed out, one after the other, and dressed.

"Darn!" said Pamela. "Just when things were heating up."

"Ross kissed me!" Elizabeth whispered excitedly.

"How could you tell who it was? It was dark," said Pamela, and she didn't sound pleased.

"I think he was going around kissing everyone," I said, trying to defuse a potential quarrel. "Somebody touched me underwater."

"Probably Gerald," said Elizabeth, to take *me* down a peg or two.

"It's going to be hard to go back home with Mom and Dad hovering around all the time, knowing where I am every living minute," said Elizabeth, zipping up her jeans.

"Everyone should be so lucky," said Tommie.

"Lucky how?"

"Most of these kids don't have anyone to hover."

"I guess so," said Elizabeth. "Just the same, tonight was really fun."

"Till Richard's dad showed up, anyway," said Pamela. "I suppose Richard's the establishment spy."

"I don't think so," I said. "He's too nice."

"Then how else did his dad know to come swimming with us? *Some*body must have told him that the guys were swimming nude last week," said Tommie.

Suddenly I remembered.

"Lester!" I cried. "He was talking with Jack Harrigan before he left."

"Kill him for us," said Pamela.

I felt the need to call home. I was going to give Lester a piece of my mind, for one thing, but what I really wanted was to hear Dad's voice and find out how he was doing. I went to the office later that night and dialed. The phone rang so many times I was afraid I'd get the answering machine, but then Dad picked it up.

"Dad? Did I wake you?" I asked. "Did you go to bed early?"

"Alice! No, I was just sitting out on the porch. How are you, honey?"

"How are *you*, Dad? I'm really sorry about Sylvia's sister."

"Well, so am I. It was a big disappointment for both of us, but there's nothing to be done. Nancy's seriously ill. Septicemia is a worrisome business, and we're just hoping she pulls through okay."

"Can't the doctors do something? Give her antibiotics?"

"Well, of course. That's what they're doing. But it's tricky. They have to figure out just what combination of drugs will work. Meanwhile, the infection can spread to the brain, the heart—almost anywhere."

"Oh, Dad. You've waited so long."

"I can wait a bit longer, I guess. Right now the important thing is Nancy's health."

"Is Sylvia coming back to teach in the fall?"

"Everything depends on Nancy. Sylvia's already told the principal she probably won't be here for the start of school. We'll just have to wait and see."

We were both quiet for a few seconds. "I wish I was there," I said finally.

"Now, Alice, what could you do? You are exactly where you are supposed to be, and I hope you're having a good time. Are you?"

"Well, yes. I didn't know that being an assistant counselor was so exhausting, though. I mean, I'm tired even when we don't do anything physical. Just trying to keep the peace wears me out."

He laughed, and it was good to hear that familiar chuckle. "Kids are a handful, all right," he said. "I can remember times you and Lester about drove me up the wall."

"Not recently, I hope."

"Not too recently, no."

"Has anyone asked about me? Called or anything?"

I could almost hear Dad's brain working at being tactful.

Playing it safe. Trying to decipher what I was really asking.

"I think most of your friends know you're away, hon," he said. "There aren't any phone messages. I don't know about e-mail. Everything going okay there at camp? You and Gwen hitting it off as cabin mates?"

"Gwen's wonderful," I said. "Pamela and Elizabeth are in separate cabins, thank goodness, because they both like the same guy—there are a *lot* of cute boys here—but other than that, we're doing okay." I didn't want to get into the nude swimming bit.

"Well, you'll be home in another week, right?" he said. "Call when you get in. I don't know who will pick you up, but somebody will drive over."

"Dad? Have you heard from Sylvia since she left?" I asked.

"Oh, yes. She's called twice—once after she got there and again from the hospital. Right now Nancy's holding her own, but we won't know anything much for a while. Sylvia's where she needs to be too, Al. That's life. We take things as they come."

He was saying all the right things, but how did he really *feel*?

"I love you, Dad," I said. "Rivers."

"I love you too, Al. Oceans."

I had a hard time falling asleep that night. I kept thinking about Pamela and Elizabeth. We'd been friends for a long time, and I didn't want anything to come between the two of them. We'd come to camp excited and looking forward to three weeks of fun together. It had been that and even more for Elizabeth, but I'm not sure about Pamela. And the letter from her mother didn't help.

I got up finally, and, throwing on my jacket, I slipped out of the cabin and made my way down the narrow lane. Night noises were all around me, and a breeze rustled the leaves of the aspens. When I got to cabin twelve, I noiselessly opened the screen door and moved across the floor to Pamela's bunk. She was lying with her face to the wall.

"Pamela," I whispered.

At first she didn't move. Then she rolled over and peered at me through the darkness. "Alice?" she said. She stared at me for a moment, then scooted over to make room. I lay down on my side and rested my cheek on one hand.

"I'm worried about you and Liz," I said.

"Well, don't be."

"I just hate to see you fighting over some guy. Even Ross, nice as he is."

"We're not fighting." Her voice was flat. "This isn't the first time I've lost out. It won't be the last," she said, and she sounded resigned. Defeated.

I tried to see her face in the darkness. This was *Pamela* talking? The talented, sexy Pamela Jones whom I'd envied so much in sixth grade? Then I remembered how she had pulled out of the high school Drama Club last year because she figured she didn't have a chance at a lead part. Now *I* was worried.

"You know," I said, "if ever a girl needed to have a guy be loving and tender with her—a guy her own age—it's Elizabeth."

"I know that," Pamela whispered back. "I was lying here thinking the same thing. And it's not just tonight; I've been noticing how much he likes her. The way he watches her. When I'm feeling mature about it, I wish Ross lived closer so they could go out once camp's over. When I'm feeling sorry for myself, I'm glad he's in Philadelphia."

We were both quiet awhile.

"I hate to see you feeling so low," I whispered finally. "It's . . . it's partly your mom, isn't it?"

There was a catch in her voice. "I get sad thinking about how we used to be, when we were a family."

"I wish you'd consider yourself a part of *my* family for a while," I said. "I wish you felt you could come over whenever you wanted and talk to me and Dad."

I could hear a note of mischief creeping into her voice. "Lester too?"

I knew Lester would kill me, but I said it anyway. "Sure. Just consider him your big brother. G'night, sis."

"Good night, Alice," she said.

10
THE GREAT KELPIE HUNT

On the Fourth of July, each cabin was given a flag to hang out front, and the camp held a picnic. We had relay races and potato sack races, and the full counselors performed in a makeshift band with a tin whistle, a potato chip can for a drum, a harmonica, and a washboard. We hand-cranked peach ice cream, and each kid had a chance to turn the handle.

I thought this might be something Latisha would particularly enjoy, but if Latisha enjoyed anything, she kept it to herself. Gwen and I saw a modest improvement in most of our girls. Ruby quit trying to smuggle food from the dining hall, which to us meant she was more comfortable here at camp—didn't feel as though there might not be enough food to go around. Kim was less fearful, Josephine more adventurous, Mary less protective. Even Estelle showed less prejudice toward Ruby and Gwen and, to some extent, toward Latisha.

But Latisha was like a sphinx. If we saw a change at all, she was a bit more quiet, but not, it seemed, less angry. Some of the Coyotes had asked to make a second twig basket to take home to someone they loved. But Latisha showed no interest in making more. She enjoyed contact sports, anything that allowed her to bump or push or pull or wrestle. Otherwise, she sat on the sidelines and glowered at everyone else.

On our last Friday, assistant counselors' night out, the guys were planning to take us on the promised "Kelpie Hunt," led by Phil. It was supposed to be a preview of what our little campers would get the following night.

"You can never tell what the guys have up their sleeves," said Doris. "I think we ought to wear bathing suits under our shorts, just in case."

"Hey! How about *nothing* under our shorts? I'd like that better," said Pamela.

"I'm going to be sorry when camp's over," said Tommie. "I wish we had another week here. Craig and I were just starting to get chummy."

"You could always write," I said.

"Oh, you know how summer romances go," she told me.

Elizabeth was thoughtful. "Well, Ross and I really like each other, and I wish ours would go on forever," she said. "You know who I feel sorry for?" I hoped she wouldn't say Pamela. "I feel sort of sorry for G. E. Why don't we each try to say something nice to him before camp's over? I mean, something spontaneous and sincere."

"Like what?" asked Gwen.

"Anything. That you like his T-shirt. Or just sit and talk with him a few minutes. We don't want him to know we agreed to do it, but it would give him something nice to remember about Camp Overlook. He must feel like the odd man out."

"He *is* the odd man out," said Doris.

"But you know how you'd feel if it were you," I said.

"I suppose we can manage to find something nice to say," said Tommie. "He's not a total dork in *every*thing."

When the kids had gone to the dining hall and the full counselors took over for the evening, we assistant counselors gathered at one of the trailheads, where the guys were whispering among themselves.

I was relieved to see that Phil was there, obviously in charge. Sue had said that the Kelpie Hunt had become a tradition, sort of an initiation for all the new assistant counselors, but you could tell that the guys knew what was coming and the girls didn't. It sounded like fun, though, and we went along with their joke— sort of like a haunted house at Halloween, except that the guys got to be the ghosts.

"*O-kay!*" Phil said. "Is everybody *ready*?" And the guys all grinned at us.

"For *what*, exactly?" asked Gwen.

"Here's the deal," Phil said mysteriously. "There's a creature here at Camp Overlook that lives on the river bottom, and few have ever seen it. A kelpie is half ghost, half horse, and if it calls your name, you'll feel this irresistible compulsion to climb on its back, where it will take you down under the water and you'll never be seen again. *Our* job is to find the kelpie before it finds you."

"Great," said Pamela. "And which of you guys gets to play the kelpie?"

"Hey, ye of little faith!" said Richard. "It's an old Scottish superstition, but doesn't every superstition have something real behind it?"

"So what are we supposed to do?" asked Elizabeth. I noticed that Ross was standing behind her with his arms wrapped around her, face against her cheek. Elizabeth was stroking his hand.

Phil continued: "Well, the kelpie knows you're here. It knows everything about us—who's here, who leaves. We'll try to spot it when it comes to the surface for air—capture it, if we can. If you hear it, of course, you have to go toward it. The trick is to keep from climbing on its back. That's what the guys are here for, to protect you."

"Yeah, sure," we said, laughing. "And if it calls *your* name?" The guys all looked at Phil.

"Oh, it's gender-specific," Phil said. "It only calls girls' names."

We laughed again and set off—some of the guys in front of us, some behind, with only the small beam of Phil's flashlight to guide us. We figured that Gerald must have been assigned the role of the kelpie, because he wasn't with us.

"Why are we going uphill if the kelpie's in the river?" I asked.

"To throw him off guard," said Richard, and the boys whispered some more.

We continued climbing, the guys holding back branches that would have scratched our faces, until finally we came out on a ridge in the moonlight. I hadn't been on this trail or this ridge, but I could tell by the way the wind tossed my hair that we were up pretty high. There didn't seem to be anything between us and the sky.

"What we've got to do," said Phil, stopping, "is rappel down the cliff, where the kelpie would least expect us."

"In the dark?" asked Doris.

"How far down is it?" asked Elizabeth.

"Only fifty feet or so."

Several of us gasped at once. *Isn't there any adult supervision up here?* Lester had asked when he'd visited. I wondered how old Phil was—twenty-two, maybe? Still . . .

And then we heard a faraway call. "Pam-e-la! . . . Pam-e-la!" Gwen and I smiled at each other. We figured one of the guys here had a cell phone or a walkie-talkie; how else could the call come just as we'd reached the top?

"Uh-oh," said Andy. "I'll be brave. I'll go with her."

We jeered.

"Strange, but I don't feel the slightest urge to go toward it," Pamela said. "I think the kelpie's losing its magic."

"You don't fool around with a kelpie," said Andy. "You sure don't want it coming looking for *you*. C'mon."

"Watch it, Pamela," said Craig.

"If it's a choice between Andy and the kelpie, take the kelpie," said Ross.

Phil produced a couple of harnesses and ropes that seemed to be tied to a tree, just waiting for us. I couldn't believe Pamela was actually going to do it, but she gamely stepped forward and put her feet through the straps of the harness, pulling it up around her.

"I think all the *guys* should go fight the kelpie and we'll stay up here," said Doris.

"Yeah, me too," said Tommie.

"Oh, that wouldn't work. We have to have bait to catch a kelpie, and he's partial to girls," said Richard.

I began to get a panicky feeling in my chest. This was dangerous. Was this one of those times Lester had warned me about, when you have to use common sense and say no?

In the moonlight Phil was demonstrating to Pamela how you hold the rope to rappel yourself down the side of a cliff.

"Pam-e-la! . . . Pam-e-la!" the faraway voice called again.

"We'll go together," said Andy, getting in the second harness. In a matter of minutes Pamela and Andy dropped over the edge, and all we could hear were their feet scuffling along the face of the cliff. Then suddenly, eerily, all was quiet.

As the moon went behind a cloud, then emerged again, Phil stood with one finger to his lips, listening, waiting. Then he and

Richard began to pull on the two ropes, and after a while the harnesses came up over the edge, minus Pamela and Andy.

"Al-ice! . . . Al-ice!" came the call.

Suddenly I could feel my body trembling. I didn't know if I was going to be sick or faint, but I just crouched down, my hands over my stomach. I felt Richard's arm around me as he crouched down too.

"Hey!" he said. "You're shaking!" And then he put his mouth to my ear. "It's safe," he said. "Trust me."

I thought of all the stories I'd heard about guys talking girls into stuff they shouldn't do. Girls getting into cars with guys who were stoned. Was I about to rappel myself over the edge of a fifty-foot drop in a flimsy harness to my death? But no one here was drunk. No one was stoned. Phil was the head counselor, and Richard had kept me safe on the horse. I decided to trust.

"You'll love it," said Craig.

I got up shakily. "That's what they all say," I told him. "Will you still respect me in the morning?" Everyone laughed.

They helped me into one of the harnesses while Richard got in the other. Then, side by side, we were lowered over the edge. I was breathing so fast, I wondered if my heart would give out. What a coward I was! First the horse, and now this!

"Al-ice! . . . Al-ice!" came the voice from below.

I let myself down a little more, a little more, almost glad for the darkness so I couldn't see the river. All of a sudden Richard grabbed hold of my rope and swung me over beside him. I gave a small shriek, afraid we'd both go crashing down. But all he said in my ear was, "Shhhh. Don't make a sound."

And the next thing I knew, my feet were on solid ground. We couldn't have traveled more than ten feet.

In the moonlight I could see Pamela and Andy grinning at me, fingers to their lips. I looked around and stepped out of the harness. The "cliff" was only a high bank over a hill below. The real drop was a lot farther on, but in the dark, from above, we couldn't see that. I put my hands to my face and suppressed a giggle.

"Tom-mie! . . . Tom-mie!" the voice came, and I sat down in the wet grass beside Pamela as we waited for all the girls' names to be called, wondering how many times this trick had been played on the assistant counselors—the girl counselors—at Camp Overlook. Had the guys decided in advance who was pairing off with whom? I wondered as we waited for Tommie to come down. But it was great fun, scary as anything, and when all the girls were down, we were allowed to talk again. We hooted and laughed at ourselves.

"Alice was hyperventilating," said Pamela. "I could hear her all the way down the bank."

"I was afraid she'd pass out on me," said Richard.

I think Elizabeth was having the best time of all. It was hard to see her and Ross in the dark, but whenever they stepped into moonlight, they were together. They didn't hug or kiss in front of the little campers when they were on duty, but I would see their hands touch momentarily, the smile that passed between them, the softening of Elizabeth's face when she watched him, and it almost made me want to stand up and shout, *Yes!* Here in the woods, though, they didn't have to hide how they felt about each other.

It was a long way down on the path to the river, but our ordeal wasn't over yet. Halfway there, Phil stopped us again.

"Okay, we've come to a tunnel," he said, "and we'll have to crawl through one at a time."

By now I was feeling more confident of myself. If I could ride a horse, I could rappel down a bank. If I could rappel down a bank, I could crawl through a tunnel. So I volunteered to be first in line after Phil, Pamela behind me. I wedged my body through the narrow opening on my hands and knees, feeling quite sure we were simply between two large boulders. I bet we could easily have walked around them, but this time I felt certain I was up to it.

Halfway through, though, one strap of my overalls came loose and, dangling between my legs as I crawled, caught its buckle on something. I couldn't go backward or forward, and the space was so narrow that I couldn't maneuver my arms to reach it.

"You coming?" Phil called over his shoulder.

"What's the matter?" asked Pamela, bumping into me from behind.

"I'm stuck!" I yelped. "My buckle's caught on something."

"Can you reach it?" Phil asked.

"No."

"I'll help you," he said.

"No!" I insisted. "Pamela, you've got to do it."

We were both wrestling with the strap, her hands between my legs, with scarcely enough room to move our arms, while somebody else bumped into Pamela. All we could do was laugh. It's a wonder we got me loose at all.

Free at last, we were still laughing about it when we reached the river, but there was the kelpie—someone with a huge rubber horse mask, complete with mane, swimming about in the water. Of course he came charging out as soon as he saw us, and of course a mock battle ensued, ending with all of us in the river. We had a great time.

"Hey, Gerald," I said when I noticed him sliding into the water. "You make a great kelpie."

"What do you mean?" he asked innocently. "I just got here. It's the guy with the horse's head you should be talking to."

"I mean the voice. Voice of the kelpie. You should work for Voice of America or something."

I could tell he was pleased.

The guys had brought sodas and chips, so we sat on the bank, talking and swatting at an occasional mosquito. The "kelpie," one of the older counselors, joined in. Phil and Craig told us stories of past Kelpie Hunts—the night even Phil had lost his way, for instance, and Jack Harrigan had to come looking for them.

Finally, though, we girls headed back to the showers to wash the river water from our hair. Pamela moved up behind Gwen and me. "Anybody see Elizabeth?" she asked.

I looked around. "She was with us all evening."

"Not on the bank, she wasn't," said Pamela. "At least I didn't see her."

We all stopped and looked about.

"What about the guys?" I asked. "Weren't they all there too?"

"All except Ross," said Tommie.

Pamela and I looked at each other. She didn't say a word; her face said it all.

11
GIRL TALK

We went on to the showers and took off our wet clothes. Even lukewarm water felt good to us after the cold of the river. I knew that the topic of conversation was going to be Elizabeth, but just that moment she walked in.

Her hair was tangled and there were leaves on the back of her T-shirt. Her face was flushed and she was breathless.

"Oh, *here* you are!" she said, as though *she* had been looking for *us*.

"Aha! She's got grass on her back!" said Tommie.

"Somebody check out Ross," Doris kidded.

"Naw. He'd have grass on his knees," said Gwen.

Elizabeth just took off her clothes and turned on a shower.

"Where did you go?" Pamela asked. "We've been wondering where you were."

"Ross and I went for a walk, that's all," Elizabeth said. She closed her eyes and turned her face up toward the spray.

The rest of us looked at each other and grinned.

"Uh-huh," said Tommie knowingly. "The way we figure, Liz, you've been missing for about forty-five minutes. Maybe longer."

"So it was a long walk," said Elizabeth, smiling.

But Pamela and I wouldn't let her off so easily.

"Well," I said, "what happened?"

"What do you mean? Nothing. We just talked."

"Elizabeth . . . !" said Pamela.

"Her cheeks are red," said Gwen.

"And getting redder," said Doris.

"You might as well tell us," Pamela teased, and I think she was beginning to enjoy it. "If you don't, we'll go ask Ross."

Elizabeth suddenly turned and faced us triumphantly. "Well," she said, "I *did* it."

There was no sound at all in the showers except running water. Pamela reached up and turned hers off, and we continued staring at Elizabeth as though she had just risen from the dead. *Elizabeth? Elizabeth* had done IT before any of the rest of us? Elizabeth *Price*?

"*Really?*" It was all I could think of to say.

"With Ross?" Tommie asked.

Still grinning stupidly, Elizabeth nodded.

"Elizabeth?" I said again, disbelieving. "*Really* really?" We were flabbergasted.

"Did you use a condom?" Gwen asked her.

Elizabeth blinked and stared back at us. "Not *that!*" she exclaimed.

I let out my breath. "*What*, then?"

Elizabeth smiled. "I . . . let him touch me."

Gwen rolled her eyes. "First base, second base, third base . . . *what?*"

"My breasts," Elizabeth whispered. I mean, for Elizabeth, this was major! *Major!*

She just kept on grinning. "I . . . I never let a guy do that before," she said.

Well, I hadn't either. Not even Patrick and I had done that.

"Details! Details!" I said. "Did you take off your bra or what?"

"I wasn't wearing one," said Elizabeth.

I turned my shower off too and wrapped my towel around me. Pamela and I sat Elizabeth down on the bench at one end of the room as Tommie and Doris and Gwen gathered around.

"Okay, slowly. One step at a time. You *planned* this?" I asked, really curious.

"Of course I didn't plan it. I didn't even know what we'd be doing on the Kelpie Hunt. I just knew it would be dark."

"And Ross . . . ?"

He just invited me to go for a walk. And we kissed. And—"

"And . . . ? Don't stop, Elizabeth!" Pamela scolded.

"And he worked his hands up under my sweatshirt in back while he was kissing me, and . . . and when he discovered I wasn't wearing a bra . . . his hands came around and he touched me in front. And . . . I let him. I wanted him to."

We relived every second of it with Elizabeth.

"Is that all?" I asked finally.

"No. . . . Then he . . . he kissed them."

He *kissed* them?

"Kissed your breasts?" I asked. Oh, this was wild. I couldn't believe it!

Elizabeth just grinned.

Gwen gave an exaggerated, romantic sigh that broke the tension, and we laughed a little. "Hey, girl, you don't have to spill everything," she told Elizabeth. "You going to take us along on your wedding night?"

"It's just that . . . we promised once—Pamela and Elizabeth and I—that we'd tell each other everything," I explained.

"Ha! Not even guys do that, I'll bet. Only the parts that make them look good," said Doris.

"I don't think I should be telling you this," said Elizabeth, now that she'd told. "Ross said he wouldn't tell anyone."

"We won't ask any more," I said.

"There isn't any more to tell," Elizabeth said, and sighed happily.

We began talking about other things then, but I couldn't help remembering that only two years before on a train trip to Chicago, a man had touched one of Pamela's breasts, and

Elizabeth had wanted her to go to a priest the next day and have it blessed. It was a different Elizabeth who sat rapturously now in the shower house, grinning still. I wondered what she'd tell the priest this time when she got home. Or if she would tell him anything at all.

Saturday was a day of "last times." The big canoe race, then our last lunch together, our last volleyball game, our last swim.

The hour before dinner was devoted to packing up, making sure all the campers were taking home everything they'd brought with them. And after dinner, while the kids watched cartoons, the assistant counselors were sent back to scour our cabins and see if we could find anything that remained unpacked that we wouldn't need in the morning. We looked under the bunks, behind the door, up on the rafters.

As we went back and forth to the trash can outside, throwing out broken shoelaces and pieces of pretzel and torn pages of comics, Tommie called over, "We should have some sort of ceremony—the six of us. Toss something in the river to show we'll return."

"Like the Bible says, 'Cast your bread upon the water'?" asked Doris.

"Huh?" said Pamela, coming down the lane from cabin number twelve.

"Well, something like that," said Tommie.

"We *should*!" said Elizabeth. "Flower petals or something!"

Gwen suddenly smiled. "What about a six-pack?"

"What?" I said. "A *six*-pack?"

She went inside our cabin and returned with the box of Trojans. While we gathered around in amusement, she tore open one end and took out six little foil wrapped condoms, dropping one in each of our hands.

"To the river!" she said, thrusting one fist in the air, and, giggling, we set off.

At the water's edge each of us made a wish, then tossed her little foil packet out into the river.

"I want to come back someday to Camp Overlook," said Tommie, tossing hers.

"I want to see Ross again," said Elizabeth, going next.

"I want to see *Joe* again!" said Gwen.

Doris thought for a minute. "I want to get through geometry next year." Out went her condom into the water.

I didn't have to think long about my wish. "I want Dad and Sylvia's wedding to finally come off this fall." I threw over-handed, and my condom sailed out way past the others.

Pamela was just drawing back her arm when Craig came down the path to secure the canoes.

"What's this? What's this?" he asked, squinting at the little foil packets that were bobbing about on the slow-moving current. Then he looked at the one in Pamela's hand. "Is that what I think it is?"

"Yeah," said Pamela. "An end to summer."

"Well, hey! Don't let it go to waste!" Craig said, trying to grab it from her.

Pamela threw. "It's all yours," she said.

"Have a good swim!" Gwen said with a laugh, as we turned and made our way up the bank.

"You didn't tell us what you wished," I said to Pamela.

"The same old," she said. "About my mom."

Saturday night, of course, started with the Kelpie Hunt for the young campers. It was a little different from ours. They could squeeze through "the tunnel" if they wanted, with plenty of light from the lanterns, but no one rappelled down a bank, and only the bravest, the most eager, heard their names called. The rest were closely guided by counselors, so that everyone got the excitement of going into the woods at night, but only a few confronted the beast head-on. And when they got to the river's edge, the counselor who played the kelpie let some of the boys pull off his horse mask so that all the kids knew it was a fun joke.

After our showers later we changed into our pajamas and had our last session around the campfire. It was a quiet, sentimental affair, with the campers clinging to their counselors, reluctant to let go. Some of them clung to each other, their newfound friends. Estelle had taken to Gwen, despite all her racist remarks, but Latisha seemed as aloof as ever. When I put an arm around her shoulder, her body was stiff, and she almost imperceptibly shrugged me off.

"I wish," Connie said at the campfire, "that I could send a little bit of Camp Overlook home with each of you. You all have your collection of pine cones, of course, and the twig baskets we made. But what I hope most is that you will take back the knowledge that there are a lot of people who are different from you in some way, and yet you can get along."

The campfire flickered on all the little faces that somberly stared into the flames.

"What we *especially* hope," Connie said, "is that you remember that of all the people there are in this world, there is only one you. Nobody else is exactly like you. You are special. In fact, it's your very differences from other people that make you *you*. Some of you came here thinking that you could never sleep away from home. You found out that you could. Some of you thought you could never go into a dark woods, or paddle a canoe, or ride a horse. You did. Some of you learned to swim while you were here. So right now I want you to turn to the campers sitting next to you and pat those people on the back."

The kids started laughing then, and patted each other a little too hard, getting slaps on the back in return.

"And now," said Connie, "I want you to pat *yourselves* on the back."

This made the kids really whoop it up. They grabbed each other's hands to help them reach their own backs. There were a lot of "ow's" and "oof's," but almost everyone was smiling.

When they calmed down at last, Jack Harrigan took over and led the kids in the Camp Overlook cheer:

"Clap your hands!
Stamp your feet!

Our Camp Overlook
Can't be beat!"

We sang the camp song, then Connie read some poems, and after that the campers and counselors quietly, almost reverently, made their way back to their cabins, like deer going into the forest, as Connie always said.

Except that our Coyotes wanted to linger a while longer, and so did the girls from Doris and Pamela's cabin. So we all sat together on the logs, watching the flames die down in the bonfire, listening to the crackle and pop of the wood.

"Well," said Doris, "tomorrow at this time, you'll all be home again, and tonight will be just a memory. It will be a good one, though, won't it?"

"Yeah. I wish I *never* had to go home," said a girl from Pamela's cabin, and I wondered if Pamela didn't feel the same way.

"Me either," said Estelle.

"There's not a thing about home you've missed while you were here?" I asked. "Not a single thing?"

"I don't miss being made fun of because I can't read as good as my sister," said the girl named Virginia.

"I don't miss bein' hit upside my head 'cause Daddy say I shootin' off my mouth," said Latisha. "I wish I didn't *never* have to go see him."

We were all quiet for a moment.

"I'd just like to have something to miss," said another girl.

"And somebody to miss *me*," said Estelle.

I think that Gwen and Doris and Pamela and I all reacted to that the same way, because we put our arms around the nearest girls and pulled them toward us.

"*I'll* miss you," I said to Mary and Kim, trying to pull Estelle over as well.

"We'll miss you too," said Josephine.

Some of the girls went right to sleep when we reached our cabin, but others were reluctant to let go of the evening.

"Good night, everybody," came Josephine's sleepy voice from her bunk.

"Good night, Josie," said Ruby.

Kim, however, was weeping because she didn't want to say good-bye the next day.

"Hey, Kim! Your aunt's going to be waiting for you! And is she ever going to love that twig basket you made!" I said.

"But I don't want to leave *you!*" Kim wept.

"Shut up, girl," came Latisha's voice from above.

"Latisha," I said, "do you think that on this last night here at camp, you could manage to say something nice to Kim?"

There was silence. And then Latisha said, "Could you quiet down, Kim? I'm trying to sleep up here."

And for Latisha, I guess, that was progress.

12

HOME

It was strange. The kids were more subdued going home than they were coming up to Camp Overlook. I would have thought it would have been the opposite.

"Hardly any of them knew each other on the way here, but they whooped it up like old friends," I said to Gwen.

"Whistling in the dark," she told me. "They were trying to hide their nervousness, that's all."

"And when you consider what most of them are going back to, there's not much to whoop about, I guess," said Elizabeth.

As we'd boarded the buses that morning outside the dining hall, Ross had kissed her just before we got on. Ross's brother had driven down from Philadelphia to pick him up, so Ross and Elizabeth were saying their good-byes early as we loaded the kids. Everyone was watching, but I don't think Elizabeth even cared.

We stopped halfway home to get the kids lunch at McDonald's, and when we got on the bus again, I sat next to Elizabeth. She was looking about as peaceful as I'd ever seen her, smiling to herself. I would have thought she'd be weeping.

"Must be having a Ross thought," I said.

"He's one of the nicest guys I've ever met," she murmured.

I settled in close to her, our shoulders touching. "What did you like most about him?"

She thought for a minute. "He . . . he just sort of let me come to him, you know? He didn't rush me."

"In other words, *you* put the moves on *him*."

She laughed. "Not exactly. It was just . . . well, a mutual thing."

"I guess that's the way love's supposed to be," I said. But I still couldn't figure why she wasn't more upset about leaving camp. Leaving Ross. I glanced over at her but didn't say anything. She was the one who put it into words:

"I know we may not see each other again. But just to know that . . . that there are guys *like* him . . . I mean, that I could feel the way I do about him. . . . Well, that's hopeful."

"Very," I said.

I had hoped, I guess, that Latisha would give some sign that she was sorry camp was over—that we had been kind to her, at least. But when she got off the bus, she saw someone waiting for her. She just gave us a shrug, and went over to him, dragging her bag behind her. It didn't look as though he said two words to her. They just walked over to his pickup, he tossed her bag in back, and they drove away.

"I wish . . . ," I began.

"I know," said Gwen.

Kim was the most affectionate, tearfully hugging us before she embraced her aunt. Mary and Josephine were pleased to see their foster mother and went rushing over to tell her about camp. Estelle's caretaker was waiting for her, Ruby's grandmother for her, and the only good-byes left were to the other assistant counselors.

Gerald, of course, went around awkwardly hugging all the girls, and we hugged back. "I'm going to listen for you on the evening news," I told him, and he grinned. We were a little more enthusiastic with the rest of the guys, and we all traded e-mail addresses.

It was Joe and Craig and Andy who did the major hugging. We'd already said good-bye to Richard and of course Ross, as well as to Phil and Sue and all the other full counselors, back at camp.

"What's this? 'Muddybiker'?" I said, looking at the screen name Craig gave me.

"Used to be 'Nearly Naked,' but I've grown up," Craig said, and we laughed.

Finally—coming around the far end of the parking lot—was Elizabeth's mom in their Oldsmobile.

"Hi," she called. "I'm the designated driver for the four of you."

Mrs. Price parked a few spaces away from where we were standing and—smiling warily, because she never knows when she's going to set Elizabeth off—she got out and opened the trunk for our bags.

"Hi, Mom!" Elizabeth said, and actually walked over and hugged her. Mrs. Price was so surprised she dropped the car keys, but quickly hugged her back. All I could figure was that after listening to the kids at Camp Overlook describe their home lives, Elizabeth must have decided that she was awfully lucky after all and that what mistakes had been made in the past were forgivable.

Dad was waiting for me when I got in the house, and I gave him a bear hug—two for good measure.

"Sure seems like camp agreed with you, honey," he said, looking me over.

"You mean I'm *fat*?"

"I mean you look like you got plenty of fresh air and exercise."

"I did. I ate everything in sight, but I guess I managed to work it off," I told him. "Any word from Sylvia?"

"Things have settled down a little. At least Nancy's no worse. The antibiotics appear to be working, but her kidneys have shut down and she's on dialysis. Doctors are hoping that after a rest they'll begin functioning again. But it's going to be a long road, I'm afraid."

I couldn't bear the sadness in his voice. "Dad, does this mean that the wedding's postponed indefinitely?"

"No. Sylvia's already decided that once the danger's past, we'll set a date, whether Nancy can be in the wedding or not."

If Nancy didn't show, would that make me maid of honor? I wondered selfishly. What I said was, "Well, that's good news, then. How's Lester?"

"Well, he's been out most of the time, but from the little I've seen of him, he's fine."

I liked coming home to find things going okay. Not perfect, but okay. Up in my room my rubber plant needed watering, but the jungle bedspread looked inviting, and everything seemed larger than it had before. There's nothing like a bunk bed in a primitive cabin to make you appreciate the comforts of home.

There was a lot of e-mail waiting for me. I love to see the little yellow flag pop up on my mailbox, meaning that someone's thinking about me, telling me something. There was even a message from Patrick. I read that one first:

> Don't suppose you can access your e-mail
> from camp, but here's a "Hi" anyhow. Taking
> two summer school courses—European
> history and psychology—they're more work
> than I thought. Let me know when you get
> back.
> Patrick

Figured you'd want to know there are girls
swarming all over me here in Texas. They seem
to like a guy who s-s-stutters. Wish you were
here to fend them off. (Don't I wish!) Just wish
you were here.
Eric

Saw Patrick at the mall, and he says you're at
camp already. Nobody tells me anything.
Jill

I called you last night, and your dad said you
were at Camp Overlook. Sounds like something
Leslie and I might like to do. We were talking
about that the other day—how our ideal job
would be guides in national parks. We both like to
hike. Call me when you get back if you want to.
Lori

I told Jill you would be at camp. I don't know
why she thinks everyone's in the loop but her.
Karen
P.S. Did you know that Mark and Penny are
going out?

Whoa! I thought. Maybe Patrick and Penny really *were* kaput!
Lester came in about four. He'd been playing tennis all after-

noon and was wet with perspiration, but I hugged him anyway.

"Careful. You'll smell like eau-de-armpits," he said.

"I don't care. I'm just glad to be home," I told him. "Everything looks good to me, even you." Then I remembered. "Listen, Lester," I said, pulling away from him. "It was *you* who blabbed to Jack Harrigan about the guys swimming naked, wasn't it?"

Lester faked surprise. *"Moi?"*

"Yes, you! What did you tell him?"

"I did not tell him the guys were naked."

"Well, what *did* you say?"

Lester wiped his face and neck with his towel. "I merely said that I understood there had been a shortage of swim trunks the other night and that I'd be glad to supply some."

"Les-ter!" I bellowed.

"What's this? What's this?" Dad called from the kitchen.

"Nothing," I said, and gave Lester a look.

Dad was making one of my favorite meals, shrimp gumbo, and we could smell it all over the house. It drowned out the smell of Lester's sweaty shirt. "Who were you playing tennis with?" I asked. "Not Eva, was it?" That was one old girlfriend of Lester's I couldn't stand.

"No, there's no woman in my life at the moment," he said.

"Too bad," I said, settling down on the couch with a magazine. "Take lots of cold showers."

"Cold showers? Do I have a disease or something?"

"So you won't keep thinking of sex, Lester."

He laughed. "Cold showers can't keep me from thinking

of sex, Al. Acupuncture wouldn't keep me from thinking of sex. Riots, floods, and heavy artillery wouldn't do it. It's carved in a man's brain. There's a little section up there between the right and the left hemispheres that's labeled S-E-X. Besides," he added, "from what I heard, there was a lot going on at camp besides toasting marshmallows."

Dad came in just then with some lemonade for us while we waited for the shrimp gumbo to cook.

"Am I interrupting something?" he asked cautiously.

"No, we're discussing sex," I teased. "Lester thinks there was a lot of it going on up at camp, but he's dead wrong."

"Glad to hear that. Nothing more serious than a little petting, I hope," said Dad, trying to sound enlightened and cool.

"Petting?" I asked. He made it sound like a *zoo*!

"Letting a guy feel you up," Lester translated. Dad sounds so *antiquated* sometimes.

Dad winced. "What has happened to the English language?" he complained. "That sounds so vulgar, Les. Can't you at least say 'fondle'?"

"'Feel' . . . 'fondle' . . . one has one syllable, Dad, and the other has two," Lester said.

Dad smiled a little, shook his head, and went back to the kitchen. It was good to be home. I wanted Dad to stay like he was forever—wonderfully warm and caring and old-fashioned—and Lester to stay hip and funny. Then I wondered if I really knew *what* I wanted. Some things to change, I guess, and others to stay the same. Yet if things stayed the same, Dad would never marry. Pamela's folks would go on fighting. You can't pick and choose, I decided. Life happens, ready or not.

It wasn't till later that evening that I remembered to call Patrick. Does that mean you're over a breakup, I wondered, when you even forget to answer an ex-boyfriend's e-mail?

I dialed his number. "Hi," I said. "I'm back."

"O-*kay*!" he said. "How was it?"

"Hard. Fun. Interesting. Exhausting."

"Sounds so academic."

"We went skinny-dipping," I said.

There was a pause. "I stand corrected," he said. "Just the girls?"

"Guys and girls together."

"Not very academic at all," said Patrick.

"So what's up?" I asked him.

"I wondered if I could get some help on an assignment," he said. "I could come over."

"*You're* asking for *my* help?" I said. "Patrick, I didn't know there was any subject in the world you couldn't handle."

"Surprise!" he said. "In psych we have to do an interview, and I wondered if I could interview you."

"Why?"

"We're doing some kind of statistical thing. Data gathering and statistical correlation."

Patrick's advanced-placement courses always sound so impossible to me. "What do you want to know?" I asked.

"Well, I thought it would be easier if I just came over. That okay?"

"Sure."

"About nine? It would help if you had a baby book or something—a record of childhood illnesses and stuff."

"Yeah, I'll look for it," I said.

"See you," he said.

"Patrick's coming over," I told Dad. "He wants to see my baby book."

"Oh?" said Dad.

"Your *baby* book?" Lester said. "Call him back and tell him there's still time to cancel. Does he know you were born bald?"

I gave Lester a look. "Where is it? My book?" I asked Dad.

"The bottom drawer of my desk," he answered.

It was a white book with pink letters on the silk cover: BABY DEAR. And there, on the very first page—I remembered it now—was the photo of me just a few hours after I was born, my eyes closed, mouth puckered, fists clenched. Lester was right. No hair whatsoever.

I carefully leafed through the book, because some of the photos were pasted in, some were loose. *First Outing*, it said at the top of one page, and there was a picture of Mom in a pretty spring dress, holding me up to the camera, a cotton sunbonnet on my bald head. *Baby's Friends, Baby's Favorite Toys, Health Record, First Birthday* . . .

Stitched to the page describing my third birthday was a lock of fine silky hair, blond with a faint orange tint to it. *We've got another strawberry blonde in the family,* Mom had written below.

A photo of me at Christmas on Dad's lap, a photo of Lester, gingerly handing me a small car . . .

Mom's notes: *Alice Kathleen—a bright happy little soul!* . . . *Around the age of two, when Alice would discover a parent missing temporarily, she would say, "Where's a mama?" or "Where's a daddy go?"* . . . *Upon waking from a nap and seeing Lester's shoes on the floor, she asked, "Where did feet go?"* . . .

And further on: *Age three: Was inspecting the beloved but raggedy bear she took to bed every night, which had long since lost its face, and said, "Daddy, we've got to buy this kid a mouth,"* . . . *Alice calls Lester her "bruzzer."*

Then three small pictures of my mother—holding me on a merry-go-round, blowing soap bubbles with me, kissing my forehead. . . . Suddenly that sinking, smothering, sad feeling. It comes on so suddenly that I don't even feel it till it knocks me over, like a wave in the ocean. I gulp, I blink, I catch my breath, and then it's gone. Sometimes it comes again within a week, and sometimes months go by without my feeling it. I told Dad about it once and he said, "It's called longing, Al. It's missing somebody."

13
VIVA LA DIFFERENCE

Patrick always seems taller when I haven't seen him for a while. He stood at the door in his tennis shorts and T-shirt, his fair skin freckled, his red hair hanging down one side of his forehead.

I think my heart will always skip a beat for Patrick. They say that's true of your first boyfriend. The big question, of course, was whether his heart still skipped a beat for me. I doubted it. Still, I couldn't help wondering just how far he would have to bend down to kiss me now.

"So, hi," he said. "Welcome back."

"Come on in," I told him. I noticed he had a notebook under his arm.

Dad was stretched out on the couch listening to music, and Lester was in the kitchen. We took over the dining room table, and Dad waved to Patrick, then closed his eyes again. When he's missing Sylvia, he always listens to the music they've enjoyed together.

"You look great," Patrick said to me.

"So do you. What have you been doing, besides school?"

"Teaching tennis."

"Really?"

"Yeah. At day camp. Five afternoons a week. My courses are both in the mornings." He saw my baby book open to the photo of me just after I was born. "Let me see that," he said, and I slid the book toward him. He studied it and grinned. "Didn't have a lot of hair, did you?"

"Bald as a grapefruit," I said.

He went back to his assignment sheet. There was a series of questions about "firsts," and I found the right page in the baby book and read them off to him. First laugh? *Twelve weeks.* First crawl? *Eight months.* First word? *Thirteen months, "ba" for "ball."* First step? . . .

"Why do you need to know all this stuff, Patrick?" I asked.

"It's just an exercise in gathering data. It's not very scientific, and that's probably what we're supposed to learn from this assignment."

"Why not just go through *your* baby book?"

"That would be too subjective."

"Okay. What else do you need to know?"

"Social development," said Patrick. "Did you have any of the following?" He slid a paper toward me. "Just put an 'X' in the appropriate box."

I looked the paper over. "I haven't the foggiest idea!" I turned toward Dad. "Dad," I called, "when I was little, did I suck my thumb, throw temper tantrums, exhibit separation anxiety, or wet the bed?"

Lester stuck his head in from the kitchen. "What's this? Did she wet the bed? Why, she was a first-class, grade-A, government-certified soaker!"

"Lester!" I said, and looked at Dad again.

"Gosh, Al, that's something Marie would have remembered," he said. "If it's not in your baby book, I don't know. You sucked your thumb till you were three, I remember that, and you cried if we left you with a sitter, but as for the rest . . ."

"It's okay," said Patrick. "I'll put down two 'no's and two 'yes's.'" He looked over the assignment again. "All right, on a scale of one to ten, one being the lowest and ten the highest, how would you rate your abilities in science and math?"

"Two," I said.

"I don't believe it," said Patrick.

"Okay. One," I said.

He smiled, shook his head, and wrote down 2.

"Your abilities in social studies—history, sociology, stuff like that?"

I shrugged. "Seven, maybe?"

"Art?"

"Seven."

"Language arts?"

"Nine and a half," I told him. Patrick wrote down 9.

"I can't understand what you're going to do with all this stuff," I told him after we'd gone through another fifteen minutes of questions.

"We're trying to see if there's any correlation between things that happened to us when we were small and our abilities in high school," said Patrick. "But I talked to a guy who took this course last semester, and he says what it's really going to show is all the things that could make for a false correlation. We learn how to do a study right by doing it wrong."

"Whatever," I said.

Patrick's always so far ahead of me that I'm not sure I know what he's talking about. Maybe he really *is* the kind of guy who should get through four years of high school in three.

"Take it from me," Lester called from the kitchen, "she really *was* a soaker."

"Lester, will you shut up?" I said. "Go out for the evening or something."

"I will. I'm just waiting for a babe to call. If the phone rings, guys, I'll get it," he said, and it sounded like his mouth was full of potato chips.

"Okay, we're almost done," said Patrick. He glanced over at me. "Can I get you anything? Water? Tranquilizers?"

"This is my house, remember?" I said.

"Oh, right!" said Patrick. "This is the last set. On a scale of one to ten, how would you rate your popularity?"

I thought I'd probably check in at about a six or seven, but I wasn't going to tell Patrick that.

"Eight," I said. He wrote it down.

"On a scale of one to ten, how comfortable are you with members of the opposite sex?"

"Ten," I lied.

"How many boys have you kissed in your lifetime, excluding family members?"

"Patrick!" I said.

He didn't even look up. "How many guys did you kiss at Camp Overlook, and on a scale of one to ten, how would you rate them?"

I laughed. "This interview is over. The whole thing was bogus, wasn't it?"

He laughed too and closed his notebook. "No. Cross my heart. Except for the last set, which I sort of sneaked in there. Hey, it's a nice night out. Want to sit on the porch for a little bit?"

"Sure," I said, and we got up and went to the door.

It was a beautiful clear night out, and it reminded me, with a pang, of the night Patrick and I had that fight and broke up. I almost didn't want to sit in the swing with him for fear it would take me back to that place where my world . . . well, my social life, anyway . . . seemed to revolve around Patrick. Before I got involved with the backstage crew of the Drama Club at school. Before I felt as comfortable with myself as I do now.

But then, there was Patrick holding the screen door open for me, so I followed him out and we sat down a few inches apart.

"Been a while since we did this," he said, and smiled at me.

"Yeah, it has," I said, and smiled back. We pushed against the floor with our feet.

"So . . . are you going out with anyone?" he asked.

"Not at the moment."

"Me either. I'm girl-less."

"So I heard."

He shrugged. "I guess school and band and track and tennis are about all I can take on this year."

"So . . . no time for romance, huh?"

"You could say that. Anyway, it was a dumb idea to think you'd like it if I went out with you both. Penny thought so too."

"Chalk one up for Penny," I said dryly, then decided to go for it. "So why *did* you two break up?"

"She was just . . . Well, Penny's a nice girl, but she was way too demanding of my time, and I can't blame her."

I didn't say anything.

"Besides," Patrick said with a grin in my direction, "she wasn't you."

"Well, of course she's not me," I said.

He leaned sideways and kissed me lightly on the forehead before he stood up. "Viva la difference," he said. "See you later. Thanks for your help, Alice."

Viva la difference? Now what did he mean by that, exactly? I've heard Lester say it before when he's talking about the differences between men and women. Talking about a woman's curves, for example.

Did Patrick mean that he was glad Penny and I were different from each other because he liked variety? Was he saying he was glad that I'm me because he found something missing in Penny? He said she was demanding. Good. At least I'd found *something* about her to hate.

The fact was, I wasn't really hurt that Patrick hadn't stayed longer—that he hadn't given me a real kiss. That he hadn't asked me to go with him again. Relieved mostly, I guess. Maybe both of us wanted to see what else—*who* else—was out there. Besides, did I really want a boyfriend who was more interested in getting through high school in three years than he was in me? I don't think so.

"'Bye, Patrick," I said to the breeze, and went back inside the house.

Aunt Sally called about ten. Sometimes I think she makes a note on the calendar when it's time to check up on us. I know she promised Mother to look after Lester and me, and since we moved to Maryland, she feels the least she can do is call. How she and Uncle Milt raised Carol, their only daughter, to be the free spirit she is, I don't know, but Dad says that talking to Aunt Sally sets him back forty years.

It was Lester who answered the phone. Les always says as little as possible to Aunt Sally because he hates the way she tries to pry personal information out of him.

"Hi, Sal!" I heard him say. "Things are fine here. How are you?" And then, "Oh, I think she enjoyed camp a lot. She's right here; I'll let you talk to her."

"Thanks," I muttered as I took the phone. Then, "Hi, Aunt Sally."

"Oh, dear, I just wanted to know how things went at camp. What a wonderful experience for you! The children must have been so grateful!" came her voice.

"Well, I can't say that, exactly, but I did have a good time," I said.

She laughed self-consciously. "But not *too* much fun, I hope."

I didn't answer for a moment. I could have told her about skinny-dipping, I suppose. I do things like that sometimes just to hear her flip out. But Aunt Sally's probably doing the best she can, so I said, "No, it was just right."

"That's good," she said. "I know you're growing up, Alice, and I try to prepare myself for the day you'll be a young woman, but I never know quite what to ask. I try to think what Marie would have wanted me to tell you, but I'm just not very good at this. I'm afraid Carol had to raise herself in the sex department."

I envisioned a store with a sex department between housewares and shoes.

"You're doing fine," I told her. We talked then about Sylvia and the wedding being postponed, about how Uncle Milt and Carol were doing, how Carol had just mailed off a box of clothes she thought I might like, and how I was going to spend the rest of my summer. I think this was the closest to a real conversation

Aunt Sally and I had ever had. I decided that from now on, now that I was "growing up," I would try to be a little more understanding of Aunt Sally.

After I hung up, I checked my e-mail one more time. There was a message from Gerald:

> Hi, Alice. Just want to apologize for what
> happened at camp. I knew I came on too
> strong. I tend to do that. Scare girls away, I
> guess. Anyway, I wanted you to know that I'm
> taking your advice and going to audition as a
> reader for Books for the Blind. I'll see how well
> I do and if they think I'm any good, maybe I'll
> major in broadcast journalism. Thanks for the
> support. Take care.
> G. E.

Dad insists that I get a checkup at the dentist's and doctor's every summer. Most of my friends see a doctor only when they're sick. But Dad says it gives him peace of mind, so I go. This year, to get it over with, I scheduled them both for the same day.

I went to the dentist first.

"You know, Alice," he said, "last time you were here, I said you have a little bite problem—the way your teeth come together in front. You might want to see an orthodontist about it. I can recommend someone if you like."

He *had* mentioned it, but in such an offhand way that I

had put it out of my mind. I felt my shoulders sag. "You mean braces, don't you?

"Probably, but I don't think it's a serious problem. I've seen a whole lot worse."

"Well, I'm not doing anything till after my dad's wedding," I said. "I don't want to be wearing braces then."

"Fair enough," the dentist said. "When's the wedding?"

"This fall sometime," I told him, and made up my mind I wouldn't even *think* about braces until the wedding was over.

But I was thinking about them anyway—how much I'd hate them—when I signed in at Dr. Beverly's later. Once inside the narrow hallway, though, I knew the routine. The nurse weighed me and measured my height, then gave me a paper cup with my last name on it and told me to go in the restroom and leave a urine specimen in the cup.

It's sort of weird, you know? You're supposed to urinate a little in the toilet, then hold the cup under you and pee into that till it's about half full—you don't want it running over and dripping all over the place—and then pee the rest in the toilet. When you're all through, you open the tiny cupboard door in the wall and set your cup on a shelf lined with a paper towel. On the other side of the wall is another tiny door leading to the doctor's laboratory. A technician on the other side opens the other door every so often, takes out any cups that are there, and does an analysis of the urine—like living in a nunnery or something, where you can communicate with people only through a hole in the wall.

I flushed the toilet. Then, carefully holding my half-filled cup, I leaned over and opened the cupboard door. At that very moment the door on the other side opened, and I found myself looking smack into the face of a fortyish woman with glasses and a mole on her cheek.

Good grief! What was I supposed to do? What was I supposed to say?

"Hi," she said.

I was so flustered, I set down my cup and quickly banged the door shut.

Instantly I felt my face flush. Now why had I done *that*? It just seemed so personal somehow, like I wasn't supposed to be looking at her. But *she* wasn't the one with her underpants down to her ankles! Why couldn't I have said something funny like, *We've got to stop meeting like this!* When would I quit doing such stupid, embarrassing things? But I already knew the answer to that. Never, ever, ever.

14

THE BIG ANNOUNCEMENT

"So how are you?" Dad asked at dinner. "Everything okay?"

Lester always cringes when Dad asks that, because I used to embarrass him hugely. I'd always have something to tell about what went on at the doctor's office because . . . well, who else was there to tell? Family, I mean.

Elizabeth and Pamela are shocked that I can talk to my dad and brother about the things I do, even though Lester says he doesn't want to hear it, which I don't believe for one moment. I guess it's because I don't have a mother. I started out asking Dad and Lester questions when I was too young to be embarrassed, and once I got started, it just seemed natural to keep on asking.

But by the time I got home, I'd recovered from my embarrassment. Besides, I was getting a stepmom, and I couldn't wait till Sylvia and I were having *intimate* conversations. Just the two of us. So when Dad asked how things went with my doctors' appointments, I replied, "Fine. No problem." I decided not to even mention braces for now. Dad didn't need this to deal with too.

"Whew!" said Lester. "That's good to hear."

"It certainly is," said Dad.

"No puddles on the examining table? No gagging when he examined your throat?" Lester asked.

"Nope," I said. "I'm good for another year."

"Well, *I've* got news, then," said Lester.

"Oh?" said Dad, suddenly focusing on Lester.

"I got an offer I can't refuse," said Lester.

"Not from a woman, I hope," said Dad.

"No, and I think even you will agree to this, Dad. The last time I talked about finding a place of my own, you said to at least wait for a while after Sylvia moves in so she won't feel like she's breaking up the family, remember?"

"Yes . . . ," Dad said warily.

"Well, I was playing tennis with Paul Sorenson this morning, and he says that a friend of his father's—an old-timer named Otto Watts—needs someone to live in the second floor of his house. He's got one of these big Victorian houses in Takoma Park near the D.C. line. They made the upstairs into an apartment for their younger daughter when she was in college, but she's out on her own now, and Mrs. Watts is dead. His children think he ought to be in a retirement home, but he won't hear of it. So here's the deal: Because he knows Paul's father, Mr. Watts is offering the apartment to Paul if he'll get two other guys to share it, with the understanding that one of us will be there evenings all the time in case Mr. Watts needs us. He has an aide come in during the day. We'd have to do all the light maintenance around the place—mow the grass, paint, trim the bushes, that kind of stuff—and pay for our utilities. But other than that, it's rent-free. George Palamas is going to move in with Paul, and they asked if I wanted to be the third."

I sat as still as the baked potato on my plate. I was too stunned to even think whether this was good news or bad news. Dad looked surprised too. Lester leaving?

"I know Paul. Do I know George?" Dad asked.

"He's been here, but you may not remember him. He's responsible. Works for an insurance company."

"Well, it certainly does seem like a good deal, Lester. But what about visitors? What about noise? Is he going to complain if you play your CDs or have late parties?"

"He's deaf," said Lester. "But he's sharp as a tack. Funny, too. Paul asked him if we could have friends in, if the noise would bother him, and he said he'd just remove his hearing aid."

Dad smiled. "Do you think you can keep the promise that one of you three will be there every evening?" Dad asked.

"That'll be the hardest part, but for a rent-free place, we're willing to do it. If it were just two of us and we could never go anywhere together, I don't think so. Besides, anytime Mr.

Watts's family takes him somewhere—out for the evening or on vacation—we can all be out too. It's not like we're prisoners forever."

Dad toyed with his veal chop. "You've talked of moving closer to campus, though."

"I know, but I'd never get as sweet a deal as this one, Dad. I really want to try it, and now that the wedding's postponed, I think I ought to move out, give you and Sylvia some privacy."

I kept looking from Dad to Lester, Lester to Dad. Just because Dad was marrying Sylvia, did *every*thing have to change? I suddenly wanted to retract everything I'd said about wanting something to happen this summer. Was *I* going to have to move out too to give them privacy? How much privacy did they need? They could always close their door. Then I realized that Lester's room is right next to theirs. Maybe that *would* be a little awkward.

"Well, it certainly seems like a good opportunity," Dad said at last. "Paul is in school too; it's a lucky break for you both."

Lester beamed and looked at me. How could I say it was okay with me? Lester had lived with us my entire life. I'd be lost without him! I could see me eating breakfast alone on Saturday mornings. Making dinner by myself when it was our night to cook. Standing at the doorway of Lester's empty room when everyone else had gone to bed and I had a worry that only Lester could understand. I hated the tremor in my voice when I asked, "Will I be able to visit you?"

"Sure!" Lester said. "It's only a couple of miles from here. We'll have you to dinner! You can drop by on weekends."

My mind suddenly did a turnaround and started racing in the other direction. I could see me eating lunch on Sundays in my brother's apartment with two other handsome guys. I could see making spaghetti sauce for them when they had a party. I could see me driving over there after I got my license and sitting on the front porch on summer nights and being introduced to Lester's friends.

"Well, I think it's a wonderful idea too!" I said. "I think it's time that Lester had a place of his own."

Both Dad and Lester looked surprised, like they'd expected a protest.

"Well, then, I'll tell Paul I'm in," said Lester.

"When will you be moving out?" asked Dad.

"Mr. Watts is having the place painted, so it won't be ready till the middle of September, but he says there's no reason we can't move some of our stuff in if we keep it in the middle of the floor."

I imagined Lester and Paul and George inviting Pamela and Elizabeth and me to dinner. I imagined George and Paul and Lester going to the movies and inviting me and Elizabeth and Pamela to come along. I imagined Paul and Lester and George going shopping at Safeway to stock their refrigerator and Elizabeth and me and Pamela going along to help. I imagined . . .

"So what's going through *your* mind?" Les said to me. "Planning to take over my room the minute I move out?"

"No," I said brightly. "Just thinking about the future, that's all."

* * *

It was the first thing I wanted to talk about when our gang met the next Sunday at Mark Stedmeister's pool. It was hard to find a time we could all get together at once, because most of us had part-time jobs. I was working days at the Melody Inn; Elizabeth was baby-sitting her little brother; and Pamela was working part-time for a dog-walking service.

The biggest change I'd noticed in our group was that we sat around and talked more. The guys weren't constantly trying to push each other in the pool, or seeing who could make the biggest cannonball and splash everyone on the deck.

In junior high our conversations were mostly the boys joking about something and the girls laughing. Joke . . . laugh . . . joke . . . laugh. Now we were actually having real conversations. I was impressed at how adult we sounded.

"Big news. Lester's moving out," I said as we lounged about on the deck, our bodies covered with sunblock.

Pamela and Elizabeth stared at me. "Oh, Al-ice!" they wailed in unison.

"Aren't you sad?" asked Elizabeth.

I began to wonder if this really was a tragedy and I just didn't know it yet.

"Well, he's only a couple of miles away, and he's sharing an apartment with two cute guys," I said, stretching it a bit, since I didn't know either Paul Sorenson or George Palamas.

I could see the wheels turning in Pamela's head. "Could we see his apartment?" she asked.

"Oh, sure! Lester said we could visit anytime." Now I was

stretching the truth so far I could almost hear it snap.

Elizabeth was all enthusiasm. "Oh, Alice, we could help them decorate! We could go over on moving day and cook for them and everything!" she said.

"We could have a housewarming party for them. In their apartment!" said Pamela. "Oh, man, this is *major*!"

"Maybe they'd let us have the apartment some night for our own party," said Brian. "Now that would be cool."

"Sweeeeet!" agreed Mark.

I began to feel as though Lester's apartment was getting a lot more publicity than he would have liked.

"When's moving day?" Pamela asked.

I knew I had to back off. "I'm not sure," I said. "I'll let you know." And I was relieved when the conversation turned to other things.

"Anyone seen Patrick lately?" Justin asked. "I thought his courses would be over by now." Justin was sitting by Elizabeth. One minute it looked like they might be getting chummy again. The next minute Jill was in his lap.

"Patrick came by the other night," I said, waving off a fly.

Everyone looked at me.

"He was doing a psych assignment," I explained, "and needed to interview someone."

"Can you imagine Patrick asking anyone for help?" said Karen.

"I can't," said Penny. "Patrick Long is the most self-sufficient person I know."

Somehow I resented her answering, even though Karen had

asked a question. I guess I'd wanted her to sound surprised—
hurt, even—that he'd come by to see me, now that they'd broken
up. I ignored her.

"What's this I hear about Gwen and Legs splitting up?" Mark
asked. "Leo says he drove up to see her at that camp and she was
making out with some guy there."

Pamela and Elizabeth and I broke into laughter, remembering
that movie-star kiss. "Yeah, sure. She was making out, all right," I
said. "And Legs couldn't be happier that he can go out now with
the girl he's been two-timing Gwen with in the first place."

Mark hadn't known that we knew about Leg's new girlfriend. The conversation got general then—who was going with
whom, what everybody had been doing over the summer.

Patrick came just as we were taking orders for calzones.
Take-out Taxi will deliver.

"My man!" Brian said when he saw Patrick, and they punched
each other on the shoulder. Guys have such *stupid* greetings!

"How you doing?" Patrick asked, looking around the whole
group. His smiled extended to me. I was mainly watching Penny,
though. She just turned her head away from him. It was then I
noticed that she and Mark were playing footsie. Things sure do
change. It hadn't seemed so long ago that Mark and Pamela were
going out, but then Mark dumped potato salad down the back
of Pamela's bikini bottom, and it was good-bye, Mark!

I was tired of baking in the sun, so I got up and jumped in
the pool. Elizabeth and Patrick jumped in too.

"How did you do on the psych interview?" I asked Patrick.

"Got an A minus," said Patrick.

"Why the minus?"

"Because I should have asked a few more questions."

"What kind of an interview was it?" asked Elizabeth.

"I had to interview someone about childhood experiences so we could see if there was any connection between what had gone on in childhood and what was going on now."

"Sounds interesting," said Elizabeth.

Patrick grinned. "She was an interesting girl."

"So was there any correlation?" I asked.

"That's what we're working on this week, when we pool our results. It's not a valid study."

"I'm grateful for that," I said. "I'd hate to have you know something about me that I didn't know."

I wasn't paying as much attention to Patrick right then, though, as I was to Pamela. She was sitting around with the others, but it looked as though her mind was a thousand miles away. I realized what I'd been missing this summer—the old, outrageous, fast-track Pamela, who always seemed a step or two ahead of the rest of us. Even at camp she'd seemed to take a backseat in whatever we did; and watching her now—her knees pulled up to her chest, her eyes on a tree—I vowed to give her more time and attention before school started.

"Okay," she said the next day when I called her, just to talk. "I got the whole story." I could hear a new CD by the Velvet Pistols playing in the background.

"Of what?" I asked.

"Of what happened between Patrick and Penny."

"Who did you get it from? Patrick or Penny?"

"Karen."

"Oh, come *on*, Pamela! You can't believe half of what Karen tells you. If she doesn't have any good gossip, she'll make it up."

"She got it straight from Penny."

"I'll bet."

"Well, do you want to hear it or not?"

Of course I did.

"Penny just felt that she came second in Patrick's life."

"Second to what?"

"I'm not sure, but that's what she told Karen. His courses, maybe. Probably you."

"Don't be ridiculous."

"She said that a couple of times Patrick even made the mistake of calling her 'Alice.'"

I had to smile. "I can imagine how Penny took to *that*!"

"Well, it wasn't just that. She also said that a lot of the time she didn't think he was all there."

"Now what did she mean by that? Patrick's one of the brightest guys I know!"

"She meant that he wasn't all that focused on her. He had his mind on other things."

"That's Patrick," I said. "But I can't imagine why she'd suspected I was in the picture again. Except for that e-mail message from Patrick, we hadn't seen or spoken to each other since school let out."

"That's not what Penny thinks."

"So why doesn't she ask *me*?"

"Oh, come on. She wouldn't humiliate herself like that. Admit it, now. Doesn't it give you even the slightest satisfaction to know that *she's* jealous of *you*?"

"Yes," I said, laughing.

"And isn't there just the teeniest, tiniest bit of satisfaction in knowing that after she took him away from you, he was the one who lost interest?"

"Yep," I told her.

"You and Patrick ought to go out sometime right under her nose, just to get even."

"Oh, I don't know," I said.

"I don't understand you, Alice. It's not a sin to want to rub it in a little."

"Maybe I like my new freedom," I told her.

In the background, the lead singer for the Velvet Pistols was shouting out the words. I'm not even sure you could call it singing:

> *"I wanna make you,*
> *I wanna break you,*
> *Baby, you're mine tonight."*

And then the band, all the guys together, started moaning a sort of syncopated "*Uh*-huh, *Uh*-huh, *Uh*-huh," which was supposed to sound like they were having sex, I guess.

Finally, Pamela said, "I'm really down, Alice. Everyone else has a job with *people* for the rest of the summer. All I've got for company are dogs. Find out exactly when Lester's moving, will you? I want at least one thing to look forward to."

15
THE GO-BETWEEN

Dad seemed to need me more around the house once I was back. I'm not sure what it was, but it was as though he'd lost his bearings after Sylvia postponed the wedding. I guess I'd call him distracted, but not quite coming apart at the seams. Maybe everyone has a limited amount of patience, I thought, and he had about used his up.

I mentioned this at the Melody Inn.

"His mind is on Sylvia, that's the problem," I said to Marilyn Rawley, after we had unpacked some boxes UPS had delivered. Marilyn is one of Lester's old girlfriends, who works for Dad as his assistant manager.

"I've noticed," Marilyn said, scooping up her long brown hair in back and planting it firmly on top of her head with a wide comb. "I had to remind him last week that our paychecks were due. The music instructors hadn't been paid."

But I was staring at her hand. I reached up and took hold of her ring finger. There was a small oval diamond set in white gold.

"Marilyn?" I said, studying her face, and she broke into a wide smile. "That guy you've been going out with? Jack?"

She nodded.

I didn't know whether to smile or cry. I had so wanted Lester to marry Marilyn! More than any of the other girls he ever dated—Crystal Harkins, even—I'd wanted it to be Marilyn.

She understood, because she put a finger to my lips and said, "Don't say it."

I swallowed, then managed to congratulate her. "Have you told Dad?" I asked.

"No. Jack just proposed last night."

"Oh, Marilyn, Jack is so lucky! I hope he knows how lucky he is, and I hope you'll be deliriously happy every day for the rest of your life!" I burbled.

She hugged me and laughed. "Nobody is happy every day of her life, Alice. But when he asked me, I just knew he was the right one."

I spent the rest of the afternoon straightening the merchandise in the Gift Shoppe and wrapping purchases and making change and wondering how you knew when you'd met the "right one." How soon had Dad known that about Sylvia? A lot sooner, I guess, than Sylvia knew that about Dad. Gwen had even thought for a while that Legs was "the one" for her. Just how wrong can you be?

"Your shirts aren't back from the laundry yet because you didn't send them out," I told Dad one evening. "Your laundry bag is still in your closet. Want me to take them in for you?"

He looked exasperated. He also kept forgetting to pick up milk and bananas—the things we use up faster than anything else—so I'd begun checking the refrigerator regularly and walking to the 7-Eleven to get them when I saw we were running low. Checking his shirts. He had worked so hard to get the house ready for Sylvia, and who knew when she'd come back?

After dinner he went out to putter around in the garden, pulling weeds, spreading a little mulch, watering. Then he went up to his room, and I saw him sitting at his desk when I walked by.

Later, when Les and I were cleaning up the kitchen, Sylvia called.

"Dad's up in his room writing a letter to you," I said. "I'll get him."

"Well, let me talk to you first, Alice. How *are* you? I don't think we've talked since you went to camp." Her voice was as lilting as ever.

"Oh, I'm fine. I had a really good time, but I like being home for the rest of the summer," I said.

"I know how you feel. I wish I could be home. How's Ben holding up? Really."

"He's missing you," I said.

"Oh, I know. And I'm missing him terribly."

"How's Nancy?"

"Better. Her kidneys are starting to function again. She still needs dialysis, but not as often. We're hopeful."

"Will you . . . will you be back before Christmas?" I asked plaintively.

"Oh, definitely," she said. "But I don't want to get Ben's hopes up that I'm coming back too much sooner until we know for sure. How are *you* doing, Alice?"

"I'm marking time," I told her.

"How?"

"Everything's on hold."

"The wedding, you mean."

"Yes." I swallowed. "I looked at the calendar this morning and . . ."

"I know," she finished for me. "The day we were supposed to be married. I've been feeling sad all day."

"Me too. But the one exciting thing that's happening is that Lester's moving out," I told her. "Well, exciting and sad both, I guess."

"What?"

"It's really a good deal. He gets the apartment rent-free. I'll let Dad tell you all about it, but Lester said I could visit whenever I wanted." Somehow it seemed that the more people I talked to about Lester's moving, the more generous I made Lester sound. "I just wish you were here, though, to take care of Dad, Sylvia. Then I'd have one less person to worry about."

"Why? Alice, what's wrong?"

"He's sad. He's forgetful. He forgets to take his shirts to the laundry, to stop at the store, to pay all the bills. All he does is mope around and work in the garden."

"You'd better get him to the phone, Alice. I think your dad needs to hear some sweet talk about now."

I grinned. "Okay."

I started upstairs to get Dad just as he was on his way down to refill his coffee cup.

"It's Sylvia, Dad," I said.

His face lit up like Christmas. "Sylvia?" He lunged for the phone, pulled out the telephone stool, and sat down, his back against the wall. His face broke into a hundred little smiling crinkles.

"Sweetheart," he said, adjusting the phone to his ear, and in that moment I heard her say, "Hi, you old, forgetful honey bear. . . ." And I knew it was time for me to clear out.

I went upstairs to sort through my things for the laundry and saw the glow of Dad's lamp coming from his room. I walked to the doorway. There were his reading glasses on the desk beside a pen and paper. As much as I knew I shouldn't, I tiptoed over to his chair. *I told Sylvia he was writing to her*, I said to myself. *All I'm going to do is take a quick peek and make sure I'd told the truth.*

He must have started the letter on the other side of the

page, because the first line was a continuation of something else. But then I read: *Sylvia, darling, do you know this poem? It's all I can think about these days. Sixteenth century, I think:*

> *O western wind, when wilt thou blow*
> *That the small rain down can rain?*
> *Christ, that my love were in my arms*
> *And I in my bed again!*

I swallowed and tiptoed out of the room. Never mind the first two lines. I wasn't even sure what they meant. But the last two! There was something about that poem so urgent, so intense. I could almost feel the longing rise up from the paper. How different it seemed from that Velvet Pistols song: "I wanna make you, I wanna break you. . . ." If anyone deserved to be deliriously happy for the rest of their lives, it was Dad and Sylvia.

I was at Pamela's house the following week when something happened. Both Elizabeth and I were there. We were lying on Pamela's bed, actually, looking through a magazine, when we heard the doorbell ring and Mr. Jones's footsteps crossing the hall.

"Is it for me, Dad?" Pamela called, and we waited.

Then, almost seconds after we heard the front door open, we heard it close again, hard, with a bang. There was a loud knocking, and then somebody obviously was leaning against the doorbell. *Dingdong-dingdong-dingdong-dingdong . . .*

"Dad?" Pamela called, and we all sat up, listening.

We heard the door open again, a muffled angry exclamation from Mr. Jones, and then a woman's voice saying, ". . . just to talk. Please!"

Bang! went the door again.

"Mom!" gasped Pamela.

"Oh no!" said Elizabeth.

Dingdong-dingdong-dingdong-dingdong . . .

"Do you want us to leave?" Elizabeth asked Pamela. "We could go out the back."

"No! I don't want to be here alone with those lunatics!" Pamela said, grabbing hold of us. "He could at least talk to her."

At that moment the doorbell did stop ringing.

"Did you know she was in town?" Elizabeth asked.

"I knew she wanted to come, but I didn't know when." Pamela absently flipped a few more pages of the magazine, but she wasn't looking at them and neither were we.

All at once something hit our window. Pamela rolled off the bed so fast she kicked me in the leg and pulled us down with her. On the way down she grabbed at the light switch, and the light went out.

"Don't even breathe," said Pamela.

We sat on the floor, our backs against the bed. Another piece of gravel hit the window.

"Pamela," her mom called from outside.

Downstairs the front door opened again, and we heard Mr. Jones say in a low voice, "If you don't leave, I'm calling the police."

"Go ahead. We're not divorced, remember. You can't keep me out of our house," Mrs. Jones yelled at him.

"Dad," Pamela shouted as he shut the door again. "Don't you dare call the police. At least *talk* to her! Maybe then she'll go."

"In a pig's eye," said her father.

But there was no more gravel at the window. No more calling.

"Do you think she's gone?" I whispered.

"Heck no," said Pamela.

Ten minutes went by, though, and nothing happened. But Pamela wouldn't turn on the light. Her dad went back to the TV.

"Man, I wish she'd stayed in Colorado," Pamela said.

"But maybe . . . if she's really sorry for walking out on you . . . he could just give her one more chance?" said Elizabeth.

"How can he give her one more chance if he hates her?" Pamela asked. "She humiliated him. I don't think he'll ever forgive her."

"That's a sin," said Elizabeth.

The phone rang.

"Gwen said she'd call," Pamela told us. "I'll get it," she called to her dad, and picked up the extension in her room. It was Karen.

"Are you ready for this? Big news," we heard her say. *What else can happen tonight?* I was thinking.

Pamela held the phone out so we could all hear even better. "Okay, what?" she asked.

"Guess who's sleeping together."

We looked at each other.

"Sam and Jennifer?" said Pamela.

"They broke up," said Karen.

"They did?" Pamela said, giving me a surprised look, because Sam used to like me.

"Just after school let out," said Karen. "But I'm talking about someone else."

"Who, then?" asked Pamela. "Elizabeth and Alice are here. Tell us."

"Good! Then I won't have to call them. Guess again."

"Penny and Mark?" Elizabeth guessed.

"Not that I know of. I mean, I don't go around *asking*, for Pete's sake!" said Karen.

"No, she just goes around telling," I whispered, but that didn't stop me from listening.

"We give up," said Pamela.

"Jill and Justin."

"Justin?" said Elizabeth. Justin used to like *her*.

"Uh-oh. Have I put my foot in my mouth?" Karen asked. "Liz? You don't still like him, do you?"

"How do you know this, Karen?" I asked, taking the phone.

"Jill told me."

"Well, thanks for that little piece of information," Pamela said.

"And you know who else?" said Karen.

"Karen!" Elizabeth and I said together. At the same time, however, Pamela said, "Who?"

But Karen said, "Well, if you don't want to know . . ." and hung up.

The phone rang again almost immediately. Pamela picked it up again. "Okay, *who*?" she said.

There was a pause. And then we heard Mrs. Jones's voice saying, "Pamela, *please* make him talk to me."

Elizabeth looked around as though she wanted to find the escape hatch.

"Mom, he doesn't want to! How can I make him?" Pamela said. She wouldn't put the phone against her ear, as though it were so hot it might burn her.

"The last two years have been a nightmare," we heard Mrs. Jones say. "That was the worst mistake I ever made in my life, and I just want to tell him."

I wished Pamela wouldn't let us hear. I felt as though I should cover my ears or go in the bathroom or something.

"You already told him that. You wrote him a letter, remember?" Pamela said. "But he says it's over, Mom. It's just over."

"Well, forget my coming back. All I want is to talk to him."

"If that's your mother, hang up," Pamela's dad yelled from below.

"Dad wants me to hang up," Pamela said into the phone. She sounded like she was going to cry.

"You can't do this to me, Pamela. Please don't hang up!"

"Mom . . . !"

"Pamela!" her dad yelled again.

Pamela slowly lowered the phone and placed it back in the cradle.

"I don't think we should stay," Elizabeth said. "Do you guys want to come over to my place?"

"I'm afraid of what's going to happen if I leave, but I'm afraid of what will happen if I stay," said Pamela. There were tears in her eyes. "Well, if she's calling from a phone, she must have gone somewhere. We might as well turn on the light."

"Maybe she's calling from a cell phone," I said.

Pamela turned on the light and pulled down her shade. "I absolutely refuse to get caught in the middle!" she declared angrily. "They aren't going to make me their go-between! No *way*!"

"Maybe you could call up that nurse your dad's been dating. Maybe if your mom saw another woman in the house, she'd go away," said Elizabeth, desperate to be helpful.

"*Not* a good idea," said Pamela. She flopped down on the bed again and lay with her arms up over her head. All at once she raised her head and said, "Do you hear footsteps?"

We listened. There were footsteps, all right. The floor creaked, and the next thing we knew, Mrs. Jones was coming through the doorway of Pamela's room, one finger to her lips. Elizabeth and I positively froze.

Pamela's petite, blond mom was wearing jeans and a red polo shirt. She looked good, but her face was a lot more worn than I'd remembered it.

"Oh!" she said, staring at Elizabeth and me. "I didn't know your friends were here."

"Now, Mom," Pamela began, sitting up.

"If you just give the word, Pamela, I'll walk out of your life right now, and you won't ever have to talk to me again."

"I didn't say that, Mom. How did you get in?"

"There's a back door, you know, and I still have a key." Mrs. Jones glanced at Elizabeth and me again, as if asking us to go, but Pamela's fingers were digging into our arms. For Pamela, we stayed put.

Suddenly we heard Mr. Jones's rapid footsteps on the stairs.

"Pamela," he called outside her door. "Is your mother in there?"

Mrs. Jones lunged for the door to lock it, but before she could, it flew open.

"Get the hell out!" Mr. Jones yelled at his wife.

"Are you going to throw me out of our own house, Bill?" Mrs. Jones said.

I wished I could crawl under the bed. I wished I could pull Pamela with me. She always sounds so fast and sassy, but right then she looked like a little girl of seven. Her bottom lip trembled and her eyes were gleaming with tears. I just wanted to hold her.

Mr. Jones reached in and grabbed his wife by the wrist. Mrs. Jones screamed, and he yanked her out of the room. She stumbled against the wall.

And then, while Elizabeth and I watched, heartsick, Pamela sank down on the floor beside her bed, her arms around her legs, face on her knees, and sobbed.

Mrs. Jones turned around and Mr. Jones stopped yelling.

And in that silence, Pamela's dad went down the hall to his own bedroom and shut the door.

Pamela's mom stood where she was in the hallway, one hand to her throat. "Oh, my God, Pamela. I'm so sorry, sweetie. I'm just so sorry for all that I've done," she said.

Pamela continued to cry. Elizabeth and I continued to stare.

"Pamela, is there anything I can do?" her mother said, coming back into the room. "What do you really want me to do, sweetheart? Just tell me. Go or stay?"

How could they *do* that to her? I wondered. How could parents make a fifteen-year-old girl decide what they should or shouldn't do?

"Mom," said Pamela, and her nose sounded clogged, "will you just go?"

There was silence.

"Are you sure that's what you want?" her mom asked finally. I cringed.

"Yes," Pamela said at last.

"Sure?" her mother repeated, taking a step closer. "*Talk* to me, Pamela!"

And suddenly Pamela screamed, "Mom, I'm not *ready* to talk yet! You can't just run off with a guy for almost two years and then expect to come home like nothing's happened."

"Pamela, I didn't exactly run off. I tried to explain it to you then, and I suppose I'm doing an even worse job of explaining now. I've said it was a mistake, and I want to make it up to you. . . ."

"How can you make up for two years of not being here?"

Pamela cried. "What could you ever do to 'make it up,' Mom? And right now I just don't want to talk about it because it's all too painful!" She started to cry again. "Yes! Go! Just go!" And she turned the other way.

Mrs. Jones waited a moment longer. Then she went back downstairs, left the house, and shut the door after her. Elizabeth and I sat down on the floor with Pamela between us and let her cry. There wasn't a thing to say, really. Just things to cry.

"Do you think you and your dad might want to talk later?" I asked. "We could go home now, Pamela, if you want."

"What I want is for you guys to stay right here the rest of the night. You're the two best friends I've ever had," Pamela wept.

So we did.

I was afraid the next morning we'd hear on the news that a woman's body had been found in the Potomac. But two days later Pamela told us her mother had called and said she'd taken an apartment in Wheaton. It looked as though Pamela was going to be the go-between whether she wanted to or not.

I sat in Lester's room the following night while he trimmed his toenails. Lester has very thick toenails, and when a clipping flies across the room, you can hear it land.

"Do you *mind*, Al?" he said. "This is rather personal, you know."

I ignored him because I needed to talk to someone about Pamela. At least he listened while I described what happened.

"I have a theory," I said finally, "that life throws you something awful every five years. When I was five, Mom died. When

I was ten, you broke your leg. Now I'm fifteen, and see what's happened to Pamela? What's going to happen when I'm twenty?"

Lester sent another clipping skimming across the floor. "That's about the stupidest thing I ever heard," he said.

"Why?"

"Because it was *me* who broke his leg, not you. And it's Pamela who's got the mother problem."

"But when I think of all the scary, awful things that *could* happen, like Sylvia's plane going down on her way home to marry Dad or—"

"Stuff it, Al! You're ignoring all the good things that happen. Name something nice that's happened recently."

I thought for a moment. "Sylvia calls Dad every day."

"Yep."

"Pamela's mother didn't jump in the river."

"Uh . . . okay. . . ."

"Elizabeth and Ross didn't have sex."

"For Pete's sake, Alice!" Lester said.

I curled up on his bed and watched him finish his clipping. "Lester, here's something I've wondered about. Before the wedding does a bride have to clip her toenails and clean out her navel and scrub every square inch of her body?"

"If she thinks she has lice, I suppose she should."

"I'm serious. I just want to know the etiquette. Are you supposed to present yourself to your new husband all clean and fresh and trimmed and filed and—"

"I don't know. I'm not a woman."

"How much will *you* clean on your wedding day?"

"I suppose I'll take a shower. Give my armpits the old sniff test and see if I really need one." He grinned at me.

I thought some more about weddings. "What if a woman starts her period just before her wedding day?"

I heard Lester let out his breath. "Man, do I ever wish you had a mother," he murmured.

"I need to *know* these things, Lester."

"Do you need to know right now?"

"No, but I'd like to."

"Okay. So what if she does?"

"Well, does she postpone the wedding or what?"

"Al, that's *life*! If her husband can't handle a little thing like that, he shouldn't be getting married at all. Where did you get the idea you have to be perfect? Perfectly scrubbed and manicured and deodorized?"

"The brides all look like that in magazines."

"Magazines aren't life, Al. *I'm* life. *You're* life."

"Yeah, and Pamela's life too, but look how lousy it is." I sat up, my chin on my knees. "You know what, Lester? You know what would give Pamela a really, really big boost?"

"Yeah? What?"

"You could ask her out."

Lester stopped clipping and stared at me, his mouth half open. "You're out of your tree."

"I don't mean in a romantic way. Just take her out for a fun evening and cheer her up."

"Al, I wouldn't take Pamela out if every other girl in the state of Maryland was certifiably insane."

"Why? She adores you, Lester! It would really give her a lift. She's had a crush on you ever since she met you."

"That's exactly why I couldn't take her out, not to mention that I'm seven years older than she is."

"Party pooper," I said with a pout. "Here's a chance for you to do something kind and wonderful for someone who's really hurting."

Lester sighed. "Okay, how's this? I won't ask Pamela out, but you could invite her and Elizabeth over some afternoon to help me pack, and I'll bring in some pizza. You could help me sort through some of my stuff."

"Really, Lester?" I thought of Elizabeth and Pamela and I going through all the secrets in Lester's closet. "That's even better than taking her out! Thank you!" I cried.

"And you know what you can do for me?"

"What?"

"Crawl around the floor and pick up all my nail clippings so I don't walk on them in my bare feet."

I gave him a little smile. "Uh-uh, Lester. That's life!"

16

CONFESSION

Two weeks before school started, a box of clothes arrived from Carol. I love Carol! Every so often she goes through her closet and sends me stuff she doesn't wear anymore. She doesn't send stuff with worn elastic or missing buttons or food stains on them either. Or styles so old that you wouldn't even wear them out on your front porch.

There was a lot to do in those last weeks of August, and e-mails were flying like crazy. Jill wanted to know what everyone was going to wear on the first day of school; Elizabeth thought we ought to take the table nearest the yogurt bar in the cafeteria for lunch; Karen asked if I knew whether she still had to take

P. E. if she took diving lessons over the summer. But at the end of her message she wrote, *So do you want to know who else slept together or not?*

The Noble Alice in me would have replied, *Not interested.* But of course that was a lie, so the Truthful Alice typed, *Who?* Karen must not have been online at the time because there was no answer, so I went back to my closet to find a T-shirt to wear the first day—the one with dolphins and sparkles all over it. I held it up in front of me at the mirror and then, on impulse, smiled a toothy smile at myself and wondered how I'd look in braces—if I had sparkles on my teeth as well as my shirt.

I put dividers in my notebook and looked for a pen refill and stuck some tampons in the zip pocket of my backpack. When I went to my computer later, I'd been signed off and had to log on again. There was only one message this time. It was from Karen. I clicked READ.

The message had only ten words:

Gwen and Legs. Legs told Mark and Mark told me.

What? I thought. *She's crazy!* Gwen wasn't going with Legs anymore, and even if she was, she wouldn't do that. Karen was such a gossip.

I decided to have some friends over while we were still homework-free, so on Saturday I invited Elizabeth and Pamela and Gwen to sleep over. Dad brought up two cots for Pamela and Gwen, and Elizabeth said she'd sleep in my double bed with me.

"Hey! Camp!" Gwen said when she saw the cots. We laughed.

"I am so wired!" said Elizabeth, flopping down on my bed and dropping her bag on the floor. "I've got three subjects I hate this year: American politics, geometry, and biology."

"What did you sign up for after school?" I asked the others. I had already told the school newspaper I'd be on the staff again this year. Maybe do stage crew again too.

"Folk dancing," said Elizabeth. "I'm also going to be in a reading program for third graders, helping them one afternoon a week. That's credit toward the student service learning requirement."

Gwen said she was seriously considering music as a career—being a singer—either that or science. She was taking voice lessons, but she was also thinking about volunteering at the National Institutes of Health. We looked at Pamela.

"Nothing," said Pamela.

"Nothing what?" I asked.

"I'm not going out for anything. My *mother* is my extracurricular activity. 'Mother: How to Avoid.'"

We were quiet a moment. What do you say to *that*? But Pamela suddenly thrust an imaginary glass in the air. "Let's *party*!" she said.

It was a warm breezy night, and we sprawled around my room in our tank tops and drawstring bottoms. I brought up some chips and Cokes, and after we watched an old *Seinfeld* rerun, we talked about— what else?—boys.

"Have you heard from Joe?" I asked Gwen.

"Four e-mails," she said.

I looked at Elizabeth. "Ross?" I asked.

She grinned. "Two e-mails and a letter," she said. "A long letter."

"Hey!" I said.

Elizabeth rolled over on her back. "Is it true about Justin and Jill, do you think? What Karen's going around saying?"

"Don't believe anything Karen says," I told her. "She'll probably grow up to be a gossip columnist."

"But she says Jill told her that herself," said Elizabeth.

"Remember what Jill did in eighth grade, though," said Pamela. "She almost got Mr. Everett fired with that story that he came on to her."

"But what if it *is* true about Jill?" said Elizabeth. "Justin was kidding around with me over at Mark's the other day like maybe he wanted to go out again, but what if all this time he's been intimate with her?"

"*Intimate?*" we all exclaimed together.

"Who are you? Queen Victoria?" asked Pamela.

"You know what I mean," said Elizabeth.

"Well, maybe he wants to kiss one girl above the neck and another girl below," said Pamela.

"Oh, stop it," said Elizabeth. "But I don't really care, now that I've met Ross. I don't know when I'll see him again, but at least we can write. And who knows?"

"Absolutely!" I said. "Who knows? You may be assistant counselors there again next year."

Pamela and I were both smiling at Elizabeth like she was our little sister. It was so nice seeing her happy for a change. *We* were happy that Camp Overlook had been so good for her. I was proud of Pamela too, that she could back off the way she had. Maybe we *were* growing up. I thought back to the time Pamela bought her first bra. She had it in a little sack and was showing it to Elizabeth and me on the playground.

"Pamela," I said. "Do you remember when you were showing Liz and me your new Sears Ahh-Bra and Mark grabbed it out of your hands and went racing to the top of the monkey bars?"

We suddenly screeched with laughter and had to tell Gwen all about it. How we'd rushed off in a huff and refused to speak to the boys, and how they'd then gathered outside our window, calling for us to come out.

"The boys were *so* immature back then, weren't they?" said Pamela. "I can't say that Mark has improved much. He and Legs have a lot in common, I think. You're lucky to be rid of him, Gwen."

"I know," said Gwen. "Especially since I met Joe."

"That was so weird, the way Legs just showed up at camp," said Elizabeth. "And to walk up just as you and Joe were kissing!"

"Yeah. Legs called the other night and wanted to know how serious I was about Joe. Said he *needed* me. His new girlfriend must have turned him down."

"What did you say?" I asked.

"What do you think, girl? *I* don't want to see *him*. You've got to be able to trust, and he proved I couldn't trust him. If I had it to do over, I wouldn't make the same mistake with Legs. I'd wait for someone I liked a whole lot more."

I quit massaging lotion into my feet and looked up. Was she saying what I *thought* she was saying?

Elizabeth stared at her too. "Wait to do *what*?" she asked breathlessly. Now even Pamela was staring. "You . . . you let him go all the way?"

"First base, second base, third base, the whole ball game," said Gwen.

We couldn't believe it. We were actually in the same room with a girl who had done IT? It was as though we expected Gwen to look different somehow. To metamorphose right in front of our eyes.

It was Elizabeth who broke the silence: "But . . . but you go to church!"

"So?" said Gwen.

"You sing in a *choir*!" Elizabeth gasped.

We couldn't help laughing. "And she's kind to her grandmother too, Elizabeth," I said.

But Elizabeth was still gawking at her. "Did you . . . like it?"

"Liz!" Pamela said, but we all wanted to know. I mean, it was one thing hearing it from my cousin Carol. It was another to hear it from one of us!

"Some of it," said Gwen, laughing a little. "We only did it four times. Maybe if we'd had a lot more time together, it would have been better."

"Gwen, you could have gotten pregnant!" I said, sounding like Elizabeth.

"Well, at least I had the good sense to be careful. 'No condom, no sex,' I told him. That's *one* thing I did right. I can't believe how naïve I was, though." Gwen looked thoughtful. "He just seemed so *needy*! Like he was in *pain* he needed me so much—and that's sort of flattering. He's really not a bad guy, and I wanted to please him, but after meeting Joe, I realized how little Legs and I have in common."

I smiled at Gwen. "Everybody's angel, that's you. Your mom needed you, your grandmother needed you, your uncles, your aunts, your boyfriend. . . ."

"Where did you do it?" asked Elizabeth. She just wouldn't stop.

Gwen shrugged. "A picnic table at a roadside rest stop. The backseat of his car. His place, once, when no one was home."

"But . . . won't you be embarrassed when you see him around school?" Elizabeth asked. "I mean, he *knows* you down there, Gwen!"

Now we all burst out laughing.

"Well, only one more year to go," Gwen said. "He's a senior already; I won't have to see him around school after that."

Elizabeth stretched out on her back. "I don't think I'm going to have sex until I'm married," she declared. "I don't want to keep running into guys I've slept with. If other boys know you . . . *intimately*"—she emphasized the word this time, as though daring us to laugh at her—". . . I mean, don't you want to save something for your husband? Shouldn't there be something between you that's really special?"

It was something to think about. "Pledging to spend your lives together and take care of each other, maybe?" I suggested.

"There's more to marriage than sex, you know," said Gwen.

And I added, "Besides, it's different for mature men and women."

"Mature men and women!" Pamela exclaimed.

"Listen," I said, and recited the poem Dad had copied for Sylvia. I'd thought of it so often I'd memorized it by now:

"O western wind, when wilt thou blow
That the small rain down can rain?
Christ, that my love were in my arms
And I in my bed again!"

"Huh?" said Pamela.

"It doesn't rhyme," said Gwen.

"A-*gain*," I said, pronouncing the second syllable "gane." But when they still looked at me blankly, I changed the subject. I was ashamed of myself for repeating the poem that belonged to Dad and Sylvia. But I didn't tell them where I'd read it. That much I'd kept secret. And I promised myself that in the future, especially after Sylvia became my stepmom, I'd keep all these secrets to myself.

I thought everyone else went to sleep that night before I did. I couldn't get it out of my mind—Gwen and Legs. And what a jerk he was to tell Mark about it. Bragging, I'll bet.

At the same time I was remembering the day Patrick and I were alone in his house. We were down in the basement, and he was giving me a drum lesson. He stood behind me and put his arms around me to show how to hold the sticks . . . and then he was caressing my sides . . . up along my breasts. . . .

If his mom hadn't come home just then, would we have gone further than that? Did I want him to touch me there? Sure. It was *supposed* to feel good, wasn't it? Isn't that what sex is about?

"Alice," Elizabeth whispered. "What's the matter?" I didn't know she was awake.

"Nothing. Why?" I whispered back.

"You're restless."

"Sorry." I rolled over and faced her in the darkness. "I was thinking about Gwen," I said.

"Yeah. Me too. What do you think would happen if a man and woman fell in love but made an agreement not to touch each other until they were married?" she asked.

"Not at *all*?"

"Well, not their privates, anyway. I mean, if both of them— the man, too—came to marriage as pure and innocent as . . ."

". . . the driven snow," I said.

"Yeah."

"And then, on their wedding night, it was 'anything goes'?"

"Something like that."

"I don't know. I suppose they'd be exhausted from making up for lost time, or they'd have to get out a manual to see what goes where."

We both started to giggle.

"The comedians," said Gwen, startling us from her cot at the foot of the bed.

We shut up then and went to sleep.

17

CELEBRATION

One more week left before school. I looked at my dad one morning, his back to me as he fixed pancakes at the stove, and thought how he needed a night out. I'd been to camp, Lester was moving, and Dad hadn't even had a vacation. He had thought he would be married by now, back from his honeymoon, and here he was, cooking breakfast as usual.

"Dad," I said, "I'm taking you out to dinner tomorrow night. I've got it all planned." I didn't, but I'd take care of that in a hurry.

"Oh?" said Dad, turning. "What's the occasion?"

"You being my dad," I said.

"Well, that's a nice thought." He smiled. "I don't have to wear a tie, do I?"

"No. You always look good to me," I told him.

I took the Yellow Pages up to my room and looked up restaurants. I scanned all the ads and came across a restaurant called Carmen's. *The Home of the Singing Waiters*, the ad read. I remembered how much fun I'd had when Lester took me to *Tony 'n' Tina's Wedding* for my birthday last May, so I called and made a reservation at Carmen's for Sunday night at seven, then checked to make sure I had enough money to cover our dinner. The following evening I gave Dad the address.

"Well!" he said as we pulled in the parking lot. "This is a new one! I don't think I've ever been here, Alice."

"Good!" I said, and hoped it wasn't a dump that served lousy food. The prices had been reasonable.

Once inside, I was relieved to find that it was clean and smelled delicious. Artificial grapevines covered the ceiling and ran down the walls in places, and all the waiters and waitresses were dressed like Italian peasants. A tall dark-haired man with a thin mustache came up to our table.

"Good *eve*-ning!" he said pleasantly. "I'm Francis, your waiter for tonight."

"Good *eve*-ning!" I said. "I'm Alice, and this is my dad." Dad smiled. So did Francis.

We listened to the day's specials, and after we'd each ordered, Francis returned from the kitchen with a basket of bread for our table. He was just about to walk away when I saw the piano player signal to him, and Francis stopped. Then, as the music started to play, Francis suddenly got down on one knee in front of me, arms outstretched, and sang "O Sole Mio." Dad listened delightedly, his face in a surprised smile.

Francis was handsome and had a great voice, and any girl in the restaurant would have been thrilled to have this hunk down on one knee in front of her. But I didn't know what I was supposed to do! Was this like in the movies, where a man and woman sing a duet and they have to stare into each other's eyes while they do it? Was it okay to look away? To blink? Was I supposed to ignore him and start eating or *what*?

I looked into his eyes until I felt my eyeballs go dry. It was just too embarrassing, so I dropped my eyes, but *then* I found myself staring at his *lap*, or what would have been his lap if he'd been sitting. No! I couldn't do that! I tried to think what a senior girl would do in a situation like this, and I sat demurely with my hands folded on the table. But then I realized that my napkin had fallen onto the floor, right on Francis's foot. Should I leave it there? Pick it up? Wait for Francis to pick it up? What did I do when the song was over? Tip him? *Kiss* him? *Why* had I brought my father to Carmen's?

Mercifully, the song was finished at last. Francis got to his feet again, handed me my napkin, and gallantly kissed my hand, then went back to the kitchen.

"What a treat!" Dad said, reaching for the bread. "This was a nice surprise, Alice. I'll have to bring Sylvia here sometime."

I finally began to relax, because I figured nobody would

serenade the same girl twice. It was fun now just watching. Every so often another waiter or waitress would stop serving and start singing—sometimes two or three of them together— and occasionally all the servers would join in the chorus, stopping whatever they were doing to sing. Several of the songs were in Italian, and it was great to see Dad enjoying himself so much.

"Oh, listen to this one!" he said when three men sang an aria from *Cosi Fan Tutte*, which, Dad told me, means "Women Are Like That."

Later, though, after we'd finished our salads and entrées, the most surprising thing happened. A waiter was serving at a table next to ours, and a waitress across the room began singing to him in Italian.

Dad leaned forward. "Listen, Alice," he said. "This one is beautiful."

What is beautiful to my father, of course, sometimes sounds like noise to me, but then I'm tone-deaf, so that doesn't count. But because Dad loved the piece so much, I paid special attention. He was mouthing the words as the singers sang. It was obviously a duet, because the woman would sing a few measures and then the waiter would sing a few back to her. Dad sang softly along with the waiter.

And suddenly the waiter, noticing, bowed slightly and gestured toward Dad when it was his turn to sing next. The pianist waited. For just a moment Dad looked flustered; he hesitated, and then—to my astonishment—he rose to his feet and, with one hand extended toward the waitress, sang the baritone part.

When it was the woman's turn, he didn't sit down, but waited while the waitress sang to him, smiling, and then he finished the piece with a flourish. His voice faltered a little on the high notes, but he brought it to a rousing end, and the whole room broke into applause. Some of the people at adjoining tables even stood up to clap for him. All the waiters and waitresses were smiling and applauding, and I don't think I ever saw Dad so pleased with himself when he sat back down again.

I could feel tears in my eyes. He was having such a good time! He needed times like these while Sylvia was away. I vowed that until she came back, I was going to take better care of my father.

I reached across the table and gave his arm a squeeze. "You were *wonderful*, Dad!" I said. "Wait till I tell Sylvia about this. You really surprised me!"

"Sometimes I even surprise myself," Dad said, beaming.

Lester had come in before we did and was up in his room, but I didn't describe our evening because I wanted to let Dad do the telling. I went up to the bathroom just as the phone rang. Dad was locking up for the night, so he picked up the phone in the hall downstairs.

"Sylvia!" he said when he answered, and I thought what a perfect time it was for her to call. I was tempted to lift the upstairs phone and tell her that Dad had been the hit of the evening, but I didn't dare.

I knew I should go on in the bathroom and close the door, but I always like to wait a minute or two when Sylvia calls to listen for Dad's response. I don't know why, I just have this feeling that . . . that after losing Mom . . . if Sylvia were to break their engagement, it would do my father in.

How did I know that her old boyfriend, Jim Sorringer, hadn't heard that Sylvia's sister was sick and had flown out to New Mexico to comfort Sylvia? If he could fly to England to surprise her, he could fly to Albuquerque. What if after Sylvia got out there, she decided that her sister needed her more than Dad did, and made up her mind to stay?

I leaned against the bathroom door, ready to duck inside if Dad looked up or Lester came out of his room.

There was a long pause from below, then a murmur, I couldn't make out what Dad was saying. But suddenly I heard, "Oh, Sylvia!"

I think I stopped breathing. I *know* I stopped breathing. My whole body grew rigid—waiting . . . waiting . . .

And then he said, "Sweetheart, that's wonderful! That's the best news I've had all day. October it is, then. I'm so glad Nancy is doing well."

I danced silently around the hall upstairs. I waltzed into Lester's room, twirled around on his rug, and said, "Get ready to be best man in October, Lester!" And then, with Les still staring after me, I rushed downstairs, unable to control myself, threw my arms around Dad's middle, and gave him a bear hug. He just laughed and patted my head and went right on talking to Sylvia.

***

On Labor Day weekend Lester wanted to take some of his stuff over to the new apartment. "Okay," he said to me. "Call the Harpies and tell them they can help if they want."

I looked "Harpies" up in the dictionary. It said a Harpy was a creature in Greek mythology that is half woman, half bird. "Why do you call us Harpies?" I asked.

"Because you chatter like birds," said Lester.

"Then why don't you call us chicks or something?"

"Harpies are more you," he said.

I called Pamela first.

"You mean, *all* weekend? We can sleep over there and everything?" she asked excitedly.

I covered the phone with my hand and looked at Lester, who was drinking his coffee. "All weekend? she wants to know. Can we sleep over there too?"

Lester shot out a mouthful of coffee and coughed. He wiped his lips with one hand. "No, you're not staying all night. You can take your choice, tomorrow or Monday."

"Tomorrow," said Pamela when I told her.

"Tomorrow," Elizabeth agreed when I called.

"Okay," Lester said. "Tell them to be over here at ten o'clock, ready to work. We'll take some boxes over to the apartment and sort them there."

Pamela believes in dressing for success—we just have different definitions of "success"—and at ten on Sunday morning she arrived in short shorts. I mean, she didn't even have to bend over to show us her cheeks. She sported a halter top and thong sandals. Elizabeth, on the other hand, came over wearing the same jersey top she'd worn to mass that morning and had just traded a skirt for a pair of cutoffs to go with it. I was in my usual jeans and T-shirt.

Elizabeth studied Pamela, who was stretching and giving an enormous yawn while we waited for Lester. "Why don't you just wear a sign saying FEEL ME?" she asked her.

Pamela glanced down at herself. "Why? What's the matter?"

"Those shorts!"

"If you got it, flaunt it," Pamela sang.

Lester came clattering downstairs carrying two boxes, one on top of the other.

"Well, this is a start," he said. "Good morning, ladies. Open the door for me, will you, Al?"

"Good mor-ning, Les-ter!" Pamela trilled.

He raised one eyebrow as he paused beside me at the screen. "Take my keys, would you, and open the trunk? I've got a couple more boxes upstairs."

We were soon rolling south on Georgia Avenue toward Takoma Park, and because it was a Sunday and a holiday weekend, the streets were deserted. Seven minutes later we were cruising down a tree-lined street of old Victorian houses, and thirty seconds after that Lester swung his car into the driveway of a large yellow house with brown trim and a wraparound porch.

"Oh, Lester!" I gasped. "You get to live *here*?"

"Isn't it great?" he said. "I still can't believe it." He turned off the motor. "Okay, everybody out, and carry something in with you. We take the stairs at the side of the house."

We headed for the separate entrance but bumped into each other because we kept stopping to exclaim over things: a huge sycamore with peeling bark, the two dormer windows at the front of the house, a little stone statue among the shrubbery, some old wicker furniture on the porch—a swing and a rocker.

"Come on up," Lester called, holding the door open with one elbow as he balanced a footlocker on his knee.

The apartment smelled of fresh paint, and the entryway was only half finished, but there was a stained-glass inset above a window on the opposite wall that let in the morning sun.

We put our boxes down and went exploring, excitedly commenting on every new detail we found. Lester tagged along, smiling broadly, pleased, I could tell, that we were so enthusiastic.

There were two large rooms with closets on one side of the hallway, two smaller rooms with closets on the other side. In between the smaller bedrooms was a sitting room with French doors that led out onto a screened porch.

"That's what was known as a sleeping porch at the turn of the century," Lester said. "Without air-conditioning, the kids— sometimes the whole family—would sleep on cots out on the porch in the summer. But see, if we open the French doors, it extends the living room so we can get more people in."

"Party, party, party!" Pamela cried. If I'd worried about Pamela being too subdued over the summer, it didn't seem I'd have to worry about that now.

Back inside, Lester pointed out the door that had been cut between the sitting room and one of the small bedrooms. The closet in that room had been removed and a kitchenette installed—a sink, a counter, a refrigerator, and a stove and oven.

"Not the best kitchen I've ever seen, but it'll do," Lester said.

"So who gets the two larger bedrooms, and who has to take the small one?" I asked.

"Paul and I get the big ones, and George gets the small one, because he's not sure he'll be here next summer. We might have to look for someone else."

"Boy, Lester, you are so lucky!" I said. I imagined Elizabeth and Pamela and I sharing an apartment like this when we went to college. Sleeping out on a porch.

"Okay. Work time!" Lester said suddenly. "Here's what I want you to do. These are boxes of stuff I've had since grade school. Some of them, anyway. I want you to go through everything and sort them into three piles: stuff that looks like I should definitely keep, stuff you're not sure about, and stuff I could possibly throw away. I'll go through them after you decide, but this will make it easier. Got it?"

"Got it," said Elizabeth.

Lester went into his bedroom with some hardware and began adding more shelves to his closet.

We sat down on the floor, each of us with a box between her legs, and began. It was obvious Lester wasn't going to let us go through anything current—love letters from former girl-friends and stuff. But this would be interesting enough, we figured. Opening the first box, I found an odd assortment of stuff: an ashtray made of clay with Lester's initials on the bottom, a pin for perfect attendance, a flag, string, thumbtacks, a model jeep, scissors, wrapping paper, an old wallet. . . .

Elizabeth kept finding the most interesting stuff in her box. "Oh, m'gosh, his first-grade class picture!" she cried, and gave a little shriek. She showed us the photo with an arrow at the side pointing to a little boy with two missing teeth, grinning broadly. "Is that *Lester*?"

We howled and dug around some more. We could hear the tap of Lester's hammer back in his closet. I felt a little like a preschooler, having been given a box to entertain myself so I wouldn't get in the way.

"Having fun?" Lester called when he heard all the laughter.

"Oh, definitely!" said Elizabeth.

Lester wandered in to see what was so funny. He looked at the picture. "I was a real ladies' man, all right," he said, and went back to work.

Pamela seemed to have all Lester's school papers and notebooks. Every so often we'd hear her chuckle, and then she'd read something to us. But then we heard her say, "What's this?"

We watched her untape a yellowed piece of tablet paper,

used as a wrapper around something else, it seemed. We stared in surprise as out fell a small pair of cotton underpants with lace around the legs.

Elizabeth clapped her hand over her mouth in amusement as we looked wide-eyed at each other.

"What does the paper say?" I asked.

Pamela turned it over. "It's just a spelling paper. Looks like first or second grade with Lester's name at the top."

"What do you suppose . . . ?" Elizabeth said.

Suddenly Pamela took the underpants and pulled them over her head like a hat.

She motioned us to follow her and walked across the hall into Lester's bedroom.

"Boy, you find all kinds of stuff in boxes, don't you?" she said. "Ta-da, Lester!"

Lester backed himself out of his closet and turned around. He stared at Pamela, then at her head, squinting slightly. "What's that?" he asked.

Pamela took the underpants off and read the label on the inside. "'Buster Brown, size 6,'" she said. "Hey, Les, you weren't a cross-dresser back in elementary school, were you?"

And suddenly, right before our eyes, Lester's face and neck and ears grew as pink as Elizabeth's jersey top. He reached out for the underpants, but Pamela snatched them away and held them behind her, eyes flashing mischievously. "Not until we hear the whole story, Les!" she said.

We hooted.

He laughed a little. "Some things were meant to stay private," he said.

That only make us more curious. "Tell us!" we begged.

He groaned and gave us a look. "Well, I was in second grade, and there was this little dark-haired girl named Maxine—Maxie, we called her—that I had a wild, secret crush on, and I was too shy to tell her."

"You? *Shy?*" cried Elizabeth.

"But not shy enough to take off her pants, huh?" teased Pamela.

Lester held up one hand.

"Go on," I said.

"One day on the playground Maxie jumped off the swings, and when she landed, she must have wet her pants. I didn't know what had happened at first, I just saw her jump and fall, and then she had this strange look on her face as she glanced around. A few minutes later, though, I was on the monkey bars and saw her go off behind the bushes in one corner and take off her underpants. She just left them there. When the bell rang, she came back and stood in line like everyone else, and I was the only one who knew she was naked under her dress."

"And you spent the afternoon trying to peek?" asked Pamela.

"No, no. But I kept thinking of her all afternoon, and when school was out, I went back there and got her underpants. They were wet, and there were ants all over them, but I took them home and rinsed them out. I was going to let them dry and then take them back to her the next day, but I was too embarrassed. So I never did. I kept them."

"Awwwwww!" we sang out together.

"She never knew?"

Lester shook his head. "Nope. One of the tragedies of second grade. And that's why I am what I am today."

"A lech?" asked Pamela.

"No! Hey!"

"A ladies' man," I said.

"Right," said Lester. "And now may I have Maxie's underwear, please?"

Pamela handed them over. "What are you going to do with them?" she asked.

"I don't know. I'd forgot all about them. But if ever there's a grade school reunion and I go back to Chicago and find Maxine, wouldn't it be something to walk up to her and say, 'For you, madame' and hand her the Buster Browns?" He stuffed them in one pocket.

"Ah! You never forget a first love," I said.

We went back to search for more of Lester's secrets, but that was the major find of the day.

Around two o'clock Lester went out to get some pizza for us. The minute he was gone, Pamela said, "I've got a great idea." She picked up the tissue paper that was in the first box and a pair of scissors, and while we watched, she made a life-size cutout of a pair of woman's underpants, scalloping the pant legs to look like lace. We grinned, puzzled. She cut out a bra next.

"What are you *doing*?" I asked.

"Watch," said Pamela. She took the ball of string and tied an end around an empty picture hanger on the wall of Lester's bedroom. Then she stretched it across the big window, cut it, and tied the other end around the hinge on his closet door. She took the pair of tissue panties and stapled them to the string, like clothes on a line. Then she stapled the bra. They blew slightly in the breeze.

We shrieked in delight and set to work cutting out more undies—panty hose, more underpants, another bra, a slip, even. By the time we heard Lester's car pull up again, there was a whole clothesline of women's tissue-paper undies fluttering in the breeze in front of Lester's window.

"You're a genius!" Elizabeth said to Pamela. "Oh, this is sweeeeet!"

"Break time!" Lester called, coming in the door. "Come and get it!" He took two boxes of pizza to the counter in the kitchen, and then, hearing us laughing in his bedroom, came to the doorway and stopped dead still. Suddenly he started to laugh.

"I see the Harpies are at it again," he said. "Very clever, girls, I must say."

We thought he'd rip them down, but he said, "George and Paul are coming by tomorrow with some of their stuff, and I think I'll leave it up, get a rise out of them."

We laughed some more.

"Of course, if Mr. Watts happens to check our apartment over the weekend, we could be out on our ear," Lester said. "But he may even want to borrow them for a while. Hang them up in his own window, get the neighbors talking."

We had a wonderful time!

After the first day of school I came home to find a cardboard box sitting on our porch addressed to me. The mail carrier had set it between the screen and the front door. There was a DEPARTMENT OF RECREATION sticker return address in the upper left corner, and all I could think of was that I probably left something behind at Camp Overlook and they'd finally traced it to me. Sneakers, maybe. But it wasn't heavy enough for sneakers. In fact, it hardly weighed anything at all. I sure hoped it wasn't dirty underwear. That would be so embarrassing!

I took it inside, set it on the kitchen table, and opened the flaps. It seemed to be full of shredded paper. I found an envelope, also from the Department of Recreation, with a letter inside from Connie Kendrick:

Hi, Alice.
We found this on the steps of the building last week when we came to work. There's a letter in it addressed to "Alice," and we decided that can only mean you. We're sending the whole thing exactly as we found it. Thanks for being part of our team this past summer. We loved having you.
Connie

Was this a joke? I wondered. I couldn't see how there could be anything else in the box except paper. Then I found a grocery sack at the bottom, the top folded over. I opened it and lifted out a twig basket. Inside was a note on tablet paper:

> Alice,
> This for you Becaus that nite I was hiding in the tolet and you hug me I gess you like me a little too. If you decid to keep it maybe you will think of me sometimes.
> Latisha

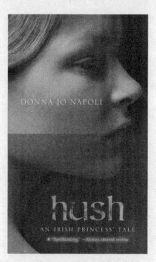

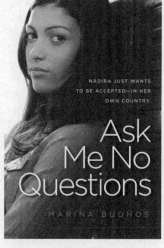
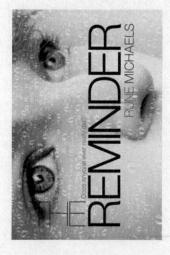

Imagine you and your best friend head out west on a cross-country bike trek. Imagine that you get into a fight—and stop riding together. Imagine you reach Seattle, go back home, start college. Imagine you think your former best friend does too. Imagine he doesn't. Imagine your world shifting. . . .

jennifer bradbury SHIFT

★ "Fresh, absorbing, compelling."
—*Kirkus Reviews*, STARRED REVIEW

★ "Bradbury's keen details about the bike trip, the places, the weather, the food, the camping, and the locals add wonderful texture to this exciting first novel. . . ."
—*Booklist*, STARRED REVIEW

"The story moves quickly and will easily draw in readers."
—*School Library Journal*

"This is an intriguing summer mystery."—*Chicago Tribune*

"*Shift* is a wonderful book by a gifted author."—teenreads.com

Atheneum Books
for Young Readers

TEEN.SimonandSchuster.com

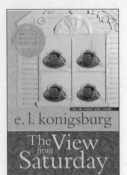
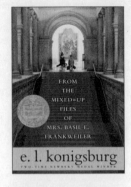

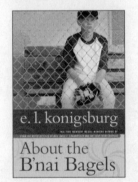
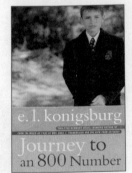